THE GRIFFIN SISTERS' GREATEST HITS

Also by Jennifer Weiner

The Breakaway

The Summer Place

That Summer

Big Summer

Mrs. Everything

Hungry Heart

Who Do You Love

All Fall Down

The Next Best Thing

Then Came You

Fly Away Home

Best Friends Forever

Certain Girls

Goodnight Nobody

Little Earthquakes

In Her Shoes

Good in Bed

THE GRIFFIN SISTERS' GREATEST HITS

A NOVEL

Jennifer Weiner

WM

WILLIAM MORROW

An Imprint of HarperCollins*Publishers*

THE GRIFFIN SISTERS' GREATEST HITS. Copyright © 2025 by Jennifer
Weiner. All rights reserved. Printed in the United States of America. No
part of this book may be used or reproduced in any manner whatsoever
without written permission except in the case of brief quotations
embodied in critical articles and reviews. For information, address
HarperCollins Publishers, 195 Broadway, New York, NY 10007.

HarperCollins books may be purchased for educational, business,
or sales promotional use. For information, please email the Special
Markets Department at SPsales@harpercollins.com.

FIRST EDITION

Library of Congress Cataloging-in-Publication Data has been applied for.

ISBN 978-0-06-344581-9

25 26 27 28 29 LBC 5 4 3 2 1

FOR PHOEBE,
MY ROCK STAR

Prologue
DETROIT, 2004

I never should have touched you," Russell D'Angelo says to the empty room.

He twists the lock, toes off his cowboy boots, and leans his forehead against the hotel-room door, against the framed placard. He's too close to read the emergency evacuation routes it details, even if his eyes weren't blurry with tears. He pinches the bridge of his nose, hard. This is an emergency, the worst he's ever been in, and knowing how to exit the building safely won't help.

He is thinking about how she looked, about what he'd said.

I never meant for this to happen, he'd told her as she'd glared at him from the hallway, her face shocked and pale and heartbroken. He'd kept talking, hating the pleading sound of his voice. *I'm sorry.*

Russell shakes his head to stop the thoughts. Three paces bring him to the bar cart. He unscrews the cap of the whiskey bottle and lifts it to his mouth, welcoming the burn of the liquor. His eyes are closed, but he can still see them both. Two sets of eyes, two faces, turned toward his. Different faces, but with the same shape to their lips, the same slope of their cheeks. Two women, waiting for an answer Russell didn't have.

"I'm an idiot," he tells the room. And it's true. He hadn't even noticed what was happening until it was too late. It wasn't until he was standing in front of an officiant, thirty of their closest friends, three hundred fellow celebrities, and a photographer from *People* magazine that he'd looked over his bride's shoulder and caught her sister's eyes, and the knowledge of the mistake that he was making hit him like a punch to the breastbone, rattling his heart. "I do," he'd said. *I'm fucked*, he'd thought. And from that moment on, a part of him has been waiting, counting down toward this place and this night.

You have to choose, she'd told him. Except there isn't a choice here. Not really. Not at all.

Twenty minutes later, half the whiskey is gone, and Russell's leaning heavily against the wall, looking blearily around the room. His eyes move from object to object without seeing. There's the bed, still made. His suitcase, open on the luggage stand, clothes spilling out from its unzipped top—his jeans and tee shirt, the silly leather pants the stylist insists on because he's the lead guitar player in what is, currently, one of the most successful bands in the country, and leather pants are what cute boys in hot bands are required to wear. There might even be a law about it.

"I never should have touched you," Russell says again. He hums a handful of notes in a minor key and decides to write the words down. Moving carefully, deliberately in his inebriation, he locates the tiny pad of hotel stationery and a pen, and writes with care, imagining piano chords, a mournful twangy guitar. Maybe the words will be the backbone of a chorus, the way into a song, he thinks. And then remembers what he's done, and how that door is closed. There will be no more songs for him.

He bends to collect his boots, sitting on the edge of the bed to pull them on before walking out into the hall. It's the middle of the night. It's quiet, and all the doors are closed. Nobody sees him as he walks through the lobby, bootheels clicking. Nobody sees as he pushes the heavy glass doors open and steps out into the cold and the dark.

Part One

Cherry

HADDONFIELD, 2024

Ten minutes," Darren said, nodding at the dashboard clock.

"Ten minutes," Cherry repeated, and opened the Prius's passenger's side door, stepping out of an atmosphere composed of equal parts pot, male body, and some kind of noxious spray cologne intended to obscure the first two things. "I've got my phone. Text me if you see anyone."

Darren nodded again. Cherry hoped he was listening, that he wasn't stoned. At eleven thirty in the morning, the house was empty, but Cherry wasn't taking chances. Extra eyes would help.

She ran around to the back door, in case the Peraltas next door or the Murphys across the street were watching and wondering why she wasn't in school. She'd left the house that morning at seven thirty, right on schedule, had endured half a day's worth of classes: the close reading of a Philip Roth story in English; sine, cosine, and tangent in algebra; a review of the past perfect tense in French. Not one single thing she'd need where she was going.

She disabled the alarm and ran lightly up the stairs to her bedroom, with its cream-colored carpeting and the flower-and-butterfly-patterned wallpaper her mom had picked out when they'd moved to this house and redone her bedroom, changing it from a boy's space to a girl's. Or, Cherry thought, changing it from a boy's space to a room for the kind of girl her mom wanted: a pretty, easygoing girlie girl who would appreciate music boxes with ballerinas inside and butterflies on her wall.

The wallpaper was now almost completely obscured beneath layers of posters, most of them featuring women with guitars. Some of the posters were the bands and singers Cherry loved best—Fiona Apple and Liz Phair, Lana Del Rey and Mitski. Others advertised Cherry's musical influences—the Breeders and Veruca Salt, Luscious Jackson and Hole. A Joan Jett poster had pride of place, a black-and-white photograph of the artist looking over her shoulder, with her guitar at her hip. Cherry's corkboard was papered with printouts of concert tickets, going back all the way to the 2015 Taylor Swift show she'd attended on her tenth birthday, during that brief window when music was something she and her mother enjoyed together, not the thing that had come between them. Her bass and guitar rested on their metal stands; her amplifier, covered in stickers, squatted in the corner. The duffel bag she'd packed the night before was at the back of her closet, obscured by a layer of dirty laundry. She unearthed it, unzipped it, and stuffed in her notebooks full of lyrics, the toiletries and makeup she hadn't wanted to pack the night before, in the event—unlikely, but not impossible—that her mother would notice their absence.

When the bag was full, Cherry slid her guitar into its padded case, the one she could wear like a backpack, and pulled the straps over her shoulders. She grabbed the duffel and hurried down the stairs, stopping in the kitchen, thinking she'd have just enough time to slap together a peanut butter sandwich for the road. She had just pulled the bread out of the bread box when she saw her stepbrother's name on the over-sized calendar on her mother's desk. *Bix dentist* was written in the space for Wednesday of the next week. Cherry winced and found her gaze moving toward the basement, where her piano lived. A few months after they'd moved to this place, Cherry had sat down to practice. She'd smelled something sour, just as her feet touched the wet, sticky mess dripping from the piano's body, pooling under the pedals. Bix had opened the instrument's lid and dumped a glass of chocolate milk into the body, soaking the tuning pins, the felt-covered hammers, the strings and the soundboard. When Zoe, in her gentle stepmothering voice, had asked Bix what had happened, Bix had shrugged. "I think Cherry left her glass there," he'd said, tapping the top of the piano with one long, somehow insectile fingertip. Like Cherry didn't know any better. Like she'd ever bring anything like that near the piano; her good, old friend; the ancient, battered upright that had once been her aunt's; the instrument she'd convinced her grandparents to give her. "Nobody ever plays it," Cherry had said. Her Pop-pop had bit his lip, looking troubled, and her Nana had actually left the room, which was when Cherry remembered that nobody was playing the piano now, but somebody had played it once. She'd opened her mouth to apologize when her grandfather had said, "You know what, kiddo? You're right. It's not doing anyone any good just sitting here." His voice was hoarse, but he'd given her a crooked smile. "We'll call it a housewarming present. Or an early Chanukah gift." Two days later, the movers had shown up in Haddonfield with the piano. Cherry had been thrilled. Her mother, not so much.

"Put it in the basement," Zoe had said, her face crinkling in distaste. Cherry hadn't cared. A piano in the basement was a hundred times better than no piano at all. And then Bix had ruined it. They'd had it cleaned and tuned, but it had never sounded the same, and that sour, spoiled-milk smell still lingered.

Cherry knew Bix had done what he'd done on purpose. But when she told her mother, Zoe had just sighed and said, "You need to get along with him, honey. You need to try harder." That was the pattern. Bix transgressed; Cherry got in trouble. Bix was believed; Cherry was not. Bix was coddled, excused, given second and third chances, and lots of extra help. Cherry was instructed to try harder, to make allowances; was reminded that Bix had lost his mother; was told that she should be his friend. It was hard, too, because most of what Bix did was so subtle it was almost impossible to describe. "What do you mean, he's looking at you?" Zoe would ask, her tone frustrated. Or, "Cherry, he's allowed to be on the couch at the same time you are." Cherry had tried to explain that it wasn't just that Bix was on the couch; it was that he was sitting too close to her, breathing too loudly, that when he looked at her it was always with a smirk curling his thin lips and a gaze that felt probing and invasive, like he was picturing her naked. "Is he touching you?" her mother would finally ask, her face very serious, and Cherry would always have to tell her mom that Bix wasn't, that he hadn't. She didn't know how to explain that it still felt like he was and he had.

Bix was nineteen now, a year older than Cherry. He should have been away, in college, but instead he was still living at home, attending classes at one of Penn State's satellite campuses, with the hope (vain, in Cherry's opinion) that he'd be admitted to the main campus someday. Meanwhile, he lived in a bedroom not ten yards from her own. And he was still, always, looking at her.

Not anymore, Cherry told herself, pressing her lips together tightly while spreading peanut butter on a slice of bread. She'd be free of Bix at last, far away from her mother and her mother's judgments. Free to follow her destiny; free to chase her dreams; free to become the only thing she'd ever wanted to be: A singer. A musician. A star.

Cherry reached into her pocket and pulled out her new phone, the one she'd paid for herself, the one that wasn't on the family plan. She thumbed the screen into life and, for the hundredth time that morning, checked the email she'd received from the producers of *The Next Stage*—the one that began with the word *Congratulations* and included attachments to her plane ticket, her hotel reservation, details about when the next round of auditions would commence, and copies of the documents she'd signed. There was a release, allowing the show to broadcast footage of her, and an NDA full of stern warnings about not telling anyone—not friends, not relatives, not vocal coaches or band-mates or even parents—that she'd made it to the semifinals, with lots of threatening language about the millions of dollars she'd owe the production company if anyone she knew went public with that news and spoiled the show.

Cherry's audition for *The Next Stage* had been back in September. She'd arrived at the Philadelphia Convention Center at eight o'clock, a full twenty-five hours before auditions began, to ensure that she'd be toward the front of the line when the doors finally opened. The producers had divided people into groups of twenty, and so, just past nine A.M., Cherry and nineteen other wannabes had walked into the vast expanse of the auditorium. There were a dozen tables, each one manned by a pair of producers. One after another, the members of Cherry's group had stepped forward, to sing for approximately twenty seconds apiece. Cherry had sung the Black Crowes' "Hard to Handle" for a pair of bored-looking producers barely older than she was, who'd gotten gratifyingly less bored-looking as her allotted twenty seconds had unspooled. When she'd finished, one of the producers had gone trotting off, eventually reappearing with another, more senior-looking producer and a cameraman, and had Cherry sing again, this time with a camera filming her. The producer had tapped something on his iPad and sent Cherry off to the bleachers to wait some more. Eventually she'd been ushered into a featureless conference room, where there were more producers and another camera waiting.

They'd asked her for a different song, and so Cherry had performed Kelly Clarkson's "Since U Been Gone." Sometimes, when she was singing, she was completely in her head, thinking about the next note, the next phrase, the next breath she'd take, but that morning, she'd been able to hear herself, to become the audience as well as the performer. Objectively, she knew she sounded good. Her belt was full-throated and yearning, the chorus and the "yeah, yeahs," she'd sung sounded plaintive and so pained that she gave herself goose bumps. She knew, even before the judges' nods, that she'd made it through, but she couldn't keep herself from jumping into the air, pumping her fist triumphantly, feeling gratified and thrilled, when they'd delivered the news.

"Come back tomorrow," they'd told her. "And make sure you look exactly the same." Same clothes, same hair, same everything. Cherry figured the plan was to edit everything together and make a two- or three-day process look like it had all happened in a single day. At home she'd ignored her mother when Zoe had complained about Cherry running the washing machine with just a single outfit inside. The next day she'd skipped school, again, and had gone back to the convention center, where she'd sung, for a third time, in front of one of the show's most senior producers. For that round, she'd gotten an entire sixty seconds to impress them: thirty seconds for the Black Crowes, thirty seconds for Kelly Clarkson.

"Very nice," the producer had said. She'd asked Cherry questions— how old was she? How long had she been singing? What kind of music did she like, what were her other hobbies, who were her favorite bands? Cherry answered everything, repeating the questions before giving her answers. She said she was eighteen, that she'd been singing as long as she could remember, that she liked all kinds of music, but singer-songwriters especially, that she played keyboard and guitar, that she had no other hobbies of note, and that her favorite band was the Griffin Sisters. By the end of the day, she'd gotten the good news. By the end of the week, the show's producers had sent her a plane ticket, instructing her to be in Los Angeles the first Monday in February. She could be sent home that same day . . . or, if she made it to the finals, she could be out there as long as four months, until the judges crowned the winner of *The Next Stage* and gave him or her one hundred thousand dollars and a recording contract.

In spite of the NDAs, Cherry had heard rumors that most teenage contestants ended up telling their parents. Cherry had not. She was legally an adult. She didn't need her mom's permission to compete, and she didn't want to have to deal with Zoe trying to stop her. She did not want to sit through another lecture about the terrible state of the music industry today, or all the ways the business would hurt her. "Men treat women like they're pieces of meat," Zoe would say, shaking her head. "I could tell you stories . . ."

I could tell you stories, Cherry would think, scowling. *I could tell you that there's already a man treating me like a piece of meat, and that the call is coming from inside the house. Only you don't want to hear it.*

She snagged a bottle of seltzer from the refrigerator and stood in the kitchen, taking in the suburban profusion, all the stuff her family owned. There was a blue ceramic bowl full of tangerines on the white marble counter; the wine refrigerator, humming underneath it; the tulips in a vase on the table in the corner; the silver-framed photographs of her little brothers, Noah and Schuyler, on the wall; all that cool, shining order. She could smell fabric softener and lemon Pledge, the ghost of cloves and amber from Zoe's Coco perfume; a leftover from her mom's rock-and-roll days, Cherry figured. Most of the ladies her mom knew, the ones from the book club and barre class and the PTA, stuck to barely there Jo Malone.

On her way out of the house, she allowed herself one last look toward the basement and saw that the door was open, just a crack. She knew if she opened the door all the way and looked down, she would see, hanging on the wall that faced the kitchen, a framed platinum album: the one relic from her previous life that her mother had kept.

It was strange. From what she'd read, people who'd won Emmys and Oscars and Tony Awards either gave their trophies pride of place or did something ironic. They'd set a Tony in the powder room or tuck an Oscar in with a bunch of random family photos on a side table. *Nothing to see here. No big deal,* such placement seemed to say.

Her mother was different. She actually seemed sincere in not wanting to put any evidence of her previous life on display. Cherry knew that it had been her stepfather's idea to hang the album, that he'd been the one to talk Zoe into pulling it out of storage. Zoe had consented, as long as she got to pick the location. *Really?* Cherry remembered him asking, when Zoe had pointed toward the basement. *That's where you want it?* She remembered his tone, curious and a little disappointed, and, above all, careful. Jordan, her stepfather, was always careful with her mother, especially on this topic. He treated her like she was a soufflé, or made of spun sugar, like she'd collapse if he looked at her too hard or shatter if he spoke to her too sharply. Cherry remembered her mother's tight-lipped smile. *Yes,* Zoe had said. *That's where I want it.*

Cherry didn't understand it, not any more than Jordan did. Maybe her mother didn't want to remind anyone of what she'd once been. Maybe she didn't like remembering herself. Zoe would never talk about her days in the band, no matter how much Cherry pestered and pleaded, or how many times she'd asked for details beyond what she could find online, on Subreddits and on the Griffin Sisters' Wikipedia page. Zoe wouldn't talk about the band, wouldn't talk about Cherry's actual, biological father. *Jordan's your father now. And he loves you. You're very lucky, Cherry. I hope you know that.*

Cherry did know. Her actual father might have died before she was born, and that was a bummer, but she'd hit the jackpot with Jordan. Jordan loved her and did the best he could. But Cherry was always aware that she was his adopted daughter, not his biological one; that she was in a different category than the boys. She'd have known it, even if, when she was six years old, Bix hadn't turned to her, when they'd both been on the couch, watching cartoons, and said, "He's not your father. Your father's dead." Jordan had offered, more than once, for Cherry to call him Dad, but she'd never been able to fit her mouth around the word.

Jordan loved her. But they'd never talked, just the two of them, about how Bix looked at her, or how his looks made her feel, about how he would hide her sheet music on the days she had piano lessons, or how he'd accidentally-on-purpose set her sixth-grade final-project diorama on fire, or how he'd put a dead mouse in her shoe, or how, once, when she was eleven, she'd woken up in the middle of the night to find him standing by the side of her bed, pale face looming over her like a moon made of rotten cheese. But Jordan must have known something, because Bix had been shipped off to boarding school when he turned fourteen. Cherry had never been as happy as she'd been that morning, watching the loaded Range Rover pulling out of the driveway. She thought he'd be gone forever, but Bix had turned out to be a classic failure-to-launch situation. After high school, he had boomeranged right back home and started tormenting Cherry again.

Time to go, she thought. She popped her sandwich into a plastic bag and hurried out of the kitchen, resetting the alarm and locking the back door behind her. After stowing her gear in the trunk, she climbed into Darren's car and clicked the seat belt into place with three minutes to spare.

"Okay?" he asked.

"Perfect," said Cherry. "Thank you."

Darren patted her shoulder awkwardly. "Gonna miss you," he said, and started driving toward the airport. Darren had been her bandmate since they'd met as sixth graders at the School of Rock. They'd played Stevie Wonder together, and they'd both been promoted to the house band in ninth grade. Darren played the drums, and Cherry played lead guitar, and keys, and she sang for as many songs as they'd let her. In tenth grade, she and Darren had formed their own band, StickyFingers (all one word). They'd learned the entire Rolling Stones catalogue and had performed on any stage that would have them—in clubs in New Jersey and across the river in Philadelphia, at all-ages nights at bars and street festivals, at open-mic nights and school talent shows.

At the curb underneath the American Airlines sign, Darren put the car in park and patted her shoulder again. "Break a leg," he said. "I'll be watching."

"Don't just watch," she said. "You've got to vote, too."

"Early and often," Darren promised.

Cherry pressed a quick kiss to his cheek, gathered her bag and her guitar, and rechecked her phone for her ticket, reminding herself that she didn't need to keep looking over her shoulder. Her stepdad was at work. Her brothers and her stepbrother were at school. Her mother was at barre class or hot yoga—"maintaining my girlish figure," she'd say, straight-faced. Then she would be shopping or at lunch with her friends. No one would be home for hours. Cherry knew no one would notice she was gone for hours after that, maybe not until after dinner, maybe, if she got lucky, not even until the next morning. By the time they'd start to worry, she'd be in Los Angeles. The next time they saw her, or heard her voice, she would be on TV.

Janice
PHILADELPHIA, 1982

No." Janice Edelman's feet were still in the stirrups when the doctor, balding and avuncular in his white coat, gave her the news. "I can't be."

"You can, and you are," Dr. Gaines announced, pulling off his gloves and tossing them into the trash can. "About twenty-two weeks, I'd say."

"Twenty-two . . ." Janice closed her eyes, struggling to reorder her thoughts. "I can't be," she repeated.

The doctor sat on his wheeled stool and used his heels to scoot himself over to her chart, spread out on the counter beside the sink. Zoe was in her stroller, snoozing peacefully, her rosebud lips parted, her hair curling and her cheeks adorably pink. Janice swallowed hard as Dr. Gaines scribbled something in her file. "Were you using birth control?" he asked.

"I'm still breastfeeding! I never even started my period again! I thought . . ." She pressed one hand to her forehead. The truth was, after her daughter's birth, just seven short months ago, it had never even occurred to her to go back on the pill. In those blurry, sleepless months, sex felt like something she'd done in another life, or possibly on a different planet. She'd gotten the go-ahead to resume marital relations at her six-week checkup, but Sam, her big, brave, police-officer husband, had been too scared to touch her. Eventually, they'd managed to make careful, tentative love, an act repeated just a handful of times in the subsequent months, and Janice suspected she'd fallen asleep midway through a few of their intimate encounters. Even easy babies needed nighttime feedings, and when Janice was in bed, it was hard to stay awake, no matter what else was happening at the time.

"I understand that this is a surprise," said Dr. Gaines.

"A surprise," Janice repeated. She licked her lips and made herself ask, "Is it too late to . . . to terminate?"

"Yes," said Dr. Gaines, without meeting her eyes. "You're well over the cutoff, unless there's a danger to your health."

"Does my mental health count?" Janice asked, only mostly kidding. Twenty-two weeks meant she'd be having another baby in four and a half months. It barely seemed possible. She and Sam had been married for two years before they'd started trying. When she'd found out she was pregnant with Zoe, she'd been thrilled. She'd gone to Modell's to buy a tiny Eagles onesie, which she'd folded up and set at his place at the kitchen table. He'd stared at the green-and-silver garment when he'd come down for dinner, then whooped with happiness, scooping Janice in his arms, whirling her around, raining kisses on her cheeks and lips and forehead. "Our little family," he'd said softly.

And that was the thing: a little family was what they'd wanted. Sam had three brothers, Janice had two brothers and three sisters. Sam had grown up in a rowhouse in Olney, and Janice had lived in a ranch house in Somerton, a few miles away. They'd both shared bedrooms and bathrooms with their siblings. They'd both worn hand-me-downs throughout childhood. They'd both wanted things to be different for their children. *I want my kids to have their own bedrooms*, Janice had said, remembering how she'd yearned for privacy and a place that belonged to her alone. *I want them to have their own clothes*, said Sam, who had been eighteen before he'd owned a new winter coat. They'd both wanted a house that had been newly constructed, or at least recently renovated. No aluminum awning over the front stoop; no worn, grimed linoleum floors or cheap laminate countertops in the kitchen; no walls that had absorbed the scents of tens of thousands of meals and the energy of tens of thousands of fights.

One kid, they'd decided. Maybe two. And only two after they'd saved up for a down payment on a big-enough house, somewhere in the Great Northeast, because Philadelphia cops were required to live within the city limits. Another baby, before Zoe's first birthday, was absolutely not part of the plan. There wasn't any room. There also wasn't any money.

But Janice was not prepared to discuss that with her gynecologist. At least, not until she'd put her underwear back on.

"How can I not have known?" she asked. "How could I have missed . . ." She waved at her doctor, then at her belly. "Everything?"

He pulled off his glasses, with their thick black plastic frames, and polished first one lens, then the other, on the hem of his white coat. "It happens more than you'd think."

Sure, Janice thought, putting her clothes on slowly once the doctor was gone. With fifteen-year-old airheads who gave birth in the school bathroom on prom night. But she wasn't fifteen. And she'd never thought of herself as stupid. Not until that afternoon.

"Congratulations," the nurse said, giving her a little wave as Janice made her way toward the reception desk, pushing Zoe, who was still sleeping in her stroller. Janice made herself smile back at the woman, and thought, *Maybe it won't be that bad. Maybe the next baby will be easy, like Zoe.*

It was just after three o'clock in the afternoon when Janice got into her thirdhand Honda and pulled out of the parking garage. She found herself driving south on Eighth Street, heading instinctively toward her aunt's house in South Philadelphia. Out of her four sisters, Janice's mother was the one who'd made it, married to a man who earned a good living, who could buy her a three-bedroom split-level ranch (a house they'd promptly stuffed with too much furniture and many children). Janice's mother's oldest sister, Bess, still lived in a Jewish neighborhood of South Philadelphia.

Janice found her aunt right where Bess spent most of her time, when the weather permitted: on a folding lawn chair on her stoop, wearing a flowered housedress with scuffed black Keds on her swollen feet. There was a pack of Marlboros in her hand, an empty Tastykake pie tin full of ashes on the table beside her, and a lit cigarette plugged into her lipsticked mouth. Aunt Bess had a blocky build, wide shoulders and hips without much of a waist between them. Her hair was cut short and dyed a brassy magenta, a color Janice's mother referred to, through pursed lips, as "a shade not found in nature." Bess's face was jowly, grooved with wrinkles, her eyes deep set in a net of crow's-feet . . . but she loved to laugh, and throw parties, and cook for a crowd, and she always had a five- or ten-dollar bill in her pocket, to press into the hands of any niece or nephew or, these days, great-niece or great-nephew or grandchild who came to visit.

Janice sat on her aunt's porch, handing Zoe over gratefully when Bess held out her arms for the baby. Janice gave her the news, as Bess listened, considerately blowing her smoke away from Zoe's little face. "Hon, just tell him," she said in her raspy smoker's voice. "Even if he's surprised at first, he'll come around. Sammy's a good boy."

"We can't afford it."

Bess shrugged. "How much does a baby cost? You've already got your stroller and car seat and bottles and all. Zoe will grow out of things, and the new one can have her hand-me-downs."

At the word *hand-me-downs*, Janice winced. "It's not what I wanted for her," she said, low-voiced.

Bess gave Janice a kind look. "So maybe this is a little setback. Doesn't mean you won't get that nice new house in the end."

"Okay, but . . ." Janice took a deep breath, smelling cigarette smoke, hot tar (the Golds, two doors down, were having their roof repaired), and the ghosts of Shabbat dinner, fresh challah and chickens roasted in honey and lemon juice, emanating from Bess's kitchen. "What if I can't love another baby as much as I love Zoe?"

Bess smiled fondly. "I remember feeling that way, after I had Marjorie and got pregnant with Scott. I thought, *I love her so much, there's no way I'll ever be able to love a new baby even half this much.* But I surprised myself. You will too. I promise. And who knows?" She gave Janice a lipsticky smile and nodded toward her niece's belly. "Maybe this baby's going to be special. Maybe he's got something big to do in the world."

Janice doubted that. She kept her mouth shut as Bess got to her feet. "Sleep on it," she said to Janice, hugging her, and, Janice saw, slipping twenty dollars into the diaper bag. "I promise, things will look better in the morning."

Janice drove slowly, following Passyunk Avenue to Columbus Boulevard until she arrived at the house in Fishtown she and Sam were renting. *Just get on with it*, she thought, and unlocked the front door. She heard all the familiar sounds: Jim Gardner on Channel 6 broadcasting the evening's headlines, Sam snoring quietly in the bedroom. She let him sleep, waiting until he came to the kitchen, his hair sticking up in spikes around his head, and let him pour a cup of coffee before saying, "I have some news."

She ended up having to tell him twice, while he stood in front of the fridge, blank-faced, rubbing at his head and staring at her, looking slack-jawed and, she thought uncharitably, a little stupid. "Another baby?" he finally asked. Janice nodded. His face fell, and he said exactly what she'd thought when she'd learned: "Shit." And then, "What are we going to do?"

"Have another baby, I guess." Janice went to the living room where she half sat, half fell onto the sofa. After a minute, Sam sat down beside her. He put one arm around her shoulders, pulling her close. "It'll be okay," he said, sounding like he was trying to convince her, and himself. "We'll figure it out." That was when Janice finally let herself cry.

Janice did her best to think happy thoughts, to try to feel a fraction of the excitement that she had the first time around, but the remainder of her pregnancy was as hard as the first one had been easy. With Zoe, she hadn't shown at all until well into her sixth month, but as the next few weeks unfolded, she gained twenty pounds, and watched, in amazement and no small amount of horror, as her body transformed in a manner that made her feel monstrous. Her stomach and thighs and breasts bulged. Her belly button turned itself inside out and poked against her shirts like a pumpkin stalk; her feet grew an entire shoe size; her cheeks and the bridge of her nose darkened. Everything she ate gave her agonizing heartburn, and, even after she'd cut out tomatoes and coffee and dairy and chocolate, her chest and throat burned like fire whenever she lay down.

"It's going to be a boy," Sam would say, resting his hands on the outsized globe of her belly. They'd decided not to have an ultrasound—their insurance wouldn't cover it, and Sam was so convinced it was a boy that he didn't see the point. Janice was less certain. *It's going to be a monster* was what she sometimes couldn't stop herself from thinking.

Her due date came and went. When she was a week overdue, Dr. Gaines scheduled a C-section. The night before Janice was to report to the hospital, her labor began . . . but not with the contractions she remembered from Zoe's birth: pains that rose and crested, sharpening and swelling into agony, then receding long enough for her to catch her breath and even sleep for a few minutes between them. This was different, an agony that felt endless. It began in her lower back and it radiated all the way to her toes and fingertips, her jaw, her face, even the crown of her head, and the pain never stopped or even faded. It was unrelenting; misery without end, a world of hurt where she would live forever.

Sam drove her to Pennsylvania Hospital, where she labored for an eternity of red hours, screaming herself hoarse, until finally, the baby's heartbeat dipped sufficiently to necessitate an emergency Cesarean. A nurse helped Janice sit up and lean forward, and Janice could guess at the size of the needle from the horror on her husband's face, but she was too exhausted and miserable to care. She felt like an animal in a trap, ready to chew off her own limbs to escape. As the blessed numbness rolled down her body, Janice was wheeled to the operating room. A drape was unfolded just below her breasts, but she still shut her eyes when the cutting started, listening for the calls of "suction" and "suture," waiting to hear the baby's cry. By the time they stitched her up, she was shivering violently. Everything was hurting, as if the pain had never stopped. The space between her legs burned like it had been dipped in acid and set on fire. She felt as raw as if she'd been chewed.

"Another girl," Sam said, settling the bundle awkwardly against her chest. Janice remembered how dainty Zoe had felt—a tiny, warm cloud wrapped up in a blanket. This baby felt gigantic, huge and unwieldy. There was a fringe of greasy-looking dark hair around her bald head. Her eyes were squinched shut, and her lips were smacking, moving in blind sucking motions that made Janice think about sea creatures, deep in the ocean's trenches, eyeless things that never saw the light.

She held her baby and shut her eyes, waiting to feel the thing she remembered from Zoe's birth, the thing that all the books and soap operas, every girlfriend and female relation from Aunt Bess to her own mom, her sisters and sisters-in-law, had promised she would feel: a tidal wave of love, undeniable in its presence, inarguable in its force.

This time, Janice felt empty and numb; dull, and so tired. She felt like a heavyweight boxer had used her body as a punching bag after she'd slid down a staircase made of razors. Her mouth was dry. Her head was throbbing, and tears were dripping down her face to plop on top of the baby's bald skull.

"Take her," she husked, in a rasping whisper, and held out the bundle, until her husband lifted it from her arms.

The next morning, a nurse came, to try and get the new baby to nurse. "Does this little one have a name yet?"

Janice shrugged. She and Sam had been so sure this baby was a boy, they'd picked a boy's name—Matthew—and had never even talked about girls' names. Janice considered and rejected Mattie and Matilda—*Mattie* sounded too much like *matted*, and Matilda was too old-fashioned.

"Cassandra," she said. She wasn't sure where the name came from, unless it was a book she'd read about Greek myths, back in middle school. Janice had never known a Cassandra in real life and had only the vaguest notion of who the mythological Cassandra might have been. Only later would she learn—or relearn, if she had, in fact, already known it—that Cassandra was a prophetess, cursed to speak the truth and have no one believe her.

Had the name shaped Cassie's life somehow, condemning her to sorrow? Would things have been different if Janice had named her unplanned second daughter Sarah or Rachel or Jane? She would never know. But sometimes, late at night, walking the hallway with Cassie screaming in her arms, begging her baby to go back to sleep, sometimes crying herself, Janice would think of how it could have been different, if she'd waited longer to have another child . . . or, most of all, if she'd found a doctor who'd do what Dr. Gaines wouldn't, if she'd never had Cassie at all. *I will never be able to love her*, she'd think, and then hate herself for thinking. *I can't do it, no matter how hard I try.*

Cassie

ALASKA, 2024

Cassie Grossberg zipped her down parka. She put on her left glove with her right hand and used her teeth to tug her right glove over her wrist. She strapped a headlamp around her forehead, over the brim of her knitted wool hat, and opened the door. It was nine o'clock in the morning, the starless sky still black as a pot of ink outside, with an icy, knife-edged wind blowing hard enough to make the sides of her wooden house groan. Winter in Alaska felt like punishment. It was cold, of course, and endlessly dark. The sky was black at seven in the morning, when kids left for school. It was dark again by three in the afternoon, when the dismissal bell rang. The hockey teams played under floodlights; the kids on the cross-country ski team practiced with headlamps. Everyone learned to live with it. Either that, or they flew off to Hawaii.

Alaska's winters suited Cassie. The sharp-edged wind found all of the gaps in her clothing—the space between her scarf and her parka's zipper, the gap between her hat and her collar—and probed at them zealously. It felt purposefully cruel; a wind that held a grudge, that sidled close and whispered in your ear every shameful, stupid thing you'd ever done. It was unrelenting and pitiless. It felt like what she deserved.

That morning, Cassie felt the cold, but she felt something else, too—a prickle of unease at the back of her neck; an unwelcome sensation that meant that, somewhere, her songs were being played; her name was being spoken. It had been that way for years. She'd get that uncomfortably itchy feeling, that sensation of being watched, and she'd turn on the radio or the TV, and boom, there they'd be, her voice and Zoe's, singing "The Gift" or "Flavor of the Week" or "Last Night in Fishtown." And she'd be forced to think of her sister, to remember, even though remembering hurt.

When they were girls, Zoe had been Cassie's companion, her protector; once, she'd believed, her friend. Had things gone the way they should have, they would have grown up and gone in separate directions: Cassie, to a life in classical music, and Zoe, probably, to college, unless her sister had managed to find some other path to the stardom she'd always yearned for. A degree, a husband, a regular kind of job.

That hadn't happened. And now . . .

"Never mind," Cassie rasped.

Her dog, Wesley, looked up at her. His expression seemed vaguely startled. Cassie wondered how long it had been since he'd heard her talk. She crouched down to scratch behind his ears. At just under twenty pounds, Wesley was conveniently portable, easy for Cassie to scoop up under an arm or tuck into her coat as needed.

Cassie had never planned on getting a dog. Pets were a comfort. They provided companionship. Cassie hadn't thought she deserved either of those things. But six years ago, she'd opened her door to find a small dog with reddish-brown fur and white spots, his tail tucked neatly underneath him, ears quivering uncertainly as he looked at her.

"Hello," she said, before she could stop herself. He hadn't been wearing a collar, and when she'd brought him to the vet, she found that he wasn't chipped. "You could take him to the shelter," the tech said. "But, you know, older dogs . . ." Her voice trailed off, and, right on cue, the little dog had whimpered, as if he understood what he'd heard. Cassie did not deserve the comfort of a dog. She'd hurt everyone who'd gotten close to her. But the dog didn't deserve a death sentence. Cassie had paid the bill and carried the dog to her car.

"I'm not going to be a lot of fun," she warned the dog, unlocking the car's doors. Wesley regarded her warily. She put him in the back seat and googled the location of the nearest pet shop, where she bought a leash, a collar, a bag of kibble, and a crate that Wesley ended up never using, preferring, instead, to sleep curled up at the foot of Cassie's single bed.

Cassie had done her best to make a life where she saw, and spoke to, as few people as possible. She'd had enough of people; enough of attention, enough of the world. Early on, after everything had gone wrong, she'd thought about killing herself. She'd wanted to die. Only that felt like the easy way out, like she was ducking her punishment, avoiding what she deserved. Which was to live out her days alone, with the knowledge of all the pain she'd caused the people who had loved her.

She'd started out in Oregon, three thousand miles from home, in an A-frame, an hour outside of Portland. *Stunning views of the Pacific Ocean, rolling sand dunes and Salmon Creek*, the ad had read. Cassie had ordered blackout curtains to cover the windows that faced the water, and had plodded through her days. She didn't have a TV, didn't buy new clothes, didn't go out to the movies or to restaurants. She ate the same three meals each day: cereal for breakfast, a sandwich for lunch, a chicken breast for dinner. She didn't listen to any music, didn't buy a piano or sing in the shower. On the rare occasions when she needed to go somewhere, she kept the car radio tuned to the all-news channel. She shopped for groceries early in the morning or late at night and did her banking online. But there were too many people; too many eyes that lit up in recognition at her face; too many occasions when she'd hear a bar or two of the band's music and be sent hurtling back to a place she didn't want to go.

Seven months into a yearlong lease, Cassie had been at the drugstore, buying toothpaste and tampons, when she'd caught a tinny, string-heavy Muzak version of "The Gift," emerging from the store's speakers. It had been playing while she'd paid, and the checkout girl had looked at the name on Cassie's credit card, then up at Cass, her eyes wide and wondering. The name on the card was C. Grossberg. She hadn't become Cassie Griffin until the record label had officially signed off on the last name that her sister had chosen. "It's just easier," Jerry had told them, in his high, boyish voice, with a smile that showed all of his teeth. Jerry's last name had once been Nussbaum before it became Nance, a fact he hadn't mentioned, that afternoon or ever.

Did the girl recognize her, in spite of the different last name? Cassie had grabbed her stuff, declined a receipt with a curt shake of her head, and hurried out of the store. At home, she'd sat up all night, in the dark, trying to decide where she would run.

At five in the morning, she bought a plane ticket. Several hours later, she was on an Alaska Airlines flight to Anchorage. When she landed, she took a taxi to a car dealership, where she paid cash for her SUV, and forced herself to smile at the salesman.

"Where do people go when they don't want anyone to find them?"

"Excuse me?" The guy was looking at her closely. Did he recognize her? Or was she making him uncomfortable? Was she acting weird? "Stop staring," Zoe used to tell her, in nursery school and elementary school and middle school. Zoe would deliver her instructions in a murmur, standing close to her sister. When more lengthy or explicit guidance was required, she'd take Cassie's sleeve and tow her into a corner so that no one could overhear. "Close your mouth. Stop smiling, it looks weird. Just act normal." The problem was that Cassie never knew what "normal" was. She'd always relied on Zoe to tell her.

In the too-bright showroom, with its gleaming tiled floors and shiny new cars, Cassie fumbled for a story.

"I . . . My ex-husband has been harassing me." Cassie looked at herself, wincing internally. Would this guy believe that someone who looked like her had been married, and that this putative former spouse would care enough about her to keep bothering her—that he wouldn't, instead, just be relieved that she was out of his life? Cassie told herself not to worry. Fat people got married. Both of the sisters on the TV show *My 600-lb Life* had boyfriends. *There's a lid for every pot*, her great-aunt Bess used to say, and Cassie would think, *I'm going to need a very big lid*. But there was truth to what she'd said. There *had* been a man who'd said he'd loved her. Once.

Cassie remembered how he'd traced her eyebrows with one fingertip. How he'd looked down at her when she'd been flushed and rumpled and smiling. How he'd made her feel lovely and cherished. She shook her head, shoved the thought into the soft meat of her memory, and told the salesman, "I want to be far away from other people."

"Well, you're in the right state, for sure." He'd shown her a map, pointing out the cities and the big tourist spots—Anchorage and Seward and Homer, the ports where the cruise ships docked, Talkeetna, the Denali range. "But anywhere that isn't one of those places can get pretty isolated." Cassie had looked at the map, considering all of the wide-open spaces.

"What do you do? For a living?" the salesman asked. "You'll need a job, right?"

"My parents left me some money." Cassie felt bad for lying, because her parents were alive and well, still living in Philadelphia. She'd barely spoken to them since that final, terrible night in Detroit. Contact with her mom and dad was one more comfort she didn't deserve.

My fault, Cassie had said, when she'd told her mother what had happened, and why she couldn't come home. *All my fault.*

The salesman had taken her money and had given her the map, along with the keys, and she'd started driving, following the highway out of town. The road ran parallel to a river, and it was a struggle not to stare or be distracted by the grandeur of the landscape. She'd never seen land so vividly green and mountains so close. They crowded against the perimeter of the road, their peaks pushing into the misty sky. Downtown Anchorage had felt like any medium-sized city, with strip malls and fast-food restaurants, the same stores and signs Cassie had seen all across the country. But after half an hour of driving, the land felt enchanted, otherworldly and wild. Best of all, it felt very far away—different, and distant, from anywhere she'd ever been.

She'd spent the first night in a hotel in Seward, the second in Homer. She'd considered pushing on, maybe to Juneau, or all the way to the Aleutian Islands, but those, she suspected, would be just like any other small town, where everyone knew everyone, and where, eventually, people would know her.

And so she'd backtracked along the Cook Inlet, passing by some towns that had names that sounded vaguely Russian, and others that sounded Native American, and some with names that seemed to have been made up by children: Kalifornsky Beach, Kasilof, Clam Gulch, Nikiski, Anchor Point, Funny River, Sterling, Ninilchik, Soldotna. She followed narrow paved roads and bumpy dirt roads that terminated in dead ends or trailed off into forests, until she found what she was looking for: a "for sale by owner" sign on a likely-looking piece of land along a barely paved road between Seward and Homer, miles away from anything that resembled a town.

The owners were a young married couple who'd moved to Alaska to be homesteaders and live off the grid. They had lasted a year. When Cassie found them, the wife was expecting, and winter was coming, and they were desperate to move back to California. Cassie was glad to offer them the price they were asking and they were overjoyed to take it. She spent the night in a hotel, found a lawyer in Homer the next morning who'd given zero indication of knowing who Cassie was, and they'd concluded the deal in the woman's office by noon. She signed her name a few dozen times, wrote one very large check and several smaller ones, and shook the former owners' hands. And then Cassie Grossberg, once Griffin, was the official owner of fifty acres in the woods, a mile south of the Kenai River.

It was as far as she could go. It still wasn't far enough.

In the doorway of her one-room home, Cassie made a clicking noise with her tongue. Wesley's pointy ears swiveled in her direction and he trotted over, tongue lolling, looking up at her as his stub of a tail quivered. When he'd first shown up, Wesley had been half-starved, so skinny that each of his ribs showed through his fur. Now he weighed twenty pounds and had a lean, deep-chested body. His paws were white, with brown freckles, and he'd cross them neatly when he lay on the bed or the rug and looked up at her with his big, dark eyes. Soulful eyes, Cassie sometimes thought, with lines of dark-brown fur extending from their corners toward his ears, like Cleopatra-style eyeliner. He was well-fed, and never alone, but he still had a mournful aspect, and he'd stick close to her heels whenever she went outside. He sat on her lap when she was reading; he curled beside her when she napped; he licked her cheeks when she cried and seemed to listen when she talked to him, so attentively that Cassie was almost convinced that he understood everything she said.

She started down the steps. Wesley trotted beside her. When they reached the bottom, he hopped up on his hind paws to give her one of what Cassie called his Patented Looks of Beseechment. Cassie pulled a piece of salmon jerky out of her pocket and tossed it to him. While Wesley daintily devoured his treat, she double-checked her bucket to make sure it held everything she'd need for her morning. All-purpose cleaning spray for the counters; a spray jar full of a water-and-vinegar solution for the windows; toilet cleaner and a scrub brush; microfiber cloths for dusting; and rags for scrubbing the floor. Murphy Oil Soap and Lestoil; Lysol and Febreze.

Cozy Treehouse in the Woods! was how the Airbnb ad she'd written described the tiny houses she'd had built. She'd moved into the trailer the married couple had left behind and spent a year working with an architect and a general contractor, until the construction was complete. The three houses had been built on stilts, tucked into the forest, completely invisible from the road, and from their neighbors. They perched above the tree line, overlooking the river and the treetops and, at night, the wide-open, star-filled sky. Each house was just one rectangular room, plus a bathroom and a kitchenette, thoughtfully constructed, with built-in storage and creative use of space. Cassie had hired a decorator to furnish two of the interiors with a comfortable king-sized bed, a two-burner stove and a miniature fridge, as well as a small, high table with two barstools, a love seat, and a writing desk. The floors were hardwood, except for the bathroom, which had heated tiled floors. She'd hired a kid with a drone to take aerial photographs of the houses, the land, and the river, and a professional photographer to shoot the interiors. Then she'd posted ads on different websites, writing the descriptions like she'd once composed songs, working to find the rhythm of the language, tweaking the listing for maximum response.

The two rental cabins were booked an average of two hundred nights a year, at an average of one hundred and fifty dollars per night. Even minus the expense of upkeep and utilities, they brought in more than enough to keep Cassie and Wesley clothed and fed and happy, their expenses covered, their taxes paid. They lived in the third tree-house, located even farther into the woods, at the end of an unmarked dirt path. Her street had no name, her house had no number, and Cassie had never had visitors. No other human being had ever set foot inside her home; no other voice had ever moved through its atmosphere, set-ting subatomic particles bouncing off each other until time ran out and the world ended. *Every piece of music you've ever played is still playing, at a level too quiet for anyone to hear.* Her first piano teacher had told her that, and Cassie had been fascinated by the concept. It was a kind of immor-tality. Once, she'd liked to imagine the pieces of music she loved going on forever. Later, it made her shiver with pride to think that every song she'd ever sung was still out there, echoing in the world. Now it just made her feel guilty and sad.

She walked with her headlamp lighting the way and Wesley trot-ting beside her, their breath puffing out in white clouds as they followed the snow-covered path in the darkness. A squirrel chit-tered, and Wesley darted ahead of her, his head in constant mo-tion, turning left, then right, then left again. She'd never seen him actually catch a squirrel, but he'd gotten a bird once. Cas-sie had watched as he'd snatched the tiny brown feathered body right off the ground and gobbled it down, still twitching, in three gulps. It had been horrifying. The bird's wings had been beating in-side of Wesley's mouth, in his throat, still, as he'd swallowed. *There's a song here*, she'd thought. Something about those desperate, tiny wings, something about that casual savagery, and how you could just be mov-ing, heedlessly, through your life, never knowing how close you were to its end. A scrap of the *unatanah tokef*, the prayer she'd once recited with her parents at Yom Kippur, came to mind: *On Rosh Hashanah it is written and on Yom Kippur it is sealed: how many will pass away and how many will be created, who will live and who will die; who will come to his timely end, and who to an untimely end; who will perish by fire and who by water; who by the sword and who by beast.*

Who by tooth and who by claw, Cassie thought. *Who by knife and who by gun. Who by love.* She'd made herself stop, clamping down on the thought, hard and fast, like she was cauterizing a bleeding artery, sealing a wound with fire. There would be no more songs. Not ever. That was the deal. She'd traded music for her life, such as it was. She'd struck a kind of fairy-tale bargain she'd thought would comfort her or, at least, would let her live with herself. Some days, it worked. Other days—most days—she could admit that it didn't. Most days, Cassie felt like she was wearing a shirt made of thorns, like she'd swallowed a ball of fishhooks. She was in constant torment, a crushed-glass sorrow that would never end. There would be no forgiveness for her. Not ever.

She trudged through the unyielding darkness with her bucket in one mittened hand, its handle biting into her palm, chin tucked toward her chest, letting her feet carry her body up the eight steps to the first treehouse. She knocked on the door. "Hello! Housekeeping!" When she'd started renting the cabins, she'd set up a system to ensure that her guests never saw her. The doors had digital locks. Cassie would text her tenants a code to unlock them the day they arrived. She'd communicate with them exclusively by text, answering questions about restaurants and the Wi-Fi password and what to do if the microwave wasn't working, never using a name, never revealing that she lived on the property. If her guests ever spotted her, with her bucket in one hand and her broom and mop in the other and a little dog trailing at her heel, they'd think she was the housekeeper, the hired help. They'd have no reason to believe she was the owner, or that she'd once been someone else entirely.

As soon as Cassie had the cabin door open, Wesley beelined for the unmade bed, hopping up and nosing at the pillows to make himself a nest.

"Oh, no you don't. Off," Cassie said. Wesley's ears and tail drooped as he hopped off the bed and curled neatly in front of the wood-burning stove in the corner. He crossed his paws, left over right, and rested his head on top of them with a sigh.

Cassie pulled off her parka and pulled on a pair of nitrile gloves. At the kitchen sink, she filled up her bucket with hot water and cleanser, and started on the floors, sweeping, then mopping, welcoming the exertion, the mindless repetition. Work would ground her in her current reality, and get that unsettled, prickling sensation to go away. It would remind her what she really was, and help her not to think of how, once, she'd been something else.

Cassie worked quickly, with the efficiency born of experience. When she was done, she refilled the basket of treats she left for her guests: a bag of locally roasted coffee, a bottle of wine, and a tiny carved wooden bear keychain (she bought them in bulk from a woodworker in Homer). She set the basket in the center of the bed, then stood by the door and looked around. "What do you think? Good enough?"

Wesley had fallen asleep. At the sound of her voice, he worked one eye half-open, and his tail gave a desultory quiver. Cassie reloaded her bucket. She clicked her tongue for Wesley, and locked the door behind her. At eleven o'clock, the sky was as light as it got in the winter, less inky black, more dove gray. Cassie walked down the path, thinking about Treehouse Two and what she'd find there, when she heard raised voices. She lifted her head and saw two women, bundled up for the weather, trekking across the yard.

Cassie froze, but it was too late. They'd seen her, and one of the women was waving. "Hi! Hello there! Can you help us?"

Cassie hunched her shoulders and dipped her chin. For one moment she found herself wishing, desperately, to be who she'd been, to be what she'd been, twenty years ago. There were things about life in the public eye that she'd hated, but Cassie had learned that fame conferred a strange kind of invisibility. When she was out in the world, she had people—her bandmates, at first; security, eventually; not to mention managers, hairdressers and makeup artists and stylists, and all of their assistants, plus assorted hangers-on. She could place herself in the center of the scrum, where she couldn't be seen. She could let her sister take the brunt of the attention. Let Zoe wave and pose and smile, while Cassie plodded forward, head down, eyes on her feet and people all around her. Safe.

And onstage . . . Cassie felt her eyes slip briefly shut. That was how she'd sing, with her eyes closed for as long as she could get away with it. It was, she knew, a little kid's trick, pretending that if she couldn't see the audience, they couldn't see her. But it had worked. When she had to look, the spotlights would erase the audience, those avid faces and hungry eyes. And sometimes, with her hands on the keyboard, or wrapped around the microphone stand, with her sister on one side of her and Russell on the other, she would feel something even better than invisible. She would feel appreciated. Respected. Loved.

The woman was still waving. "Yoo-hoo!" she called. "Can you hear me?"

Yoo-hoo, Cassie thought, amused in spite of herself. She hadn't heard a *yoo-hoo* since she was a kid, in the company of her great-aunt Bess, whose thick Philadelphia accent had delighted her and her sister.

"Say *water*," Zoe would instruct her, sitting at her kitchen table while Bess rolled out dough for rugelach, or stirred chocolate chips into cookie batter.

"Wooder."

"Say *Eagles*."

"Iggles."

"Say *bagel*."

"Beggle."

Cassie pushed the memory away and held still, not responding, but not running, doing her very best impression of someone who was not quite right.

It was funny, she thought, as the woman approached (a little hesitantly, Cassie was pleased to see). For a long time, Cassie had done her very best to approximate normalcy, trying as hard as she could to look and talk and behave like a regular girl. She could remember reading the Archie comic books and Nancy Drew mysteries that Bess had in the bookshelves of the third-floor bedroom where her daughters and nieces and nephews, including Cassie's own mother, had once slept, and Baby-Sitters Club books that Zoe brought home. Cassie had read them carefully, paying attention to how the characters spoke to other kids, thinking it would help her. It had never worked. Especially because she hadn't realized that some of her great-aunt's books were quite old, and nobody her age said that things were "swell," or referred to their friends as "chums." She'd wanted friends—or, at least, a friend. And if she couldn't have that, she wanted the other kids to leave her alone. After a dozen bruising years, she realized that neither of those things was likely to happen. She was fat, she was ugly, and there was something fundamentally different about her, something strange and wrong. Nobody was ever going to like her. She would never have a friend. The best she could hope for was to go unnoticed.

"Hi there!" The woman was trotting toward her, still waving. "Hello! Do you work here?"

Cassie nodded, raising her bucket of cleaning supplies, hoping the two gestures, combined, would say, *I am but a humble, possibly mentally challenged cleaning lady.*

"Um, we were just wondering if there's anywhere near here we can buy . . ." She lowered her voice to a stage whisper. "Feminine supplies."

Cassie did her best not to flinch away from the woman's inspection. She tried not to hear the echo of long-ago voices, to notice how the women's gaze reminded her of every other girl and woman who'd ever looked her over and found her pathetic. She cleared her throat. "Fritz Creek General Store," she muttered, and pointed in the correct direction.

"Thank you!" The woman bobbed her head and went trotting back to her rental car. Cassie kept walking. That buzzing, unsettled feeling was back: the prickle under her collar, that wobbliness in her knees, and the air was so cold it stung.

At home, she gave Wesley a bowl of kibble and a breath-freshening bone and looked around. Sometimes, she imagined Zoe inspecting her house, taking in the single bed tucked against one wall, the cheap plastic-walled tub in the bathroom, which lacked the fancy tiles and heated floors she'd used for the rentals. Zoe would walk around slowly, with eyebrows arched, taking note of what was there, and what was not, how there was no art on the walls, no photographs on display. She would ask Cass if she was trying to live like a nun, or when she'd be announcing her candidacy for sainthood. She'd rub Cassie's comforter between her fingers and ask if there wasn't a bed of thorns available. *You're beating yourself up*, she'd say. Her eyes would look silvery and cool in the thin winter sunshine. Her voice would be light and mocking. *You're punishing yourself. And how's that working out for you? Do you really think you could ever punish yourself enough to make up for what you've done? That you could ever suffer enough for anyone to forgive you?*

Cassie groaned out loud, which made Wesley come trotting over. He hopped onto his back legs, set one paw on her thigh, and looked up at her. Cassie thought his expression was concerned. But maybe—probably—that was a lie. Wesley cared about her only because she had opposable thumbs and access to the dog food. If she died, he'd probably move along to the next doorstep. Possibly after eating her face, just like he'd eaten that bird. She wasn't special. She didn't matter. Not to him. Not to anyone.

In the tiny kitchen, she brewed a cup of peppermint tea and sat at the table, letting the fragrant steam warm her face. A small pleasure, one she decided she could allow. *It's okay. You're okay*, she told herself. *You're safe. No one will find you, and you won't hurt anyone else.* The songs she'd sung could go on without her, vibrating at increasingly minuscule increments. The music she'd made would have its own life. Her lyrics would be sung by girls she'd never meet, the fat girls, the frizzy-haired girls, the strange ones. Girls who were lonely, like she'd been, who felt invisible, like she'd felt. Maybe her songs would comfort them. Maybe that comfort would help to offset the devastation she'd left when she'd fled. Maybe God would take it into account, and when she died, there would be nothing. Not torment. Not heaven. Just nothing. That was all she allowed herself to hope for.

When her phone rang, Cassie jumped, and couldn't keep a tiny screech from escaping her lips. She stared at it for a minute as it buzzed and vibrated on the counter like a thing possessed. If it was a tenant, she'd let the call go to voicemail, she decided. Why did people insist on calling, anyhow? Didn't everyone text these days?

She looked at the screen, frowning. There were only three people in the world she actually knew who had her number. One was her mother. ("You don't have to talk to me, Cassie, not if you're not ready, but at the very least, Dad and I need to know that you're alive.") Cassie wouldn't pick up the phone when Janice called, but she would text her mother a monthly proof-of-life message, keeping it as short as she could. *I'm here. I'm fine.* If she didn't speak to her mother, she couldn't be tempted to ask questions whose answers she did not deserve. The second person was Aunt Bess. "Talk to your sister," Bess had told her, after Cassie had called from Detroit on that terrible morning. "Whatever happened, Cassie, you'll feel better if you talk about it." But that was a lie. Cassie would never feel better.

The third person—the one who was calling—was the band's former manager, CJ, who'd also insisted on having a way to reach her. The stated reason for this was so he could keep her apprised of any band-related financial or legal issue that arose. The reality was he'd call to tell her about proposed Vegas residencies ("They're offering a fortune, Cassie, an absolute fortune, and it would just be one show a night, five days a week") and possible jukebox-style Broadway musicals ("It's the team that did *Head Over Heels*, and listen, if it does a tenth of what *Mamma Mia* did for ABBA, your children's children's children will be rich") and rappers who wanted to sample a snippet of one of their songs ("It could be good, could introduce you guys to a whole new audience"). Cassie always told him no, whenever it was in her power to refuse, which was not always, but still, no matter how many times she told him no, CJ would insist on calling, dangling opportunities in front of her like they were plums. Or, she thought sourly, apples in the Garden of Eden.

CJ didn't call more than three or four times a year. But every time he did call, Cassie would endure a moment of breath-stealing, skin-crawling dread, terrified that, this time, it wouldn't be a question about tax payments or Broadway shows or reunion tours; that, instead, it would be more bad news, and he would be calling to tell her that someone else had died.

"Hello?"

"Cassie! Good to hear your voice." CJ always began the same way, and from his bluff, hearty tone, she could tell that this wasn't the call she was dreading.

"What's going on?"

CJ paused. Cassie tried to picture him, not as he'd been, with his round face and easy smile, but how he would look now. His dark blond hair had been thinning when she'd known him. Had he gone bald? Or had he gotten hair transplants or a toupee? Had he gained weight, or lost it, becoming one of those middle-aged guys that she'd seen in Portland, fit almost to the point of gauntness, zipping around on their carbon-fiber bikes like Lycra-clad strips of fruit leather? Maybe he'd had kids. She realized with a jolt that it was even possible he had grandkids by now.

"Listen," he was saying, speaking rapidly. "And please hear me out before you say no. We're coming up on the twenty-fifth anniversary of the album . . ."

"No."

CJ kept talking. "And there's this show on Netflix, *Evermore* . . ."

Cassie closed her eyes. CJ had begged and pleaded and used every weapon at his disposal to get her to agree to giving *Evermore*'s producers permission to use a handful of the band's songs. She would have said no, the way she always did, except CJ had told her that Russell's niece was a production assistant on the show. "It would mean the world to her," he'd said. "It would be a kindness." Left unsaid was how many unkindnesses the family had endured; how Cassie owed them. *Fine*, she'd finally told CJ. *Okay. Fine.*

"*Evermore* is the top-rated show for the past month. The past *month*, Cassie. It's completely unprecedented. The director's a Griffin Sisters superfan. She's given interviews talking about how much she loved your music when she was in high school."

Cassie didn't say anything.

"The songs are blowing up. They're actually charting again." CJ was talking faster and faster, like if he got the words out quickly enough Cassie would be fooled into saying yes. "If there was ever a moment to capitalize—there's all of this new interest, all of these new kids connecting with your music, and I think—"

"No."

"Cassie." His voice became gentler. "Your songs meant something to girls. And girls are in trouble right now. You read the news, don't you?"

Cassie did not. She didn't bother telling CJ that.

"This country is having a mental health crisis," CJ said, assuming a lecturing tone, "and women are getting the worst of it. The pandemic was devastating to kids. Especially teenagers. Especially teenage girls. They need you," he said. Which set off an echo in Cassie's brain, a familiar voice saying, *What's the point of being able to sing like you can if no one hears you? What's the point of a gift if you don't share it?*

Shut up, Cassie told the voice.

"What?" CJ asked, sounding offended. Cassie realized she must have said it out loud.

"No one needs me." She felt herself flush as soon as she heard how self-pitying it sounded. "They've got the songs. Isn't that enough?"

"I think that you have more to give."

I think you're wrong, Cassie thought. "Goodbye," she said, and ended the call. Her hands were shaking. Her knees felt watery.

She sat at her desk, opened her elderly laptop, logged into her banking account, and blinked when she saw that a sizable sum had been deposited the previous week. That, at least, explained the prickling sensation. Something had been happening with the band's music. It must have been the show CJ had mentioned.

As quickly as she could, like a criminal hiding evidence, Cassie got rid of the money in a series of four-figure donations: one to the animal shelter where Wesley had almost ended up; another to the national office of Big Brothers Big Sisters. Doctors Without Borders, the ACLU, the NAACP. An organization that helped new immigrants find jobs; another that helped abused women. Anything that uplifted the sick and the needy, the young and abused, the powerless of all races and nations.

When the money was gone, she looked over her bank statement, to make sure that her utility bills were being paid and that the on-line security expert CJ had found for her, a young woman whose job was to keep mentions of Cassie off the Internet, had gotten her monthly retainer. Then she pulled a notebook off the stack of papers beside her laptop, opening it to a fresh, blank page. She picked up a pen. Once, she'd used notebooks like these to write down lyrics, bits of melodies, ideas for songs. Then she'd tried writing letters. *Dear Mom and Dad. Dear Zoe. Dear CJ. Dear Tommy. Dear Cam. Dear Mrs. D'Angelo.* But no matter what she said, it all came down to two words, which became her routine.

I'm sorry, she wrote, in neat cursive, in black ink. She wrote it again, and again and again, over and over, in neat rows, until the page was full, and then she flipped open a fresh page and kept writing.

Cassie knew that apologies, sent or unsent, wouldn't do what she wanted. A hundred thousand notebooks filled with a million repeti-tions of *I'm sorry* would still never be enough. But writing filled the empty hours. It kept her hands busy. And if it didn't make her feel any better, at least it didn't leave her feeling any worse.

Janice
PHILADELPHIA, 1987

When Zoe was almost five years old and Cassie was almost four, Janice came to the synagogue for the twelve P.M. preschool pickup, and found the teacher, Miss Lori, waiting at the door. "Can I talk to you for a minute?" Miss Lori asked, as the other moms and nannies streamed past her.

"What is it?" Janice asked wearily, preparing herself for the *This school is no longer a good fit* conversation. Every minute of Cassie's life had been a struggle—a struggle to get her to sleep when she was a baby; a struggle when she wouldn't walk or talk when she was a toddler. Janice was unsurprised that preschool had become a problem too. Still, she had no idea what she'd do if the teachers told her they couldn't handle Cassie, or what that would mean for her daughter's move to kindergarten.

But Miss Lori didn't seem angry, which would have been bad, or concerned, which would have been worse. There were pink ovals high on her cheeks and her voice, normally low and lulling to the point of being hypnotic, was high and animated. "How long has Cassie been taking piano lessons?" she asked.

Janice was certain she'd heard wrong. Maybe Miss Lori was trying to sell them on some additional programming, or the extended-day sessions, which Janice would have loved, but which she and Sam couldn't afford. Sending two kids to preschool, even with financial aid, was already straining their budget. "Oh, no, we can't afford lessons. Or a piano. Ha-ha-ha!"

Miss Lori looked at her strangely. "So Cassie isn't taking lessons somewhere?"

Janice shook her head.

"Because Miss Carlie played the 'Good Morning Song' on the piano this morning. And then, when it was circle time, Cassie didn't sit with the rest of the class." *As usual*, Janice thought, but, before she could apologize for her daughter, Miss Lori continued. "Cassie went over to the piano, and she played the whole song. Perfectly. She didn't miss a note!"

Janice stared at the teacher. Her brain felt sluggish. "She did?"

Miss Lori nodded. Janice followed her into the classroom, which was cozy, low-ceilinged and warmly lit, and still smelled like the muffins the kids had baked for snack. Zoe was coloring at a toddler-height table with a group of other children, the ones whose parents could afford extended days. Zoe's hair was still in neatly braided pigtails, her outfit still pristine. Cass was alone in the corner, crouching in front of a pile of Lego Duplos, building something hulking and shapeless. Her light-brown curls were matted, and her pants had a new rip at the knee.

"Cassie," called Miss Lori, "can you come to the piano for a minute?"

Cassie got to her feet, glancing toward the table.

"Go ahead," said Zoe, with her eyes on her construction paper. "It's okay."

Cassie walked to the piano and clambered, laboriously, onto the bench. Janice watched, wishing, for the thousandth time, that her second child possessed some of her first one's grace, just a little bit of Zoe's ease or charm. Being pretty made life easier for girls, Janice thought. It wasn't fair, but it was true.

Miss Lori crouched down to put her face at Cassie's eye level. "Cassie, do you remember the song you played this morning?" she asked, speaking slowly and clearly. "Can you play it for your mommy?"

Cassie was still expressionless, but she set her hands on the keys and began to play. Janice stared, watching Cassie's fingers moving nimbly, hearing the music, and the words to the song in her head: "Good morning, good morning, good morning to you! Good morning, my friends, and it's nice to see you, too!"

Cassie wasn't just picking out the melody with one finger, either, Janice saw. She was playing with both hands, moving them both fluidly, her fingers unerringly finding the right keys, like she'd been doing it all her life.

Janice blinked. "Cassie," she said. Her tongue felt thick and strange. "Who taught you how to do that?"

"No one," Cassie mumbled.

"So how do you know how? How did you learn?"

Cassie shrugged.

Miss Lori looked at Janice before turning back to the piano. "Cassie," she said. "Can you play 'Happy Birthday' for us?"

Again, Cassie looked at her sister. "Go ahead," said Zoe. Cassie's fingers moved over the keys, right hand picking out the familiar melody, left hand playing chords. "My God," Janice murmured.

"Do you have musicians in the family?" Miss Lori was asking. "Are you musical yourself?"

Janice shook her head and laughed, a little wildly. "I can't carry a tune in a bucket. One of my brothers played the clarinet in the high-school marching band."

"You should get her a teacher," Miss Lori said. "She has a gift."

Janice looked at the floor, thinking, guiltily, that if Zoe had been the one to evince this unsuspected talent, Janice would have been delighted. She would have rushed to tell her husband and immediately started scheming about getting a piano and finding the money for lessons. She felt her face flushing at the evidence—at least the fifth or sixth piece of it since she'd woken up that morning—that she didn't love Cassie as much as Zoe, that she was failing her daughter. Even if Cassie was hard to love, Janice was her mother. Loving her children—both of her children—was her job. And she couldn't do it.

"We don't have a piano," she finally managed. "And—they're expensive, aren't they?"

"She can use ours," said Miss Lori. "She can come early, or stay late."

Shit, thought Janice, feeling helpless and trapped. "Do you know anyone who gives lessons?" she made herself ask. Miss Lori said she didn't, but that Miss Rachel would, and excused herself, leaving Janice alone with her daughters.

"Cassie knows lots of songs," Zoe announced. "She likes to sing."

This, too, was news to Janice. "Cassie sings?" she asked, hating how surprised she sounded. What kind of mother didn't know something like that about her own daughter? What kind of mother had to be informed by a teacher that her kid was some kind of genius?

"We sing together," Zoe said.

Janice walked to the piano bench, where Cass was still sitting, legs dangling, back slumped, looking, for all the world, like an appliance that had been unplugged. Janice made herself put her hands on Cass's shoulders. They felt stiff and unyielding as blocks of wood. "Can you sing me something?" she asked.

Cassie just shook her head.

"She only sings for me," said Zoe.

"Ah," said Janice. "That—that's nice." *How did I miss this?* she wondered again. Was it possible that Zoe was lying? And if she was lying, why?

When Miss Lori came back with a phone number on a Post-it note, Janice folded it carefully and slipped it into her wallet, hoping she at least gave the impression of love and competence.

"What a gift she has," Miss Lori said softly. "You're very lucky."

Lucky, Janice told herself as she navigated the icy sidewalk toward her car, holding her daughters' hands. This was a good thing. Cass had a gift, a wonderful gift. Then why did Janice feel so burdened, like she'd been given bad news instead of good news? Why did she feel like she'd been cursed instead of blessed?

That night, Janice fed the girls dinner, bathed them, and supervised toothbrushing. She read them a story (Zoe listened attentively and helped turn the pages; Cassie listened quietly). "Good night, girls," Janice said, when the story was over, and kissed their cheeks. An hour later, she crept back up the stairs, and held her breath as she stood in the hallway, outside their bedroom door.

Sure enough, they were singing. It took Janice a moment to recognize the song as "Can't Help Falling in Love." Janice's aunt Bess was a big Elvis fan. She must have played the girls one of her records when she'd babysat. Zoe still had trouble with her *l* sounds so *love* came out *wuv*, but it wasn't her older daughter's articulation that made Janice's breath catch in her chest, as she stood, rapt and unmoving. It was Cassie's voice. It was low, and tuneful, and rich; adult, somehow. It was lovely and wistful and sad. It was gorgeous, so beautiful Janice found herself shivering with something that felt like awe. She stayed frozen in place as the girls finished the song, and didn't even notice that she'd started to cry until she felt a tear drip off her chin and onto her collar. She stayed in the hallway, listening, until their voices faded, and, presumably, they'd fallen asleep. She felt a little bit like she was dreaming as she went back down to the kitchen.

The next morning, when Zoe was in the bathroom, Janice got Cassie by herself in the bedroom, as she was climbing out of bed.

"Cassie, I heard you singing last night."

No answer.

"Cassie. Can you look at me?"

Nothing. Cassie was in her pajamas. Her hair was a snarled mess, and she had her thumb plugged in her mouth. She was already an inch taller than her sister, and eight pounds heavier; a blocky, thick-bodied girl with muddy brownish-green eyes. Janice put her hand on Cassie's chin, tamping down her frustration, reminding herself to be patient. Zoe would have looked at her, offering answers. Zoe had no trouble having a conversation. But Cassie wasn't Zoe.

"Can you sing me something?" Janice asked.

"She won't sing for you." Zoe emerged from the bathroom and padded, on her bare feet, to the dresser the girls shared. "Is there toast?"

Janice went downstairs, popped two slices of bread into the toaster, and poured two cups of milk with hands that felt like they belonged to someone else. "Why not?" she asked her older daughter. "Why won't Cassie sing for me?"

Zoe looked thoughtful. "I don't know. She just won't." She took a sip of the milk and said, "She only sings when I sing with her."

The next night, after the girls had been put to bed, Sam and Janice both stood outside their bedroom for the concert, which featured songs from *Mary Poppins*. Sam's eyes were wide, his expression awed. "Holy shit," he said.

"Can anyone in your family sing like that?" Janice whispered.

"No one in my family can sing at all," Sam whispered back. "You've been to synagogue with us. You know."

Janice nodded. Her husband wasn't lying.

When Sam came home from his shift the next night, he had an electronic keyboard tucked under his arm. "Got it at a pawnshop," he said, setting it on the kitchen table. Janice wondered if *pawnshop* meant *evidence locker*. She decided not to ask.

The keyboard's speakers had been covered in glitter, and a few of the black keys had been decorated with flower stickers. Sam loaded in new batteries and set the keyboard on the kitchen table.

"Play us something," he said to Cassie. Janice held her breath, waiting to see if Cassie would refuse, the way she'd refused to sing. But instead, Cassie climbed obligingly into her booster seat and played "Happy Birthday."

"Okay," said Sam. "Play . . ." He paused, trying to think of a song.

"Play 'Think of Me,'" Janice said. For their anniversary, Sam had taken her to see *Phantom of the Opera* when a touring production came to the Academy of Music on Broad Street. "Do you know that one, Cassie?"

Cass nodded, bent over the keyboard, and started to play. Janice watched as her daughter's hands moved confidently over the keys, and the song poured out. Cassie's eyes were closed, her face was tranquil, and her mouth was curved into something that was almost a smile. She looked happy, Janice thought. Happier than she'd ever seen her looking before.

"We need to find her a teacher," Janice told Sam.

"Why?" her husband asked. His eyes were still on Cassie. He looked mesmerized. "If she can already play like this, why does she need a teacher?"

"So she can learn to read music?" Janice said, knowing she was on shaky ground. Her own musical education had concluded after sixth grade, when participation in the schoolwide chorus was no longer mandatory. "So someone can help her?" *So someone can help us,* was what she meant. *So someone who understands all of this can tell us what to do with our strange and gifted daughter.*

And maybe, she thought, this was Cassie's chance. The best chance her daughter had to find a calling. A hobby. Maybe even a career. It was Cassie's best chance to be happy, or something close.

Later, when reporters came with questions, when friends and acquaintances and neighbors and even the UPS guy all wanted to know if Janice had seen it coming, if she'd always known that her girls were special, destined for stardom, for greatness, she would think back to her daughters' parent-teacher conferences and recitals. Not any specific conference or any one recital, because they were all, in their way, the same.

At every conference, the teachers would begin with Zoe. They'd praise her cheerful nature, her sociability, her ease with the other kids. *She needs to pay attention and focus*, they would say, but they'd say it with a smile. The teachers never smiled when they discussed Sam and Janice's second daughter, whose homework was competent and whose test scores suggested intelligence, but who never spoke in class, never raised her hand, and had no friends. *Does Cassie talk about feeling left out or lonely?* they'd ask, looking concerned. *No*, Janice would tell them, honestly. Maybe Cassie did feel that way, maybe she longed for friends and companions, but she never said so. And Cassie had her sister. She wasn't completely alone.

Janice would leave every conference feeling disheartened, convinced that she was failing her daughter, that, no matter how hard she tried, she'd never do any better.

But then, the same week as the parent-teacher conferences, there'd be a recital, and everything would be different.

Cassie was always the last kid to play. She would walk to the piano, head down, feet dragging. Her shoulders would be hunched, her curls tangled and hanging in her face in unlovely clumps. *Sit up straight*, Janice would think, trying to communicate with Cassie via mental telepathy. It never worked. Eventually, Cassie would set her hands on the keys, head cocked slightly sideways, eyes closed, like the piano was telling her a secret, and she was listening as closely as she could. And then she'd begin to play. Her body would sway a little to the music, bending close to the keys, as if the notes were flowing down her arms, from her fingers to the instrument. *She's good*, Janice would think, and she would find herself smiling as her daughter played, all the anxiety and guilt she usually felt replaced with happiness and pride. She wanted to stand up and announce, *That's my daughter*. Never mind that Cassie was clumsy or ungainly, that her dress didn't fit and her hair was a mess. Never mind that she had no friends, that Janice found her hard to understand and harder to love. *That's my daughter, and she has a gift.*

Zoe

HADDONFIELD, 2024

It was seven thirty on a Thursday night, thirty minutes into the planning of the PTA's annual winter gala, and Zoe Rohrbach's butt had fallen asleep. She rocked from side to side at her kid-sized desk in the first-grade classroom, where her knees were up in the vicinity of her chin, and wondered what kind of emergency she could fake that would let her leave the room, or at least let her stand up long enough to get the circulation going again.

She looked around at the other women who'd pulled their desks into a semicircle and were introducing themselves, for the benefit of the committee's newest member. There was Hadley Inslee, who ran the PTA, and Laurel Weaver, Hadley's second-in-command. Next to her sat Penny Lifshitz, Zoe's best friend in Haddonfield. Next to Penny was the newcomer. She wore caramel-colored suede boots, dark-rinse jeans, a white angora sweater, and a hefty diamond on her ring finger. Her hair was cut in shoulder-length waves; her expression was friendly. "I'm Caitlyn Graves, and I moved here over the summer. My daughter, Maddie, is in kindergarten, and my son, Jasper, is in second grade."

"Welcome! We're happy to have you on board." Hadley nodded at Zoe. "And, last but not least . . ."

"I'm Zoe Rohrbach."

Zoe saw the moment it happened. She watched Caitlyn's eyes get wide, saw the other woman's hand rise to press against her lips. She always knew when she'd been recognized, because the signs were always the same. First came the *I-know-you* face: wide eyes, the quiet gasp, the dropped jaw. Then the naming would commence. "Oh my God," Caitlyn breathed. "You're . . ."

Zoe glanced at her fellow moms. Hadley was poking at her iPad, running through the snack possibilities. Laurel was sidebarring with Monica, probably trying to sell her the skincare products she was currently trying to off-load (the previous year, it had been leggings, and the year before that, jewelry). Penny was watching the byplay, a small smile on her lips.

"You're . . ."

Zoe leaned forward, lifted a finger to her lips and mouthed, *Shhh*. Caitlyn, her eyes still big, nodded like a bobblehead doll. Zoe sat back, knowing she'd failed to avoid the interrogation. All she'd done was postpone it.

As soon as the meeting was over—the silent-auction donation-gathering chores assigned; the egg-, nut-, dairy-, and gluten-free snacks approved; the language for the program agreed upon—Zoe stepped out into the cold winter air. She said goodbye to Penny, pulled her key fob out of her pocket, and had just unlocked her Range Rover, when Caitlyn hurried across the parking lot to intercept her.

"Oh my God," she said. "You're Zoe Griffin."

Zoe gave what she hoped was a pleasant smile, even though she felt no pleasure at all. Just a kind of numbness and the memory of old regret and shame. "That's right," she said. "I am." *I was* would have been more honest, but never mind.

"Oh my God. You're here. In New Jersey. How are you . . . when did . . . oh my God," Caitlyn said, and stopped talking in favor of gazing at Zoe with her hands clasped at her heart. Caitlyn's clothes and purse and jewelry were all expensive. She had all of the armor and accoutrements of a well-heeled wife and mother in her thirties, but the expression on her face, that soft-eyed, unalloyed awe, made her look younger, like a fourteen-year-old who should have been dressed in head-to-toe Hot Topic, with knockoff Doc Martens on her feet.

"You guys were my favorite," she said to Zoe. "My absolute favorite. Your music saved my life."

Zoe didn't have to ask who Caitlyn meant by *You guys*, or which songs had saved Caitlyn's life. It wasn't any of the music she'd made after the Griffin Sisters. God knows it hadn't been her solo stuff, which no one remembered. "Not your fault," CJ had told her, after her album flopped and her label dropped her. "The industry's changing," he'd said. Radio play didn't matter; streams and downloads did. You couldn't even get discovered by having a TV show use your music, because there were just too many shows. When Zoe had asked, "What now?" he'd said, "Send my assistant your new songs when you've got them, and she'll pass them along." Zoe knew what it meant when you got shunted to an assistant. It was *You're not making us any money, so you're not getting any of my time.* It was *Don't call us, we'll call you.* Zoe had decided, years ago, to save herself the postage, to quit while she was ahead and find a new life when she was still relatively young and lovely and her fame wasn't too distant. If that made her a has-been, Zoe reasoned, it was better than being a never-was.

In the elementary school parking lot, she made herself smile. "Thank you," she said. "That's very kind."

Caitlyn nodded toward the school, and the other mothers. "Does everyone know that you're . . . you know. You?"

Zoe kept her smile in place. "I'm just a mom now. I'm not anyone anymore."

"Oh, but . . . I mean . . ." First came the recognition. Then came the awe. They'd now arrived at Zoe's least favorite part of the experience: the questions. Why are you here? What happened? Why aren't you making music anymore? Sometimes her interlocutor was aware that Zoe had done things after the Griffin Sisters broke up. More often, their knowledge of her career began and ended with her first band—which, as far as they were concerned, was her only band. Zoe should have been used to it, but it always stung.

"My husband and I have two boys," Zoe told Caitlyn. "Noah and

Schuyler. They're in second and fourth grade. So I've got my hands full." She didn't mention Cherry. She never talked about Cherry.

"I'm actually running to the grocery store. Boys. They never stop eating!" Zoe gave the other woman a conspiratorial look. *You get it, right?*—and hoped that Caitlyn would know what it meant, which was that Zoe was so busy, with the carpooling, the shopping, the cooking and the cleaning and the cheering at T-ball games, the unpaid emotional labor of running a household and caring for a family, to even consider writing a song or playing a show. It was important that the other woman believe the lie, which was that Zoe no longer had the time to make music, and did not suspect the truth, which was that what Zoe lacked was not free time but talent.

Caitlyn, meanwhile, hardly seemed to be listening to her.

"I can't believe this," she was saying. "God. If I could go back in time and tell my sixteen-year-old self that I was at a PTA meeting with Zoe Griffin . . ." She closed her mouth and eyed Zoe shyly. "I was kind of a wreck when I was a teenager, and your music meant so much to me. And I was devastated when—" Zoe saw her throat work as she gulped. "I mean, obviously, not as much as you were. Of course not as much as you were. But it was just—I mean, I felt like I knew you. All of you. Like you wrote those songs just for me."

Zoe nodded, the way she had a hundred times—regally, a little mournfully, like a grieving queen. *I'm never going to get out of here*, she thought. She'd either have to skip the grocery store or be late picking up Schuyler. The other woman must have seen some of that in Zoe's expression, because she pulled herself together. "Thank you," she said, and ducked her head, bending her knees and dipping her head in a gesture that was almost a bow. "Thank you for your songs."

"Of course. You're welcome," Zoe said, and tried to smile like she meant it.

Your music meant so much to me, Zoe thought as she drove to the Whole Foods. How many times had people said that, in the years since the band's dissolution? How many spoonfuls of her self-esteem had been scooped away every time she heard it? Because when the fans said *your music*, they meant the Griffin Sisters. And they had no idea how much one sister had been responsible for those songs, and how little the other had contributed.

Zoe had done her part, of course. She'd swung her hips and shaken her tambourine, sung the occasional harmony, and even played guitar, if the part was simple enough. She'd gotten famous, had been showered with love, swimming in money, if only briefly. She'd had thousands of people cheering for her; she'd been on the covers of magazines, had gotten everything she'd thought she'd ever wanted, and none of it had mattered in the end. She hadn't written those famous songs about loneliness and longing. She'd performed them, but their lyrics had never meant much to her, because she'd never been lonely or felt unloved. That had all been Cassie.

And now Zoe was stuck, trapped in amber, locked in a moment from twenty years ago. In the public's mind, she would always be the girl from that famous photograph, fragile and lovely, holding a bouquet of red roses, in a black leather jacket and a black lace veil, on a rain-misty morning in Boston. The other bands and her solo career could not compete with the legacy of the Griffin Sisters. They'd been doomed before they'd drawn their first breath.

Zoe had learned how to deal with the way people looked at her. She knew the tone to take when she'd say, *I'm glad our music meant so much to you.* She knew better than to complain, because nobody wanted to hear someone who was rich (or so they imagined) and famous (or, at least, had been famous, once) complaining. Zoe had forfeited her right to have problems somewhere between the time the first single had charted and the week her wedding had been on the cover of *People* magazine.

She thought, sometimes, about the bargain she'd made. As a girl, she had envied her sister's talent, her ability to stop conversations and draw every eye in the room the instant she struck the first keys on her piano. Zoe had coveted Cassie's skills. She had wanted that attention for herself. Then, when she'd gotten it, it had ruined her. Still, she wondered, if some supernatural creature, some witch or wizard or genie from a bottle, had approached her and told her how it was going to go, she would have made a different choice. If that genie had said, *You can have everything you've ever wanted, you can sing and dance in front of thousands of people, your songs will be played on the radio, you'll be on the covers of magazines with your gorgeous boyfriend, but you won't write any of the songs that will make you famous, you'll barely be able to play an instrument and most of your singing will be edited out of the recordings,* how would Zoe have responded? If the genie had gone on to say, *You will feel like a fraud whenever someone thanks you for the songs you didn't write and barely sang, and that man will love someone else,* would she have still agreed to the deal? Zoe liked to imagine making a wiser choice, saying, *Thanks, but you know what, I'll just be a nurse or a teacher or a regular old housewife instead.* She suspected differently. There was no version of herself that would not say *Yes, I'll do it,* probably before the genie had gotten the last words out of its mouth.

She felt very old as she wheeled her shopping cart past the organic lettuce blends and the twelve-dollar plastic clamshells of cut-up pineapple. All week long, at barre class and in coffee shops, Zoe listened to her friends talk about how they didn't want to sleep with their husbands; how they had crushes on their oral hygienists or their personal trainers or their kids' soccer coaches. "Was it like that for you, after you had the boys?" a yoga classmate named Nina had asked her, over kale and protein-powder smoothies after class. "Did you ever feel like if one more person touched you, if one more person wanted something from you, you'd throw something heavy at their head?" Zoe had said, "Sometimes," because that was the right answer. The truth was, she'd never stopped wanting Jordan. Maybe because her subconscious wouldn't allow it, and some part deep inside of her knew how dangerous it would be, if she stopped wanting Jordan or if Jordan stopped wanting her. She seemed to be immune to other longings, and the questions that kept her friends up at night. Zoe remembered how once, after they'd shared a bottle of wine at dinner, Penny had asked, "Do you ever worry you're not a good person?"

Zoe had given her the right answer again. *Sure*, she had said. *Sometimes*. That, too, was a lie. It wasn't *sometimes*, it was *always*. And she never worried. She knew, for sure, that she was not.

Zoe paid for her groceries at the self-checkout station and carried her bags back to her car. She was only a few minutes late picking Schuyler up from swim practice. In the car, she asked the same questions she always asked: What was the best thing that happened? What was the worst thing? What was one thing that made you laugh? She barely listened to his answers, offering the occasional "Mm-hmm" and "That's nice," and reminding him not to leave his wet towel in the car. She was seeing Cassie instead of her son; Cassie at eight or nine years old, silent, stocky, slumped, eternally alone. When Janice took them to the playground, Cassie would go off by herself. She'd push an empty swing, not even getting on it, just pushing it; staring covetously at the kids playing tag, never courageous enough to join them. At birthday parties, Cassie would stand in the corner, watching intently, ignoring the games and the entertainment. Cassie had needed looking out for, and it had been Zoe's job to do it—to keep Cassie safe, to speak for her. At the park, she'd have to get the other kids to include her sister. At birthday parties, she would have to explain that Cassie couldn't play games like musical chairs ("She gets dizzy," she'd say). More often than not, Zoe would end up sitting beside Cassie, instead of playing herself. At the town pool, Cassie was afraid to go in the water. Zoe remembered a miserably hot day, sweat gluing her swimsuit to the small of her back, sitting next to her sister with their legs dangling in the blue water. "I'm just going to jump in for a second," she'd said, and Cassie had made a panicky grab at her forearm. "Don't go," Cassie said, gripping hard enough to bruise. "Don't go, don't go, don't leave me. You said you'd stay. You promised," Cassie would say. "You promised."

Zoe had promised . . . so she'd ended up sitting on the edge of the pool, sweating in the sun, dreaming of the day she'd be a famous pop star, with a touring bus and a handsome boyfriend and a private jet to swoop her away, out of bondage and into the sky, and the big, free life that she knew was waiting.

Cassie, she knew, would be okay. Her sister would eventually finish high school and go on to the Curtis Institute in Center City, which had the twin benefits of being one of the foremost conservatories in the world and also being close enough to home that Cassie could continue to live with their parents while she studied. Curtis students paid no tuition. Their education was supported by the school's endowment, funded by many thousands of dollars given by music lovers over many years. Students enrolled at eighteen—or earlier, if they were especially gifted. They stayed until their teachers decided they were ready to graduate. Once they'd gotten their degrees, they went to play in the world's top orchestras or opera companies, or to start solo careers. That would be Cassie's future.

Living with a prodigy, Zoe had often thought, was like having an especially beautiful lamp, with an unusually powerful bulb, plopped down in your living room. The light it cast was dazzling, undeniable. You couldn't look away. And not only did it outshine everything around it; it made everything else look shabby and unremarkable by comparison. Zoe's parents loved her. They applauded her normal-kid achievements. They enjoyed her company. But they would never look at her with the same kind of awe she saw on their faces around Cassie. She would never matter as much. Not to them. Not to the world.

Zoe drove slowly, half listening to Schuyler chattering about some video game, or a movie, or a video game that was being turned into a movie. She reminded herself that she was no longer an envious teenager or a famous twenty-one-year-old, and that no one cared if she'd chosen the life of a wife and a mother, or if she'd fallen into it because it was the only option left. She was here now. She would do her best.

She collected Noah at the hockey rink and asked him the same questions, trying to shake off the strange mood that had overtaken her, to ground herself in her real life again.

At home, Zoe put away the groceries in the kitchen she'd just had redone, with sage-green paint on the cabinets, pale yellow tiles along the backsplash, and a built-in dining nook. She pulled a pan out of a cupboard and the olive oil from the pantry shelf, cut the sweet potatoes into wedges, seasoned the burgers, washed lettuce for a salad. As she called to her sons to set the table, she remembered a night from her childhood. Zoe had been watching *Inspector Gadget* on TV, and Cassie had been practicing, as usual, when Zoe had looked outside the window and had seen that it was snowing, the twilight sky a lovely indigo, the snowflakes silvery in the streetlights, swirling on the gusts of wind, piling up on the ground below.

"Let's go outside," Zoe had told Cass. "We can make snow angels!" She must have been—five? Six? Too young to realize that there wasn't anywhere near enough snow for snow angels or that the frozen ground would be bumpy and painful against their bodies, that it was going to hurt. She could remember zipping her sister's coat, the sound of Cassie laughing, for once; the snowflakes melting on her cheeks, like tiny, cool kisses, and her sister's hand in hers, holding on tight.

How long had they been outside before their mom had come running after them, coatless and wild-eyed? Janice had hauled them inside, talking in a low, angry voice about how they'd scared her half to death, how she'd turned around and found the door open and both girls gone, how there were kidnappers and bad people, and they were never, ever to scare her like that again.

Both of them had gotten twigs and dead leaves in their hair, and the sleeve of Cassie's new winter coat had ripped. Janice had had plenty to say about that too. *Do you think we're made of money? Do you think new coats grow on trees?* It hadn't mattered . . . or it hadn't been enough to erase the joy of being outside in the dark, in the snow. *Remember the time we made snow angels?* Zoe would ask her sister, for years afterward, and Cass would always smile.

In her kitchen, Zoe arranged the turkey burgers on a platter, washed her hands, uncorked a bottle of wine. She set a place for Cherry, even though, more times than not, her daughter wouldn't join them. Cherry would text to say she was out with friends, or at rehearsal, that she'd grab a hoagie or a slice of pizza on her way home . . . and that was if she remembered to let them know. Her daughter didn't want to be at home, and, the truth was, it was harder for everyone when Cherry was around. Cherry was angry at Zoe, so permanently outraged that it felt like her resentment had taken an actual physical form, that it was a thing that sat in its own place at the dining-room table, or hung in the air like a fog. If Zoe said anything about music, or college, or Cherry's future, Cherry's mood would go from indifferent to furious in a handful of seconds, and she'd go storming out of the kitchen, down into the basement, where she'd sing something atonal and angry, or send sour, warped sounds from her bass up through the floor.

Zoe told herself that was normal teenage-girl behavior, that Cherry was doing what a book she'd read called the *work of separation*. Teenage girls always pull away from their parents, especially their mothers. *It's their job*, the book had said. Zoe took comfort from that. She also thought, guiltily, that she was doing a better job with her sons than she'd done with her daughter. Which made sense. Of course a woman who was settled, with a partner and a house and money in the bank, would be a better mother than a scared, hurt, angry girl barely out of her teens, who was all alone, who'd lost her band and, thus, her job and her identity, and whose heart was still mostly broken.

"Daddy!" The boys rushed into the hallway at the sound of the garage door opening, and hurled themselves at Jordan as soon as he came through the door. Zoe waited until her husband hugged them both before she gave him a glass of wine and a kiss, and tried not to feel hurt that he seemed to appreciate the former more than the latter.

"How was your day?" he asked her.

Zoe wondered what would happen if she told Jordan the truth: *I met a new woman at the PTA meeting, and I told her the same old lies, and now I can't stop thinking about the band and my sister and I feel sad and ashamed and sick with guilt, and I don't think I'm happy and I don't think I ever will be.* She smiled a little, imagining Jordan's absent *That's nice, honey*. Her husband loved her. That didn't mean he wanted to be burdened with her troubles. At least, not when he'd just come home from work and still had a head full of his own. "My day was fine," she said. "Come on in. Let's sit. Dinner's on the table."

The next morning, Zoe tried to push through her sluggishness. She forced herself into her exercise clothes and suffered through an hourlong barre class. When she finished, there was a voicemail from Cherry's high school on her phone, informing her that Cherry wasn't there.

A prickling foreboding crept over Zoe's body as she shouldered her gym bag and sat behind the wheel of her Range Rover, in her black leggings with the sheer cutout panels and her snug racerback tank top. Cherry's phone went straight to voicemail, and the Find My iPhone feature revealed that Cherry's phone was still in her bedroom, where Cherry, unquestionably, was not. She'd call Jordan first, Zoe decided. Then Cherry's friends. The boy with the blue hair; Lillian, who played bass in Cherry's band; the kid with all the piercings whose pronouns Zoe could never get right.

Instead of dialing, Zoe just sat there, her hands on the wheel, frozen and immobile. Again, the thoughts from the previous night surfaced: *This isn't the life I want. I miss my sister.* It made no sense . . . unless it was the idea of responsibility that connected her current situation to her previous life. Cassie had been her responsibility, and Zoe had failed her. And now she'd failed her daughter, too.

Part Two

www.reddit.com/letstalkmusic/griffinsisters

MariahScary: Okay, so I am new to the Griffin Sisters' music (Evermore fan here!) and I've been listening to their album and I love love love every single song but especially The Only Lonely Girl and Flavor of the Week and Last Night in Fishtown. I have looked and looked but I can't find more songs. Is this it?

HatLady: Oh my sweet summer child

Bonobo: Who's gonna tell her?

Richard_Jones: Google is your friend

HatLady: Don't be a dick u/Richard_Jones.

HatLady: Yes, u/MariahScary, the band only recorded one album before they broke up. No more music. And it was Cassie Griffin and Russell D'Angelo who wrote almost all of their songs.

ScreamingMimi: Um, FYI, Russell was not JUST the Sisters' band's songwriter and guitar player. He founded a band himself—they were called Sky King, their music is pretty good. Think Gin Blossoms meets Mumford & Sons.

HatLady: Cam Gratz went on to play for other bands, including—I think?—Bluebonnet and Bloody Sundae. Maybe others? Tommy Kelleher became a studio player. Zoe Griffin, last I heard, is remarried and has kids. Nobody knows where Cassie Griffin went.

MercyMe: One of the unsolved musical mysteries of our time.

Richard_Jones: LOL shes too big to disappear.

Moderator: Reminder, no fat-shaming or negative body talk here! u/Richard_Jones, this is your first warning! Let's keep it positive, everyone!

MariahScary: Just FYI, I did google. I also saw the big "Where Are They Now" story in People, but I thought maybe you guys might know more.

99Problems: Wish we did. Wish there was more to know.

Bonobo: TGS were ahead of their time. Cassie especially. It breaks my heart they never did more than the one album.

MariahScary: Can famous people really just disappear, though?

HatLady: I don't know if "people" can. But Cassie did.

Cherry

We're live in five," the producer murmured, and gave Cherry's shoulder a squeeze. Cherry nodded. She was in Los Angeles—Los Angeles! She could still barely believe it—standing in the wings in a cavernous studio, with her guitar's strap over her shoulder, watching as a stagehand adjusted the angle of a microphone stand and a makeup artist whisked a powder puff over Jason Carr's handsome face.

It was her fifth day in Los Angeles, and the crowd of six hundred semifinalists had already been relentlessly winnowed down. On the day she'd arrived, Cherry had met the first in a series of roommates. "Don't bother unpacking," the girl had told her, sitting on a bed in the room they shared at the Sheraton in Burbank. "They said we've all got to be packed up again at seven thirty tomorrow morning, so we're ready to go straight to the airport if we get sent home. Brutal, right?" *That's not happening to me*, Cherry had thought, but she'd just taken out her cosmetics bag, pajamas, and clothes for the next day, leaving everything else folded in her duffel.

In the morning, they'd been bussed to the theater, on the CBS lot in Radford, a huge, echoing soundstage with six hundred empty seats, the same place where game shows and soap operas and, once, *Star Search* had been taped. There had been individual performances, a version of the Philadelphia audition's test, where the singers were grouped in lines of ten, and each of them got to step forward and sing for thirty seconds, before getting either the thumbs-up or thumbs-down. Cherry's roommate had been cut, along with three hundred or so other wannabes. The next morning, each contestant had been assigned a phrase or a word, and had been told to come up with at least thirty seconds' worth of a song. Cherry's phrase had been *reach for the stars*, and her song had mostly involved belting out repetitions of the words in the key best suited to her voice. *Reach for the stars / I know you can do it / Just reach for the stars / Like there's nothing to it.* Not her best work, but good enough to get her through. The day after that, they'd been put into groups of three or four, and assigned some old song from the 1980s or 1990s to which *The Next Stage* had secured the rights and told to come up with a performance, from arranging the music to inventing a dance. Cherry had been grouped with a girl named Jacinda and a boy named Braden, and they'd been given a Hall & Oates song— "Kiss on My List"—that, of the three of them, only Cherry had heard. But Jacinda had taken six years of tap and ballet, and she'd put together some basic choreography while Cherry and Braden had come up with an arrangement of the vocals. By the end of that day, Cherry and Braden had been put through, and Jacinda had been sent home, and after five days, fewer than a hundred singers remained. The next morning, each one of them sat for a slightly longer tell-us-about-yourself interview with the producers. In the afternoon, they'd each gotten to sing an entire song, uninterrupted. Cherry had decided to go all out. She'd chosen her favorite Griffin Sisters song.

And now it was Saturday. There were twenty-four of them left. Twelve of them were competing that night. Six would make it through, becoming the season's first six finalists. The show was taped, not live, but, for the first time, an actual audience had been recruited to watch them. Cherry could hear the audience members talking as they'd been brought in, and imagined she could feel them, out there in the dark. Standing backstage, trying to stay calm, Cherry realized that her mother had been about her age when she'd been discovered. How had it felt? Zoe had never told her. All through Cherry's childhood— the years when it was just her and her mom, and then, later, when there was Jordan, and her brothers—the message had been clear and consistent: her mother did not want to talk about the past. She did not want to talk about the Griffin Sisters, or what had happened; not the good times, not the bad ones. If it had been up to Zoe, Cherry would never have even known about the Griffin Sisters.

Her mom hadn't even been the one to tell her about the band. Cherry had found out accidentally, when she was six years old, and she'd been with her mom in a used bookstore on Bainbridge Street, a sprawling warren of rooms that stretched the width of a city block, with dusty hardwood floors and ceiling-high shelves crammed with books about every imaginable topic.

Her mom had been looking for cookbooks, and Cherry had wandered off and found a bin of CDs. David Bowie had stared up from the first one, a star painted around one of his eyes. Cherry had started to flip, enjoying the clicking of the plastic cases, past Natalie Imbruglia and Jewel and Mandy Moore, past Britney Spears, wearing a red shirt with a white tank top underneath and a miniskirt that left her tucked-up legs bare . . . and then her fingers froze. She looked carefully, making sure that she wasn't imagining things, but there it was. Her mother's face, on a CD case. Her mother's eyes, staring up at her.

Zoe's hair was different, a lighter brown than Cherry was used to, with some strands dyed red. She wore red lipstick, a short, lacy black dress, and lots of dark makeup around her eyes, and she was standing outside, on a rolling green hill, in front of a leafy green tree. Another lady stood beside her. This woman, too, wore black, but a suit, not a dress, a big, boxy, loose-fitting jacket with padded shoulders and creased pants, and a hat pulled down over one eye. She had a soft, round face and a larger body, which the suit, the tree, and her pose all seemed intended to hide, just as the hat was meant to disguise her face. There were three more people, three men, behind and to the sides of Cherry's mother and the black-suit lady. One had long hair and a leather vest, and the other two wore a button-down shirt and a skinny tie.

"'The Griffin Sisters,'" Cherry read, sounding out each word carefully. She didn't understand it. Her mother's last name was not Griffin. She didn't have a sister. And she didn't like music. She never played records or CDs at home. When they were in the car, the radio was tuned to the all-news station.

Cherry pulled the CD out of the bin and found her mother in front of the cash register, frowning as she rummaged in her wallet. "Mom!" Cherry said, and tugged on Zoe's sleeve. "Mom, look!"

When her mother finally glanced down at what Cherry was holding, she went very still. Her shoulders stiffened, and her face settled into a familiar expression, lips pursed, forehead furrowed, eyes glaring. In a low, steady voice, Zoe said, "Put that back where you found it, please."

Cherry saw the young woman behind the counter look down at the CD case, then up at her mom. "Oh my God," she whispered. "Oh my God, oh my God, oh my God." Her voice rose higher and higher, until it was practically a squeal. "You—you're Zoe Griffin!"

Cherry looked at her mother curiously, but Zoe did not correct the young woman, who was standing with her mouth a little open, leaning forward like she wanted to touch Zoe but couldn't quite work up the courage. Words were spilling out of the lady's mouth, almost too fast for Cherry to hear them. She was saying that the Griffin Sisters was her favorite band and how she'd heard them twice in concert and how she didn't think she would have survived high school without their songs. "Your music was everything," she was saying, and it sounded almost like she was going to cry.

"Thank you," Zoe replied, in a voice just short of curt.

"Do you think you'll ever make more music? Or play concerts again?"

Cherry's mom gave the woman a hard, bright smile, one that showed her teeth. "Never say never, right? Anything can happen." She reached down for Cherry's hand. "Excuse us," she said, and tugged Cherry—not gently—toward the door, as the woman called, "Wait! Don't you want your books?"

"Who are the Griffin Sisters?" Cherry asked. Her mother hadn't answered. Cherry had a hundred other questions. *How old were you when you were in the band?* and *Who are the other people in the picture?* and *Why don't you do music anymore?* and *Why was that woman almost crying when she recognized you?* But Cherry had learned to read the emotional weather in her household, to check the forecast on her mother's face before she spoke. Ask the wrong question at the wrong time, Cherry had learned, and Zoe would yell, or snap at Cherry and send her to her room, or, worse, go quiet and moody for hours or days. *I'll wait,* Cherry decided. *And I'll find out what's going on, even if I have to ask someone else.*

"Here you go," said a stagehand, tucking the microphone pack into the back of Cherry's pants. *Glamorous,* thought Cherry as she felt the hard plastic against the band of her underwear.

"Ten . . . nine . . . eight . . ."

Cherry took one last, long inhalation and, at the producer's nod, walked out from the wings and into the spotlight, not too slow, not too fast. Head held high and confident, shoulders back, like she had every belief in her own abilities and nothing had ever hurt her.

"Cherry," Jason, the emcee, said, giving her his professional, twinkly smile. Up close, Cherry could see how the makeup had evened out his complexion and settled into the lines around his eyes. "How are you feeling?"

"Nervous," said Cherry, with the self-deprecating grin she'd practiced in her hotel room the night before.

"Fair enough. It's a big night." Jason nodded toward the judges—or, rather, he nodded toward the audience, and the desk where Cherry knew the judges were sitting. The spotlights had turned the auditorium into a blank black space. That was probably a good thing.

A disembodied voice emerged from the darkness. "Cherry, welcome to the semifinal round of *The Next Stage.*" That posh British accent belonged to Sebastian Knoll. Sebastian was a music producer. Fifteen years ago, he'd come up with the concept of *The Next Stage* and had been the executive producer, head judge, and, the contestants joked, Lord High Executioner for each of its thirty-six subsequent seasons.

"Thank you," Cherry said, and was pleased to hear her own voice sounded steady. "I'm very glad to be here."

"Cherry, you've got a very distinctive look." That was Lizzie Blair, a country singer known for twangy ballads about men who'd done her wrong, and whose own look involved wavy blond hair extensions that hung to her waist, acres of cleavage, and brightly colored cowgirl boots paired with cutoff denim shorts.

Cherry touched her spiky, freshly bleached hair, the braided rattail that hung over her shoulder. *The Next Stage* had a stylist who'd signed off on Cherry's clothes: high-waisted pants in a checkered gray plaid, a white cropped tank top, and black suspenders. The studded leather cuff on her wrist was her own, as were her lucky Doc Martens, a sixteenth-birthday present—the last thing her mother had given her that Cherry had actually liked. The pants were just a little too big, and the tank top was a little too small. The combined effect was to make Cherry look waifish, even boyish. Plenty of the other girls were doing sexy. Cherry was happy to do something else.

"You're a singer-songwriter?" asked Sebastian.

"That's right," Cherry said. "I've been writing my own music since I was fourteen, and I hope to have the chance to perform some of it for you."

"And you're eighteen, right? Tell us a little more about yourself, how you got here." This was the third judge, Aurora Bloch, a model-slash-actress. Aurora managed to sound genuinely curious, as if she didn't already know the answer, as if this exchange hadn't been scripted and rehearsed as recently as the run-through two hours previously. Cherry was impressed. She'd never thought Aurora was that good of an actress.

"Music is all I ever wanted. I auditioned at home, in Philadelphia. I skipped school and waited in line for twenty-four hours." She gave a self-deprecating smile. "Sorry, Mom!" This was where, Cherry knew, they'd insert footage of her audition.

"What about your family?" Aurora again, staying on script.

Cherry gave the answer she'd rehearsed. "My mom and my step-dad love me, but I don't think they understand how much I want this. I think they'd prefer it if I'd gone to college." That was the redacted version. If Cherry made it to the finals, she'd have to tell more of the story, including who her mother was and who her father had been. She hadn't even started to figure out how to talk about that. Right now, as far as anyone here knew, she was the daughter of a housewife named Zoe Rohrbach, who had no connection at all to Zoe Grossberg, who'd once been Zoe Griffin of the Griffin Sisters.

"That must be hard for you," Aurora murmured.

Cherry gave a little shrug, and a smile she hoped was charming. "I'm not the only person who wants to perform whose parents don't approve." It was actually parent, singular, who didn't approve. Jordan, she knew, would have been fine with whatever made Cherry happy, but his first priority was Cherry's mother, and keeping the peace in the house. "But this is all I've ever wanted. And I'll do whatever I have to do to try to make music my life."

"Because you want to be rich and famous?" Sebastian's voice was a bored, cynical drawl.

"Because this is it for me." Cherry hadn't realized how serious she'd sound until she started talking. "This is what I love, and it's what I have to give. This is how I share myself with the world." She'd considered those questions, and thought out answers, which she'd written down and practiced in front of her hotel room's mirror, but when she said the words out loud, into the darkness, they didn't sound rehearsed. They sounded true. "And, look, if I end up rich and famous, I promise I won't complain." She gave a little smile. "But it's not about that. Not really."

"And if this doesn't work out?" Sebastian asked.

"Then I'll keep trying," Cherry said. "I'll stay out here, in Los Angeles, and see if I can get hired to work in a studio. I'll sing backup or record other people's demos. I'll put my stuff out on social media. I'll play in bars, or on street corners, or in subway cars."

"Whatever it takes, huh?" asked Lizzie.

"Whatever it takes," Cherry repeated.

"Let's get to it," Sebastian said, his voice businesslike. Cherry could picture him, arms set on his desk, leaning forward, eager to get on with it. "What are you singing for us tonight?"

"I'm going to sing one of my favorite songs. 'The Gift,' by the Griffin Sisters."

She could hear the audience's reaction, the people who'd sent away for tickets and the ones they'd pulled in from the studio tour to fill out the crowd, and hoped that it was an approving murmur. Choosing the right songs was just as important as how well you could sing them . . . and it wasn't easy. Every morning that they hadn't been assigned a song, the show sent contestants a playlist with two hundred songs they'd been cleared to perform. Each one got a little time to talk about the possibilities with the show's musical director, an affable man named Michael Oh. There was only one Griffin Sisters song on the playlist, one that had been used on the Netflix show. Cherry had to hope it would hit the sweet spot, that it was popular but not overplayed to the point that people were sick of it.

"The floor is yours," said Sebastian, the way he always did.

And that was her cue. Cherry settled her fingers on the guitar's strings, feeling the comforting weight of the instrument's body pulling at her shoulders. She took a last deep breath and looked out into the obscuring darkness. She found that she wasn't nervous at all, just excited. Her body was thrumming, her heart beating fast.

She played the first chord, raised her chin, opened her mouth, and began.

"I can see the day I met you / All I do is hit rewind / You were tall just like my father / Your hands were big, your eyes were kind." As always, she sounded like a stranger when she sang, like she was hearing her voice from the outside. In her own opinion, she sounded good. Her voice wasn't shaky; she wasn't pitchy or sharp or flat. Even better, Cherry could feel the audience's attention . . . and, she hoped, its approval. She imagined the song reaching into people's memories, plucking on a guitar string, or singing a single note: taking them back to whatever it had made them feel.

Her fingers were steady on the fretboard, her feet were solid on the stage, and her voice was soaring, clear and strong.

"I was the girl who no one wanted / Too big, too weird, too much / Frightened of all the empty faces / Hungry for your touch."

The song was in a major key, and it sounded, at first, bright and cheery, a sugary-sweet pop confection to be sung on a summer afternoon, driving in a convertible with the top down and your crush in the seat beside you. But the last word of the pre-chorus landed on an unexpected minor note, foreshadowing that what sounded like a bouncy power-pop anthem was something different, a story that would not have a happy ending.

That was Cassie Griffin's genius. Or maybe it was the genius of Cassie and Russell together, the way they'd been able to take familiar things and rearrange them, twisting and subtly reshaping them, making pop songs that felt both familiar and new.

Listening to a Griffin Sisters song felt like walking down a familiar street in the city where you'd always lived and looking up to see a building you'd never noticed, with gargoyles perched on its cornices, and the mouth of a dark alley you'd never seen before just beyond it. The songs invited you to keep walking until you realized you were somewhere else entirely. A different neighborhood. Even a different world.

Cherry bent over her guitar as, behind her, the light display burst into a fusillade of color, and the house band came in; the bass first, its heavy-bottomed notes thick and dark and insistent, and the drums exploded, and the backup singers joined her in soaring three-part harmony. Cherry moved her mouth a crucial fraction of space back from the microphone and opened up into a belt, her chest and throat and lips all vibrating with the music. She pictured the song's subject so clearly that he could have been standing right in front of her. A handsome, heartbreaking liar, an agent of chaos. A target. A present. A prize.

> You're a gift
> You're my present
> You're the rip in my heart
> You're a star
> You're a scar
> And you tore me apart

And I know
Even so
If you come back, I won't say no . . .
And every day I'm learning
That there is no returning

The backup singers dropped out, bass and drums vanishing, the guitar fading away, until it was just Cherry's voice, all regret and longing. She poured herself into the song, every heartache and betrayal she'd ever felt, all the pain she'd ever endured. Cherry couldn't see the crowd, but she could hear them, joining in with the chorus, clapping, stomping, singing, almost shouting along.

"You're a gift / And I can't take you back."

Cherry held the last note, her voice the sound of a hundred girls' hearts being torn to pieces; the sound of a thousand girls sobbing into their pillows, and the battle cry of all of those girls, who would wake up the next morning, sharpen their swords, and come to take their revenge.

The song ended. There was silence for the space of a breath. Then came the applause, pouring over her like a wave. Cherry stood, breathing hard, flushed and glowing, knowing that she'd done well. She couldn't predict what the judges would decide, or how, or if, her particular look and sound would fit into the final selection (she'd heard stories of singers being cut because the producers already had a pretty Black girl with a gospel sound, or not-conventionally-attractive guy with a compelling backstory). But she knew she'd never sung that song better than she had just now. If she left the show with nothing else, she'd have that.

"Thank you, Cherry," came Sebastian's voice out of the darkness.

Cherry's lips were numb, and her face ached from smiling. She nodded, mouthed, *Thank you.* Then she kissed her fingertips and raised them to the sky—the gesture her mother used to make at the end of her shows. Anyone watching might have thought she was praying, and Cherry supposed that it was a kind of prayer. *For you, Cassie,* she thought. *Wherever you are.*

Backstage, the PA helped her remove the mic pack. Once she was freed, she put her guitar on a stand and stepped into the lounge, where the other contestants were waiting, watching their competition, and being filmed as they watched. They clapped for her, whooping and cheering and chanting her name.

"OhmyGod, that was AMAZEBALLS!" Tori shrieked in her ear. Cherry and Tori had been roommates for two nights, moving in together after their respective previous roommates had been sent home.

"I'm crying!" said Braden, pointing at his cheek. Braden was from New York City. He'd started his run at the beginning of the week as a sensitive singer-songwriter in cardigan sweaters and geeky glasses, only another singer-songwriter had already emerged as one of the judges' favorites, and so Braden had quickly pivoted, acquiring a cowboy hat from the Galleria mall and discovering his love of all things beer- and pickup-truck-related. "See? Actual tears!"

Cherry hugged Braden, and let Tori waltz her around the room. At another PA's instruction, she took her seat in the holding pen, a semicircle of couches surrounded by three different cameras, and watched, on monitors, as the last three performers sang their songs, then waited, while the judges conferred. Thirty minutes later, the twelve semifinalists were summoned back to the stage. They stood in a line, waiting for the verdict. One by one, Sebastian read out names. "Will David Reyes please step forward. Will Cherry Rohrbach please step forward. Will Tori Johanssen please step forward. Will Crystal Jones please step forward. Will Braden Welsh please step forward. Will Tamara Easton please step forward." The six of them whose names had been called stood at the front of the stage, hands linked. Tori's eyes were squeezed shut, and David's hand was slippery. The pause, before Sebastian spoke again, felt endless. Cherry held her breath. Sometimes it was the people whose names got called who'd made it through to the finals, and sometimes they were the ones who got sent home. Every year was different, and you never knew, until you heard Sebastian say . . .

"Congratulations. You six are on to the Next Stage."

Tori screamed so loudly that Cherry was sure her eardrum had suffered permanent damage. David kissed the cross he wore around his neck. His lips moved soundlessly. Cherry guessed he was having a conversation with Jesus (personally, she couldn't imagine a deity taking interest in a singing contest, but what did she know?). Cherry's heart was beating so hard she could feel her pulse throbbing in her wrists, in her throat, in the hinge of her jaw.

"Except . . ." Sebastian was talking again, his voice cutting through the shrieks and the shouts and the intimate chats with Jesus. It took a minute for the audience and the contestants to quiet down, but finally, he had silence. "This year . . ."

All the contestants went very still. Cherry could imagine the editing: the ominous chord that television viewers would hear just after Sebastian's pronouncement. David grabbed Cherry's hand again, squeezing hard, and Cherry squeezed back.

"This year," Sebastian continued, "our theme is 'Mentors.' Each of our finalists will be paired with an established figure in the music industry. This person will serve as a teacher, a coach, and a performing partner, because, this year, for the first time, our finals will include a duet." David's grip on Cherry's hand had tightened to just shy of painful. On her other side, Tori said quietly, "Oh, wow." Cherry couldn't see it, but she could picture Sebastian's smug smile, and his face, all bright teeth and cold eyes, looking them over like eggs in a carton, wondering which one would crack first. Her knees felt wobbly, her throat and chest felt hot. *Shit*, she thought. Because she didn't want whoever they would give her. There was only one person she wanted, one person who made sense . . . and Cherry had no idea how to find her.

Zoe

It was the week before Christmas, and JC Dobbs on South Street was hosting its annual Battle of the Bands. By that time, the world had survived Y2K and 9/11. Britney and Justin had wowed the crowds in matching denim at the American Music Awards; George W. Bush had declared Iran, Iraq, and North Korea the "axis of evil"; and Kelly Clarkson had won *American Idol*'s first season.

Of those headlines, Zoe Grossberg cared the most about only the last one, and she took it as a promising sign. If a regular girl from Texas could vault to superstardom, a regular girl from Philadelphia could too. Zoe had turned twenty that winter. She was still living at home, attending a desultory handful of classes at the Community College of Philadelphia, still chasing her dream of pop stardom. Which seemed perfectly attainable, something she could achieve with the right set of circumstances, sustained effort, and a few lucky breaks. And why not? Young women all around her were ascending to the ranks of superstardom. Some of them were enormously talented. Zoe was the first to acknowledge that she couldn't sing like Christina Aguilera or Mariah Carey or write music like Alanis Morissette or Jewel. But there were also the Mandy Moores, Jennifer Lopezes, and Britney Spearses of the world, who were cute instead of beautiful, who were talented dancers, competent actresses, and good-enough singers but were mostly, in Zoe's perception, extremely hard workers, willing to throw themselves into a fast-moving, sharp-toothed machine and not care that it might hurt them.

Some of those girls had started their careers with stints in Disney movies or television shows before moving to music, sometimes with a detour through reality TV, always with plenty of attention from the tabloids. They'd been polished and packaged and sent out into the world: pretty and shiny and slightly interchangeable. And then those girls had become rich, famous, and adored. They showed up on red carpets and on TV, and in the pages of *Us Weekly* and *In Style* and *People*, and, Zoe assumed, they stopped conversations in every room they entered. That was what Zoe wanted. She was pretty enough, talented enough, and, even though she'd been an indifferent student, she knew that she could work hard, when the goal was something she actually cared about.

In high school, Zoe had put together a band called Girl Power! (the exclamation point was part of the name). The group was composed of four of her friends: three girls plus Tommy Kelleher, who'd been Cassie's classmate at the Curtis Institute. Zoe had met Tommy at the last of her sister's recitals she'd deigned to attend. She'd barely noticed him back there, banging on the timpani, but Tommy had noticed her, and at the punch-and-cookies reception, he'd come sidling up to shyly introduce himself. She'd learned his name, and that he'd moved to Philadelphia from Minnesota when he turned seventeen, and that his mom had moved out with him—a not-uncommon arrangement among Curtis's youngest prodigies. That September, his mom had gone back to Duluth, leaving nineteen-year-old Tommy with his own apartment on Pine Street and her old minivan to drive.

Tommy wasn't bad-looking. He was taller than Zoe, a little chunky, with curly brown hair and a shy smile. He had a twangy Midwestern accent, he spoke with a bit of a lisp, and he was obsessive about music, the way all the kids at Curtis were. He seemed nice enough, and her band needed a drummer, and she could tell right away, from the besotted look on his face, that Tommy would be happy to help. The minivan was also a plus, insofar as her parents and her bandmates' parents had all gotten sick of the girls monopolizing their cars to transport their gear. And so Zoe had gone out for coffee with Tommy, at La Colombe on Rittenhouse Square, where she'd told him that she had a boyfriend (a lie) and that her band needed a drummer (the truth). Tommy, perhaps hoping that he'd start as a bandmate and end up as a boyfriend, had happily come on board.

Girl Power! covered other female musicians' work, pop songs

from Britney and Christina and Shania Twain. They'd been playing every gig they could get since Zoe had finished high school. That night, at Dobbs, the plan was for them to perform "Wannabe." Zoe would take the part of Baby Spice. She had clip-in hair extensions, the better to re-create Emma Bunton's high white-blond ponytail; white platform basketball sneakers; and a powder-pink latex mini-dress, purchased at Zipperhead on South Street, that was hell to put on and even harder to take off. A Miracle Bra, uncomfortable but effective, pushed her breasts up and out, creating impressive cleav-age. Three of her four bandmates had done their best to approximate their assigned Spice. Janelle Garces, the girl playing Sporty Spice, wore loose-fitting tracksuit pants and a sports bra; Sammi Johnson, as Scary Spice, had used a pick to push her short Afro to its absolute limits. Olivia Friedelle, as Ginger Spice, had a Union Jack minidress and red pleather platform boots. Poor Tommy, assigned the role of Posh Spice, had declined Zoe's offer of a wig, and wore his usual jeans, white tee shirt, and the black leather vest that he'd decided, some-how, encapsulated the essence of rock and roll. Zoe had figured, after a childhood and adolescence spent in concert blacks, Tommy would be thrilled by the chance to branch out, but it was always the same: white shirt, black vest, jeans.

It was fine, Zoe told herself . . . and Tommy in drag might have been more of a distraction than a boon. She'd drilled the girls on the dance moves, she'd packed the audience with a few dozen classmates and friends. Victory was, if not assured, at least strongly possible. Not only was there money for the contest winner; there was, allegedly, go-ing to be a scout from a record label at the show—at least, that's what everyone was saying. A person with the power to give Zoe the life she wanted would be there, watching her perform.

And then, mere hours before the show, Zoe's friends kicked her out of the band.

The trouble began at their run-through, the afternoon of the show, when Janelle, the girl playing Sporty Spice, had accused Zoe—

correctly, it eventually emerged—of flirting with her boyfriend. Zoe denied it, but Scary and Ginger both took Janelle's side. The band had voted, and, even with Tommy defending her, Zoe was out.

After Janelle delivered the news, Zoe drove herself home to Fishtown and locked herself in the house's single bathroom, where she stuffed her fist into her mouth to stifle her screams of rage. Then she wiped her eyes, touched up her mascara, and looked at herself in the mirror, waiting for options to present themselves. It didn't take her long to realize that there was only one real possibility. Zoe nodded, gave her ponytail a tweak, and went downstairs, in search of her sister.

She found Cassie, as usual, at her piano, the battered upright that Sam had purchased, secondhand, after Cassie's teachers told him that the electronic keyboard would no longer suffice. Her sister was working on some dense piece of classical music that Zoe didn't recognize, playing the same phrase over and over and over, with her eyes closed and her mouth slightly opened, swaying a little in time with the notes. She looked possessed, Zoe thought, and wondered, for the thousandth time, how Cassie could be so unaware of how she presented herself, why she didn't try to look even slightly more normal.

Never mind, Zoe thought, as she put on her brightest smile. She leaned over the top of the instrument and waited, looking down at Cassie, who was wearing a version of what she wore every day: a double-extra-large sweatshirt that hung almost to her knees, pale-blue high-waisted jeans that bagged at her ankles, and a pair of bulky, padded white sneakers. Her hair was scraped back from her face and knotted at the nape of her neck. Zoe knew that her sister combed her hair when it was wet, pulled it back, and went to sleep, on her side, leaving her with a bun that resembled a squashed squirrel's tail. It was beyond depressing, Zoe thought. And so unnecessary. Some mousse at her roots could take away the frizz; an actual hairstyle would be a vast improvement, and a few swipes of bronzer would make Cassie look more like someone who occasionally encountered sunlight. Even if Cassie was bigger than most girls, she didn't have to dress like a senior citizen on her way to walk laps at the Oxford Valley Mall. *Never mind,* Zoe thought again. Never mind Cassie's appearance. What she needed was Cassie's voice.

"I need you to do me a favor," she said, when her sister finally noticed her presence and stopped playing. Cassie looked at her warily, as Zoe said, as quickly as she could, "My friends kicked me out of the band, and I need you to sing with me at Dobbs tonight."

For a moment, Cassie just stared. Then she shook her head, turned back toward her sheet music, and started playing again.

Zoe plopped down on the piano bench next to Cassie, nudging her with her hip until her sister was forced to lift her fingers from the keys. "Please," she said.

"I don't sing anymore," Cassie muttered.

This was true. The impromptu concerts they'd performed in bed as little girls had stopped years ago. Zoe wasn't sure exactly when, or why. They'd never talked about it. Still, Zoe could remember Cassie's voice, rich and clear and comforting as a hug in the darkness. "You can sing," Zoe said. "And I need you."

"Why?" Cassie said to the keyboard. "Just get up there and sing by yourself."

"You're the one with the really good voice." Cassie didn't reply to the compliment, or even seem to notice that she'd been complimented. Zoe stared straight ahead and forced the admission past her lips. "If I sing by myself, they'll laugh at me. Janelle and Olivia and Sammi." She looked her sister in the eyes, her expression saying, *You know how that feels, don't you? You know how much it hurts when people laugh.*

Cassie shook her head. Zoe gave her sister a hard look that said, *You owe me.* You owe me for the time at Natalie Freeman's birthday party in first grade when the kids said you couldn't play musical chairs because you'd probably break the chairs and I said I'd tell Natalie's mom unless everyone said they were sorry. You owe me for the sixth-grade camping trip when no one wanted you in their cabin and I told my friends they had to let you stay with us. You owe me for the time we went to the King of Prussia Mall and those boys followed us around oinking and mooing and I yelled at them and made them stop. You owe me for every time I sat with you on the bus and let you come trick-or-treating with my friends. You owe me a lot. *Take care of your sister*, their mother had told Zoe over the years. The words had played like a mantra in her head from the time they were little girls, and her mom had made Zoe wait a year so that she could start kindergarten with Cassie, and be her protector. Cassie owed her for everything Zoe had sacrificed, for everything it had cost her to spend so much time taking care of her sister.

Zoe didn't say any of this. She just waited, silently, until, finally, Cassie muttered, "I can't."

"Can't what?"

"Can't sing. Onstage. People are going to stare at me."

"So what?" Zoe asked, not even trying to deny that people would, indeed, be staring. "Who cares if they're staring? You're good!"

Cassie pressed her lips together tightly, shaking her head.

"And it'll be dark. And most of them will probably be drunk, anyhow. And I'll be there." Zoe left the rest of that sentence implied— *they'll be looking at me, not at you.*

Cassie shook her head again. Zoe could feel herself getting angry. Getting desperate. Only what were the levers that would move her sister?

"I don't understand you," Zoe finally said. "Everyone goes on and on about how talented you are, about what a gift you have." Zoe let herself sound angry, let the words *talented* and *gift* come out especially barbed. She made an abrupt gesture, raising her hands, palms open, in the air. "What's the point of being able to sing like you can if no one hears you? What's the point of a gift if you don't share it?"

For a moment, Cassie sat motionless, doing her best impression of a statue. Zoe wondered what Cassie was thinking before deciding that wondering would do her little good. She had no idea how Cassie's brain worked. So she waited, until, finally, Cassie asked, without looking at her, "What do you want to sing?"

Zoe hopped into the air, squealing with joy. "'Save the Best for Last'?"

"Won't work," Cass said shortly. "Let's do 'Why.' You know? Annie

Lennox?" She hummed a few bars. Zoe knew that Cassie might play only the works of composers who'd been dead for hundreds of years, but her sister listened to all kinds of music, from girl groups from the 1950s and 1960s to country to R&B, current Top 40 hits, and Broadway musicals. Cassie played the organ for churches and synagogues, accompanying their choruses and cantors. As far as Zoe could tell, every penny she earned went to purchasing CDs and sheet music, plus a high-end stereo and fancy compact disc player. God knew her sister wasn't spending any of it on makeup or clothes.

Zoe suspected that her sister's interest in popular music had to do with filling in the blanks left by Zoe's departure. By the time they'd finished elementary school, Zoe was done being Cassie's intermediary, her normal-human-being translator, her emotional-support animal. Cassie was stuck trying to figure people out all on her own. The songs must have helped. Especially the ones from musicals, where, instead of simply doing something—kissing the guy, breaking up with the girl, leaving home, or coming back—the characters sang about it, explaining their actions and choices and motivations in ballads or anthems or jaunty patter songs. Maybe it helped.

"Can't we do something happy?" Zoe asked.

"That," said Cass, her face stony, "or nothing."

Zoe nodded, and closed her eyes, trying to recall the words. "I may be mad / I may be blind / I may be viciously unkind / But I can still read what you're thinking," she said in her silvery soprano, which was a little thin, but still sweet and mostly on tune.

Cassie sang the next line, her face expressionless, her eyes on the floor. It was still enthralling. Zoe listened, skin prickling with goose bumps. She wondered what it would be like, how it would feel to have that voice, to know that you could open up your mouth and have a miracle pouring past your lips. Mostly, Zoe was thinking that if she actually got Cassie up on that stage, the contest was as good as won. Oh, she'd make those bitches sorry!

"So you'll do it?"

"Fine," Cassie sighed.

Zoe gave another jump in the air, and hugged her sister, smacking her lips against Cassie's cheek before bounding out of the room, running back upstairs to find the lyrics and check her hair and make sure her makeup was perfect.

Two hours later, Cassie and Zoe were backstage at Dobbs, Zoe in her shiny pink dress, Cassie in the sweatshirt Zoe hadn't been able to get her to change. "You said no one was going to look at me," Cassie had said, and Zoe hadn't wanted to tell her otherwise, or that a giant sweatshirt wouldn't make her invisible. Zoe's friends had just finished a credible version of "Wannabe" (Janelle had forgotten half of the dance routine, as usual, Zoe noticed, and Olivia's boots had come unzipped). They'd been followed by a young man with an acoustic guitar, who was currently onstage, doing terrible things to "The Freshmen" by the Verve Pipe. While Zoe and Cassie stood in the wings, a young woman with a shiny dark ponytail who'd introduced herself as Chloe checked a clipboard, then asked, "Do you guys have a name?"

"Zoe and Cassie," said Zoe, and looked at her sister, who'd gone pale as skim milk and was visibly trembling. "Cassie and Zoe?" she asked, as if maybe that would help.

"I can't do this," her sister muttered, her eyes flickering toward the exit.

"What? No! You have to!" Zoe said.

Cassie ducked her head and muttered a word that sounded like *people.*

"What?" Zoe asked.

Cassie repeated what she'd said, more clearly. "All those people are going to look at me."

Zoe stared at her sister. Her sister, who'd never evinced the tiniest bit of stage fright at any of her recitals, and some of them had been in front of sizable crowds. But at those performances, Cassie hadn't been singing, and those audiences hadn't been drunk, or rowdy, or inclined to boo, or full of people her own age.

She thought about saying *So what?* Or even *You look fine!* But neither of those would be right. Or effective. Or true. People were going to look . . . and Cassie's appearance was not what people expected, or wanted, from a woman on a stage. Nor was there time to do anything about it.

As Chloe stared at them impatiently, tapping her pen against the paper sign-up sheet, Zoe stepped close to her sister. She looked into Cassie's eyes and took Cassie's hands.

"It doesn't matter how you look," she said, her voice firm, ringing with conviction. "You have talent. You have a beautiful voice, and you deserve to be up there." She squeezed her sister's fingers. "You can do this. You deserve this. I believe in you." *And if you don't do it, I'm fucked,* Zoe thought, but did not say.

Cassie's eyes were squeezed shut as Chloe and her clipboard went onstage and introduced them. "And now, Cassie and Zoe!" Zoe had to half drag her sister onto the stage and more or less dump her at the piano. She heard people murmuring, heard a few of them laugh, and prayed Cassie hadn't noticed. "You got this," she whispered, as Cassie settled herself on the bench with a relieved sigh. "Just close your eyes. I'm right here. You'll be fine." Zoe strutted to center stage and stood behind the microphone, holding her breath. For what felt like a long, long moment—long enough for Zoe to think that it wasn't going to work, that Cassie wouldn't sing, wouldn't accompany her, wouldn't even open her mouth—there was nothing. Then came the sound of the first few bars of the song, slow and rippling and sad.

Zoe took the first verse. "How many times do I have to try to tell you / That I'm sorry for the things I've done."

Cass still had her eyes closed. Zoe wondered if she was pretending she was at home, at her piano, or in their bedroom with the door locked, with no one listening. "But when I start to try to tell you / That's when you have to tell me / Hey, this kind of trouble's only just begun . . ." she sang. Zoe felt the reverent hush that fell over an audience whenever Cassie played piano—a hush that extended, for the first time, to include her, and felt not just impressed but awed. It was a heady, euphoric feeling, that sense of commanding every bit of the attention from every single person in the audience. It made her feel powerful: that she could take people out of the real world and into the world she was creating with her voice; that she could make them feel what she wanted them to feel. And Cassie could do this all the time. Whenever she wanted, Zoe marveled, feeling the first threads of envy gathering inside her, twisting and knotting into something nasty and sharp-edged. *Just keep singing*, she thought. *Keep singing, and you'll win.*

Cassie's back straightened, her voice getting louder, more confident. "I may be mad / I may be blind / I may be viciously unkind . . . / But I can still read what you're thinking . . ." And then Cassie surprised her, singing over the verse that should have been Zoe's: "And I've heard it said too many times / That you'd be better off / Besides, why can't you see this boat is sinking."

Zoe's eyes opened wide in surprise. Part of her wanted to turn and storm off the stage, go back home, lock herself in the bathroom, scream some more, at yet another betrayal. Instead, she dropped her voice low, humming along as Cassie sang, "Let's go down to the water's edge / And we can cast away those doubts." What had started as a duet was becoming more like a solo. Zoe didn't know how to stop it, or even if that was what she wanted to do. She could hear the audience's rapt silence as Cassie reached the end of the song, a recitation; a lament. A farewell. "This is the book I never read / These are the words I never said . . ."

Zoe sang softly in the background, the repeated words, "You don't know," a counterpoint to the song's sharp-edged anguish. "I don't think you know how I feel," Cass sang, making her voice quieter and more intense, almost whispering the final line. "You don't know what I fear."

There was a long beat of silence . . . and then an explosion of applause so loud that it was startling. Cassie's eyes flew open and she looked around, her mouth slightly agape, her expression startled and fearful. Zoe caught her sister's eyes across the stage and mouthed the words, *Thank you.* In that moment, the jealousy was gone. All she felt was gratitude. Not envy at how much better Cassie was, not resentment, not anger at how deftly and completely Cassie had stolen the spotlight. All of that would come later. In that moment, all Zoe was conscious of was the applause and the pleasure of knowing that she'd won. Without planning on it, she kissed the tips of the first two fingers of her right hand, and raised them toward the sky, thinking, *Thank God. Thank God for Cassie.*

As she stepped offstage, Chloe stopped her and touched her shoulder. Her face was slack with wonder, her eyes wide and shiny. "That was," she said, and swallowed. "That was astonishing."

"So where is he?" Zoe asked.

"Who?" Chloe replied.

"The scout?"

Chloe just shrugged. "I think that was just a rumor," she said. Zoe's shoulders slumped. Of course, she thought. Of course, after all that, it was a lie. She told herself that maybe it was for the best. A scout who'd seen that performance would have wanted Cassie, not her.

Chloe hadn't lied. There was not a music scout at the show, but there was one on his way to Philadelphia. While she and her sister were onstage, a man named David Katz, a record-label executive and the eventual agent of their destiny, was on an airplane, in a middle seat two rows up from the rear of the plane, flying from Los Angeles to Philadelphia, where he'd spend the last two weeks of December with his sister, meeting his newest niece, and trying not to think about his ex-wife. He hadn't been there, but his nephew Simon had.

Ten hours after the Dobbs show ended, David Katz stood in his sister's kitchen in Narberth, nibbling the edge of a latke, and listened to his nephew with a faintly condescending smile. "Back up. Tell me again."

"They're sisters. Cassie and Zoe Grossberg. I went to school with them. Cassie's at the Curtis Institute now, and Zoe's at CCP. She did the talent shows at school and plays around here. I've heard her, but not with Cassie. Last night, they played in a Battle of the Bands at a club on South Street, and they were incredible."

David considered his nephew's starry-eyed expression and thought that Simon probably had a crush on one or the other of them, or maybe both. The fact that one sister was at Curtis certainly suggested musical legitimacy . . . but if they were that good, wouldn't Relic's scout, who attended open mic nights and triple-A baseball games and minor-league hockey tournaments up and down the eastern seaboard, just in case the kid singing the national anthem was another Whitney Houston, have heard of them?

That was likely, David knew. But, he had to acknowledge, it wasn't impossible that the sisters were an unknown quantity. It did happen. Boyz II Men had been Philadelphia high-school students once . . . and, a few generations back, so had Daryl Hall and John Oates, although they'd been in college, at Temple University, when they'd been discovered. Talent had to come from somewhere, and these girls were young. It was possible they hadn't played on a stage where a scout might have heard them. When he asked his nephew if one or both of the girls had ever made the anthem rounds, the boy just shrugged. "I don't think so. Cassie's really, really shy—like, she barely talks—and I think Zoe's more into the, um, performing piece of it. The dancing, you know?"

Wonderful, David thought. A pathologically shy girl and a dilettante. But after hours of his new niece drooling on his shoulder, he'd be eager to get out of the house, happy to have an excuse for a few hours' worth of freedom. The next morning, he bundled up in his brother-in-law's borrowed winter coat, and, with Simon in the passenger's seat of his sister's car, he'd sped off along the Schuylkill Express toward Fishtown, scowling at the falling snow. He and Suzanne had moved west right after they'd gotten married, and David had sworn he was done with Northeast winters forever.

David loved LA. He loved the little two-bedroom house that he and his bride had rented, high in the hills, on the edge of Laurel Canyon. He loved the weather, loved stepping into the yard to pluck lemons and avocados and silvery-skinned plums; loved that he didn't need to buy rock salt or snow tires, and no longer owned a scarf or gloves. He'd been happy. For seven years, he and Suzanne had been happy together.

Don't think about it, David told himself as he eased the car along the icy ruts that had formed on the narrow streets. "Don't the plows come through here?" he asked as the car fishtailed and wobbled. Simon just shrugged. Finally, David parallel parked and made his way along a barely shoveled sidewalk to knock on the rowhouse's front door. "Hello!" he'd said, his voice bluff and nonthreatening. "I'm David Katz."

His first impression was not promising. Zoe, who'd opened the door almost before he'd finished knocking, was pretty enough, fine-boned and slim-hipped, with the kind of oval face and regular features he knew would photograph well.

The second sister was a different story. She was heavy, with deep-set eyes and hair that was a dingy, flat brown and somehow looked both thin and frizzy. Even with a diet, even with implants, even with all the things that cosmetics and lighting and stylists and surgeons could do, David couldn't see it. He sighed mentally, resigning himself to a wasted half hour. The pretty sister had dressed for a beach outing instead of a snow day, in tight jeans and a checked plaid shirt, knotted at her midriff, and clunky black sandals with platform soles. The other sister wore black leggings and a loose-fitting black jersey tunic, with seasonally appropriate dark-blue wool socks on her feet.

David shook hands with Zoe. He nodded at Cassie, who ducked her head and muttered something that might have been *hello*. He met their parents, whose names he forgot as soon as they'd said them, and he let himself be ushered to the sofa as the fat girl settled down behind the piano, and her sister stood beside her, with a guitar strap over her neck, her fingers resting awkwardly on the strings. "Cassie's taken piano lessons for fourteen years," Zoe said, her voice breathy and rushed.

David did the math, realizing that Cassie would have had to have started her lessons at four years old, and decided her sister was lying.

Through the window, he could see a snowdrift in cross-section, with half a dozen ribbons of grime running through it. There was a splatter of yellow along its side and a cigarette butt frozen midway down, a geological sampling of urban life. *Twenty more minutes*, he reminded himself, and thought of his lemon tree, back in Los Angeles.

"Whenever you're ready," he said, forcing a smile. The girls' parents were standing side by side in the doorway, staring adoringly at their daughters, in the manner of every parent at every school concert and play ever. An old line from a poem he'd learned in high school came swimming to the top of his brain: *and I, Tiresias, have foresuffered all.*

Then Cass struck the first notes on the piano, and the sisters sang together, their voices ringing through the small, low-ceilinged room. "I've been cheated / Been mistreated / When will I be loved," and David Katz forgot about English-class poetry; forgot to think, forgot to breathe. The hairs at the back of his neck prickled. His forearms bristled with gooseflesh as he tried to keep still, tried to keep his face from showing what he was thinking . . . which, as soon as his brain stopped flashing exclamation points, was *These girls are the real deal,* quickly followed by *They're going to make me so rich.*

The fat girl's voice was a marvel: agile and supple and full of shades from bright to dark. She sang with power and control, with a range of at least three octaves, maybe more. She could belt, and then sing in a delicate head voice, then drop down into a rolling vibrato. If he'd closed his eyes, he could have been listening to Linda Ronstadt, or Carole King, or Carly Simon, one of the all-time greats.

David stared, fighting the impulse to hustle the girls out of the house and into his sister's car, so he could drive them straight to New York City and sign them before they played another show or even just left the house and gave someone else the chance to discover them. His mind sped ahead, from getting the girls signed to finding them a songwriter to recording the first single to releasing the first album to having it go platinum, a sixty-second fast-forward that ended with David in a new mansion, with an entire grove of lemon trees, declining, through his assistant, to take his ex-wife's calls.

Even as he made his plans, he was already grasping the essential problem. Any reasonably pretty teenage girl could be made to look beautiful, and Zoe Grossberg was more than reasonably pretty. Cassie Grossberg was a disaster.

There were fat girls of whom people said, "She has such a pretty face." There were also your Cass Elliots, your—he hesitated to even think the name, then gave himself permission—your Arethas, whose talent was so goddamn enormous that it didn't matter, in the end, what the container that held it looked like. All that mattered was the voice.

Maybe they could fix Cassie. And if they couldn't, maybe they could hide her. But first they had to sign her. And her sister, who seemed to be part of the deal. Which meant charming Mom and Dad. David mentally spat on his hands, reviewing his tactics, preparing to go to work.

"Nice," said David, careful to sound approving, impressed, but not too eager. "Very, very nice." He put on his most winning smile, a smile custom-built to elicit confidence from the parents of young and impressionable girls. "Tell me what kind of training you've had," he said. Zoe answered for both of them. In a high, girlish voice, she told him about all of her dance classes at the local YMCA, and the band she'd formed in high school.

"And Cassie just sat down at the piano at her nursery school and started playing," said the mom. "It was amazing."

"Amazing!" Zoe repeated.

Cassie still said nothing.

"Do you play mostly classical music?" David asked her.

Cassie nodded, very slightly.

"But she can play anything by ear," said the dad. "Anything at all."

"Voice lessons?" David asked. The girls shook their heads. David took a brief moment to marvel at it, to wonder about Cassie's untapped potential, to let himself imagine how good she could get.

"And Zoe, how about you? Have you taken any guitar lessons?"

It turned out she hadn't. It further emerged that Zoe knew only three chords, which her sister had taught her the night before, on the guitar, which was on loan from a neighbor. No matter. David's heart was beating faster than it had since the last time he'd done cocaine. "Do you have any original music?" he asked.

Zoe shot an anxious glance at her sister. "It's fine if you don't," David said quickly. He was already flipping through his mental Rolodex, thinking about who was available, who'd be the right fit, as another part of his brain tried to remember which island his boss, Jerry Nance, and his supermodel girlfriend were currently visiting. Anguilla? Antigua?—one of those *A* places. David wondered if the move was to get Jerry on the phone, tell him what he'd heard, and insist Jerry fly back to New York before anyone could get their hooks into these girls, or if he, David, could just get Cassie and Zoe to a conference room in the label's New York office, put them on speakerphone, and let them play for whichever execs he could round up in the week between Christmas and New Year's. The good news was that his boss wasn't the only one who'd decamped to some sunny paradise. Other bosses had, too, which increased his chances of being able to slip the girls into the city quietly and sign them without other labels finding out.

"Do you have a name?" he asked.

The sisters exchanged a fast glance. "The Grossberg Sisters?" asked the fat one.

David schooled his face, thinking, *Absolutely not. Under no circumstances.* "We'll see," he said instead.

"How about the Griffin Sisters?" said the pretty one.

The fat one looked at her, puzzled.

"Who are the Griffins?" asked Dad.

"It's a made-up name. It'll be better," said the pretty sister. "For, like, our privacy."

"And for anti-Semites." The fat girl's voice was low, but not so low that David couldn't hear her.

"Carole King changed her name," he offered. "And Bob Dylan, of course. Lots of Jewish people in the, ah, performing arts do it."

"Natalie Portman!" said the pretty sister, coming in with a reference more pertinent to her world than either Carole King or Bob Dylan.

"It just makes breaking through a little easier," David said.

The pretty sister was nodding. The fat one looked unconvinced, and the parents just looked bewildered.

"The Griffin Sisters," David said, tasting the words. Testing them. "I like it." What he liked even more was that the sisters were willing to be flexible, and they hadn't gotten attached to something silly. The Beach Boys had once been the Pendletones; the Red Hot Chili Peppers, God help them, had called themselves Tony Flow and the Miraculously Majestic Masters of Mayhem and some version of David had been tasked with talking them out of it.

"If you'll excuse me, I'm going to make a few phone calls," David said, reaching for his BlackBerry as he got to his feet. He practically skipped outside, barely feeling the cold as he called his assistant in Waukesha, Wisconsin.

"Find Jerry," he instructed her, speaking quickly. "Tell him he's got to get back to New York as fast as he can. I found an act he's got to hear. No one else knows about them yet—they're teenage girls, just out of high school."

"Got it," said Kelly, who knew when to just keep her mouth shut and listen.

"Call Helen," he continued. "If she can't be there, find out who from A&R can. Tell her to round up anyone who's in town, tomorrow at noon. Got it?"

"Got it," Kelly repeated.

David adjusted his coat and straightened his smile. He walked back into the rowhouse's living room, prepared to use whatever combinations of tactics the day required. He'd sweet-talk Mom and strong-arm Dad (or sweet-talk Dad and strong-arm Mom). He'd dangle all the prizes in front of them: money and fame, dream houses and fancy cars. He'd invoke the divine, if he had to: *your daughters have a gift, and with gifts come responsibilities; it is God's will that they use their talents to give back to the world* (he'd once used that line to coax a reluctant Mormon into postponing his two-year mission to South Africa and signing a development deal instead). *Whatever it takes*, he told himself, and looked at the girls, and announced, with absolute, unwavering sincerity, "I think the two of you are fantastic. I'd feel very honored to bring you to New York City to meet my boss. I'm pretty sure he'd like to offer you a deal."

Less than twenty-four hours after David Katz heard Cassie and Zoe Grossberg singing in their parents' living room in Fishtown, he had the girls, plus Mom and Dad, bundled into a rented SUV, cruising north on the New Jersey Turnpike. The previous evening, he'd made his apologies to his sister and brother-in-law, promised his nephew courtside Lakers seats if he signed the sisters, and had gotten the message to Jerry, once they'd reached him (the *A* place turned out to be Aruba). *These girls are the real deal. We need to lock them down before someone else finds them.*

The timing, David mused, as he piloted the enormous vehicle along the fast lane, could actually work in his favor. Typically, by the time an artist made it to one of the big labels—Atlantic, Arista, RCA, Capitol—they were known quantities. They'd been discovered as kids and come through Broadway or the Disney machine—à la Britney, Christina, Ryan Gosling, and Justin Timberlake—or they'd been scouted as young adults, playing at a bar or a concert hall or an open mic night, usually after they'd been at it for a year, or years, plural, and had built up a fan base. All the labels had scouts; all the scouts went to the same shows and listened to the same stations; they attended the same open mic nights and Battles of the Bands. If one label had heard of a group or a performer—if there was a church soloist in West Philadelphia who sang "Ave Maria" like an angel, or a boy from South Jersey whose "Star-Spangled Banner" at the ribbon-cutting for a new Costco brought tears to the attendees' eyes—chances were, all of them had, which made it unlikely for a deal to be one-and-done: one performance for one label, followed by a signed contract.

That was the feat David was hoping to pull off. He'd asked—repeatedly—and his nephew, both girls, plus their parents had told him the same thing. Zoe had performed at school talent shows, and Cassie at piano recitals, but they'd never performed together in public until two nights ago, where David's nephew (God bless him and keep him) had heard them.

It seemed almost too good to be true . . . but, David figured, the

Universe owed him. He was broke, his wife had left him (for a woman! his brain insisted on adding, as if that made it worse). His back hurt when he woke up, more mornings than not, and his hair was visibly thinning. The point, he thought, as he drove through the Lincoln Tunnel, was that he was due for a win. He zipped through the tollbooth and visualized how it would go, assuming that Cassie and Zoe would impress Jerry as much as they'd impressed him.

The label would find the girls a songwriter who could write them a hit. Figure six weeks to write it and record it, to put a band together and see if they could get Cassie looking a little more presentable. The label would release a single, and the girls would be sent on a cross-country radio-station tour, visiting three or four or five stations a day, performing for the DJs and the program directors, or at small concerts the stations would set up.

And then they would wait. Maybe a big station's programming director would fall in love with their song, would march it down to the DJ's booth and order it played every hour. Maybe a music director would want it for a big TV show or a commercial. Once, an artist might have been condemned for letting his or her art be used for commerce, but these days, it seemed, there was no such thing as a sellout, and commercials were just another way to introduce your music to the masses. David had some half-formed idea that rap music, with its celebration of material wealth and penchant for name-checking brands, had done something to erase that stigma, but he hadn't completely worked out how.

Once the car was parked and his party had been loaded into an elevator, David told the girls how it would go. "You'll just be performing for a few people. Jerry runs the label, and Helen Leary's part of the A&R division."

Timidly, Mom inquired, "What's A&R?"

"Artists and repertoire," David told her. "It's just a fancy way of saying talent development. The A&R people scout artists, and, once they're signed, they help to manage the recording process. Then, once the record's out, they help with the marketing and promotion."

"Got it," said Mom, who'd pulled a small notebook out of her purse and was actually scribbling down notes as David spoke.

"They'll both have assistants there. And then you'll meet Sean, who scouts in Philadelphia . . ." *And who'd have found you already, if he'd been doing his job,* David thought but did not say. "And me. That's it." He put on what he hoped was a friendly smile. "Not even as many people as the Battle of the Bands, right?"

Zoe nodded. Cassie looked queasy. David hoped she didn't choke. He'd seen it happen: bands or singers who were fine in front of friendly hometown crowds who could barely strum G major when it mattered.

"I've been working on my guitar playing," Zoe said shyly. Which probably meant she knew four chords, instead of yesterday's three, David thought. But no matter. Jerry and Helen would hear Cassie, and it would be as good as over.

David's mind whirled and clicked as he led the girls into the conference room. There was an electronic keyboard on a stand, plugged into a pair of speakers, with a small wheeled stool behind it and a microphone in front. A second mic stood on a metal stand. Jerry sat at the head of the table, all five feet three inches of him, with his doll-like features and his fresh island tan, his dark hair combed neatly over his forehead, the cuffs of his blue oxford shirt rolled up to display his narrow wrists. It was good, David thought, that his boss, although pushing fifty, still looked like one of the Cleaver brothers, that he wasn't some sleazeball in snakeskin boots and a silk shirt unbuttoned to his navel.

Cassie was still wearing her bulky parka when she walked over to the keyboard. When she plopped down on the stool, David sent up a quick prayer that it wouldn't collapse. Zoe, who'd gotten herself gussied up in a denim minidress, a black velvet choker, and high-heeled black boots, was smoothing her hair, shifting her weight from foot to foot.

David cleared his throat. "Jerry. Helen. Ladies," he said, nodding at the assistants. "I'm pleased to introduce Cassie and Zoe from Philadelphia. The, ah, Griffin Sisters."

He nodded at the girls. Zoe looked at her sister, and Cassie started to play. David felt the hairs at the back of his neck prickling, a shiver rippling through his body as his heartbeat sped up and his scrotum tightened. He recognized the song: "(You Make Me Feel Like) A Natural Woman," by Aretha Franklin. The vocal equivalent of Mount Everest. If you couldn't scale its peaks, if—like most mortals—you compared unfavorably to Aretha, you'd fall to your doom. He would have steered them away from it, if they'd given him the chance, but here they were. All he could do was hope.

Cassie's face was peaceful, tilted slightly upward, like she was basking in a ray of sun that none of them could feel, and her voice was like scuffed marble, a pour of molten gold with a raspy growl on top. "Before the day I met you," she wailed, with her eyes shut, "Life was so unkind . . ." She belted the first two lines of the chorus, then went into a head voice as sweet and delicate as a line of icing piped expertly onto a cake. Her voice floated lightly above the melody, dropping down to kiss it for a note or two, then soaring airily upward.

It took only a measure or two more before David caught Jerry's infinitesimal nod. By the time the girls sang "When Will I Be Loved," Jerry was tapping his fingers on the table, and Helen's lips were pressed together tightly, like she was trying to keep herself from shouting with delight. David wondered if they, like him, were imagining an arena full of people, arms and lighters and cell phones held aloft, everyone giving themselves over to the music, forgetting their problems, their regrets and their sorrows, the bills they had to pay and the wives who'd walked out on them, and just basking in the joy of it, raised up by the music, dancing and singing along (and then lining up to buy albums and tee shirts and ten-dollar beers in commemorative cups).

As soon as the last note had faded, Zoe grinned and pressed her fingertips to her lips, kissing them before raising them up toward the sky. Jerry nodded at the girls, then at David. He got to his feet and left the conference room without saying a word. Zoe bit her lip, and Mom looked anxious. Cassie kept her hands on the keys, like she wished she was still playing.

David smiled, giving himself a moment to gloat as Helen walked over to the girls and their mother, hearing her speech. *So impressive . . . incredible talent . . . we'd love to start working on a deal memo . . . happy to recommend a manager.* He wondered if he should encourage them to go find their own manager. It would show the girls that he was on their side. Then again, Helen's suggestions would all be legitimate, reputable, well-connected professionals. There was no point in steering artists toward incompetents—it only meant that the execs would waste time fixing someone's fuckups. And God only knew who the sisters might dig up in Philadelphia. David remembered a rapper he'd found in Minneapolis, a seventeen-year-old boy who called himself Lunchmeat, and his brother/manager, an obnoxious fellow who'd clearly modeled himself on every sleazy agent he'd ever seen in a movie. The would-be manager kept pounding on Jerry's desk, shouting, "What are you going to do for us?" and "Show me the money!" while Lunchmeat (real name: Kyle Donovan) giggled in the corner.

"Ladies!" said David, spreading his arms wide. "How about we let the team get to work? We can get some lunch, and I bet by the time we're done they'll have something for you to look at." If they didn't, he thought, there would be some serious ass-kicking. Speed was the name of the game, and if Helen couldn't rustle up a few business affairs types from whatever beach or ski resort they'd gone off to, before the girls realized their own value and invited other bidders to the table, Jerry would want to know the reason why.

"Do I—should we get a lawyer?" asked Mom.

"That's up to you," said David. "But if you want to have a lawyer look this over, that is fine." The deal, he knew, would be straightforward, with standard terms. The sisters would get an advance, plus royalties on any sales, and Relic would own the rights to any music they wrote and recorded for the term of the deal, which would probably be eighteen months. And would Mom be able to find a lawyer, with no notice, in New York City? Doubtful.

They took the elevator down to the lobby. David's brain was still spinning. He'd talk to Helen about a stylist. A stylist, a trainer, maybe a doctor—he knew a few who understood the assignment and were known to be liberal with their prescription pads. They'd get Cassie some heavy-duty diet pills, or a plastic surgeon who'd be fast and discreet, or both. He'd need to find the girls a place to stay—the label usually had an apartment or two that could be made available for situations like this, and—

"Hi!" The woman lurking by the building's entrance was young—maybe all of twenty-five—and smiling. She was bundled up in a dark-blue down coat and duck boots, and her flushed cheeks suggested she'd been standing there for some time. Ignoring David, she looked at the girls. "Are you the Griffin Sisters?"

Cassie and Zoe looked at each other. Cassie's expression was uneasy. Zoe's was thrilled.

"Yes," Zoe said. "We are."

"Oh, that's great! It is so good to meet you. I'm Jolie Davidow from Park City Records. We would love for you to play for our team."

Three sets of eyes swung to David, who ducked his head and slipped his hands into his pockets so two generations of Grossbergs wouldn't see them balled up into fists. *Fuck*, he thought. This was, no doubt, the work of Helen's assistant. Annie or Penny or something like that. She'd been there for the first song, and for the end of the second song, but she'd slipped out in between, and she must have called this girl, a fellow assistant at a rival label. *Fuck.*

"Is that—would that be okay?" Zoe asked David timidly.

"You haven't signed anything yet, have you?" Jolie said, before David could answer. "I mean, of course you haven't," she said, rolling her eyes at the very possibility of anyone doing something so dumb. "You wouldn't sign anything without a lawyer looking it over."

"No," said Mom, giving David a look that was far too suspicious for his comfort. "We haven't signed anything."

"Then you can play for whoever you want to play for," said Jolie. "His label, my label, every label in town. Right?" She turned to David, wide-eyed.

David swallowed hard and forced a smile. "Of course."

"Which is what I'd tell you to do, if you were my friends. Not just us, either. Everyone." She smiled, a big, relatable grin better than David's own. A smile suggesting that she was the good guy and David was the bad guy; that she was being transparent and forthcoming and was looking out for the girls' best interest, while David had his own best interests in mind and was attempting to hustle them into a deal before they could meet with other labels and turn it into a competitive situation.

Which, of course, was more or less what he'd been doing. Fuck!

David knew, as the old Kenny Rogers song went, when to hold 'em, and when to fold 'em. He smiled weakly, unfisted his right hand, and pulled a business card out of his wallet.

"Keep in touch," he said. "We'd like to stay in the running."

Mom accepted the card as if it had been lightly coated in slime. And for the rest of his life, whenever David heard the Griffin Sisters' songs on the radio or on TV or on the Muzak in Trader Joe's, he'd think back to that moment and wonder how different everything would have been if the girls had slipped through his fingers, if they had signed with another label. Would everything have changed? Would Cassie have written the same songs with someone else, or different songs, even better ones? Would their album have been a hit? Would Cassie and Zoe still be making music together? Would they have met Russell D'Angelo some other way . . . or would the story have played out the same, just with a different man, or even a woman, taking Russell's spot in the triangle?

It wasn't worth dwelling on. David knew that. But sometimes he couldn't help himself from wondering. Lying awake in Los Feliz, in the six-bedroom house the Griffin Sisters had bought him, listening to the rustling of the desert wind and the distant howling of coyotes, he would wonder if he should have seen it coming, and if he could have stopped it. Some nights, the winds would carry the sharp scent of lemons. They'd always smell like despair and triumph, mixed together, the pain of losing his wife, the joy of landing the sisters. He'd breathe in the bittersweet tanginess, feeling lucky, feeling sorry, and he would wonder where Cassie Griffin had gone, and if she was still making music, all by herself, somewhere far, far away.

Cassie
ALASKA, 2024

There was only one grocery store in Homer, a Safeway, with a big parking lot and the town's only Starbucks inside. Once a month, Cassie would have to brave the big market for staples, pet food, and cleaning supplies.

The Safeway stayed open until eleven o'clock, so ten thirty, give or take, was when Cass came in to do her monthly shopping. She locked her car and hurried inside through the darkness, thinking that it was going to feel like winter for months longer, but at least the holidays were over. She wouldn't be confronted by Christmas trees in plastic netting, or Christmas music on the speakers. She'd made it through that particular gauntlet of reminders of what she was missing.

The Grossberg home hadn't always been filled with holiday cheer. But her parents would try. Janice would polish the brass menorah that she'd inherited from her mother, and for eight nights, they would light the candles and sing the blessings. Once each Chanukah, they would join the extended family at Bess's house for a feast of brisket and latkes with homemade applesauce, or sour cream and vivid orange curls of smoked salmon, with a teaspoonful of caviar on top. Those were Janice's sister Stephanie's contribution. "Fancy-schmancy!" Bess would say. On the way home, Janice would mutter to Sam about how pretentious her sister was, and Sam would remind her that Steffi and her husband might live in a brand-new five-bedroom mansion on the Main Line, and that their oldest son might have gotten into Penn ("Early decision!" Steffi had crowed), but neither of their kids was a musical prodigy. Cassie always wondered whether Zoe heard those whispered conversations, and how they made her sister feel.

In the parking lot, Cassie clenched her hands around the shopping cart's handle. She swallowed hard and squeezed her eyes shut. *Breathe,* she thought . . . but the memories kept coming.

The smells came first: Aunt Bess's brisket, cooked for hours in a sweet-and-sour sauce of ketchup and cranberries and brown sugar. Chanukah candles, burning in the menorah. The smell of the bedroom she and her sister shared: Zoe's hairspray and mousse and Opium perfume. "You can borrow some if you want," Zoe would offer, but Cass never did. She didn't want to smell appealing, didn't want guys inhaling some alluring, sexy fragrance, then turning to see the girl that alluring, sexy scent was attached to, and ending up disappointed. It would be like the Goodyear Blimp trailing the scent of lilies and lilacs. False advertising. Asking for trouble.

Then there were tastes: the crisp fried latkes and sufganiyot, the creamy nutmeg smoothness of the eggnog Steffi's husband, Frank, would bring to dinner. Frank wasn't Jewish, and eggnog wasn't a traditional Chanukah libation, but the Grossberg clan adapted to it fast. Janice would give each girl a teacup full, with nutmeg and cinnamon sprinkled on top, and sneak a shot of rum into her own cup when Sam wasn't looking, to sip as the party went on.

Outside the Safeway, Cassie made herself get moving, pushing her cart through the automatic door. Her boots squeaked on the linoleum floor. The cart's wheels rattled in counterpoint. *Squeak, squeak, rattle,* F, F, D sharp, the noises resolving into notes without her having to give it any thought as she grabbed her staples: a bag of oranges, for the vitamin C; a gallon of skim milk, for the calcium. Two pounds of carrots and five pounds of onions and three heads of romaine lettuce, because, after her time in the band, and the diets they'd had her on, Cassie couldn't prepare herself a plate that wasn't at least fifty percent filled with vegetables. She grabbed a container of yogurt and a package of chicken breasts. Kidney beans, black beans, a bag of rice, low-fat cheddar cheese. Boxed chicken broth. In the frozen foods section, she pulled out a box of turkey burgers and a single loaf of Ezekiel bread, which felt like an icy brick and tasted, she'd always thought, like tree bark and spite.

Cassie often wondered why she bothered to keep up the fight against a body that clearly wanted to be bigger. Who cared anymore? Who was going to look, now that she lived so far away from family, from strangers, from everyone? There weren't any classmates to make fun of her, no boys who'd moo or oink or call her names. She wasn't just fat; she was fat and middle-aged and, thus, doubly invisible. Couldn't she be a little kinder to herself?

Sometimes she tried. She'd buy heavy cream and buttermilk, cocoa powder and Ghirardelli chocolate chips, and she'd bake carrot cakes with luscious cream-cheese frosting or make pot roast or eggs Benedict for Sunday brunch. She'd think about her great-aunt Bess, who had always been big, and who had still done what she wanted, including taking a Caribbean cruise and posing for pictures in a polka-dotted bikini by the pool. Janice had never put Cassie on a diet, although sometimes Cassie wondered if that had to do with her mother's general lack of interest in her second daughter than a progressive, forward-thinking acceptance of Cassie's size.

Whatever the reason, between Aunt Bess's example and her mother's indifference, Cassie's real trouble with her body hadn't started until the band. The managers and the music video directors, the stylists and photographers—they'd all cared. A lot. To them, Cassie's body was a problem to be solved, a thing to be reduced or disguised or hidden. By the time the band broke up, dieting had become a habit, one that was as hard to lose as the pounds had been. *You don't need that*, the voices in her head would whisper, if she reached for a cookie in the bakery or a container of ice cream when she was picking out her sprouted-wheat bread and frozen spinach. *A minute on the lips, a lifetime on the hips*, she'd hear . . . or, *That's an hour on the treadmill right there*, or, worst of all, *Remember, you're going to be standing next to your sister*.

"Hello there!" said the woman at the cash register as Cassie put the last of her items onto the belt.

"Hi," Cassie muttered. The cashier's name tag read "Marcia" and she was tiny and frail. She had an airy meringue of white hair and a tanned, wise, wrinkled face. She looked like a kindly walnut. A walnut with glasses, and a necklace made of miniature Valentine hearts, flashing red lights, blinking on and off on top of her pink sweater.

"Two hundred and eleven dollars is your damage!" the woman said. She was wearing bright pink lipstick, the same shade as her top. Cassie saw that a little had smeared onto one of her front teeth. "Would you like to round up? We're raising money for cancer research."

"Sure." Cassie handed the woman her credit card. The woman handed it back, then hesitated. Cassie's entire body tensed. But instead of *Don't I know you?* or *You look so familiar* or *Weren't you in that band?* the woman turned around at the sound of someone calling. Cassie followed her gaze and saw a skinny, dark-haired girl approaching from the direction of the deli. "Naomi and Pete both went home," the girl said.

"Oh Lord," the older woman replied. "So that's, what, three of us?"

"Four," said the girl, whose name tag read "Erica." "Including you."

The woman clicked her tongue against the roof of her mouth, then looked at Cass and said, "Are you in a hurry?"

Before Cassie could answer, the woman—Marcia—continued to talk.

"It's just that we're doing a little birthday party for Carl." The woman aimed her chin in the direction of a young man carefully wiping down a conveyer belt with paper towels. Cassie had seen him. He'd even bagged her groceries once. He had a round face and was short and stocky, always smiling. She'd heard him talking, in a slow, slightly thickened voice, greeting people, asking them how their day was. She had always been careful to never stand in his line, so that he wouldn't try talking to her.

The cashier leaned toward Cassie and lowered her voice to a whisper. "Carl lives with his dad, who I doubt even remembered it's his son's birthday, so we're going to have a cake and sing 'Happy Birthday' right after we close."

Cassie nodded, because, clearly, some response was required.

"The trouble is," Marcia said, "there's only going to be four of us. It's a pretty skimpy crowd!" Looking around, Cassie realized that she was the only shopper left. The cavernous store appeared to be entirely empty. Normally, that would be a good thing; exactly what she wanted. Not tonight. "If you could just stay for a few minutes and sing, it'd mean the world to Carl," said Marcia, as she gave Cassie a twinkly grin. "It can be your good deed for the day."

Cassie opened her mouth to refuse. "I—" she began. *I can't. I'm late. I'm busy. I have to get back home, to my dog. I can't sing, not ever. I'm not allowed.* She swallowed hard. Her eyes were stinging, and her throat felt tight and hot. She started to shake her head, to open her mouth and croak out a refusal. What came out, instead, was, "Okay."

"Oh, thank you!" The cashier clapped her hands in approval. The hearts on her necklace bounced. "Wonderful! Okay, so, we're going to set up the cake in the back corner, by the bagel bins. I'm Marcia, by the way."

"Cass." Cassie cleared her throat and tried again. "I'm Cass."

"Nice to meet you, Cass. Come with me."

Cassie put her groceries into her cart and followed Marcia toward the back of the store. She wished she'd thought quickly enough to give a fake name. She braced herself for questions—*Do you live here, or are you just visiting? How long have you lived in Alaska? Where do you live?* and *What do you do?* She wondered if she could say she was a day-tripper from one of the cruise ships that stopped at Homer, letting the passengers off to spend the day hiking the Grace Ridge Summit, or taking a snowmobile tour of the glaciers and fjords, or kayaking in Kachemak Bay. Only why would a day-tripper be shopping for groceries at eleven o'clock at night?

There was a table set up in the corner by the bakery, draped in a cheerful tablecloth with a pattern of dinosaurs in party hats blowing noisemakers and dancing around its borders. A small, round cake with white frosting and the words "HAPPY BIRTHDAY CARL" piped on top in green icing sat at its center, and two other people with name tags on their aprons stood around it. Cass recognized a sullen-looking middle-aged white guy from the deli. His name tag read "Sven," and he had lank, long hair and a thick beard. A young woman with cropped dark hair whose name tag identified her as Louise was also familiar from the deli counter, even though Cass had never ordered anything from the deli. She bought the prepackaged stuff from the refrigerated shelves, sparing herself a human interaction, even if she would have preferred a different kind of cheese or cold cut.

"Everyone, this is Cass. She's going to sing with us. I'll go get Carl!" Marcia scampered off. Cass felt, or imagined she could feel, everyone's eyes turning toward her.

"Got roped into this, huh?" said Louise. She was petite and cute, with big, blue-gray eyes and a tiny jewel glittering in her right nostril. Sven had a pockmarked face, a pug nose, broken blood vessels in his cheeks, and a Semper Fi tattoo crawling up his neck.

"Marcia asked every customer who came through her line," Sven said abruptly. "You're the only one who said yes." He had a nice, deep voice. Cassie wondered if he could carry a tune.

"And here's the birthday boy!" Marcia said. She was walking behind Carl, with one hand on his shoulder to guide him and the other hand covering his eyes. When they were almost at the table, she let her hands drop and said, "Open up." Carl opened his eyes and stared at the cake. His eyes went wide behind his glasses. "For me?" he asked.

"That's your name, isn't it? Do you see any other Carls anywhere?" Marcia asked. She bent down, pulling a box of matches from her pocket, and lit the three candles that were sticking up from the icing. She looked around at the group, nodded, and then, in a cracked, quavering voice, began to sing. "Happy birthday to you . . ."

Sven took up the song in a low rumble. "Happy birthday to you . . ."

Cass jammed her hands into her pockets. Her plan had been to just stand there, adding her body to the crowd, singing only if she had to, and as quietly as possible. But when the song began it was as if her voice, so long denied the pleasure of music, had made its own plans.

Cassie found that she'd opened her mouth and raised her head, that she'd drawn her spine straight and her shoulder blades down and had automatically pulled in the right amount of breath.

"Happy birthday to you," she sang. She could hear herself, the words emerging clear and tuneful in the empty supermarket, echoing off the shelves and the high rafters. "Happy birthday, dear Carl . . ."

Cassie hadn't noticed how, by the song's conclusion, she and Sven were the only ones still singing. They did the last four words alone, in harmony, her voice rising, his going down. "Happy birthday to you."

Then it was over. And everyone was looking at her. Marcia's mouth had dropped open, and Carl, the birthday boy, was so busy staring that he had neglected to blow out his candles.

"My God," Sven murmured. "Who *are* you?"

"Nobody," Cassie said, low-voiced, hunching her shoulders. She looked at Carl and nodded at the cake. "Blow out your candles."

"Oh!" Carl bent down, took a deep breath, and blew out all three candles in one extravagant gust. The little crowd applauded, calling, "Make a wish," and "Happy birthday!"

Carl looked at Cassie again. He had his hands clasped against his chest, and his eyes, his whole face, were shining. "You sing," he said, "like an angel."

Cassie felt her eyes fill with tears. She shook her head. "Angels play harps," she said, and gave her drawstrings a tug, trying to hide as much of her face as possible behind her hood. *Weak*, she thought scornfully, hating herself. *Oh, you're so so weak.*

"Do you know more songs?" Carl asked. "I love singing. It's my favorite thing. Will you sing some more?"

She wanted to laugh. She wanted to cry. "I should go," she said.

"Oh, please!" said Carl, and then everyone was asking. Carl was looking at her, his face open and expectant and hopeful, and it was his birthday, after all. She didn't have a present, but she could give him something.

"What's your favorite song?" She realized, as soon as she'd asked, that she might be setting herself up for trouble. Carl might love some rap song or a new piece of Top 40 fluff that she hadn't heard of.

But Marcia, thank goodness, jumped in to save her. "How about a Christmas carol?"

Carl thought for a minute. "'Silent Night'?" he said.

Cass nodded. "Okay." She cleared her throat, took a few deep breaths, and began. "Silent night, holy night / All is calm, all is bright / 'Round yon virgin, mother and child / holy infant, so tender and mild . . ."

She looked at Sven, who nodded, joining in, his voice an octave below hers. "Sleep in heavenly peace . . . Sleep in heavenly peace."

Cass should have been on guard. She should have been paying attention, noticing what was going on. But she was so intent on the music, the pleasure of singing, that wonderfully freeing sensation of being nothing but voice—no face, no body, no history, just song. Carl was looking at her like she was an actual Christmas miracle. *You have a gift.* How many times in her life had she heard that, from how many different people? All of her piano teachers, the parents who came to her recitals. The people at the record label. Their manager. Her sister. *You have a gift,* they'd all said . . . and when God had given you something that you hadn't earned and might not deserve, it came with responsibilities. When you'd been given a gift, you had to use it. You had to share it.

"Thank you," Carl was saying, still clapping, long after the last note had faded. "Thank you thank you thank you!" He rushed forward and hugged her. It was so unexpected that Cassie was rocked back on her heels. She had to grab his shoulders and hug him back to keep from falling, trying not to think about how long it had been since anyone had hugged her.

"I—I have to go," Cassie stammered. Her heart was beating too hard, and she felt dizzy, like there wasn't enough oxygen getting to her lungs. She turned, heading toward the front of the store, hurrying through the supermarket, toward the waiting dark, with Carl and

Marcia and Sven and Erica and Louise calling "Thank you" and "Take care" as she went.

Forget it, she told herself as she unlocked her car and piled bags of groceries into the back seat. *Just forget it*, she thought as she drove fifty miles through the darkness, carried her groceries inside, and put them away. She gave Wesley his dinner, heated a can of soup for herself, took a longer-than-usual shower, pulled on her flannel pajamas, and got into bed, where she lay awake for what felt like hours, trying to calm her racing heart.

Eventually, she fell into a thin sleep, and in the morning she jolted awake in the darkness, remembering what had happened, what she'd done, scrambling out of bed and onto her feet as Wesley stared at her in alarm. She splashed cold water on her face, got dressed, gathered her cleaning supplies, went out into the cold. A few hours of scrubbing made the impromptu birthday party feel like a dream, and by the end of the day, she'd almost managed to put it completely out of her mind. Back at home that afternoon, she found an app that would let her schedule grocery deliveries. *PLEASE LEAVE BAGS AT FRONT DOOR. DO NOT KNOCK*, she wrote, in the space left for "special instructions."

There, she thought, shutting the laptop. Problem solved. She'd never go back to the Safeway, or see any of the five people in Homer who knew that she could sing, ever again. That night, she fell asleep easily, convinced that she'd navigated a difficult situation to the best of her abilities and that there would be no lasting damage, no fallout, and certainly no requests for an encore.

Cassie was not on social media. The World Wide Web had barely been a thing when the Griffin Sisters had launched. They'd had a MySpace page, which the record label ran and, eventually, a Facebook page, where some intern posted clips from their video and their concerts. Things like Snapchat and Twitter, Instagram and TikTok had all come along during her time in Alaska. She knew that they existed, but she'd never downloaded any apps. It was easier, that way, to avoid the temptation of looking up old classmates from Curtis, or checking in on her relatives or bandmates or her sister. CJ had found her a person who could keep her name and her whereabouts out of the online world. Cassie paid her, and hoped the young woman was as good as CJ had promised. Cassie herself never went online to see what was out there.

Which meant she had no way of knowing that Louise from the deli counter had filmed Carl's birthday party and sent the video to her co-workers. Or that forty-two seconds of shaky footage of Cassie singing "Silent Night" had gone live on Marcia's Facebook account an hour after Cassie had left the store.

Marcia had only 87 friends, but one of them, a first cousin who lived in Tuscarora, reposted the video on his page, sharing it with his 357 friends. One of those people, a former classmate who'd moved to West Hartford, Connecticut, reposted the video to her 1,267 followers, and one of her followers, a sorority sister turned makeup artist/influencer, had 10,000 friends. After a few dozen likes became a few thousand, the platform's algorithm began feeding the video to accounts far and wide. Within forty-eight hours, the snippet of Cassie singing "Silent Night" had been seen by close to a million people and reposted thousands of times. From TikTok, the video moved on, to Twitter and Instagram, circling back to Facebook, finally jumping over to the Subreddit devoted to the Griffin Sisters.

All that had happened in the twelve hours it took Lior, Cassie's Internet scrubber, to discover the video, trace it back to its source, and get it taken down.

As it turned out, that was just long enough.

Zoe

After Cherry disappeared, Zoe had done everything she could think of to find her, in the real world and the virtual one. She'd gone through Cherry's bedroom in painstaking detail, rifling through each drawer, reaching under Cherry's mattress. Online, she'd rummaged through months of Cherry's social media history, tugging at the threads of every connection, contacting friends and everyone with whom her daughter had interacted. *Have you seen her? If you have, can you ask her to call? Tell her that her mother is worried about her. Tell her we miss her. Tell her I'm not angry. Tell her that whatever's wrong, we'll fix it.*

She didn't say those last parts. She knew—or thought she knew—what had prompted her daughter's flight. Cherry wanted to be a musician, a performer, a star, and Zoe, who knew first-hand what that world could do to women, had shut her down at every opportunity. "It's impossible," she told Cherry, the first time her daughter talked about the band she was putting together, how they were going to be discovered, how they'd become the next big thing. They'd been in the kitchen at the condo in Margate, where they spent most of the summer. Zoe had been in the galley kitchen making dinner, shrimp and corn and fresh sliced tomatoes she'd bought at a farmstand on the Black Horse Pike, the four-lane road Jordan always insisted on taking, because he believed it got them to the beach faster than the newer, wider, and much more popular Atlantic City Expressway. "The industry has changed."

Cherry had rolled her eyes, in that special, scornful way only teen-age girls could manage. "Maybe it's changed since you were perform-ing," she said, in a tone suggesting that those performances might have taken place before the invention of electricity. Or language.

Zoe had handed Cherry a stack of plates through the pass-through, and while her daughter set the table, she'd told Cherry how it was.

She'd explained to her daughter that musicians toured because that was the only way for them to make money from their music; that the streamers paid next to nothing to anyone except for the very biggest acts; that nobody bought albums or CDs anymore; that selling concert tickets and merchandise was the only way to earn a profit; and that these days, very, very few musicians did.

Cherry, who had milk crates full of old vinyls, who would, as often as Zoe would let her, take the PATCO train to listening parties at the record stores that had sprouted in Center City, like toadstools after the rain, had arched an eyebrow at that, but Zoe had plowed on. "When the Griffin Sisters were around, we sold albums. And we had a song on a big TV show—"

"People are still doing that," Cherry interrupted. "TV shows still need songs."

"A big TV show today gets maybe a million people watching, right?"

Cherry muttered something about how not everyone watched a show the day or even the week that it aired. Zoe plowed ahead. "A big show back then, or a commercial that played during the Super Bowl, you'd have tens of millions."

"What about *American Idol*? *The Voice*?" Cherry asked.

"Tell me one person who's gotten famous from winning those shows."

"Kelly Clarkson? Carrie Underwood?" Cherry offered.

"One person in the last ten years."

Cherry opened her mouth, then closed it. She glared at her mother. "You don't think I'm good enough," she said, and set the last plate down on the table with a thump.

"It's not that." Zoe could see a flush crawling up Cherry's neck. Cherry's eyes were narrowed and her lips pressed tightly together, and she was so pretty, even when she was scowling. Even with her piercings and her boy's clothes, even after she'd chopped off her hair. Zoe knew what the music industry did to pretty girls like that, girls who were eager to make their dreams come true. She'd been one, once.

"I think you're very good," she said carefully. "I also think that it's next to impossible to get discovered these days, and even harder to succeed if you do. There used to be a clear path to making it as a musician. There were steps you'd follow, and now, there aren't. I don't know how to help you—"

"I'm not asking for your help."

Which left Zoe with nothing to say except, "I don't want you to get hurt."

"You can't Bubble Wrap me and protect me from everything!" Cherry's voice was high and indignant. "Getting hurt is part of having an actual life. Things happen." As if Zoe didn't know that. "I'll survive." *She thinks she's invincible,* Zoe thought sadly. She could remember feeling exactly the same way, when she'd been Cherry's age: bulletproof, and furious at anyone who'd tried to hold her back, to suggest, by deed or implication, that her dreams would not come true.

Zoe hadn't been surprised that her daughter had left. That didn't mean she wasn't sick and sleepless with anxiety about where Cherry had gone, what she was doing, and what was being done to her. Jordan had soothed her as best he could, reminded her that Cherry was smart and capable, nobody's fool, but Zoe still felt almost feral, half-crazed with worry about her daughter, her only girl, out there in a world with sharp teeth.

Zoe had gone to her mother, which had been bad ("What do you mean, she's gone? She just left?" Janice had asked. "And you didn't try to stop her?"). She'd gone to her great-aunt Bess, who'd been Cassie's favorite, and then Cherry's, and that had been worse. Bess had just looked at her with her penciled eyebrows lifted and her voice expressionless. "No, I haven't heard from her," she'd said.

At night, in bed, with Jordan sleeping on his back beside her, his CPAP mask strapped in place and his hands crossed on top of his chest, Zoe would stare up into the darkness, where a thousand horror movies played in limited-engagement runs on her bedroom ceiling. Cherry murdered, dismembered, dead in a ditch. Cherry sipping a drink that had been roofied, or swallowing a pill that turned out to contain a lethal dose of fentanyl. Cherry raped; Cherry sold into a human-trafficking ring. Cherry walking along the highway, late at night, not realizing that the cars couldn't see her.

"Be patient," Jordan told her, after the Haddonfield cops sent them away. The sergeant had explained, in what Zoe found to be an extremely condescending fashion, that her daughter was legally an adult and under no obligation to share her whereabouts. ("Count yourself lucky," he'd said, after he'd taken Zoe's report. "At least she's not hitting you up for money like my kids do.")

A few weeks after Cherry's disappearance, Zoe came home from her errands to find a bright yellow Mini Cooper parked in their driveway. She felt her heart sink. Bix's car had been a Christmas present from Jordan, a combination gift and bribe. After none of the nineteen colleges to which he'd applied offered him admission, Bix wanted to find a job. Jordan had convinced him to take classes instead. He'd bought his son a car and, over Zoe's objections, had allowed him to move back home.

Zoe hadn't wanted him there. Zoe had wanted to send him away, to do a thirteenth year of high school at some boarding school. Zoe wanted her stepson nowhere near Schuyler and Noah, and especially not Cherry. She'd never liked him, not from the first time she'd met him, when he'd been just five years old, a fine-boned boy with big, dark eyes and delicate features.

"Bix, this is Zoe," Jordan had said. Jordan hadn't proposed yet, but they'd talked about it. Zoe knew that meeting Bix was the final hurdle, the last test she'd have to pass before she got her guy.

They'd met at the Please Touch Museum, just the three of them. Janice and Sam were babysitting Cherry. Jordan and his son had been waiting on the white marble steps leading up to the museum, which was housed in Memorial Hall in the middle of Fairmount Park. Zoe knew it well. She and her daughter had spent many rainy afternoons there, loading a tiny shopping cart with plastic food and wheeling it through the pretend supermarket checkout line, or riding the carved wooden horses on the antique carousel.

"Hello, Bix. I'm Zoe." She'd crouched down to bring her eyes to his level. Bix had regarded her gravely, his expression oddly adult and unreadable as he'd studied her face, then let his gaze slide along the length of her body as she'd straightened up. Zoe told herself she was being silly, as she resisted an urge to rub her hand against her skirt and tried to ignore her first impression, which was that there was something sly about his expression, something unsettling about his stare.

Zoe had done her best. She had tried to befriend Bix, with the goal of being a supportive and loving adult in his life. "I know I can't replace your mother," she'd told him, in a speech she'd cribbed from one of the stepparenting websites she'd consulted, optimistically, after her third date with Jordan. "All I want is to be an adult in your life who loves you." She'd said all the right things. She'd even thought—she cringed to remember—that Bix and Cherry, who was just a year younger than Bix, could be friends, that they would grow up like brother and sister. It would have been good for both of them to have a companion, an ally, a peer. But Zoe had abandoned those fantasies almost immediately. Six weeks after that first meeting, where Bix had walked through the exhibits ignoring them; ignoring her, talking only to his father, Jordan had invited her and Cherry to his place in Margate. The house was a two-story, three-bedroom condo with beige vinyl siding that Zoe disliked, and two porches—one on the second floor, one on the third— and it stood just a block away from the beach. There was a neat square of yard in the front and an outdoor shower on the side of the house.

On their first afternoon, they'd spent a few hours together at the ocean, before Zoe noticed Cherry's skin turning pink, and had walked her back to Jordan's place. In the outdoor shower, Zoe pulled off her daughter's swimsuit and her own, and was shampooing Cherry's hair when she saw a single dark eye peering through from a hole in the door.

She'd screamed, and snatched Cherry into her arms. "What happened?" Cherry asked her. "What's wrong?"

"I saw a spider," Zoe said, through numb lips. Quickly, she'd rinsed Cherry's hair and body, bundling her into a towel and wrapping another towel around herself. By the time she opened the door, she'd figured, Bix would be long gone. She was surprised to find him standing there, in his blue board shorts staring at Zoe with his wet dark eyes.

Zoe had sent Cherry inside to get a juice pop. She waited until the door had slammed before turning to her boyfriend's son.

"Were you looking at us?" Zoe's lips felt stiff with fury. She could barely breathe, could barely form words. She was trying not to yell, reminding herself that he was just a kid, and that all the books she'd read had been very clear about how discipline was the parent's job, not the stepparent's.

Bix hadn't answered. He'd just kept staring at her, his thin lips lifted in the tiniest of smirks. His expression said, *I know what you look like naked.* Which, she supposed, he did.

"That's—that isn't—that is not an okay thing to do."

Bix had extended a spindly white finger, pointing toward her crotch. "You have hair down there."

Zoe stared at him, numb with shock. "Most grown-ups do," she finally managed.

"My mommy was prettier than you are," Bix announced.

"Your mother was very pretty," Zoe said, a little stiffly, because her lips still felt frozen. She was remembering some advice she'd read, about validating your stepchildren, no matter how uncomfortable they made you feel. Plus, she refused to let the little weirdo know how much he'd hurt her. "Bix, what you did is not okay."

He didn't respond. He turned and started walking toward the house and didn't stop until Zoe caught up with him, putting her hand on one small, bony shoulder and holding him still.

"Spying on people is not okay. You need to apologize to me, and to Cherry, and I'm going to be discussing it with your father."

"Sor-ry," he'd singsonged, his voice and face both utterly insincere. And he'd strolled off, still with that little smirk on his face. Inside, Zoe had gotten dressed and had paced the length of the bedroom, trembling, hating herself for becoming the kind of woman who'd say, *Wait until your father gets home!* How had it come to this? Once, she'd commanded stages in front of tens of thousands of people (or, at least, she'd been on stages, in front of tens of thousands of people, even if her bandmates had done most of the commanding). She'd been on TV! She'd been on the cover of *Elle* and *People*! How had she ended up here, undone by a five-year-old boy?

Zoe sat, stewing, until Jordan hurried into the house, with his towel wrapped around his shoulders, dark hair wet and his cheeks pink with new sunburn.

"Zoe?" he'd called from the back door. He sounded out of breath and panicked. "Did Bix come back with you guys?"

"He's here now."

"Thank God. I couldn't find him, and I got worried. I'm going to grab a shower."

"I need to talk to you."

"Can it wait?" he'd asked, indicating his bare chest and sandy feet. Zoe shook her head and stepped into the backyard, taking a seat in one of the chairs around a metal firepit. Jordan had looked at her curiously, then taken the chair across from hers. As Zoe told him what Bix had done, she assumed that Jordan would be just as outraged as she was. She was wrong.

"You're saying he made a hole in the door to look at you?" Jordan had asked, after Zoe had walked him through the unsettling event twice.

"I don't know if he made the hole or found it. But he was definitely looking at us." *And it was creepy*, she wanted to say, but did not. *Your son is creepy*.

Jordan had sighed, rubbing at the bridge of his nose. "Look," he finally said. "I'm not condoning this, at all. But boys get curious."

"So help me, if you say 'boys will be boys' . . ." Zoe made herself be quiet. She reminded herself that she was an adult and that Bix was a child, a kid who'd lost his mother. Of course boys were curious, and of course Jordan would stick up for his son. Jordan's loyalty was one of the things she loved most about him. Still, she couldn't help feeling angry and betrayed, and ashamed about being seen naked, a violation that felt almost biblical (had it been Noah whose sons had been punished for looking at him unclothed?). Most of all, she was worried about Cherry.

"I'm not saying boys will be boys." Her husband's tone had become patient and lawyerly, just shy of condescending. "And I understand that you're upset. Look. I'll give his therapist a call, see what's going on. And I'll talk to Bix. I'll let him know it's not okay, and that he can't do it again."

"You don't think . . ." Zoe stood up and started pacing again, walking from one end of the tiny yard to the other. "You don't think he'd do anything to Cherry, do you?"

Jordan tilted his head, frowning at her. When he spoke, his voice had cooled by a few noticeable degrees. "What do you mean?"

"Like spy on her. Or bother her. Or—" Zoe didn't know exactly what she was suggesting, or how exactly to communicate her feelings. *He's creepy*, she thought again. But she couldn't say that. Jordan would get defensive, and angry. He'd take his son's side, and Zoe would be his enemy, and she'd end up right back where she'd started, looking for a needle in a haystack, a winning lottery ticket, a unicorn—a good, stable, employed, non-crazy man who'd want to marry her and support her unskilled, has-been ass. Her, and her daughter.

Jordan sounded aggrieved when he said, "Look, Zoe. I understand that this was upsetting. But let's not blow things out of proportion. I'll talk to him. He won't do it again." He'd dropped a kiss on her head and headed off to the shower, leaving Zoe unhappy, unsatisfied, and deeply unsettled.

The next morning, Jordan had patched up the hole, nailing a square of wood over it, and told her he'd spoken to Bix. She'd resisted her urge to press for more information, to ask what he'd said and how Bix had explained himself; whether Bix was going to be punished and whether Jordan had had this kind of trouble with Bix before. She resolved, instead, to keep a close eye on the little creep, even as she tried not to think of him as a little creep. Over the years, she'd done her best to make sure Cherry was never alone with him, but when her own sons had come along, Zoe admitted, her focus had shifted. Cherry had been older, and Bix was mostly out of the house by then. She'd always thought that her daughter had been safe.

No, Zoe thought, as she sat behind the wheel of her Range Rover, staring at Bix's yellow Mini Cooper. She could be honest, even if it was just in the privacy of her own head. She hadn't thought that her daughter had been safe. She'd just stopped thinking about Bix at all. She'd pushed all of her concern, and her memories of what he'd done, into some dark corner of her brain, where all her regrets resided, and she'd left them there, ignored, but not resolved. She hadn't wanted to push too hard, hadn't wanted to risk upsetting Jordan. Hadn't wanted to—what did the kids say?—*blow up her spot.* Risk her comfort. Rock the boat.

Slowly, Zoe climbed out of her car. She pulled her purse and gym bag over her shoulder and walked into the house. She found Bix in the kitchen, drinking almond milk. At nineteen, he was still slight, pale-skinned, fine-boned, with a carefully blank expression that still struck her as sneaky and sly. "He gives me incel vibes," she'd told Penny.

Zoe made herself smile at her stepson. She fought the urge to fidget, or to pull the zipper of her cashmere hoodie all the way up to her chin. "How was your day?"

Bix smirked and gave a shrug.

"How are your classes?"

"Fine."

Bix was smart—at least, according to the standardized tests—but he'd always been an indifferent student. He did just enough work to get by, sometimes managing a B in math or science, getting Cs or even Ds in the courses that relied more on essays and class participation than memorization or multiple-choice tests. The only subject he seemed to enjoy was computer science. The better to hack the government, or to invent an app that would digitally undress images of celebrities, Zoe thought.

"You haven't heard from Cherry, have you?"

Bix shook his head. "Nope. Sorry." He didn't sound sorry at all.

"You don't have any idea why she left, do you?"

Bix stared at her blankly.

"Or where she might have gone?"

He shrugged a little and shook his head. "If I hear anything I'll let you know." He tossed the empty carton into the trash (not, Zoe noted, the recycling bin, where it belonged) and went upstairs.

Zoe moved the carton into the proper bin and washed her hands, staring out through the window above the sink, into the backyard. Sleety rain was spitting down. The sky was a listless gray. She wanted to shower—barre class had left her sweaty, and talking to Bix had left her, as usual, feeling greasy and soiled—but she hated being naked when she was alone with Bix in the house, no matter how many locked doors were between them. So she refilled her water bottle and sat at her desk in the kitchen, paying bills, checking her daughter's social media accounts, untouched in the weeks since Cherry's departure, until she'd come up with a plan. A quick trip to the liquor store let her buy the bait she needed, plus ingredients for dinner. Once she had what she needed, she went to pick up the boys.

At home, Zoe gave everyone dinner, then cleaned everything up, all the while keeping tabs on the bottle of whiskey she'd purchased and set on the bar cart in the dining room. She'd seen Bix eyeing it, had watched how he'd licked his lips.

At some point, between the time she'd put the last dish into the dishwasher and when she'd gone upstairs at eleven P.M., the bottle disappeared. *Good*, Zoe thought. She set an alarm on her phone to go off at three in the morning. When it woke her, she crept out of bed and padded down the hall.

Bix's bedroom door was closed but unlocked. Zoe stood with her hand on the doorknob, for what felt like a very long time. She did not want to open the door, did not want to go looking for what she was afraid she might find. But she had to do it. She couldn't keep pretending.

Heart pounding, mouth dry, skin prickling with nerves, she opened the door and shuffled her bare feet along the carpet, letting her eyes adjust until she could make out the contours of the dresser, the desk, the bookcase, the bed. Bix slept on his back, like his father. His mouth was open, and she could hear him snoring softly.

She looked at his dresser, at the backpack, unzipped and crammed with what she was sure was dirty laundry she'd be, at some point, expected to wash . . . but Bix was sly. If he had evidence, or—she shuddered—trophies, he wouldn't keep them here, to be discovered. No. Like every other member of his generation, Bix lived on his phone. If there was anything for Zoe to find, she'd find it there.

His phone was charging on his desk. She unplugged it, hoping against hope that it was unlocked, unsurprised when she saw that it wasn't. Holding her breath, Zoe tiptoed over to her stepson's bed and aimed the screen at his face, holding her breath until his features had unlocked it. Once she saw the rows of apps appear, she slipped out of his bedroom again and stood in the hallway, heart pounding, holding her prize.

She started with his photographs, scrolling through dozens of shots: Bix at school, Bix at parties, Bix smirking as he held a joint in someone's passenger's seat and a beer in someone's dorm room. She swiped through November and October and September, until she was looking at August's pictures, which was where she hit pay dirt. There were two pictures of her daughter at the beach, in her swimsuit, bending down to retrieve something. The pictures weren't especially revealing, save for the fact that the subject was clearly unaware she was being photographed.

Zoe's blood felt blazing hot. She clenched her fists to keep herself from kicking Bix awake and raking her nails over his face. She could almost smell onions and male sweat, could almost feel a man's hands on her bare breasts, calloused fingers pinching, too hard. *Come on. You're not a prude, are you? Let's give the people what they want.*

She pressed her fist to her mouth, moaning softly when she scrolled to a picture of Cherry wrapped in a towel, in the bathroom just down the hall. For a moment, she couldn't do anything except stare at the screen, feeling punched and breathless, furious at Bix, but even angrier at herself . . . because she'd known. At some level, in some part of her mind she didn't let herself visit, she had known. Not suspected, but known. "He looks at me," Cherry had told her, back when Cherry had been how old? Eight? Nine? Her voice had been tiny, her little face downcast, and Zoe could hear her own voice, sharp, almost hectoring, as she'd replied, "Did he say anything to you? Did he touch you? Did he try to make you touch him?" Cherry's head had wobbled as she'd shaken it, back and forth. "No, Mom. Only . . ."

"Only what?"

"Only he's always too close. He stands too close and he sits too close. And he watches me." Cherry had shivered. "All the time."

Zoe should have listened. Believed her daughter. Defended her. Forced Bix to confess. Fixed it. Instead, she'd been invested in making things with Jordan work, and so she'd told herself that Cherry was being too sensitive, that maybe Bix annoyed Cherry but that he wasn't actively harming her. She'd ignored her daughter, ignored her instincts, tried to silence the voice in her own brain saying *This is not good, do something.*

And now Cherry was gone.

Zoe's hands were steady as she pulled her own phone from her bathrobe's pocket and snapped pictures of Bix's screen. She was already imagining what Jordan would say, how Jordan would find a way to excuse this: *he's unhappy,* and *he lost his mom,* and—her favorite—*he's in therapy.* Jordan's voice would be calm, his expression sincere. *These pictures aren't that bad,* he'd tell her, and—oh God, the thing he always said, the thing that made her want to put her hands around his neck and squeeze and not stop squeezing—*No harm done.* The way he'd use the passive voice made her skin prickle with loathing—the way Bix wasn't even a part of the sentence, as either subject or object; it was just harm, just some random thing that hadn't happened and had not been inflicted by any particular person, most certainly not his unnamed son.

Zoe bowed her head. When her heartbeat slowed down enough, when she was certain she wasn't going to vomit, or scream, Zoe slipped into Bix's bedroom and replaced the phone. She walked back to her bedroom. Jordan was still asleep on his back, mask in place, the covers drawn up neatly under his chin. Zoe looked down at him for a long moment, wondering, *What would happen if I told him the truth? What would he say if I told him everything, about me, and Russell, and Cassie? Would the world crack open? Would he throw me out?*

And what would happen if she didn't tell? Would the secret start leeching its poison inside of her, rotting her from the inside out, ruining her even more than she was already ruined?

Zoe lay down beside her husband. She stared up into the darkness. And then, very quietly, she started to cry.

Part Three

"NIGHT RIDE TURNS TWENTY-FIVE"

Thanks to the Netflix hit *Evermore*, the Griffin Sisters, the early aughts pop-rock colossus, is enjoying a second life. With a new generation of fans finding their songs, can the band's true believers hope for new music?

MARGARET FRANTZ
Rolling Stone

Poetic. Emotional. Intimate. Confessional. Read enough articles, reviews, and blog posts about the Griffin Sisters, and there are words and phrases that come up again and again. But when you ask someone who was there—someone who was just the right age, at just the right time and place and moment in her life to hear their music or see them live—you might not get any words at all. Instead, you'll get the same expressions, identical gestures. You'll watch a woman's gaze go unfocused as she searches for ways to explain what the band's music meant to her when she was fifteen and felt freakish, or sixteen and the boy she'd had a crush on told her he just wanted to be friends—then started dating her thinner, prettier best friend. Hands will move through the air, trying to conjure the words to communicate how the band's lyrics made them feel connected, not invisible and not alone. Eyes will fill with tears; heads will shake; shoulders will lift in shrugs. "There is no way for me to explain it," said Amanda Shaw. Now in her forties, married with children, Shaw saw the band perform live, twice, in Pittsburgh, when she was eighteen. "It's all of the clichés. It felt like someone read my diary, or read my mind; like someone took everything I was thinking and feeling and turned it into songs, and made my life make sense. Or, at least, let me know that I'd survive it."

Other bands have fans. The Sisters have acolytes—mostly female ones, many, but not all, of whom are white—women who were tweens and teenagers and young women when the band was ascendant. They are now grown-ups, who've tattooed the bands' lyrics on their bodies and worked them into their wedding vows, who've named pets and children after Cassie and Zoe Griffin, who, along with guitar player and songwriter Russell D'Angelo, drummer Tommy Kelleher, and bass player Cameron Gratz, made up the band. They've designed tee shirts featuring Zoe Griffin, in silhouette, making her signature concert-closing gesture of kissing two fingers and raising them to the sky. They've made pilgrimages to the Philadelphia and Philly-adjacent places name-checked in the songs like "Last Night in Fishtown"—Broad Street, the Schuylkill River, the Camden aquarium, and the Benjamin Franklin Bridge. They keep tribute bands and karaoke parlors in business and spend their free time on Discord groups, Slack channels, and Subreddits devoted to the Griffin Sisters' music. Some of them write fan fiction about the band's members and give Zoe and Russell the happily ever after that real life did not. Some of them write songs themselves.

It's a disproportionately outsized legacy, considering that the Griffin Sisters recorded just a single album, the triple-platinum *Night Ride*, which was released in September of 2003. The album came out in a world that had breathed a sigh of relief when the horrors of Y2K failed to materialize, only to live through the tragedy of 9/11. Heroin-chic models shared magazine covers with plaid-and-babydoll-dress-wearing grunge goddesses; reality TV shows, with their star-making power, were on the rise; and the Britney/Justin breakup made head-lines all over the world. For a moment, radio had room for a panoply of women artists, confessional singer-songwriters, R&B girl groups, and singing, dancing pop princesses. The Griffin Sisters gave listeners the best of both worlds—the raw, intimate lyrics and expert musicianship that Cassie Griffin provided, along with the sex appeal and showmanship that were Zoe Griffin's hallmarks.

"It's hard to explain just how big they were," said Allison McCrae, a profes-sor of women's studies and pop culture at Rutgers University. "By 2004, there were thirteen million copies of *Night Ride* sold. One out of every ten households in America owned a copy of the album. It was unprecedented. There's been nothing like that, before or since." McCrae's book *In One Voice: Women Singer-Songwriters from Joni Mitchell to Taylor Swift* calls the Griffin Sisters one of—if not the—definitive groups of the early aughts.

More than twenty years after their breakup, the story of how the girls were discovered, just out of high school in Philadelphia, how the band was formed, how Russell D'Angelo fell in love with Zoe Griffin, and all the tragedies that ensued—from D'Angelo's death to the band's dissolution to Cassie Griffin's disappearance—has become a legend, a story the acolytes know by heart.

"I knew right away that they were something special," David Katz, an executive for Relic Records, recalled. His nephew saw the sisters perform at a Battle of the Bands in Philadelphia, and Katz, in town for the holidays, went to their Fishtown rowhouse and heard them the very next day. Katz immediately brought the girls to New York City, where they ended up playing for three different labels, before signing with Relic.

"I had never heard a voice like Cassie's, not before, and not since."

By March of 2004, the band's first single, "The Gift," climbed the charts to number six. Then "Stay the Night" was released, and after that the hits just kept on coming. Over the next nine months, four more of the album's thirteen songs hit the charts. Two of them—the girl-power banger "Bloom" and the ballad "The Only Lonely Girl"—made it to number one.

"Even though Cassie Griffin was the lead singer, Russell D'Angelo was an essential part of what made the Griffin Sisters what it was," said McCrae. D'Angelo was co-credited, along with Cassie Griffin, as songwriter for twelve of the album's thirteen songs. "Russell was a world-class songwriter, and he did his best work with the Griffin Sisters," said Kevin Douglas, a former colleague of D'Angelo's and a Grammy-winning songwriter whose hits have been sung by Kelly Clarkson and Meghan Trainor. "When he was writing for a boy band, he could sound like a sixteen-year-old boy with a crush. When he was writing with Cassie, he sounded like a young woman, whether she was lonely, or angry, or head over heels in love."

What would have happened if Russell D'Angelo had lived into his thirties, and middle age? Or if the band had had a more standard trajectory, a more normal breakup? "Maybe Cassie could have found another writing partner or written more songs on her own," McCrae said. "Maybe she and Zoe could have performed together, as a duo, or formed another band."

There are dozens of what-ifs, hundreds of possibilities. What's certain is that the public's love for the Griffin Sisters' music, the poetry of its lyrics wrapped around driving pop-rock hooks, has never diminished. With the album's twenty-fifth anniversary approaching, and the band's music finding new fans via Netflix, that appetite has only sharpened. The only question is whether the band's remaining members have any plans to sate it.

Cherry
ALASKA, 2024

Imagine you're Cassie Griffin, Cherry told herself, as soon as the plane's wheels had touched down, screeching, on the runway in Anchorage. She'd gotten a seat in the very last row, and it took her forever to make her way to the front of the plane, using her phone to film herself as she went. *Think like Cassie,* she repeated as she hustled through the airport and, finally, collected the keys to the rental car the show had arranged for her (she wasn't yet old enough to rent one on her own, and she suspected money had changed hands to allow it). *Your bandmate, your sister's husband, your writing partner, is dead. Your band's broken up. You're running.*

Cherry remembered how she'd pestered her mother about the CD she'd seen in the used bookstore. Who were the Griffin Sisters? What were the names of the other people in the band? Where did they live? Were they her friends? Did any of them have kids, and could Cherry meet them? Could she invite them to her birthday party, which was going to have a unicorn theme?

Zoe hadn't wanted to answer. "The Griffin Sisters was a made-up name," she'd told Cherry. And, "It was all a long time ago. I don't want to talk about it." It had been Aunt Bess—Zoe's great-aunt, Cherry's great-great-aunt—who'd finally told her that the Griffin Sisters were Cherry's mom and Cherry's mom's sister.

"My mom has a sister?" Cherry had asked. "Where does she live? And who are the Griffins?"

"Griffin was a made-up name," Aunt Bess said, smiling a little. "And yes, your mom has a sister. She moved away. She lives a long way from here."

"What happened?"

Aunt Bess had looked troubled as she smoothed Cherry's hair. "The band broke up, and your aunt went away. It was . . ." Aunt Bess paused. "Very hard. And sad. A hard time for everyone."

Cherry wanted to ask a million more things, but Aunt Bess's expression was so grave, her face and body both stiff, the same way Cherry's mother's face and body got right before Zoe told her to stop pestering her already and go find a coloring book or a game. And so Cherry had waited. Eventually, the Internet had filled in more of the blanks. Cherry had learned more of the band's history, and more about her aunt, although, as she got older, she was both bemused and insulted to learn that nobody seemed aware that Zoe Griffin—now Zoe Grossberg again—had even had a baby. Nor did anyone seem to know where Cassie Grossberg had gone.

It hadn't taken long for Cherry's imagination to turn her absent aunt into a kind of magical, musical fairy godmother: a woman who'd understand and support her, the way her own mother did not. Instead of a gown and a horse-drawn carriage, Cherry imagined Cassie waving her magic wand and bestowing fame and fortune; connections and phone numbers; a clear path to musical stardom. If Cherry could ever find her aunt and ask her for her help.

As she waited in line to leave the airport parking lot, Cherry thought, again, that she still couldn't believe how lucky she'd gotten. Years ago, she'd set up Google Alerts for Cassie's name and for any mention of the Griffin Sisters. Every time there was a new mention—whether it was in a magazine or a newspaper, a Pinterest page or some crackpot's blog—Cherry's inbox would ping. The morning after she'd made it to the finals, she'd been in her hotel room and had checked the day's links, thinking they would be the usual mix of stuff that she'd already seen: old articles that had been reposted, videos of singers who were not Cassie covering her songs. But the third link had led to a Subreddit and a grainy snippet of a video of a woman in a supermarket singing "Silent Night." Cherry had plugged in her earbuds, thinking it would be the typical non-Cassie nonsense. But seconds after she hit play, Cherry felt the whole world stop. She froze, holding perfectly still, like the song, and the singer, were a soap bubble, and the tiniest move would cause it to pop.

". . . all is calm, all is bright."

"That's her," Cherry whispered to the empty room. "Holy shit, oh my God, that's. . . ." She'd turned up the volume and listened to the snippet again, just to be sure, and then she'd gone running to find Braden, to show him what she'd found and get an objective confirmation.

"Is that really Cassie Griffin?" she'd asked, staring at her cracked phone screen, taking in the details—the big black parka with its fur-trimmed hood, the snow boots. "Tell me I'm not making this up."

"Yes." Braden's voice was hushed and reverent. "That's really her."

That was the good news. The bad news: the comments that had been posted in the ninety minutes between Cherry viewing the video and its disappearance had quickly ID'd the performance venue, which turned out to be the Safeway supermarket on Sterling Highway in Homer, Alaska. Cherry had printed out a map of the region and, with a highlighter, had drawn a circle with a fifty-mile circumference around the supermarket. If Cassie was hiding, as Cherry surmised, she wouldn't live in Homer, or anything close to an actual city or town. She'd be off the grid, in the woods, in one of the camps or cabins that dotted the forests and the foothills of the Kenai Mountains. *A needle in a haystack*, Cherry told herself . . . but Cassie was an extremely shiny needle. And Cherry was extremely determined.

The Next Stage producers had, as promised, paired each finalist with a mentor. Cherry's had been a woman named April Lange, who was twenty-two and whose one hit song had gotten popular mostly because a big city's Major League Baseball team had started playing a remixed version at games whenever anyone hit a home run. April was reasonably accomplished and friendly enough, but her songs didn't speak to Cherry the way the Griffin Sisters' music did. If she performed one of their songs—the music that was her inheritance, the songs that were literally part of her bloodline—she'd win, for certain. So she'd petitioned for an appointment, explaining everything to Sebastian's assistant, who had eventually brought Cherry to make her case to Sebastian himself.

"Zoe Griffin," Sebastian had repeated, looking Cherry over the way a man in a grocery store might have inspected a melon. She braced herself, waiting for him to ask about her aunt, or her father, but, instead, he just said, "I saw the Griffin Sisters in Las Vegas. It was twenty years ago, but I still remember—they were incredible." His expression, which had been, briefly, fond and nostalgic, shifted back to calculating. "It'd be huge for ratings," he mused. "Would your mother sing with you? Even if we can't get Cassie, that would be something."

Cherry tried not to grimace at the idea of her mother being her performing partner, when Cassie was the one she wanted. "No," Cherry had said. "She wouldn't be interested. But I don't want her. I want my aunt." Never mind that she'd never met Aunt Cassie, and hadn't known where to find her. Sebastian had been intrigued enough (and, Cherry figured, ratings-hungry enough) to give her seven days, ten thousand dollars, and instructions to film her quest, so the producers would have plenty of background video to use when the show aired. Those same producers had given Cherry instructions on how to give them what they'd need ("Shoot horizontally, vertically, in HD, 4K, at sixty minutes of footage, from as many angles and POVs as possible!").

When Sebastian dismissed her, Cherry had racewalked back to her hotel room, where Braden had been waiting to hear what the producers had said to her.

"So what are you going to do?" he'd asked. Braden himself was planning on returning to his sensitive singer-songwriter roots for the final round, now that his closest competition had been sent home (the day after it had happened, Cherry had joined him on the hotel's roof, for a ceremonial burning of his cowboy hat).

Cherry pulled her suitcase out of the closet and began gathering her clothes. "I'm going to Alaska to find her."

Braden looked thoughtful. He belly flopped onto her bed and looked at her with his chin cupped in his hands. "What was it like?" he asked.

"What was what like?" she asked, even though she knew what he was asking. It was what everyone asked when they learned her mom had been in the Griffin Sisters. They wanted stories. Details. Up-close-and-personal tales of being raised by a rock-and-roll goddess. Had Cherry been taken on tour, given a kid-sized pair of noise-canceling headphones, perched on a bodyguard's shoulders so she could watch concerts from the wings? Had she attended the Rock & Roll Hall of Fame induction ceremony? Had she met Bruce Springsteen or Celine Dion? Was Joni Mitchell her godmother? Did Dolly Parton come over for Christmas? Had there been mansions, private jets, yachts, and vacations all over the world?

Cherry didn't have any stories like that. Zoe had not taken Cherry to concerts or introduced her to other musicians. She had no memories of her mother singing—ever. Not even in the shower. When she'd ask—and she had asked—her mom would refuse. *Cassie was the singer,* she'd say. *Not me.* And they'd been the opposite of rich. In Cherry's earliest memories, they'd lived with Zoe's parents. Her mother had been gone a lot, playing shows at night, writing music in the daytime, sometimes spending weeks in Los Angeles or New York City with one writing partner or another. Her mom had never lied to her, never pretended that Janice and Sam were actually her parents and that Zoe was her big sister and not her mom, but that was how it had felt sometimes. Janice was certainly a more constant, more present caretaker, while Zoe flitted in and out, slipping into Cherry's bedroom to press a kiss on her forehead late at night, leaving behind the smell of her perfume, gone before Cherry was even entirely awake.

"It wasn't anything special," Cherry told Braden. "She wasn't Zoe Griffin when she had me. She was just a regular old mom."

"Sure. Just a regular old mom," Brendan said, giving the words a mocking lilt. "Along with your regular old dad. Dude, you're, like, basically music royalty."

"My dad is dead." Cherry's voice was flat. "And my mother did everything she could to stop me from becoming a musician." She ran her hands through her hair, stiff with hairspray, and started to pace. "I had to pay for my guitar lessons with my own money."

"Poor you," Braden said insincerely.

Cherry glared at him. "I was eight."

Braden's look was not unsympathetic. "Let me know if you need any help. I should go practice." He picked up his guitar and let the hotel room door shut behind him.

Cherry fell back on the bed Braden had vacated, thinking about how truly shitty it was. She'd open herself up to all the criticism that every kid with famous parents got, even though she'd never enjoyed a single one of nepotism's benefits. Her famous father had died before she'd been born; her famous mom had actively worked to thwart her. "You don't know what it's like," Zoe would say. "The music industry chews up girls and spits them out. You'll get hurt. I won't let it happen."

Cherry had spent years trying to tell her mom that things were different now. Fame, she'd tell Zoe, had been a rare commodity twenty years ago. These days, anyone with an Internet connection and talent—or a scandal, or just a good story—had a shot at becoming a bold-faced name. "Famous for nothing," Zoe would scoff, about the reality stars and Instagram influencers, the Kardashians and the Teen Moms Cherry would tell her about. "No," Cherry would say. "You're wrong. They're not famous for nothing. They're famous because they've made themselves interesting enough for people to care. That is a talent." Zoe would just roll her eyes.

As the line of cars inched forward, creeping closer toward the person in the booth to whom they'd have to present their paperwork.

Cherry found herself thinking about the day they'd moved in with Jordan. She remembered sitting on her new bed, marveling at how big it was, and how clean. A dresser, and a closet, and a desk with a lamp, all for her! A bookcase, with just her books! She and her mom had shared a dresser, back in the apartment. There'd been one desk, and it had been strictly off-limits.

She'd been running her fingers along the pink-and-cream rug when Bix had come in without knocking. He'd stared at her, with his big, dark eyes and too-red lips, in a way that made her feel like he'd dropped an ice cube into her shirt and left it there to leak chilly drips down her spine.

"This was my room," he'd said.

Cherry didn't know how to respond. Was he angry at her? Did he want the room back?

"I'm sorry," she said. He'd licked his lips in a way that made her stomach feel strange and her skin go cold, and he'd looked at her, a long, slow, insolent kind of look. Then he'd walked out the door.

Bix was creepy. But what could she have told her mother? That he didn't knock? That he was too quiet? That he looked at her in a way that made her feel uncomfortable? That, sometimes, she'd notice things missing from her room, little things like pens or books or earrings, a single shoe, and she was pretty sure he was sneaking in and taking them?

Cherry knew what Zoe would say: *His mother died, Cherry. He's having a hard time at his new school.* Zoe would tell Cherry that she was imagining things and that if there were things missing from her room, it was probably due to Cherry's carelessness. So, after a while, Cherry stopped trying. She kept quiet, and did her best to stay away from her stepbrother, which got easier when he went away to boarding school, but she couldn't avoid him completely. And whenever they were together, she'd feel him looking, his gaze like a sweat-damp hand at the small of her back. One more reason for her to leave; one more thing pushing her out the door.

"License and rental agreement?" asked the woman in the tollbooth. Cherry handed them over and double-checked her directions to the Safeway in Homer.

"One way . . . or another . . . I'm gonna find ya . . . I'll getcha, I'll getcha, getcha," she sang softly to herself, following the highway for what would be, according to her phone, a five-hour drive. She had a suitcase, the winter coat she'd purchased secondhand at a used clothing store in West Hollywood, a checking account with nine thousand dollars left of the money the producers had given her, and a stack of fifty copies of a flyer she'd made up on the seat beside her. There were two photographs, side by side, one of Cassie in the Griffin Sisters' heyday, the other an enlarged still from the supermarket video. Cherry's own name and cell phone number were printed at the bottom.

She had a week. Seven days, to track down and convince Cassie to come to Los Angeles and sing again. Sebastian had made it clear the show wouldn't be paying April to hang around as a backup plan. Failure was not an option. By charm or by force, by begging or guilt-tripping, by promising Cassie an actual kidney or her theoretical firstborn child—whichever Cassie would prefer—Cherry was ready to do whatever it took. She was going to convince the most fabulous of the two Griffin Sisters to step back into the limelight, where she should have been all along.

Zoe

PHILADELPHIA, 2003

Can't we just sing covers?" Zoe had asked, after the deal had been signed, and the record-label bosses—Jerry and Helen and David—told the girls what would come next.

"Trust me," Jerry had told them, "you need to break out with a song of your own." He'd started to say something else, but then Cassie had raised her hand, like a kid in an elementary school classroom. Zoe had cringed as Jerry pointed to her sister with an indulgent smile.

Cassie's voice was all but inaudible. "How long do you think you'll need me?"

Shit, Zoe thought, and kicked Cassie under the table.

"What?" asked Jerry, eyebrows shooting up.

"I have a recital in two weeks," Cassie said. "At Curtis. I have to go back to school."

"I don't think you're going back to school anytime soon," Jerry said. Zoe was grateful that he was speaking kindly, that his voice was gentle. "I think you can consider yourself graduated."

"But—"

Zoe grabbed her sister's hand and squeezed it, a little desperately. The squeeze was meant to communicate a number of things. Most essentially: *You have your whole life to play classical music, and I need you here. Now.* That, plus the thing that no one had said, but that Zoe knew to be true, even if she was unwilling to even think it. *They don't want me without you.* In a low voice she said, "Please." Then she held her breath until her sister sighed, closed her eyes, and gave an almost imperceptible nod.

At the head of the table, Jerry had smiled. "So: a hit. A brand-new song, just for you. And I think I know just the young man to help you write one."

The young man's name was Russell D'Angelo, late of Medford, Massachusetts, currently living in Los Angeles. Relic had signed his band, Sky King, six years ago. Sky King had failed to catch fire, and had eventually fallen apart, but Russell had written their songs and had sold a few more songs to other female singers—Cyndi Lauper, Norah Jones. "He's a great guy. I know you'll love him."

"Is he here?" Zoe had asked.

"He's in LA right now," Jerry had said, tapping his fingers on the table. "But we'll get him back East this week, and we'll send him along to you."

As if this guy was a package, to be wrapped up and shipped overnight. The thought made Zoe smile. On their way to the elevator, when they'd pulled far enough ahead of the group that no one could hear them, Zoe had grasped her sister's arm. "I'll never be able to thank you enough for this."

Cassie hadn't replied. She looked numb, and terrified, and Zoe couldn't blame her. Zoe herself couldn't quite believe what had happened, or how it had all happened so fast. The Battle of the Bands had been on a Wednesday. On Thursday morning they'd sung for Simon and David Katz. On Friday morning they'd been in New York City, and, by the end of the day, they'd visited four different labels and decided to sign with Relic. Janice liked Jerry, who, it turned out, had grown up in Cherry Hill, just over the bridge. Cassie had liked the way the keys of the keyboard the label had supplied felt under her fingers while she played. Weird, but whatever. As for Zoe, she liked the three boy bands who were signed to Relic.

Just after the New Year, Cassie had gone to Curtis to deliver her news and, probably, break all of her professors' hearts. Zoe had happily un-enrolled herself from the spring semester at the Community College of Philadelphia. When that task was complete, she'd spent hours on the phone, telling every single one of her friends and most of her acquaintances that she and her sister had been signed to a major label (she didn't bother telling her enemies, confident that word would make its way to them without her). "What about me?" asked Tommy, the only member of Girl Power! with whom Zoe was still speaking. "Your band needs a drummer, right?"

"I don't know," Zoe said. "The people at the label were talking about putting together a band." *The people at the label* was a phrase Zoe was using as often as she could. "He's already got a songwriter. Cassie and I are meeting with him today."

"What time?" Tommy asked. "I can come. I can help."

Zoe rolled her eyes a little. Tommy was musically gifted, she knew—a prodigy, just like her sister—but she didn't think she'd trust him to take his thoughts and feelings, such as they were, and translate them into songs. "I'll see what the people at the label think," she told him, enjoying how those magical words felt in her mouth, how they sounded when she spoke them. "I'll call you."

As soon as that pleasant task was discharged, Zoe had borrowed the family car and driven to the Cherry Hill Mall, where she'd charged seven hundred dollars of new clothes at Nordstrom, knowing she'd have no trouble paying the bill as soon as their signing payment arrived.

On Tuesday morning, Sam was at work. Janice had been banished to the kitchen, where she was wiping the counters, which were already extremely clean, and eavesdropping, Zoe was positive. She'd told her mom to go somewhere—anywhere!—but Janice had refused. "You've never met this person. I want to make sure you're safe."

Zoe was wearing one of her new outfits—boot-cut dark-rinse jeans and a light-blue halter-style crop top, with long sleeves, a high, ruffled collar, and a hem that left a few inches of her belly bare. She'd used a curling iron to put waves in her long, light-brown hair, and had taken her time lining her lips and her eyes.

Cassie was at the piano, as usual, in a sweatshirt and loose-fitting high-waisted jeans. No makeup, as usual, but her hair looked recently washed, and her top and pants were both clean. "Are you ready?" Zoe asked.

Cassie just sighed. Zoe ignored her. No one—not even her weird, silent sister—was going to ruin this fairy tale. Her dreams were coming true, and Zoe meant to enjoy it. When she heard a knock at the door, she smiled her prettiest smile, licked her glossy lips, and crossed the living room with a spring in her step and a swing in her hips.

Russell D'Angelo entered on a gust of wintry air with a guitar in one hand and a notebook tucked under his arm. His hair was wind-tousled. His cheeks and his knuckles were red from the cold. "Hello!" he said. "I'm Russell."

Zoe took his coat and looked him over. She'd expected . . . well, she hadn't known what to expect, exactly. *Songwriter* conjured a number of things. There was the *writer* part—pale, poetic, romantic; a man with a tender heart and sensitive eyes who'd maybe wear a cape or have a scarf thrown around his neck. But the *song* part, plus Russell's past tenure in a band, brought to mind something different: long hair, tattoos, booze and nicotine and worse; an air of dissolution, a whiff of the forbidden. A guy who'd wear sunglasses inside, and look rumpled, from sleeping until noon.

This guy did not resemble either Mr. Darcy or David Lee Roth. He looked, Zoe thought, like a substitute teacher. He was a little taller than she was. His brown hair was cut in a modified mullet, shorter on the sides and top, long enough to curl over the collar of his blue crew-neck in the back. His full cheeks and big, soft brown eyes gave his face a boyish appearance. He looked young, maybe in his mid-twenties. No cape or scarf. No earrings. No visible tattoos.

Zoe knew she was staring, but she couldn't make herself stop. She still couldn't get over how guys in bands were also just regular people, who bought groceries and ate frozen pizza and replaced the toilet paper when it ran out.

"I'm Zoe, and this is Cassie," she said, leaving out their last names for the time being. "Can I get you something to drink? Water? Coffee?"

Russell smiled a little and lifted a Wawa to-go cup. "I'm all set."

His expression was open and curious as he looked around their living room, taking in the stiff couch and love seat, the coffee table with a bowl of dusty potpourri (why hadn't she tossed it?) and Janice and Sam's wedding album (why hadn't she moved it?) arranged on top. The family photos (ugh) on the mantel above the ornamental fireplace, the school pictures (double ugh) hung beside the staircase. Cassie's piano against the wall, and Cassie, sitting on the bench in front of it.

Later, Zoe would think that afternoon was when she'd realized that they were poor. Or, not poor, but definitely not middle-class. She knew, of course, that there were people who lived differently. Tommy, for example, had told her about the house where he'd grown up, which had four bedrooms and a swimming pool in the backyard. She guessed, from his carefully neutral expression, that Russell had also been used to more than this. She wondered if he pitied them. But she couldn't tell from his tone, which was businesslike and brisk, or his face, which gave nothing away.

"Okay!" he said. "Jerry tells me you ladies are going to be the next big thing. Are you ready to write a hit?"

Zoe looked at Cassie, trying not to appear uncertain. They'd talked about it the night before, about how it was going to work. "Probably he'll just bring us a song," Zoe had said, with a confidence she didn't completely feel. "One he's already written. Like, maybe something he wrote for Norah Jones that she didn't want."

"So we're getting someone's leftovers?" Zoe couldn't see in the dark, but she had imagined Cassie making a face.

Zoe had sniffed. "They're not leftovers," she'd said. "They're just, like, songs there wasn't room for on an album. Or maybe songs someone didn't like, or couldn't sing."

"Leftovers," Cassie had repeated. After a moment, she'd asked, "How's he supposed to bring us a song if he doesn't even know us? How does he know what we'll like?"

Zoe had considered. "He knows about us. He knows how old we are. Maybe Jerry played him that tape they made, so he knows how we sound."

Zoe wondered if Russell had also been told how they looked—if he knew that one of the sisters was beautiful and one was not. If he had feelings about it, again, she couldn't tell. He looked at them the same way he'd looked at the furnishings—open, and curious, not judging, just taking it in. "We're ready," she told him, and tossed her hair.

"Great," said Russell. "So, I've got a couple of things I've been fooling around with." He'd brought in a spiral notebook with a soft red cover, the kind Zoe had used in school. He set it on the coffee table, on top of the wedding album, and opened the guitar case, his movements deft and practiced. Zoe watched as he settled the instrument against his body and began to tune it.

"How does this work?" Zoe asked.

Russell looked at her. "What do you mean?"

"I mean, how do you write a song? What comes first? The lyrics or the music?"

Russell strummed a chord, and then gave one of the tuning pegs a twist. "It's probably different for different songwriters. It's different for me. Sometimes I'll get a line, or even just a few words, stuck in my head, and I'll build a song around them. Sometimes it's the music. A phrase, a chord progression." He strummed some more. Zoe watched the motion of his fingers, the tendons flexing in his wrists. He didn't look like a substitute teacher when he played. He looked like an expert, accomplished and smart. "But I thought we could start just by talking." He looked at them, first Cassie, then Zoe. "What kind of music do you like?"

Zoe felt her mouth go dry as she struggled to come up with the name of a single musician. When she couldn't, she looked at Cassie. "Aretha Franklin," Cassie began. "Tina Turner—the early stuff, especially. 'Fool in Love.'" Her sister's voice was less low and muttery than it normally was. She wasn't quite smiling, but she wasn't frowning either. "Dolly Parton and Emmylou Harris and Patsy Cline and Tammy Wynette."

Russell gave Cassie a teasing smile. "Anything in the last five, ten years?" he asked. "Someone, perhaps, of a more contemporary nature?"

"Alanis," said Cassie. "Ani DiFranco. Liz Phair."

Zoe saw how Russell's expression was becoming more impressed with every name Cassie spoke. "I like Christina Aguilera," she said, feeling an urgent need to insert herself into this conversation. "And the Backstreet Boys, and *NSYNC. Popular songs," she said, her chin raised. "That's what we're trying to do, right? Be popular? Because that's what they told us. That you were going to write us a hit."

Cassie gave Zoe a narrow-eyed glare and mouthed three words that Zoe herself had said to her sister probably a million times since preschool: *You're being rude.* Zoe felt a sense of dislocation, like the world had flipped over and she was tumbling through a void, turning upside down and right side up and upside down again.

Russell's chord strumming turned into fingerpicking, a swift flurry of notes that moved up and down the scale. "I think popular songs get popular because they're saying something true. Something that feels real, that resonates, even if it's just a song about partying and having fun. And the best ones combine that with music that . . ." He gave a half smile. "Strikes a chord. So to speak."

"So where do we start?" Zoe repeated.

Russell played a few chords again. Zoe didn't recognize them. Cassie probably did. She probably knew if they were major or minor chords too, what notes were involved, and how to replicate them on the piano. In terms of music, Cassie was far ahead of her, which made Zoe's sense of dislocation, of wrongness, feel even stronger.

Russell, meanwhile, was still talking. "What do you two want to talk about when you sing?" he asked, looking from Cassie to Zoe. "What do you want to say?"

"You mean, like, a message?" Zoe asked. Her heart was sinking, a hollow feeling replacing the elation of the previous days; like she'd walked into a classroom and found herself forced to take a test she hadn't prepared for. She hadn't thought about messages or what she wanted to say. She'd just imagined singing . . . something . . . in front of a crowd that would adore her. There were a hundred pop songs she loved, but where had those songs come from? And had their music or their lyrics come first? She'd never given those questions much thought.

"Not exactly a message," Russell said. "More like a conversation with the audience. With give-and-take."

Zoe frowned. She didn't want to sound stupid, but she also did not want to screw this up. "But we're performing, and they're listening," she said. "So how is it a conversation?"

Russell raised his eyebrows and didn't answer. Zoe realized he was waiting for her to figure it out. She groped for a response, but, before she could find one, Cassie spoke up. "People have questions. Songs are the answers," Cassie said, her voice too loud in the small room. Russell looked at Cassie, startled, then smiled with approval.

"That's it. That's exactly right."

Cassie ducked her head. Her skin turned an unlovely blotchy pink. Zoe felt her belly clenching, that sense of being turned upside down returning, intensifying.

"So who's your audience? What are your people asking you?" Russell let his fingers drop from the strings to thump against the guitar's body, tapping out a rhythm.

Quickly, Zoe said, "Love. Everyone wants to know about love." She sat up very straight, chin lifted, shoulders back. She was determined to reclaim her position as the smarter, savvier sister, the one who knew things, who was, perhaps, less musically knowledgeable, with less native talent, but was also, unquestionably, the one best equipped to navigate this world.

Russell nodded at her. "Okay. So you want to write a love song." He looked at Cassie. "What about you?" He arched an eyebrow and waited, as the silence stretched, until Cassie mumbled, "Love is fine."

Poor Cassie, Zoe thought. Outside, the morning's clouds had lifted; the light coming in through the windows was brighter, and Zoe thought she detected the faint remnants of pink lipstick on Cassie's lips, like she'd put it on, then wiped it away. *Poor thing,* Zoe thought.

"Pick something else," Russell said to Cassie, his voice light, his expression coaxing. "Don't overthink it. Just tell me—what's on your mind?"

"Loneliness," Cassie blurted, and then turned even blotchier. Zoe felt herself flushing in sympathy, knowing how much of herself Cassie had exposed.

Russell nodded. His expression was calm. He didn't look disgusted, or even surprised, as he strummed those three chords again. Zoe could feel them forming a groove in her brain. *A hook,* she thought, and felt her heart beating faster.

"Love and loneliness," Russell said.

"What about, like, a crush?" Zoe said. "Like, someone you want but can't have. That's love and loneliness." She sat back, feeling pleased with herself.

"Or what if," Cassie began. She swallowed and licked her lips. Zoe was startled. Cassie rarely spoke at all and, certainly, not more than she had to when there were strangers around. Was it possible that Cassie felt competitive? It gave her a stab of unease, until she decided that it couldn't possibly matter. Cassie was so awkward, and so weird. If this was a competition for Russell's attention, for his regard, Zoe knew she'd win.

Zoe crossed her legs as Cassie slowly said, "What if it's a love song about disappointment? Like, a girl in love with a guy, and she's lonely when they're apart, and then, after they get together, she's even lonelier?"

Russell leaned toward Cassie, his expression sharper, more interested. "Okay," he said. "So it's like, I want you, I've got you, I miss you?" He strummed the chords again, one for *want*, one for *got*, one for *miss.*

"I miss you when you're here," Cassie said, actually meeting his eyes.

Russell smiled, wide and unguarded. He looked about ten years old, just a boy, eager to show you the Lego tower he'd constructed, as he opened up the notebook, then pushed it across the coffee table, away from her, toward her sister. "Write that down," he said.

Cassie picked up the notebook, produced a pen from somewhere, and began writing. Zoe tilted her head toward Russell.

"Is it like a riddle?" she asked.

"Uh-huh. Kind of," said Russell, who barely appeared to be listening to her. His eyes were on Cassie, on her hand as it moved across the page. He strummed his guitar, playing the chords again, and sang, "In all of the darkness / I saw you so clear." He played a different chord. "But now that we're together . . ."

His voice trailed off, and Cassie sang, her voice low and clear and lovely, "I miss you when you're here."

Russell was beaming, and Cassie was smiling at him shyly. Actually smiling! Zoe, meanwhile, was shocked. A coldness was spreading in the pit of her stomach, and her face felt paralyzed. Had Cassie ever sung on her own like that, unprompted? Had she ever sung without Zoe harmonizing, offering Cassie her mantra of encouragement: *You can do it. I believe in you?*

Russell, of course, did not realize what a rare occurrence he'd just witnessed. "So let's plan on three verses. One where she wants him, then one where she's got him . . ."

"And one where she's happy?" Zoe made herself smile. She hoped she didn't look as confused as she felt. "We want a happy ending, right? People like happy endings."

"Maybe it ends when she's leaving," Cassie said, speaking rapidly, like she was hurrying to get the words out before she forgot them, or lost her nerve. "Maybe that's the happy ending. She realizes he wasn't what she thought he was."

"A breakup anthem." Russell sounded pleased. He paused, then said, "'When You're Here.'"

"That's the title?" Zoe asked, hearing the capital letters when he spoke. Hearing, too, the uncertainty in her voice. "It's about a breakup, and we're calling it 'When You're Here'?"

It was Cassie, not Russell, who answered her. "I think it's good. That should be the title." Zoe saw that he was smiling and nodding, and Cassie's pen was almost flying over the page. He'd hum a phrase of music, she'd sing a few words; he'd play another chord, she'd write something else. Later, Zoe would think it was like watching someone carving a statue: like someone taking a hunk of wood or slab of marble and unerringly cutting away the parts that weren't supposed to be there, until what was hiding inside the wood or the stone was revealed. Like the song had always been there, and Russell and Cassie were working together to find it. Like this was a thing her sister knew how to do, without being taught, without being shown how.

I saw you
And I knew
You were my heart's desire
My first clue
That we two
Could set the world on fire

You were so high, you'd never know
You on your throne, me down below

You looked, but you could never see
That what you needed, it was me

No, you can't see

In all of the darkness
I saw you so clear
Look at me
I'm right here.
Yeah, I'm right here.

Zoe watched them work, sitting in silence, a lump on the couch, frozen in her shock and her dismay. She watched her sister and Russell, as the music came pouring out of them—pouring *through* them—spilling out like a shower of gold, lyrics that Russell identified as *verse* and *pre-chorus* and *chorus*. A love story in three minutes and thirty seconds; a girl who goes from yearning to satisfied to lonely again, but stronger and wiser—heartbroken, but ready to move on.

"What do you think?" Russell asked, forty-five minutes later. Cassie looked up at him and shook her head, blinking. Her expression was startled. She looked like she'd been woken up from a dream as her eyes moved from Russell to the clock that ticked on the mantel. Clearly she hadn't noticed the time passing. Zoe, meanwhile, had felt every excruciating second that she'd been sitting there like a useless third wheel that couldn't even spin.

"It's good," Zoe made herself say, hoping she sounded enthusiastic. "It's really good."

Russell nodded without bothering to look at her. "Cassie? What do you think?"

"I think," she said slowly, "that if my piano teacher heard this he would kill me."

"Cassie!" Zoe was appalled.

Russell looked at her sister, head tilted. He didn't sound shocked as much as amused. "How come?"

Cassie looked embarrassed. "He calls this moon-June music."

"We didn't rhyme *moon* and *June*."

Cassie smirked. "Yeah. Just *fire* and *desire*."

Russell slapped his hand against his chest, like she'd shot him in the heart. "Ouch." He pulled his guitar strap over his head and put the instrument back into its case, talking as he did. "A really famous songwriter once told me that pop songs are simple for a reason. You want the audience to be able to sing along with the chorus the second time they hear it, and to have all the lyrics memorized the second time they've heard the whole song. But you can still make choices within that framework." He stood up, stretched, and ambled over to Cassie's piano, looking at it, then turning to her, eyebrows lifted, waiting for Cassie to give him permission.

Cassie nodded. Zoe wondered how her sister felt, watching Russell sit down on the bench, where only Cassie herself had ever sat. *A day full of firsts*, she thought. Russell raised his arms, wiggled his fingers, and started to play an Elton John song.

"I can't lie . . . no more of your darkness . . ." He had a pleasant voice, a light, tuneful tenor. It sounded especially good when paired with Cassie's darker, raspier alto. "All my pictures . . . seem to fade to black and white." He stopped, looking from Cassie to Zoe. "Do you hear it?"

Zoe was frowning, her brain skittering, spinning fruitlessly as she tried to figure out what he meant, to hear what he'd wanted her to hear. Because Cassie, clearly, knew the answer. Zoe watched as her sister got up, walked to the piano, and leaned over Russell's shoulder to play, one-handed.

"I met a woman / She had a mouth like yours," Cassie sang. "She knew your life / She knew your devils and your deeds."

Zoe could feel her frown deepening into a scowl. "What is that?" she asked them. "Are you making it up?"

Cassie and Russell exchanged a glance, a brief look of perfect understanding, absolute complicity. Zoe could imagine their connection like a physical thing, a golden thread stretching between them, a bright line she couldn't cross. She wanted to scream. She wanted to hit them both.

Later, she would think, *I should have gotten up off the couch and gone out of the living room, out of the house. I should have left them alone. I should have walked away and never looked back. I should have known that it would only get worse, that it would never get better.* And she'd think of the words she hadn't known yet, the part of the verse her sister hadn't sung, that felt, years later, like prophecy: "And she said / 'Go to him, stay with him if you can / But be prepared to bleed.'"

Cassie

ON THE ROAD, 2003

The Midwestern label rep's name was Daisy. She had long blond hair, an easy laugh, and a maternal air, even though she couldn't have been much older than thirty. That morning, she looked wide awake and fully caffeinated in her jeans and low, immaculately white sneakers. They were probably expensive, Cassie suspected, even though they looked like regular tennis shoes. Zoe would know. Cassie, herself, did not.

"You guys know the drill, right?" Daisy asked, as they piled out of the van that Ronnie, the previous rep, had been driving them around in, all of them grabbing luggage and instruments and following her across the pavement. Cassie's mouth tasted grungy. Her skin felt filmed with travel dirt. She was torn between desperation for a shower and never wanting to bathe again, because, at some point between Lock Haven, Pennsylvania, and Youngstown, Ohio, Russell D'Angelo had fallen asleep with his head on her shoulder, and she imagined that her sweatshirt might smell faintly like his shampoo.

She still couldn't believe it: where she was, what had happened. Eight weeks ago she'd been home, practicing Liszt, imagining the only life she'd ever pictured for herself, the only one she'd ever wanted, and now, she was here, in a band, on a tour that would take them across the country. Their manager, CJ Carver, had explained how it would work, after he'd handed them each a copy of the schedule— ten pages, double-sided, full of names of radio stations, label reps, performance venues, and hotels—before putting them on the first in a series of vans. "It's going to be a lot," he'd warned them, back in New York City. CJ was thirty-two, mild-mannered, Midwestern, and gay. (Cassie hadn't noticed. Zoe had told her.) CJ had a round, freckled face, light-brown hair that was already thinning on top, and an endless collection of Hawaiian shirts, which was all the sisters had ever seen him wear. He looked like Charlie Brown if the comic-book character had purchased his entire wardrobe in Maui.

"But when do we get to go home?" Cassie had asked. Her sister had smirked, but Russell had looked sympathetic, and he'd been the one who answered. "I think we're going to be on the road for a while," he told her.

That had been three weeks ago, and CJ hadn't lied. It was exhausting, playing two or three shows a day, carrying their own equipment to each performance and driving for hours between them. It would have been unendurable, if it hadn't been for Russell. Cassie found that she was brave enough to talk to him, as long as the subject was music, and they'd converse in the vans for hours, each playing for the other bands and songs they hadn't heard. Cassie knew much more classical and Broadway music than he did, while Russell knew a lot more pop, and they could spend hours going back and forth, trading songs. Somewhere in New Jersey, Russell had bought a splitter for his CD player that let him plug in two pairs of headphones at a time. Sometimes, he'd sit beside Cassie in the van, close enough for her to feel the warmth of his thigh and his shoulder next to hers, and give her one pair, and pull on the other, and he'd play her something, a song or an album or an artist he wanted her to hear, asking her what she thought, urging her to improvise lyrics, to add more harmony. When Russell listened to her, he had a way of going very still, his eyes heavy-lidded, half-shut, all of his focus fixed on the sound of her voice. Cassie had never felt attention like that; had never been its object. She could never have imagined a man looking at her while she talked, his face open and shining with appreciation, even awe. Those hours were perfect.

That morning, Cassie had kept her eyes fixed on the line of his shoulders as they crossed the parking lot. His hair was getting long enough to curl over his collar, she saw, as they followed Daisy into the SUV. Russell and Cam, their new bass player, put their instruments in the back, and then Russell helped Cassie settle her keyboard, making sure it was secure. Tommy, the drummer, Cassie's old classmate and Zoe's old bandmate, had stayed back in Philly. If there were any actual concerts, Jerry said, the label would fly him out, or they'd find someone local to sit in. But, for the time being, the Griffin Sisters was a foursome, with Cassie on keyboard and vocals, and Zoe singing backup, contributing the occasional harmony or, very rarely, a chord or two on her guitar, and mostly looking pretty while she shook a tambourine. Russell played lead guitar, and Cam played bass.

Tommy had not been happy about being left behind. Tommy still had a desperate and, as far as Cassie knew, unrequited crush on her sister, and he was convinced that Zoe was going to hook up with Russell or with Cam, or that she'd meet some other guy on the road.

Cassie didn't think Tommy had to worry about Cam, who was almost thirty, and who had a girlfriend back in New York, a puppeteer who worked for *Sesame Street*. Cam had bleached-blond hair and an easy smile, and tattoos of vines and mermaids, skulls and spiders crawling all over both of his arms, along with a pair of enormous wings on his back. Cam smoked, in Cassie's admittedly untutored opinion, an absurd amount of pot. He loved to do yoga poses, backbends and handstands, before every show, and he could turn anything into a bong, including a whole pineapple, but he was harmless, a cross between a big brother and a golden retriever, friendly without actually being their friend. That was a relief. It meant Cassie wouldn't have to think through the steps of every interaction with him, reminding herself what to say, how to look, when to smile. She could just give Cam a nod or say "good morning" or "excuse me" or "let's run it again," and Cam wouldn't be mad or look at Cassie like she was some creature, something barely even human, the way her sister, and her sister's friends, sometimes did.

Russell, though . . . Cassie saw the way Russell looked at Zoe, with admiration and desire. She figured they'd become a couple. The thought gave her a sick, plummeting sensation in her guts, a feeling she didn't understand. She liked Russell, liked being near him, singing with him, writing music with him, but she didn't like him romantically. What would be the point? The very thought of it was ludicrous, like an elephant falling in love with a Christmas-tree ornament. They didn't make sense together. Russell would never want her that way. Especially not with her sister around. Cassie had spent years watching Zoe effortlessly attract any man she wanted, and many she didn't. She'd seen her sister hook up with guys, then cast them aside when she got bored or when someone better came along, like they were outfits she was trying on and carelessly discarding, tossing to her bedroom floor, never to be picked up or considered again. Zoe was beautiful and charming and sexy. Of course Russell would want to be with her. What else could Cassie expect?

She tried not to think about it. She did her best to focus, instead, on everything happening around her, the unexpected novelty of this new life, and how rapidly it had all come to pass. She was still shocked that this had happened. That she was no longer at home with her parents, in Philadelphia, no longer a classical pianist in training. That she was part of a band—a band, of all things, making popular music! It had always been Zoe's dream, never hers . . . and, Cassie was sure, Zoe had never suspected that being in a band was so unglamorous, such a repetitive, exhausting grind. On the road, every day was the same. Up at seven o'clock, in a hotel room that looked the same as the room from the night before (Cassie would sometimes have to check the hotel stationery or her printed schedule to remember where she was). She'd shower quickly, so that Zoe could take her time in the bathroom, putting on her makeup, doing her hair. She'd pack up her things, and go down to the lobby for breakfast. Mostly they stayed in chain hotels that offered a free buffet. Sometimes there'd be eggs and bacon and sausage and even a waffle station. Usually it was just packets of oatmeal and containers of yogurt, paper plates and plastic silverware and a bowl full of waxy-looking fruit.

By eight thirty, they'd be in a rented car, with their label representative at the wheel. The rep would go over their itinerary, reading out the names of towns and cities, the radio station's call letters and format—Top 40 or classic rock, adult contemporary, variety, giving them the names of the station manager, the program director, any DJs they'd meet. Cassie would memorize the names on her way into the station, and then forget them before they'd left the parking lot. Once they'd arrived, they'd unload the trunk, carrying their gear into the conference room at the station. Cassie would set up her keyboard on its stand or, if there wasn't room, right on the table; Russell and Cam would plug their bass and guitar into whatever amplifier the station had on hand (the amplifiers, Russell had told Cassie, came in two categories: crappy and crappier, and he had not been wrong). The station personnel would file in. Greetings would be exchanged, with the label rep doing her best to sound as enthusiastic as she had on the very first day at the very first station. "I'm excited for you to listen to the Griffin Sisters from Philadelphia, the next big thing!"

Cassie would look around as she stood behind her instrument. It was endlessly amazing to her, how male DJs who sounded handsome and dashing and young almost always turned out to be middle-aged schlubs. Then again, she supposed, she might sound beautiful to anyone who couldn't see her.

The station managers and program directors would have newspapers, copies of *Billboard* or *DownBeat* or *Rolling Stone*, cigarettes and cups of coffee. The DJs would sip from mugs of honeyed tea or suck on lozenges. Everyone, including the interns, would look uniformly bored, disinterested, like they wished they were anyplace else. Until the music began. Then, sometimes, their expressions would change.

Cassie would lead them through a three-song set—one cover, which rotated, sometimes Annie Lennox, sometimes Aretha Franklin, if Cassie felt like showing off, and two original songs, "The Gift," which the label was trying to break as their first single, and "When You're Here," the first song Cassie and Russell had written together. At the last song's conclusion, the rep would thank the radio people for their time, hand them a copy of the band's two-song demo, and then they'd do the whole thing in reverse, packing up their stuff, loading the car, driving off to the next performance.

Sometimes, the DJs would look interested, or some of the audience members would applaud. Sometimes, Cassie would see at least a flicker of interest or appreciation, especially from the younger staffers or the interns. More often, though, their faces would give nothing away; their handshakes and goodbyes would be carefully noncommittal. No DJ had, so far, declared them the next best thing; no programming director had raced off to the DJ's booth, insisting that he play the song right this minute, and once an hour every hour after that. The reps assured them that this was to be expected, that they shouldn't worry, that all was well and the tour was proceeding just as they'd hoped. Cassie thought the reps were right. As careful as the radio people always were, as unreadably blank as they kept their faces, she could feel their attention and admiration, could tell, from how the quality of the silence changed when she sang, that they were impressed.

She didn't mind people listening when she played and sang. She hated that they were looking. The attention, even if it was positive attention, was unsettling, destabilizing and confusing. Part of her wanted to close her mouth, to hunch her shoulders and shut her eyes and say *stop looking at me*. Or, maybe, *stop looking at me* like that, like I'm impressive, like I matter. *You've got me mixed up with my sister.* Every time, in every conference room, there was a brief moment of absolute terror before she began, a moment when she could feel the notes she'd play and the words she'd sing fleeing her memory, like fleas racing off a dead dog's body, and she'd think *I can't, I can't, don't make me.* Then she'd turn her head and see her sister mouthing, *You got this*. She'd turn to the left and see Russell, his face calm and expectant, unbothered.

Between Zoe's support and her own growing desire to see that impressive, admirable version of herself reflected in Russell's gaze, Cassie would find a way, each time, to perform. She learned to endure it. And then, in one of the most startling developments of her life, she began to enjoy it. When she played and sang, she could pretend that she had ceased to be a body and was only a voice, a ghost, or some supernatural creature that had no physical form, a thing that was made of music. And oh, she loved it when she sang with Russell. That was the best feeling of all. "You make me feel," she'd sing, and his voice would join hers, low and raspy, and—Cassie flushed every time she thought it—sexy. "You make me feel like a natural woman."

"Thank you," the head of programming would say, in Altoona and Pittsburgh and Cleveland and Cincinnati. "We'll be in touch." The label rep would thank them, and Cassie would be back in her body, ungainly, unlovely, unlovable. The band would pile back into the car and drive to the next station, the next city, to do it all again.

Cam, who'd been in Sky King with Russell, and two other bands after that, was used to the routines of the road. He always sat in the very back of the van or the SUV, on the driver's side, with his eyes closed and his portable CD player's headphones on. Cassie usually sat on the other side of the back row, ceding the middle row to Zoe and Russell. Her sister would chatter at Russell, drawing him out, telling him stories; asking him questions, making him laugh. She'd brush his fingertips, his upper arm, his shoulder, with little, fluttering touches, like her hands were birds that would alight and fly away. She'd lean against him playfully, or pretend to fall asleep on his shoulder. Maybe she was actually falling asleep on his shoulder. Cassie had her doubts.

She would sit and watch, unable to make herself turn away. Not when she could see the way the corners of Russell's eyes crinkled when he smiled, or memorize the exact shade of his lips. She collected every smile, cherished every story, even if the smiles and the stories were for Zoe, not for her. And sometimes, Russell would ask Cassie to join him.

Cassie would see her sister's tight-lipped face as they traded spots, Zoe climbing into the back seat and Cassie clambering over the back of the seat, feeling enormous and ungainly, to take her place beside Russell. She'd be shy at first, her lips and tongue feeling thick and slow, her body feeling even larger than it actually was, but he'd say, "Hey, listen to this," and hand her a set of headphones, and then they'd be together in the music, and she'd find her feet again.

She loved listening to him play and talk and sing, loved hearing him laugh, loved his excitement, the way he'd gesture, moving his hands in the air when he talked about a song he liked. She knew that it was hopeless. A joke. But she could not keep herself from yearning for him, quietly, privately, in the locked rooms of her own heart. She'd imagine him coming to her, finding her alone somewhere, making a declaration, like a hero in a movie or a romance novel. *I want us to be together*, the Russell who lived in her imagination would say. Or, sometimes, thrillingly, shamefully—*I have to have you. I'll die without you.* She could imagine him saying things, taking her hand, touching her face. Beyond that, her imagination stalled. She couldn't picture Russell touching her body, much less her own hands on him.

She told herself that it didn't matter, that no one would ever have to know how she felt. Not Zoe. Not Russell. Not anyone. She would never say anything, and Russell would never guess her secret.

But then, one afternoon in Wisconsin, somewhere between Platteville and Madison, after they'd played their third showcase at their third radio station of the day, everything changed.

It was after six o'clock, not dark yet, but on its way, and Daisy was driving them to the Holiday Inn where they were staying. Cam, unexpectedly, had taken the front passenger's seat, trying to wheedle Daisy into taking them to a steakhouse for dinner ("No, I told you," Daisy was saying. "We can only do steak once a week. That's from the big bosses. And you guys got your steak two nights ago." She'd given Cam a scolding look. "You do know that the reps all talk to each other, right?")

Zoe was curled up in the corner in the middle row of seats. Cassie could tell she was asleep for real, not just sham-sleeping as an excuse to lean on Russell's shoulder. Her mouth was hanging open, giving her a slatternly appearance and the illusion of the tiniest double chin. And she was snoring: harsh, unlovely sounds. Russell turned around and caught Cassie's eye. He nodded at her sister. "Shh," he said, pressing one finger to his lips. Cassie found herself smiling at him, wondering how his lips might feel if she were the one touching them. She couldn't imagine touching his body, certainly couldn't imagine kissing him, but she could allow herself to think about brushing her fingertips against his mouth.

Russell turned around. Just when Cassie was thinking, *Well, that's that,* he turned on his side, stretching one arm back, and Cassie felt his fingers brushing her ankle, just over her sock. She stared down in disbelief, breath caught in her throat, watching herself being touched by a boy for the first time ever. Russell wrapped his fingers around her ankle and gave it a gentle, fond squeeze.

"Hey," he whispered, so softly that only Cassie could hear him.

"Hey," she whispered back.

And that was it. A quick touch, a single word. That was all it took for Cassie to fall in love, to decide that she would love him forever, even if she couldn't have him, even if she never got anything more than that single touch. She would love him quietly, secretly, in the privacy of her own heart, and maybe no one else, not even Russell himself, would ever know. But it would still be love.

They had a concert that night: an actual concert at a bar, in front of regular people, not a conference-room showcase at a radio station, in front of staff. It would be their first show in front of an audience. In the hotel room, Zoe had been beside herself with delight, trying on all the new clothes she'd bought that afternoon, during an hourlong sprint through the East Towne Mall, while Cassie sat in the food court and ate a hot pretzel and waited. To Cassie, the outfits all looked the same:

low-rise, dark-rinse, boot-cut jeans; shirts that were cropped to show her flat, fake-tanned belly; platform-soled sandals; and a half dozen gold necklaces of varying widths, some with charms dangling from the center, some with fake diamonds that would glitter under the lights.

Cassie had shrugged. "They all look good." Her sister had been given money to go shopping. Cassie had been sent a single choice: a black polyester pantsuit, a garment with the single goal of conceal-ment. They'd probably picked it out because it matched the venue's curtains, she'd thought, touching the scratchy fabric, noting the baggy arms, the absurd shoulder pads. She wouldn't look pretty, could only hope for invisible. But it didn't matter, she thought, still glowing all over from the memory of Russell's fingers on her skin.

"Okay, but this one's got silver sequins, and this has puffed sleeves," Zoe was saying, when Cassie focused again. "Come on, you've got to help me pick one." Cassie could tell that one shirt was pale purple, lav-ishly ruffled, and that another was icy-blue satin with no sleeves, but the subtler distinctions eluded her, and the more she tried to assist, the more frustrated Zoe became, until she'd gathered up all of her options and flounced off to the bathroom. Cassie had pulled on her own clothes dreamily, wondering if maybe they'd be sent on an international tour. Maybe the plane would crash over the ocean, and her sister and the rest of the band would be swept out to sea (and eventually rescued, Cassie thought guiltily), while she and Russell would drift to some white-sand, windswept island, where a diet of coconuts and mangos would finally leave Cassie thin, and the sun would turn her skin golden, and, after weeks or maybe months went by, Russell would realize that what he felt was not just admiration, or respect for her musical talent. He would see that he loved her too.

"Which one, which one?" Zoe muttered, emerging from the bath-room to stand in front of the full-length mirror. She held one blouse in front of her, then another one, turning from side to side, bending down, then whipping her neck up and back to send her hair flying.

"That one," Cassie said, pointing randomly at one of the tops.

"This one?" Zoe asked, sounding skeptical as she smoothed the shirt's fabric.

"Yes," Cassie said. "And hurry. We're going to be late."

Half an hour later, the band pulled in front of the Up North Bar, just off campus, near the University of Wisconsin–Madison. Cassie shivered as wind blew off of either Lake Mendota or Lake Monona (she'd seen, on a map, that both were nearby, but had no idea which was responsible for the breeze). She carried her keyboard across a street thronging with college students around her age. It made her feel a little superior, to be a working girl, with a job. She was earning her own money, making her way in the world. She was not a kid going to class on Mom and Dad's dime. But it also made her feel a little wistful, the tiniest bit envious. Nobody asked anything of these boys and girls, except that they show up for their classes, study, do their homework, and pass their tests. Nobody would wake them up early, day after day, drive them to radio station after radio station to play show after show, the country flickering past them like a deck of quickly shuffled cards. Watching the kids, bundled up in down coats and hoodies, hearing them call to one another—"Hey! Wait up!"— Cassie felt unmoored, unsettled. Homesick, she realized, and wondered if Zoe felt it too.

"Welcome, welcome!" said the guy running the bar. He'd given Daisy a kiss on the cheek, and ushered the band to a greenroom barely the size of a closet. At nine o'clock on a weeknight, there wasn't much of a crowd, maybe thirty or forty people. Cassie could hear the rise and fall of their voices through the flimsy walls.

"You're going to be fine," Zoe murmured, as Cassie stood in the wings with her eyes shut, wishing there was a way to teleport herself onto her piano bench. She'd gotten relatively comfortable at radio stations, but here, again, were regular people, peers, who would judge her in a different way. She knew that she could close her eyes as soon as she arrived at the instrument, but she couldn't navigate her way across the stage unless she was looking . . . and looking meant keeping her eyes open. Looking meant seeing the

crowd, knowing that they could see her, imagining their scorn. It
was terrifying. The voices felt closer, and they sounded louder; not
like dozens of people, but like the voice of a single creature, a monster from under the bed, something many-eyed and many-limbed,
hot-breathed and hungry.

"You're fine," Zoe was telling her. "You can do this. You deserve to
be here." Cassie nodded. She always heard the part that Zoe wasn't
saying—*I need you. And I'll kill you if you don't get out there and play.*
She was nervous . . . but, she realized, less nervous than she would
have been the day before. Her stomach wasn't fluttering, and her heart
wasn't thudding in her chest. Maybe it was because she could still feel
the place where Russell had touched her. She wondered if she could get
that spot tattooed, a circle of flowers or a wavy line or a row of hearts
to mark the spot.

"Give it up for the Griffin Sisters!" the bar's owner shouted. There
was a smattering of disinterested applause. Cassie walked the gauntlet,
onto the tiny stage, which was barely a foot above the bar's floor, with
barely enough room for a drum kit and a piano. She settled herself on
the bench, hoping her pantsuit did, in fact, help her blend in with the
curtains and the walls. She watched the other band members find their
places, Cam beside her, Russell and Zoe in front of her, Russell on the
right, Zoe toward her left. Their borrowed drummer clicked his drumsticks. Russell counted, "One, two, three, four," and it was like wind-
shield wipers clearing away rain so that she could see, like a cinched
corset loosening so that she could breathe. She raised her hands, knowing she could trust them, that the notes were at her fingertips and the
lyrics in her brain; that everything she needed was there, and when she
reached for it, she'd find what she required.

As the four of them had gotten more familiar with one another,
they'd sounded better together, smoother and more proficient, with
every radio station that they'd played for. They'd gone from competent to good and, by Wisconsin, had been verging on very good . . .
and that night, they vaulted right past very good and excellent. That
night, they were transcendent. It was like they'd found another gear:

the harmonies more perfectly blended, the sound more balanced, every word of every song imbued with meaning. Instead of the crowd as a terrified, many-eyed monster, Cassie felt its members as people, people who were thrilled to be hearing their songs, to be witnessing their show. The crowd sent its energy, in the form of enthusiasm, toward the stage, and the band used it as fuel, turned fuel into music, and sent their songs back out. Cassie knew she'd never sung more beautifully, and that Russell had never been more in tune with her, in his singing and in his whole self.

They closed the show with "Flavor of the Week," Cassie's and Zoe's voices twining in high harmony, Russell's voice an octave lower, grounding them, and it was glorious perfection. By the second time the chorus came around, the audience was on its feet, singing along.

> I was just your flavor
> If I saw that girl, I'd save her
> I'd tell her no
> I'd tell her go,
> I'd tell her run, and don't look back
> I was just your flavor
> If only I'd been braver
> But I was just your flavor of the week.

Cam's final chord hung in the air. There was a single breath's worth of electric silence, and then the audience was cheering, stamping and clapping, whistling, and shouting for more. Cassie looked at Zoe, watching as her sister kissed her fingertips and raised her hand in the air, exultant, a gesture she made after every show. Then she looked at Russell, and found he was looking at her, his eyes soft, mouth a little open. Dazzled and adoring. And, in that moment, Cassie could almost believe that what she felt was reciprocated, that what she dreamed of might actually, someday, come true.

Zoe
ON THE ROAD, 2003

For weeks, as the tour proceeded, Zoe watched Russell D'Angelo. She'd watched him in the van, stretched out with his long legs forward and his head tipped back, as he listened to his CD player. She'd watched him onstage, his eyes heavy-lidded, mouth a little open. She'd watched the way he'd sway, or rock from heel to toe and back again, along with Cam's bass, the way he'd rock his hips from side to side to the sounds of the drums, and clutch the microphone, singing into it like it was a lover's mouth.

She had memorized the blue veins that traced along the pale skin of his neck, the way he hooked his thumbs in his pockets when he was nervous. She knew the timbre of his voice, first thing in the morning, knew the smell of his hair, and she'd extracted as much of his personal history as he would tell her: mom, the manager of a health-food store in Boston; dad, an orthopedic surgeon. Two older sisters, a dentist and an art gallery owner, both success stories compared to Russell, who, in spite of his talent, in spite of getting his first band signed, his parents and siblings all insisted on seeing as the family fuckup. Russell related all of this with an easy smile—how his dad had said, "I wash my hands of this," when Russell had decided to go on the road with Sky King instead of to college, how his mom had, for a while, snuck him money from her own paycheck, so he wouldn't have to live on ramen and rice and beans.

Zoe wanted him fiercely. She wanted him because he was cute and sweet and talented. Beyond that, Zoe could admit that she wanted him because, for the first time in her life, she sensed resistance. Russell was the first guy she'd desired who hadn't immediately wanted her back. For the first time in her life, Zoe was feeling insecure about the dream she'd chased since she was old enough to hold a hairbrush and pretend it was a microphone. Now that she'd gotten a record deal, now that she'd started performing, now that she had what she'd always wanted, she was starting to think that maybe her dreams had been ludicrous, and that she wasn't the Griffin sister destined to be a star. Cassie was.

The unfairness of it made Zoe sick. Cassie hadn't even wanted this. Cassie was indifferent to attention. She still got stage fright and claimed that crowds made her queasy.

The problem was, Cassie disliked audiences, but Zoe could see that audiences—at least, some of the people in them—liked Cassie just fine.

In Altoona, Zoe saw how a radio-station intern, a girl even fatter than Cassie, had stared at her sister like she was watching the Second Coming the minute Cassie had started to sing; how her mouth had fallen open and how she'd been almost crying by the end of the second song. In Wisconsin, Zoe noticed one plain, plump girl, a girl who'd been watching her friends' purses while they'd danced. Zoe watched the girl edging closer and closer toward the stage as the set had gone on, like she'd been hypnotized by Cassie's singing, like Cassie had called to her, summoning her in a register only other fat girls could hear. By the end of the show, the girl was right up front, and her expression had been rapturous as she'd clapped and cheered. When they'd left the club the girl had been waiting outside the stage door, her breath coming out of her mouth in a frosty white cloud, shivering in the cold, waiting for a chance to touch Cassie's shoulder and whisper, "Thank you."

Zoe wouldn't have minded her sister getting her little fan club. She would have, in fact, been happy to cede the attention of every fat girl in the world to her sister. But Russell, too, seemed fascinated by Cassie. He'd talk about Cassie's talent with a dreamy look on his face. *Do you have any idea how rare it is?* he would ask Zoe, talking about Cassie's abilities, her perfect pitch, her innate sense of rhythm, her facility with language, and her gift for lyrics. *Do you know how amazing?*

Rare, Zoe would repeat, trying to match Russell's enthusiasm. *Amazing*.

It made her furious. Why couldn't she have been the musical

prodigy? "Because you have other gifts," her mom said, during one of the weekly phone calls Janice had demanded. "Not everyone gets to be good at every single thing." Which was sensible, but it didn't make Cassie's easy mastery of every song any easier for Zoe to accept. Why couldn't she have been the one with the gorgeous voice, the one who could pull songs and lyrics out of the air? And what other gifts did she, Zoe, have, other than just being pretty, in a world full of pretty girls?

By the Wisconsin show, she could see how things were going, could read the future as clearly as if someone had handed her a MapQuest printout. Cassie was becoming a star. Zoe was becoming extraneous. Maybe, by the time Jerry called them back to New York City, he'd have decided that the band didn't need her at all.

If Russell loved her, Zoe thought, none of that would matter. Or, at least, it wouldn't hurt as much. If she spent her nights in his bed, if he thought she was amazing, beautiful, special, something rare, to be cherished, that would take some of the sting away. So she'd watched, and she'd waited, and, eventually, she'd figured out a way to make Russell D'Angelo hers. Her plan was simplicity itself. It required just three components: booze, a movie, and a semi-willing guy with working eyes and a functioning libido.

In Dallas, another concert had ended in multiple ovations and, even better, a radio-station visit had concluded with the promise of airplay for "The Gift." Road-ragged as they were by the time they finally got back to the hotel, the members of the band were still glowing and buzzing, lit up with delight, and at the prospect of staying in place and doing their laundry the next day. Even Cassie looked happy. She'd been standing up straighter, and there'd been a bit of a bounce in her step, a little color in her cheeks.

Good for her, Zoe thought coolly. Let Cassie enjoy her musical triumph. Zoe was after something else: a victory on a different field of play.

After her sister had tucked herself into bed with a book in her hands and her headphones clamped to her ears, Zoe wiped off some (but not all) of her stage makeup, took a quick shower, and pulled on her softest pajama bottoms and a giant sweatshirt. She spritzed herself with perfume, collected the bottle of vodka she'd gotten Cam to buy, and padded, barefoot, down the hotel hallway, until she'd reached Russell's room. Normally, they doubled up—Zoe sharing a room with Cassie; Cam sharing with Russell—but the label rep had gone to spend the night with his grandmother, who lived in nearby Highland Park, so Russell was all by himself. It couldn't have been more perfect.

Zoe knocked, and waited for Russell to open the door. The clothes she'd chosen disguised her body, but Zoe thought that would work in her favor. Let Russell think about whether she was wearing a bra under the sweatshirt. Let him wonder, when he looked at the pajama bottoms, worn thin by a hundred trips through the dryer, how soft they would be under his fingers; let him consider how close he'd need to get to feel the warmth of her skin underneath them. She held up the bottle and smiled brightly. "I'm too wound up to sleep. Want to watch a movie?"

"Um. Sure. Does Cassie want to come?"

"Cassie crashed," Zoe lied. Cassie had been awake when she'd left, maybe hoping that Russell would come to her, as he sometimes would. He'd show up at their room, and he and Cassie would spend hours working on music or talking about it, sharing favorite songs, playing each other bands or songs the other hadn't heard, while Zoe either feigned interest or took herself to the hotel gym or to watch TV with Cam. *Not tonight*, Zoe thought.

"Let me just see if Cam's around." Before she could stop him, Russell had slipped past her, into the hall. Zoe frowned, then located the remote and turned on the TV. She'd play the long game, if she had to. She'd waited four weeks already, all the time they'd been on the road. She could wait a few hours more.

Russell came back with Cam in tow. "What are we watching?" Zoe asked. After Russell's suggestion of some independent film with subtitles had gotten him thoroughly razzed, they'd settled on *The Cable Guy*.

Zoe went to the ice machine to fill up the bucket, and pulled small bottles of orange juice and cranberry juice from the minibar. "You know the label's going to bill us for that," Russell had said with his familiar easy smile. Zoe knew. CJ had explained it to them, before the tour commenced: how the label would, eventually, bill them for everything—their meals and hotel rooms, their outfits and makeup, the gas for the reps' cars. Every penny spent on introducing the Griffin Sisters to the world would come out of the band's eventual profits, assuming there were any. But Zoe couldn't let herself worry about the costs of a few bottles of juice. Not with so much at stake.

She'd filled everyone's glass, making sure to go heavy on the vodka for Russell. Then she set herself up on the king-sized bed with her back against the headboard and a pillow in her lap, thinking that, if nothing else happened, at least she'd leave the sheets and blankets smelling like her perfume.

Russell watched the movie. Zoe watched Russell, sneaking glances at his lips, the curls that brushed his collar, his faintly stubbled cheeks. She kept his cup full, and she waited. Waited until the movie ended and they'd moved on to *There's Something About Mary*. Waited, until Cam announced that he needed to call his girlfriend before she fell asleep, and went back to his room.

As soon as the door had closed, Russell got to his feet, yawning ostentatiously. "Whew! I'm beat. Maybe you should go."

Zoe had smiled at him, leaning back ever so slightly. Knowing how tuned in Russell was to sound, she made sure that he could hear her hair, moving gently against the pillow she'd tucked behind her head. "Maybe I should stay."

Russell looked at her for a moment, frowning faintly as he rubbed at his head. Zoe remembered what he'd told her once, somewhere in . . . Florida? Georgia? She remembered a haze drifting off the blacktop and palm trees outside the SUV's windows. They'd been chatting, and Zoe had asked what he'd been like in high school. He hadn't looked at her; he had paused, staring at his lap, and finally, he'd said, "More like Cassie than you." Zoe hadn't wanted to push him. But later, she'd asked Cam, who'd known Russell since his Sky King days, and Cam had gotten his girlfriend to send a copy of the *Rolling Stone* magazine that had featured that band to show her. Zoe remembered the picture of younger Russell: a chunky, block-shaped boy, draped in oversized black clothes, with curtains of dyed black hair obscuring his acne-studded cheeks.

He'd slimmed down since then. His hair was no longer shoe-polish black, and all that remained of the acne were a few faint scars. But his perception of himself had been shaped by those years, and Zoe suspected that not even his subsequent status as a musician had been enough to erase those ingrained insecurities. Girls might have laughed at him . . . or, maybe, he'd never even approached them, so they'd never had the chance. Russell had probably spent much of his life believing he'd never have a chance with someone like Zoe. Now that she was giving him that chance, she was hopeful he'd take it—that he'd grab onto it, and onto her, with both hands, and be grateful. And never let her go.

In the hotel room, Zoe smiled at him. She sat up slowly, smoothing her hair over her shoulders with both hands, hoping it looked soft in the low light, that he'd want to feel it under his fingers. She watched, pleased, as he licked his lips and shifted his weight.

"Look, Zoe. I think you're great. But you and me . . . it's not a good idea."

"Why not?"

He shook his head, looking stubborn and befuddled, adorably owlish. "We're collies," he said, thick-tongued. Zoe giggled. "Coll-eagues," he said, saying the word precisely. "We work together. S'not a good idea."

"It doesn't have to be anything serious," Zoe told him. "We can just fool around. I'm not a virgin, if that's what you're worried about."

He stared at her, then shook his head. "No . . . I . . ."

Zoe let her lip quiver. "Don't you like me?" she whispered.

"Of course I like you. You're great! But . . ."

This was a moment for actions, not words. Zoe rose up and walked, on her knees, to the edge of the bed, so that her face was level with Russell's face, her thighs and chest against his body. "Come on," she whispered, so close that her sweatshirt rubbed against his tee shirt, so close that she knew he could feel her breath on his lips. "Come on, I want you to."

She waited. When nothing happened, she leaned forward, closing the gap, pressing her mouth against Russell's. At first, the kiss was just as sweet as she'd thought it would be, warm and gentle and tender, almost chaste. But Zoe didn't want chaste. She tilted her head, sighing into his mouth, tracing his lower lip with the tip of her tongue. She could feel him struggling, trying to resist, until, with a groan that sounded almost pained, Russell yanked her against him, so that they were pressed together from shoulder to groin, and she could feel every inch of him. A sweet, throbbing ache gathered between her legs, and her clothes felt too heavy, too hot.

"Is this what you want?" Russell asked, his voice low and raspy. He slid his hands underneath her sweatshirt, gliding them over the smooth skin of her back.

"Yes," Zoe whispered, biting at his neck, licking his earlobe, gripping his shoulders, then his upper arms.

Russell kissed her hard, gripping her shoulders, sounding almost angry as he asked, again, "Is this what you want?" Zoe got off the bed and stood in front of him. She slipped off her sweatshirt and stepped out of her pajama bottoms and underwear. She watched his eyes get wide as he took her in: her body licked by the faint blue light of the screen; her nipples tightening in the cool air; the curves of her waist and her hips and her thighs. She watched him raise one hand, slowly, looking at it like it wasn't a part of him, like he didn't know what it would do, and held her breath until it settled on her waist, pulling her tightly against him. "Come on," she breathed in his ear. "Come on, I want you to." She took his other hand in hers and drew it down between her legs, hearing him inhale sharply, knowing that, once he'd touched her, it was over. She'd won.

When she'd made her plan, she'd imagined that everything would be gentle, sweet, and romantic. Russell would undress her slowly, kissing every inch of her, worshipping her with his hands and his tongue, telling her that she was beautiful, maybe, even saying that he loved her. The reality was Russell pressing his mouth to her neck, then her lips, then her chest, like there was a timer running somewhere and he had to get his lips against as much of her as possible as quickly as he could. It was Russell mashing his body against her, so that Zoe felt the press of buttons and zippers, everything hard and fast and urgent, like he was desperate to be inside of her. Or, maybe, Zoe would think later, like he was just desperate to have it be over.

He walked her back to the bed, urged her onto her back, then pulled his own pants down and knelt, rolling on the condom he'd produced from somewhere. *Yay, safe sex,* thought Zoe, whose own brain had gone a little fuzzy. When she took him inside her, she was completely naked, and Russell was still almost entirely clothed, and she wasn't thinking of how good it felt, or how much she loved him. *I won,* she was thinking, as Russell began to move, slowly at first, then faster, gripping her hard, sweating and panting, like his orgasm was something that was eluding him, something he had to hunt down and subdue. Possibly with a club. Zoe pushed her hips up to meet his. She pinched his nipple and felt him shudder, bit his neck and heard him groan.

It went on and on, with Russell getting sweatier, sounding more desperate, until Zoe's legs were cramping and she'd started to feel sore. Finally, he rolled off of her and lay on his back, panting. "Whiskey dick," he said, when he'd gathered enough breath to speak. "Or vodka, I guess. Sorry."

"It's okay." That ache was still there, heavy between her legs. Zoe wanted to be alone, back in her own bed, so she could finish herself, quietly, holding her breath so she wouldn't wake up her sister. "I've wanted you for such a long time."

"Zoe." He rolled onto his side. "This—you and me—it's not—we shouldn't—"

"Shh," she said, and pressed her finger against his lips. "Shh," she said, and stroked his hair gently, and lay with him until he'd fallen asleep, her body still tense and tingling with arousal, her skin unpleasantly sticky, her brain buzzing with triumph.

Cassie

The morning after the Dallas show, when Zoe came flouncing back to their room, with her hair tangled and suck marks on her neck, and announced that she and Russell were together, Cassie had kept her face expressionless and her voice steady, hoping she didn't look, or sound, like she was falling apart, like the world was ending, like her heart had shattered into jagged, glassy pieces inside of her. "Oh," she said. "Okay."

Zoe lifted an eyebrow. "'Okay'? That's all you've got?"

"Congratulations?" Cassie ventured. She tried to sound enthusiastic and sincere, tried to look happy. "That's great." She'd expected it, she told herself. She should not have been surprised, or hurt. She shouldn't feel anything at all . . . and now, she thought, she would have to be even more careful. If Zoe ever guessed how she felt about Russell, her sister would probably be kind and sweet. *Oh, Cassie. I'm so sorry. How can I help? What can I do?* The reality of Zoe and Russell as a couple was almost more than she could stand. Zoe's sympathy, on top of that, would kill her.

Her heart was broken, but the tour rolled on: Tulsa and Kansas City, Denver and Albuquerque, zigzagging around the country, driven less by geography and more by the whims of the record label and the radio stations. Cassie did her best not to look at Russell, not to stand too close onstage or sit with him in the van, to keep the focus solely on music when they were writing or performing together. If Zoe pitying her would be bad, she knew, then Russell's pity would be impossible to survive.

But it was hard. The best songs, the truest songs, were based on real emotions—on yearning, on loneliness, on feeling loved or brokenhearted, cherished or rejected. Cassie didn't know much about love, but she knew plenty about loneliness. Russell would probe, gently, carefully, for details. "Tell me about that," he'd say, when she'd recall some bit of personal history—being picked up from a field trip by Sasha Lowry's mom, watching Sasha and Zoe and Christina Tate and Meghan Moran squeeze themselves, giggling, into the car's back seat. Hearing Meghan hiss, "No, she's not invited!" as Zoe tried to shush her. The look on Mrs. Lowry's face when she'd patted the passenger's seat and said, kindly, "Cassie, why don't you come up here with me?"

"Girls are the worst," she'd said to Russell, trying to smile.

"Really? I'd have thought boys would be the worst." He was looking at her in a Mrs. Lowry kind of way, all kind and understanding, but with a sharp gleam of interest. Mrs. Lowry knew she'd be rid of Cassie within minutes, that her daughter's friend's weird, fat sister was an unpleasant and awkward task she'd get through and pass off to someone else. But Russell was stuck with her. He probably wasn't really interested, Cassie told herself fiercely. He was probably just pretending to care. It was confusing, because Russell gave every appearance of caring. If he was pretending, he did it well.

"No," Cassie said. "Boys are obvious. They just . . . you know." She ducked her head, not wanting to say what boys did, what boys had done to her. Russell waited. He waited for her to finish the thought, and, suddenly, Cassie felt a flare of anger. Not just anger, but fury. Why should she have to expose herself like this? Why should she have to display all her pain, so that he could set it to music, then go back to a hotel room and sleep with her sister?

Russell was looking at her kindly. Considerately. Like what she was saying mattered to him. "You know, you're not the only girl to go through something like that."

"No," Cassie said. "It just feels that way. Every time it happens." She thought about the summer camp her parents had sent her to, when she was twelve. They'd saved all year so that she and Zoe could go for a week, to the Poconos, had probably gotten financial aid too. "Have a wonderful time," Janice had said, kissing them both before they'd boarded the bus. And Zoe had. Cassie, not so much. No one had wanted to be her bunkmate, or her partner during swimming lessons; she'd eaten every meal at the end of the table, with only the counselor for company. She remembered one night, going back to the cabin to change her clothes and seeing a postcard, half-written, on a bunkmate's bed. *Camp is great accept for this one girl Cassie who is fat and weird. She is ANNOYING EVERYONE. We all HATE HER.*

Cassie held the postcard in her fingers for one long, frozen moment. *You spelled* except *wrong*, she thought about saying, or writing on the postcard, crossing out the misspelled word, writing the correct one in its stead. She thought about tearing the postcard into a hundred tiny pieces, or slapping the girl in her snub-nosed, freckled face, or telling her, *I can play the piano a thousand times better than you'll ever be able to do anything in your life.* She'd done none of those things. She'd set the postcard back on the bed where she'd found it. That was how it always went. No matter what happened, she'd just take it, like a whale being jabbed with a harpoon, over and over, until the water was dark with blood. She'd keep swimming, pretending that it didn't hurt.

In the hotel room, she looked at Russell, shrugging, and tried to sound blithe and unbothered. Normal. Like Zoe. "That's what the world does, I guess. It makes you feel like you're the only lonely girl."

Russell's eyes crinkled at the corners. His smile was brilliant, electric: a firelit room on a winter night, inviting her inside. "And that," he said, tapping her nose with his pen, "is a song."

She smiled, because he'd almost touched her, because it was impossible not to smile. Russell's joy was infectious; she couldn't resist. This, she understood, was how it would be: she'd peel back layers of her skin, she'd show him every shameful part of herself, and he'd use them. It would hurt. But Cassie was powerless to refuse him, incapable of telling him no. She loved him. She could deny him nothing.

The band went west. After New Mexico came Phoenix and Scottsdale. Then Las Vegas. Then, finally, Los Angeles. Three days into what was meant to be a weeklong stay, Jerry summoned them home. "The Gift" was starting to get some airplay, and the label wanted an album. Thanks to Cassie and Russell's diligence, they had plenty of material.

The plan was to record ten new songs, make a video for "The Gift," and shoot the album cover in New York, accomplishing the last two tasks in two days (and with only one bill for hair and makeup and wardrobe). The label had rented studio space in Queens, and a director and photographer were both standing by.

Zoe was overjoyed, jumping up and down on the hotel-room bed until the people in the room below them banged on the ceiling. She'd grabbed Cassie's hands, whirling her around the room, saying, "We're going to have a music video on MTV!" Cassie feigned happiness. She tried to find joy in her sister's joy, in Russell's satisfaction, but, mostly, she faked it. The idea of a video terrified her. The album was fine, she thought . . . but, mostly, what she liked was performing, with the footlights blinding her and her eyes closed and the crowd gone quiet to listen. *She is ANNOYING EVERYONE*, she'd think, sometimes, as an ovation rolled over her, people clapping and screaming and lining up to meet her after, like she was someone who mattered, not a joke or a nuisance. *We all HATE HER. Maybe I'll send that girl a postcard*, she would think. *Now that I am someone.* That thought was satisfying too.

They flew to New York on a red-eye. On Monday morning, at six A.M. sharp, a rented van fetched them at their Midtown Manhattan hotel and drove them to Queens. They crossed the 59th Street Bridge as the sun came up over the Hudson, drawing ribbons of mist up from the water. The studio was a sprawling, single-story building, with high ceilings, painted cinderblock walls, and concrete floors, a warren of dressing rooms and offices and huge, empty performance spaces.

Cassie and Zoe's dressing room had mirrors everywhere: waist-high makeup mirrors running the length of one wall, a three-way, full-length mirror with a kind of pedestal in front of it in the corner. There were two racks full of clothes for Zoe: diaphanous gowns, leather miniskirts, artfully ripped and faded jeans and white button-downs, a gold sequined blouse with a plunging neckline that made her look like a sexy disco ball. Zoe had squealed in pleasure, pushing her hands into the fabric, pulling out a violet-gray gown made of some airy, floaty fabric, saying, "Oh my God, is this the most beautiful thing you've ever seen?"

Cassie had inspected her rack, on which exactly two outfits had been hung. There was another black pantsuit, with an oversized jacket and a spray of sequins on the lapels—like that would help anything, Cassie thought—and a long-sleeved, shin-length dress made of thick jersey material, like a sweatshirt that had gotten ambitious. Instead of sequins on the lapels, this garment had rhinestones glued around the neckline. ("I'm sorry," the stylist would tell her, when they'd finally met. "There just weren't a lot of options." Cassie said she understood.)

In a conference room, where urns of hot water and coffee and platters of bagels and cut-up fruit had been arranged, Jerry and Helen from the label were waiting. They met the director, who showed them storyboards, explaining that the video would be about a couple breaking up at a high-school house party. The label had hired dozens of extras and had built a set—living room, dining room, kitchen, and den—to resemble the interior of a suburban house. Zoe would play the song's main character. An actor named Rick Jarvis had been cast to play the love interest.

"So I'm singing, while the party's going on around me?" Zoe asked. Her cheeks were pink, her eyes were bright, and she looked, Cassie had to concede, very pretty.

"That's right," replied the director, Luke Allston. Luke Allston was a middle-aged white guy with a narrow build, a bald head, and a pointy dark-brown goatee. He wore a wool beanie and heavy leather cuffs on both wrists, and he talked fast, his eyes darting around the room, never landing on Cassie. "Zoe, you and the boy show up at the party together, and then you catch him making out with another girl, and then there's kind of a dream sequence, where you're standing on the dining-room table, and you're singing while the party goes on around you."

"Got it," Zoe said with a crisp nod.

"The rest of the guys will be at the party, and then they'll be up there with you, playing their instruments. Or, you know, pretending to play their instruments."

"And what about Cassie?" Russell had been standing toward the back of the room while the director and his production assistant walked them through the storyboards.

Cassie saw dozens of heads—including her sister's—swing around, felt many eyes looking at her. She stared at the ground. She'd been half hoping, half fearing, that there wouldn't be a part for her at all. Maybe they'd tell her that she'd be playing the designated driver, and while the party was unfolding, she'd be sitting behind the wheel of a station wagon in the driveway outside, waiting to take Zoe home.

This turned out to be not far from the actual plan.

"So, Cass, what we're thinking for you is that you're at home, and at some point Zoe calls you—you know, to tell you what's going on." The director gave her a large and insincere smile. "We'll film you on the phone with her."

"So she's at the party and I'm at home?" It made a sad kind of sense, Cassie thought. She'd never been invited to parties when she'd actually been at high school. Why should she have expected to have been included in a pretend one?

"That's right. You're supporting her. It's going to look amazing. And it'll really fit with the message of the song! You know. Women, uh, supporting each other!" The director's voice had gotten high and hurried. Maybe he'd realized how stupid he'd sounded when he heard himself out loud.

"Quick question?" Russell raised a finger. "You know Cassie sings lead vocals, right? So you're asking Zoe to lip-synch Cassie's parts? And you're not going to show Cassie singing at all?"

Cassie saw her sister's body stiffen, saw Zoe stare at Russell, tight-lipped and panicky. Russell ignored Zoe. He was looking at her instead. "It's okay," she said softly. Russell's eyes widened, and Cassie knew what he was thinking: *Why are you letting them do this to you?*

She tried, as hard as she could, to use her own eyes and face to communicate that she didn't mind—that it would be better this way. She had no desire to be on camera. She could handle attention when she was performing, behind her piano, or standing at the microphone with her eyes closed and her sister and Russell nearby, but the idea of being in a video, her face and her body on television, to be judged and analyzed and mocked, compared to her sister and found wanting, made her stomach lurch and her skin feel clammy. It would be like every rejection, every instance of mockery she'd described to Russell: the parties she hadn't been invited to; the lunches she'd eaten alone, in the handicapped stall of the girls' room; the time in eighth grade she'd opened her locker to find that someone had taped a *Free Willy* poster inside. It would be all of that, multiplied, made global, because MTV was all over the world. She held her breath until finally Russell gave a small, defeated nod, paired with a shrug. *Okay, if that's what you want,* he seemed to say, and Cassie nodded, almost faint with relief that she wouldn't have to be on TV, that no one would see her . . . and that Russell had stood up for her, arguing her case.

Back in the dressing room, Cassie sat in the mirror's unforgiving light, with the hairstylist clipping hanks of fake hair against her scalp, and the makeup artist using bronzer and contouring powder to essentially draw a new face on top of the face she already had. At the neighboring mirror, the stylist was cooing over Zoe, holding up gowns for her approval: "Cindy Crawford wore this six months ago on the cover of *Vogue,* so you're the second celebrity to wear it."

Zoe sighed happily. Cassie could picture the look on her sister's face, could imagine Zoe mouthing the word *celebrity* to herself, and suddenly, Cassie couldn't hold still.

"Excuse me," she muttered to the hair and makeup ladies. She unsnapped her tentlike smock and hurried off down the hall, feeling her thighs wobble, her breasts jiggle, every despised ounce of her body. She felt monstrous. Enormous. And, worse, she realized, halfway down the featureless white hallway, lined with framed photographs of bands that had shot their videos here and supermodels who'd posed for magazine covers, that she had no idea where the bathroom was. She walked aimlessly until she heard familiar voices, coming through a mostly closed door.

"What's going on with you and Zoe?" Jerry asked in his nasal, New York–accented voice. Cassie stopped, holding her breath.

"It's no big deal," Russell had said.

Cassie felt hope spreading inside of her, like ink coloring a glass of water. Hope, and relief, at the words *no big deal.*

Jerry's voice got louder. "It better not be. Because if you break her heart . . . if she leaves the band and goes running home to Mommy and Daddy . . ."

"That won't happen. It's just a crush," Russell had said. He didn't sound angry, but he must have looked that way, because Jerry said, "Calm down!"

"I am calm," Russell said.

Jerry's words came more slowly, his tone growing speculative. "It's good, though. Everyone loves a happy couple."

"Sure," Russell said. His voice was flat. "But, listen. If there's anyone the band can't do without, it's Cassie. Not Zoe. You know that, right?"

Pleasure, hot and shocking, had bloomed in Cassie's chest, warming her face, making her heart pound, making her glow right down to her fingertips. Russell thought she was essential. Russell thought she mattered. She should have left right there, to savor the compliment in private, to tend her new crop of hope, those fresh green shoots that had sprouted in the soil of her imagination, no matter how much poison she'd dumped on the ground. But before she could move, Jerry spoke up again.

"Can't they do anything with her?" he asked, low and angry.

"I don't know what you mean," Russell said.

"Yeah, you do," Jerry said. He sighed. "Why is it that the pretty ones can hardly ever sing? And the ones who can sing have to look like that?"

Cassie had gasped, like something had stung her. She'd hurried away, head down, cheeks flaming, a sick feeling spreading in her belly, all of her fresh pleasure erased by fresher shame. Back in the dressing room, she flung herself down in the chair. Zoe had stared at her curiously, and the makeup artist had dabbed sweat off her brow and upper lip, making Cassie feel even bigger, even more disgusting. She tried to push out of her mind what Jerry had said and focus on Russell's praise. *If there's anyone the band can't do without, it's Cassie.* She'd tucked those words away, like strands of hair in a locket—a treasure, to get her through hard times; a keepsake, to be taken out and admired when she was alone.

Cassie was barely in the video, which meant, for most of the shoot's first day, she just hung around the perimeter of the stage, in what they told her was called video village, watching on monitors as the story unfolded. She watched Zoe in an evening gown with her hair up; Zoe in jeans with her hair down; Zoe pretending to slurp a Jell-O shot, to kiss a boy, to cry in a bathroom. She watched Zoe lip-synch the lyrics Cassie and Russell had written and sung and tried to tell herself that she understood why it had to be this way, that she didn't mind. The truth made her feel like she'd swallowed a broken mirror, like every inhalation cut her open from the inside. She was envious and ashamed. Everything hurt.

Finally, it was time to shoot her scene. She emerged from the dressing room wearing the pantsuit with its stupid sequins, feeling like she must have looked like Zoe's high school principal, or, worse, like somebody's mom, and found Russell waiting by the door. Before she could say anything, he took her hand and pulled her into his dressing room, a smaller, but just as amply mirrored, version of Cassie and Zoe's room. He leaned against the counter and looked at her, frowning, his eyebrows drawn together, mouth pressed into a thin line.

"If you're not okay with this, I'll say something to Jerry."

Cassie shook her head. "It's fine."

"No," he said. "It's really not." Russell was wearing a denim jacket, a tee shirt, a pair of darker jeans. He had fewer costume changes than Zoe, who had, Cassie thought, six in all. This was his partygoer outfit. Later, he'd wear a leather jacket, for the dream-sequence scene, where he played with the band. She could see powder on his skin, and his hair had been styled into neater curls than normal, and it smelled of some unfamiliar product. Which made her realize, with some surprise, that she knew the usual scent of his hair . . . along with its exact shade, and the precise color of his eyes, light brown backed by gold, like strong tea sweetened with honey.

"I don't like attention," Cassie said.

"It doesn't matter," said Russell. "You deserve to be a bigger part of this. You're the one who sang the song. You're the one who wrote it."

"We wrote it together," Cassie said.

Russell nodded, looking troubled. "This feels . . ." He waved his hand toward the soundstage. "I don't know. Like a lie."

"I feel like Zoe's doing me a favor." That was the truth, Cassie thought. Or a true thing, if not the entire truth about how she felt. "I didn't go to a lot of parties in high school." She cleared her throat and tried to put her hands in the pockets of her suit jacket, only they'd been sewn shut. Because of course they had. "Did you?" She realized, with a hot, stinging, sudden guilt, that, as much as Russell knew about her adolescence, her high-school years, she'd hardly asked him a single question. What was wrong with her? Why did everyone else know how to do this, why had they all been born knowing how to do the give-and-take dance of a conversation, and she had not?

Russell smiled a little. "When I was in high school, I was pretty shy. So no. Not a lot of parties. Until I was in my first band. And then . . ." His smile widened. "When I was playing for people, I'd be crazy nervous at first. Like, convinced-I-was-going-to-throw-up-level nervous. But that stopped as soon as I started playing. It felt like I could be there but invisible at the same time. Like being a part of things but separate from them too." He shook his head. "I'm not explaining it very well."

"No," said Cassie. "No, I understand." His face was so soft, his eyes so attentive. "I get it."

"I know you do," said Russell. His voice was low and warm, and Cassie was suddenly aware that they were in a very small room, alone, together, where the air felt a few degrees warmer than the air everywhere else.

She groped for another question, suddenly self-conscious again. Over the past weeks, she'd gotten comfortable with talking to him. She could make eye contact, even initiate a conversation. Now all the ease she'd felt was gone, and Cassie was just as awkward as ever. "Do you still get nervous?" she asked. Blurted, really. *There*, she thought. That was a good thing to ask . . . even if it was something a normal person would already know about their bandmate. Their friend.

Russell nodded. "Oh, yeah," he said. "It's not as bad as it was, but it's still there." He smiled a little. "Have you ever noticed that I don't eat anything before the shows?"

Cassie thought. She remembered Cam eating pineapple (the better to turn the pineapple's rind into a bong), and CJ, their manager, devouring pizza, folding the slices in half in order to fit more of them into his mouth faster. Even Zoe would nibble at vending-machine crackers or at the fruit-and-cheese plates that had started arriving in the greenroom before their most recent shows (Russell, his voice unusually cynical, had explained that you could always tell where you were on the charts, and in your label's estimation, by the quality of the food your label sent).

"Why did you agree to join the band, then?" Cassie asked. "If you get so nervous? You could have just written songs." She felt her face flush and her chest tighten as soon as she'd asked it, thinking that it made her sound like she didn't want him in the band. But Russell did not seem offended. He was looking at her with an expression Cassie couldn't decipher, a patient, soft-eyed kind of look.

"Don't you know?"

She shook her head, feeling embarrassed. It was probably something obvious, something like, *I fell in love with your sister the minute I saw her,* and *I can't stand to be away from Zoe for more than a day.* Something he'd said already—maybe even in an interview!—that Cassie, stupid and oblivious lump that she was, had failed to remember. But Russell was smiling, smiling right at her, and her stomach was doing something strange and swoopy in her midsection, and her heart felt like a tiny bird cupped in someone's hand.

"At first, all I was going to do was help you write a song," he said. "I knew Jerry wanted me in the band—because you guys were so young,

I think, and I had a little bit of experience—but I told him I wasn't interested. I liked writing songs a lot better than getting up in front of a crowd and playing them. And then I heard you sing." His face was sweet and guileless, his eyes clear, like she was seeing him the way he'd looked as a little kid. "I'd never heard a voice like yours."

Cassie's mouth was very dry. Her face was hot, and her pulse thrummed in her neck and her wrists. Part of her wanted Zoe to appear, to help her make sense of this, to tell her where to stand, what to do with her hands and her body, to help her decide what to say. Another part of her thought she'd claw her sister's eyes out if Zoe dared to open the door.

Russell was still looking at her, like she was a revelation, or a puzzle he'd solved. A gift.

"You really don't know," he said, speaking as much to himself as to her. "Having you sing my songs—it's like, if I came up with a recipe and got Gordon Ramsay to cook it. Or if I wrote a play and got, like, Robert Redford to act." His hands were swooping through the air, and he was smiling. "I've never been so productive; I've never had so many ideas." He closed his mouth, going suddenly silent, looking a little abashed. Cassie could recognize that easily enough. So often, it was how she felt. "You're my muse, I guess."

His muse. Cassie did not know what to say to that. She wasn't sure she even remembered how talking happened, how tongue and teeth and breath and palate worked together to form words, how words conveyed thought. Her mind had gone silent. There was no more ceaseless, anxious chattering, no more hectoring voice that said *You're doing it wrong.* She could hear crowds of extras in the hallway, an assistant director calling out instructions in a loud, droning voice—"You, striped shirt, lose the gum; no cell phones, no cameras, if I catch anyone with a camera, you'll be asked to leave"—and, more faintly, four bars of "The Gift," playing over and over and over—*and I know / even so / if you say yes, I won't say no.* She could picture the scene. Zoe would be up on the kitchen table, in that silvery, airy ball gown, pretending to sing Cassie's lyrics, while kids danced and drank beers all around her. She'd be so beautiful.

Russell touched her arm and looked at her expectantly. Obviously, he'd just asked her something. She had no idea what. "I'm sorry. What did you say?"

"I asked if you had AIM. You know—the messaging thing, on your computer?"

"Oh—I . . ." Did she? She thought that Zoe did, but Cassie wasn't sure whether she, herself, had it or not.

"Tell you what," Russell said. "When we finish up tonight, I'm going to send you the lyrics for that song I've been playing with. 'Carry You Through.' Read them tonight and tell me what you think." He raised his eyebrows at the noise outside. "Assuming we survive this."

Cassie nodded, weak-kneed with gratitude that Russell had sensed her difficulty and had found a solution, a way for them to communicate that she could manage. A PA knocked on the door and, at Russell's "Come in," stuck her head into the dressing room.

"Russell? They need you on set."

"Gotta go." He smiled at Cassie. "I'll write."

Cassie nodded again. And then he was gone, leaving her alone in a room full of mirrors and her own reflection all around her: big and ungainly, unlovely and unlovable.

Russell sent her the first message that night, and Cassie had gone running to her laptop when it pinged, her hands a little unsteady as she opened the screen. There'd been the lyrics, as promised, and then a note. *I can tell it freaks you out when I talk about how talented you are, so I promise not to do it anymore. Just take my word for it—you're amazing. And when this album comes out, you're going to be famous. People are going to love you. I hope you can be proud of yourself, or enjoy this, even a little bit.*

All those years later, she could still recall every word he'd written. *People are going to love you.* She'd wanted to ask if he was included in people, if there was a world where he could love her, even platonically.

Talent is just luck, she'd written instead, after spending half an hour composing and discarding drafts and forcing herself to wait until morning before hitting send. *You don't ask to be born with a good voice or a pretty face. It's just something that happens. Maybe that's why it's hard for me to enjoy this. I don't feel like I've earned it.*

Russell had written back right away. *You work as hard as anyone I've ever met. And if you're implying that you don't deserve to be talented, I disagree. No one deserves this more than you.*

She should have stopped it then. Maybe it wouldn't have been too late. If he'd never sent that first message, or if she'd never written him back. If she hadn't let him pull her into his dressing room to say what he'd said. If she hadn't started to understand that it was his words, backstage, before the shows, that had started to matter; his words, and not Zoe's, that allowed her to get through the shows. There'd been chance after chance, dozens of moments where she could look back and think, *If I'd stopped it then, if I'd done this, if I hadn't done that, everything would have been different.* But she hadn't stopped it. She and Russell had exchanged messages, and onstage smiles, and Zoe didn't know about the first thing and didn't seem bothered by the second. Cassie was stung by her sister's indifference, annoyed by the idea that Zoe didn't even seem to consider the possibility of Cassie as a rival or a threat. For so long, Cassie had needed her sister, but, in this world, it was the other way around. In this word, Zoe needed her, and Zoe didn't see it.

But Russell saw.

You have a gift, Russell would tell her over and over, his eyes sincere, his voice warm. *You make people feel less alone. This is what you were born to do.* And she'd believed him. Standing onstage, hearing girls singing along with her, felt better than anything she could have imagined. Like she was a little kid, putting a quarter in the gumball machine outside the grocery store, turning the handle, and, instead of just one piece of gum, having all the candy, red and blue and yellow and green, every bit of sweetness in the world come pouring out into her hands. It was as unexpected as it was thrilling—this idea that her music was doing something that mattered, that Russell was there to encourage her and tell her she was worthy of every good thing.

She should have known not to trust something that wonderful.

Part Four

Sheryl Crow continued her world tour last night at Philadelphia's Mann Center and, as expected, she delighted the sellout crowd, who came out to the lawn on a perfect June night to hear Crow sing under the stars. Crow was in fine voice as she ran through her catalogue of hits, from the wistful anthem "Leaving Las Vegas" to the sunny, danceable "All I Wanna Do" and "Soak Up the Sun." It was exactly what the audience had come for, everything fun and familiar; summer vacation in a ninety-minute set.

There was, however, a surprise on the menu, in the form of Crow's opening act, a band called the Griffin Sisters, fronted by two—you guessed it—sisters who grew up in Fishtown. The band's sound walks the line between pop and rock, grounded by the capable musicianship of bass player Cam Gratz, drummer Tommy Kelleher, backup vocalist Zoe Griffin, and, especially, the fiery lead-guitar work of Russell D'Angelo. But the secret sauce is lead vocalist and keyboard player Cassie Griffin, who studied classical music at the Curtis Institute before rock and roll came calling. Griffin's voice is a wonder, a flexible, octave-spanning marvel that left the crowd—including Crow, who joined the band for an encore—enthralled. Griffin's airy high notes are sweet as cotton candy; her growly low notes are sexy, soulful, bone-shaking thunder. On Friday, the band played original tunes from their debut EP, plus a handful of covers. From the elegiac lament "Last Night in Fishtown" to the peppy, poppy "Flavor of the Week," from the country twang of "Coat of Many Colors," a song made famous by Dolly Parton, to the Alanis Morissette–influenced breakup anthem "The Gift," Cassie Griffin's voice was a revelation. Whenever she sang, she had the crowd in her hand.

You can hear an encyclopedia's worth of references in Griffin's singing: Aretha's vibrato; Mariah's melisma; the powder-puff, featherlight sweetness of Go-Go's; the ironic, cool-girl remove of the Pretenders or Liz Phair; the raspy rocker-chick of Heart . . . but Griffin has a sound all her own. That she's young (just twenty) and credited or co-credited for all three of the songs the band has released only adds to the impressive package.

While Griffin's voice calls to mind a panoply of pop-rock divas, Griffin's look echoes Mama Cass. But Mama Cass was an exuberant dancer, joyous and unabashed in her body, while this Cass, so far, seems uncomfortable in the spotlight. At the Mann, she barricaded herself behind her piano and seemed happy to cede the spotlight, content to let her sister dance and D'Angelo bend heroically over his guitar.

But dance moves can be learned. Confidence can be gained. A voice like Cassie Griffin's is a gift from the pop gods. She's lucky to have it. We're lucky to have her.

"Flavor of the Week" is already climbing the pop charts. Look for the Griffin Sisters to make themselves at home there in the months and years to come.

SHERYL CROW REVIEW
Philadelphia Inquirer, 2003

Cherry

ALASKA, 2024

"N up," said the guy behind the deli counter. He had a hairnet on his shoulder-length hair and a smaller net corralling a chest-length beard. In his white coat, he looked only slightly less substantial than the mountains Cherry had spent most of her drive staring at. He'd barely even glanced at her flyer before shaking his head. "Never seen her."

"Do you know who she is?" Cherry figured her best bet was to start where she knew for sure Cassie had been, and so she'd gone directly from the airport to the Safeway in Homer, without even checking into her hotel.

"Nup." The man's mouth was mostly obscured by the tangle of facial hair.

"Is there a manager I could speak to? Or someone else? Maybe people who work different shifts?" *Someone who doesn't talk like they're being charged by the syllable?*

The mountainous man shrugged without offering any more information. Cherry bit back a sigh and turned off her phone's camera. No point in getting this man to sign a release either. Nobody would ever want this footage.

Deep breath, she told herself. Start again. "Is there a manager in the store?"

"Nup."

"When will a manager be here?"

"Try tomorrow."

"Okay." Cherry walked up and down each aisle, just in case, then plodded, shivering, back to her car. The cold seeping up from the pavement went right through the soles of her sneakers, and she could already tell that the jacket she'd bought was not going to keep her warm. It was just after six o'clock. She was hungry and tired, after hours of driving with her hands tight on the wheel, eyes darting left and right. The signs along the road had warned about moose in the vicinity; she knew there were bears too. And maybe she'd see Aunt Cassie, out for a late-night stroll. Wouldn't that be lucky?

Her hotel, the Land's End Resort, was on the Homer Spit, a skinny stretch of land that reached out into the water, with a two-lane road running its length. Cherry pegged it as the touristy part of town as she cruised past the tee shirt shops, the outfitters advertising fishing trips and guided hikes and bear- and whale-watching excursions. There were restaurants offering fresh salmon and fried halibut, along with ice cream and burritos. A chilly wind ruffled the water behind them, the gleaming expanse of white and gray that Cherry knew from her time with the maps had to be Kachemak Bay. She followed the road, driving slowly, eyeing the people and the shops, thinking that this was the last place she'd ever find Cassie.

In the lobby of the Land's End Resort, Cherry gave the clerk her name, a flyer, and a hopeful smile. "Have you seen this woman anywhere?"

"No," said the girl, whose name tag read "Aline." "But I love *Evermore*, and I'm a huge Griffin Sisters fan." Aline was about Cassie's age, with pale skin, a mass of light-brown curls pulled up in a messy bun, and a ring through her lower lip. Aline looked at the flyer, then leaned over the counter. "Do you really think Cassie Griffin's here? In Homer?"

"I don't know. There was a video that's been going around, and it looked like she was in the Safeway in town." Cherry took out her phone and showed her the video she'd saved on it.

Aline looked impressed. "Wow. Yeah, that definitely looks like our Safeway." She toyed with her lip ring. "Although I guess every Safeway kind of looks the same."

Not helping, Cherry thought. "If you were trying to find her, what would you do? Where would you start?"

Aline looked thoughtful. "That's the problem. You know what they say about Alaska, if you're a single gal? 'The odds are good, but the goods are odd.'"

"Ha," Cherry said.

"They say there are people who come here because they got lost, and people who come here to get lost," Aline continued. "And most of them aren't interested in being found." She smiled kindly. "I guess I'd start by putting some of those flyers up along the spit. Can't hurt, right?"

"Can't hurt." Cherry towed her suitcase to her room and set it on the bed, not bothering to unpack or even unzip her coat. She used the bathroom, washed her face, took a stack of flyers, and went back outside. She bought a bowl of chowder at Captain Pattie's Fish Fry and then, for the next two hours, stopped into restaurants and campgrounds, outfitters and clothing stores, handing out her flyers, showing them to hostesses and clerks and ice-cream scoopers, asking if she could stick them on their bulletin boards, if they had them, asking the same question. *Seen her?*

Nobody had.

At six o'clock the next morning, yawning and bleary-eyed, Cherry went back into Safeway. This time, there was a tiny, white-haired woman behind the deli counter.

"Help you?" she asked.

Cherry made herself smile as she extended the flyer. "Hi. My name is Cherry Rohrbach. I saw a video of this woman singing here. I'm trying to find her."

"Oh. Her." The woman's name tag read "Marcia." As she looked at the flyer, her face did something complicated—eyebrows up, lips pressed in a tight line. Regret? Embarrassment? The remembered thrill of a celebrity close encounter?

"Do you know her?" Cherry asked.

The woman nodded. "She does her shopping here."

Cherry's heartbeat quickened. "Do you know where she lives?"

Marcia shook her head. "I haven't seen her in a while. I don't even know her last name."

"It's Griffin. Cassie Griffin. Does she come here a lot?"

"She—well." The woman dropped her voice. "She used to be in here every few weeks or so. But I haven't seen her since . . ."

"She sang here, didn't she? 'Silent Night'?"

"I don't think I'm supposed to talk about it." Marcia stood on her tiptoes to lean across the counter. "I got a scary letter from a law firm after I posted a video on my Facebook page."

Cherry's heart was beating so hard, she could feel her rib cage throb, as Marcia looked down at the flyer again.

"She was in a band? Well, that makes sense. I have never heard anything like her singing in my life. It was . . ." Her voice trailed off.

Cherry nodded. "She's my aunt," she said, surprising herself. She hadn't meant to lead with that—had intended to talk about *The Next Stage*, and the mentorship, and her own ambitions—but, somehow, that was what had fallen out of her mouth.

"Lucky you," said Marcia.

"Lucky me," Cherry agreed. Feeling desperate for even the tiniest crumb of information, she asked, "What does she buy when she's in here?"

Marcia shrugged. "Just regular things. Food. Dog food. Cleaning supplies. Lots of cleaning supplies. Bottles of shampoo, bars of soap . . ."

A glimmer of an idea was beginning to form. After the auditions in Los Angeles, Cherry had to wait almost a month before learning whether she'd made it to the next round. Instead of going home, she'd found a room for rent in West Hollywood and had gotten a job cleaning at a fancy hotel in Beverly Hills. She remembered pushing a cart full of towels and tiny bars of soap and miniature bottles of lotion. A single person wouldn't need to replenish those supplies regularly, but someone who owned a cleaning service or was in charge of stocking hotel rooms or rental properties would.

"Thank you," Cherry said, then pointed toward the bulletin board near the entrance. "Is it okay if I put a flyer up?"

"That's fine," Marcia said. Her expression was sympathetic. *Don't get your hopes up*, it said.

Back in her hotel room, Cherry called her friend Tova. Tova was her bandmate Darren's older sister. She was a bartender, in her second year of law school at Temple, and a true-crime podcast addict. She knew things. If she couldn't give Cherry an answer, she'd at least know who to ask.

"Start with town hall," said Tova. "Or city government offices. Property transactions are public record. If she bought a house, or a piece of land, there will be records."

"Okay," Cherry said, taking notes. The phone was on speaker mode, lying on her bed. "So I just go to city hall and ask—"

"There's probably a form you've got to fill out," Tova said.

"Okay. So I fill out a form and say, 'I'm looking for the records of any property purchased by Cassie Griffin in' . . ." Cherry thought for a minute. The band had broken up in 2003. But would Cassie have gone immediately to Alaska? Cherry wasn't sure, but she thought there might have been intermediate stops, before Cassie had washed up here, at the end of the earth. "How long of a time period will they let me search? And are they going to be able to give me an answer right away?"

"Depends. Everything should be online, but how long it takes is going to depend on whether you get a friendly clerk who isn't too busy, or whether you've got someone who's underpaid and miserable and trying to take out their misery on everyone else." From her friend's tone, Cherry guessed that the second scenario was much more likely than the first. "Also," Tova continued, "Cassie might have set up a trust to buy property."

"A trust?"

"Like, an institution, with a different name than an individual. Lots of rich people do that, to obscure where they're living or how much they paid."

"So then what do I do if she's got a trust?"

"Hope you get lucky," Tova said. "Hope that she didn't just call it Anonymous Trust. That maybe it's, like, the Griffin Sisters Trust."

Cherry frowned. If Cass was determined to stay hidden, it wasn't likely she'd choose so obvious a name.

"Try to narrow it down to the time frame you think she might have ended up in Alaska," Tova said.

Which could have been anywhere from two months ago, when the video had been filmed, to twenty years ago, Cherry thought, as her heart sank even further. But Tova was encouraging.

"You've got some idea of where she might have bought, and some idea of when," she said. "That's at least a start."

And then what? Cherry thought, as she trudged back to her car. *Assuming I manage to figure out where she is, assuming I can find her, what if she won't talk to me? Or if she doesn't want to help?*

I have to try, she told herself. She started the car and let her phone's map guide her to the office of the city clerk on East Pioneer Avenue.

That was where she got her next piece of luck.

"So you don't know when the property was purchased." The clerk, who'd introduced herself as Fran, was a middle-aged white lady, with a middle-aged white-lady haircut (a chin-length bob) and a swipe of middle-aged white-lady lipstick (coral pink) on her lips. Cherry had not been immediately encouraged by the sight of her, but Fran had agreed to being filmed, looking flattered instead of freaked out when Cherry had asked.

Cherry decided not to say *I don't even know if there is a property*. Instead, she said, "My best guess is 2004 or 2005." That meant Cassie would have come to Alaska relatively soon, but not immediately after the band's dissolution, the scenario that Cherry had decided made the most sense. Alaska felt like a last resort, not a first stop, and Cassie had grown up as a city girl. She would have tried other places before coming here, to the ends of the earth, to hide in the cold and the dark.

Fran clicked her tongue against the roof of her mouth and slid a piece of paper across her desk. "Fill this out."

Cherry looked down at the form, her eyes drawn immediately to the line that read *the City Clerk's office shall respond within ten (10) working days.* Shit.

"Listen," she said, speaking rapidly. "Here's the deal. I'm in Alaska for five more days. I'm on a reality show?"

Fran raised her plucked eyebrows. "Is it one of those dating shows? They filmed one of those here once, you know." Fran's face softened as she smiled a little. *"Looking for Love: Bachelorettes in Alaska.* You probably didn't see it."

Cherry shook her head. "My show is a talent competition. *The Next Stage?"*

"Oh, I know that one." Fran looked Cherry over, with a fresh level of scrutiny. "Are you any good?"

"I am," said Cherry. No point in being coy. "And here's the thing. I made it to the final round, and I have to find Cassie Griffin and ask her to be my mentor. She was in this band . . ."

"The Griffin Sisters!" As she spoke the band's name, Fran's entire demeanor changed. Her voice got higher, her eyes went wide, and her lips curved into a wide and entirely genuine smile. "Oh God, I loved their music so much. I saw them in concert, at the Nectar Lounge in Seattle!" Lost in reverie, Fran looked younger, and happy. "So that's who you're looking for? Does Cassie Griffin live here?"

"Here, or nearby." Cherry took her phone out of her pocket. She pulled up the video and showed it to Fran, who said, immediately, "Yep. That's her. Nobody else in the world sounds like that."

"I know, right!" Cherry held the older woman's gaze. "I want her to be my mentor. I want her to sing again."

Fran appeared to be thinking, before she nodded. "Let me take a look."

It turned out that an entity called CSG Trust had purchased a fifty-acre parcel of land in 2004. Cherry did not know Cassie's middle name, but the C and the G both worked. So did the timing. "It's zoned residential," Fran said. "So she could have built a house, or rental cabins."

Cherry considered asking Fran to make a copy of the document, decided not to push her luck, and instead took a photo with her phone. "How do I get there?"

Fran pulled out a map and a Sharpie. "Follow Pioneer Avenue to Sterling Highway, like you're heading out of town. You're going to pass a weed shop, then a mead shop and a used bookstore, and then, um, another weed shop, and right after you see a sign for the Diamond Ridge Road, turn here." Fran tapped with her pen. "Follow it west for five or six miles. That should bring you to the property line." She gave Cherry a level look. "One more thing. You should know that a lot of people in Alaska have guns. For hunting and home protection. One of my neighbors shot a bear in his backyard last year."

Cherry must have looked horrified. Fran shrugged. "The bear was trying to eat his dog. He had every right."

Jesus, thought Cherry. "I'll be careful. I promise."

"Good luck."

Cherry thanked Fran profusely. She hurried out of the building, then remembered to go back and set her phone on a ledge so she could film herself hurrying out of the building, with a smile on her face and a map clutched triumphantly in her hand. She trotted to her car and peeled out of the parking lot, murmuring, "Pioneer Avenue to Sterling Highway," imagining what she'd do if she actually saw Cassie Griffin, her musical idol, her aunt, her mother's sister, in person. Would she scream? Faint? Have a heart attack and die right on the spot, in the snow?

Keep it together, she told herself as she drove. The highway became a two-lane road, which turned into a gravel road that devolved into a rutted dirt path that went more and more deeply into the forest. Cherry inched along, sending strength to the car's suspension, easing between the encroaching bushes and branches, over the ruts, until she saw a wooden arrow that bore the painted words "Cozy Cabins."

"Thank God," Cherry whispered, and drove on. The road smoothed out—it was still unpaved, but it was wider and flatter, and someone had cut back the brush and filled in the worst of the ruts with gravel. She inched forward until she saw another arrow-shaped sign with the number "1" on it pointing left, to a fork in the road. A second, matching sign that read "2" pointed to the right. The road kept going, and Cherry kept driving, gripping the wheel tightly, following the path, which ended, as she'd hoped it would, in front of a tiny house, barely bigger than a prefab garden shed, raised up on stilts so that its windows looked out over the tree line. A flight of wooden stairs led to its front door. Parked underneath it was a smallish black SUV with an Alaska license plate. There were two narrow windows along the long side of the house, and one beside the door. All three had their curtains drawn. Still, Cherry had an uneasy sensation of being watched.

Okay. Here we go. Cherry executed a clumsy K-turn, so that the car's nose was facing the road, thinking that the noise of the engine would alert whoever was inside the house to her presence. Thinking, too, that if she needed to make a quick getaway, having the rental car heading in the right direction would help.

Cherry got out of the car, closed the door, and briefly considered her reflection in the car's windows: jeans more or less clean, hair in reasonable order. She walked up the stairs. When she'd reached the top, she opened her phone's camera app and set the phone on the railing behind her, angling it to catch the action. She hit record, and started knocking.

She rapped at the door a solid thirty seconds. No one answered.

"Hello?" Cherry called, and started knocking again. When she stopped, she heard a dog's high-pitched yip. She'd raised her fist to resume her banging when the door swung open. A woman stood in the house's dim interior. She wore a bulky black parka with the hood pulled up, concealing her face. A little dog was at her side. There was a rifle in her hands, its stock pressed against her shoulder, its barrel pointing right at Cherry's face.

Zoe
PHILADELPHIA, 2024

Zoe knocked at the door, a half dozen hard raps of her fist. When no one answered, she counted slowly to ten, then started to knock again, thinking she'd stand out here for as long as she had to, that she'd knock until her hands fell off, if that was what it took. For twenty years, she'd kept quiet. She'd stuck to the script, the handful of lines she'd memorized: *Russell D'Angelo was the love of my life.* She'd told everyone that Russell's death was a tragedy, a terrible accident, that Cassie's disappearance was just as sad but, also, nothing to do with her. Now that she'd finally decided to tell the truth, she felt like a kettle on the verge of boiling over. She thought that if she couldn't start talking soon, if she didn't get the truth out, she'd explode.

That morning, Zoe had been scrolling through Instagram, when a *People* magazine headline caught her eye: The Next Stage *announces the new season's big twist: mentors. The long-running top-rated reality singing competition will pair competitors with big names in the music business who will coach them and perform with them in the season finale.* Zoe felt the hairs at the back of her neck quiver, saw goose bumps bristle on her forearms. She knew what Cherry had run from . . . and now the realization of what her daughter might have run toward landed in her brain with a resolute thump.

Cherry was an avid viewer of all the singing shows: *American Idol, America's Got Talent, X Factor,* and, her favorite, *The Next Stage.* For years, she'd begged Zoe for permission to compete. Zoe had always told her no. But now Cherry was eighteen. She didn't need permission.

And if she'd picked *The Next Stage* and made it past the first rounds, which seemed at least possible, the only mentor she'd want would be Cassie.

Zoe started knocking again, letting herself imagine the scene: Cherry finding Cassie somewhere; Cherry asking questions and telling her aunt about everything Cassie had missed. Cassie, head cocked in silence, listening to what would surely be a less-than-generous assessment of Zoe's life and her choices. It made Zoe feel panicky and desperate. She knocked harder and harder, until she finally heard an annoyed-sounding "Hang on!" Zoe pictured Bess using her four-pronged cane to push herself up from the ancient La-Z-Boy recliner, patched with duct tape, that she refused to get rid of. The door swung open, and there was Bess. Her hair was dyed its familiar brick-red shade; the jammy coating of red lipstick on her lips and the scuffed slippers on her feet were all the same. Bess's ankles were swollen. Her hair was white at the roots. Her expression was unreadable; her gaze was as sharp as ever as she studied Zoe's face. "Hello, Zoe. What's wrong?"

Cassie had always been Bess's favorite. In the real world, Zoe was adored and Cassie was barely tolerated, but in Bess's rowhouse, Cassie was doted on, coddled and cosseted and endlessly admired. Aunt Bess had even gotten an upright piano from an elderly neighbor who was emptying his house, en route to assisted living, so Cassie could practice and play. *Your sister is a miracle,* Aunt Bess used to tell Zoe, who didn't want to hear it—not the music or the praise. *You're lucky to have a sister like that.*

After the band's collapse and Zoe's return, her parents had welcomed her back. Maybe not with open arms, but they'd taken her in, and they'd let her stay, and they'd loved her, and Cherry, as well as they could. Not Bess. She'd been cool, watchful and skeptical, and persistent, asking Zoe questions that Zoe had not wanted to answer. At first Zoe had avoided Bess, barely saying hello to her at family gatherings, declining her invitations, but, eventually, she'd needed childcare, and whatever animus Bess bore toward her, it had never extended to Cherry. Cherry, like Cassie, adored Aunt Bess, and was always delighted to spend an afternoon or a weekend with her, sleeping in the bedroom Zoe and Cassie had once shared, banging on her old piano, reading the Nancy Drew books that Janice had left behind.

"Zoe?" Bess asked again.

Cherry's still gone. That was how Zoe had imagined she'd begin. *I think Bix did something to her.* She would start there, and build to *I think I've failed her, and I can't live with myself if that's true,* and then go backward, carefully working her way to *I'm not sure I'll be able to live with myself, no matter what,* and *My whole life has been a lie.* Only what Zoe ended up actually saying was "I need Cassie's phone number."

Bess looked at her for a moment with that probing expression Zoe had come to know in the wake of the band's breakup, before finally opening the door wide enough to admit her. Zoe followed her great-aunt inside, to the kitchen, and sat at the Formica breakfast bar while Bess filled the kettle and made them both mint tea. She didn't speak again until Bess handed her a mug and stood across from her with her own mug, silent, waiting for Zoe to begin.

"I need to find Cassie," Zoe said. "I think maybe she knows where Cherry is. Or that maybe Cherry's with her."

Bess stared at her, head tilted. "What makes you think so?"

Zoe bent her head and wrapped both hands around her mug. The ceramic was so hot she could feel the skin of her palms stinging, and she welcomed the distracting bite of the pain. "I think . . ." *Just say it,* she told herself. "I think I know why Cherry left. I think Bix maybe did something to her. I found pictures—these weird, creepy pictures—on his phone."

Bess raised her eyebrows.

"Not, like, naked pictures. Just pictures he took when Cherry didn't know he was there." Bess pressed her lips together. Zoe's voice wobbled as she said, "Cherry always said he looked at her. That he made her feel weird. And I'd ask, well, is he touching you? Is he doing anything? I didn't realize—" She paused to swallow, to snatch another breath. "I didn't understand that there's other ways to hurt someone." Zoe raised her mug, trying to keep her hands steady, but couldn't curl her lips enough to sip, as a voice in her head inquired, *Aren't you the queen of pain? If there's a way to hurt someone, haven't you tried it?*

She set her mug down again. "I haven't said anything to Jordan yet. I'm going to, but I already know what he'll say—that I'm picking on his kid, who's already been through enough. Or he'll make it like I'm the problem, for violating Bix's privacy."

"And you think Cassie can help?" Bess's voice was cigarette-raspy, even though she'd quit smoking years ago. "Why? How does she fit into all of this?"

Zoe bowed her head. "I know it sounds crazy," she said, low-voiced. "But I just have this feeling . . ." She made herself look up. "Cherry's never met Cassie," she said. Which was obvious. Of course Cherry hadn't met Cassie. Cherry knew that Zoe had a sister, but Cassie did not know that Zoe had a daughter. The family knew, but the press did not. And no one from either camp had seen Cassie, not since that terrible night in Detroit. "Cherry's obsessed with the Griffin Sisters. She's probably listened to the album a thousand times. She's built Cassie up in her head as this tragic hero." Zoe took another breath. "She thinks Cassie is everything I'm not. Talented, and brilliant, and someone who would have encouraged her, instead of trying to keep her away from the industry."

Isn't she? Zoe imagined her aunt thinking.

"The fun aunt," said Bess.

Zoe thought it over. "Sure. The fun aunt." Like Bess had been. The one who'd let you stay up late and have breakfast for dinner. The one who'd paint your toenails and wouldn't worry about getting nail polish on the bedspread. A fun aunt, she realized, was one more thing she'd deprived Cherry of; one more thing she'd prevented Cassie from becoming. It was one more piece of the exploding, ongoing disaster that was the Griffin Sisters; one more bit of wreckage to be laid at Zoe's door.

She saw, with surprise, that Bess was smiling a little. Zoe wondered

if her aunt was remembering two little girls cuddled up in her big bed
with its pink satin bedspread, putting cotton balls between their toes in
preparation for their pedicures. Two little girls who used to sing each
other to sleep.

"You know where Cassie went," said Zoe. It wasn't a question, and
Bess didn't confirm, but she didn't shake her head either. "If you know
how to get in touch with her, maybe you could ask if she's heard from
Cherry?" Except how would her daughter know how to find Cassie,
when Zoe herself did not? Could Cherry have figured it out somehow?
Could Bess have told her?

Bess held up her hands, palms out. She shook her head. "I don't
know where Cherry is, and I didn't tell her how to get in touch with
your sister," she said.

"But you know how," said Zoe.

Bess looked at her steadily, a long, tense moment. Then she nodded.
"Cassie and I spoke after Russell died. She told me what happened," she
said.

Zoe shut her eyes again, hearing what Bess hadn't said: *I know Cassie's story. What's yours?* She watched as her aunt turned and shuffled
across the kitchen to refill her mug, hearing the spoon clink against the
white porcelain as she stirred in honey. She was remembering a dozen
different things, sounds and sensations. Russell's hands, gripping her
shoulders, the first night they'd slept together. Russell's voice, slurred
and lust-roughened, asking, *Is this what you want?* She remembered
how triumphant she'd felt, like she'd passed some impossible test,
claimed some rich prize.

Other images flickered through her mind. She remembered looking across the stage in the middle of a performance and seeing Russell
watching Cassie, not her. She remembered watching the roadies setting
up before a show and how, at every load-in, Cassie's piano would move
closer and closer to the audience, while her own microphone stand
inched farther and farther away. Zoe saw her hand, with long, red nails,
on a hotel door's knob. She saw her feet, in high-heeled, thigh-high
black leather boots, moving along the hotel's carpeted floor. She heard

Russell calling after her, saying, "Zoe, wait, please, let me explain." Only he couldn't, because what explanation could there have been? She could taste her fury, her rage at realizing that she hadn't passed the test at all, that she was not triumphant, that Cassie had won and she had lost. It had felt like something clawing in her chest. It had tasted, she remembered, like hot ashes.

"Oh God," Zoe whispered.

Bess reached across the table and touched Zoe's arm. "Start at the beginning," she said. "That usually works the best."

Zoe gripped her mug, shaking her head. "I wish none of it had happened," she said. "I wish I'd never . . ." She stopped talking and gestured, one hand circling. *I wish I'd never asked Cassie to sing with me. I wish I'd never been in a band. I wish I'd never tried.*

"If wishes were horses, then beggars would ride," said Bess. She gave Zoe's arm a squeeze, and her voice was not without sympathy as she said, "You'd better tell someone. It might as well be me."

Part Five

Critics of Britney Spears and Christina Aguilera charge them with making themselves into sexual objects, reinforcing unhealthy images of young women that are considered the source of a wide range of sociocultural problems. Their assertion is that, although both women retained significant control of their careers—or, at least, managed to convey that impression, early on—there is a big difference between Tori Amos singing "Me and a Gun" and Britney Spears singing ". . . Baby One More Time." The Griffin Sisters gave fans both options: a pretty pop princess in Zoe Griffin, a strong heroine in Cassie Griffin. Instead of having to choose, music fans could, for the band's brief tenure, have it all.

**—TURNING TABLES: A HISTORY OF WOMEN IN ROCK
JOEL FLOURY AND ARTHUR KOVACS**

Cherry

ALASKA, 2024

Cherry felt her breath freezing in her lungs, her blood stalling in her veins. Her hands were, somehow, in the air. It seemed as though she'd put them there without even being asked.

"Get off my property," the woman said. Her voice was low and angry and instantly familiar, recognizable in a way Cherry felt in her bones. "Right now."

Cherry was simultaneously terrified and unsurprised. Maybe because Fran had put the idea of guns in her head, she'd almost been expecting this. In that moment, she found that terror gave her thoughts an unexpected clarity. All the chatter that normally rattled around in her brain, the to-do lists and lyrics and random daydreams and recurring grudges, all of that had gone quiet. Her heart must have started beating again, because she could hear it thrumming loudly in her ears. She licked her lips. "Are you going to shoot me?"

Instead of answering, the woman did something to the gun that made a loud and ominous click. "Sixty seconds."

"Please," Cherry said. "I just want to talk."

"That's fifty seconds." The gun barrel was steady.

"Look, if I could just—"

"Forty-five."

Cherry made herself breathe. She moved backward, one hand on the railing, trying to descend the stairs and look harmless, all without taking her eyes off the woman's shadowed face.

"Turn around," the woman said, sounding—was Cherry imagining it?—the tiniest bit amused. "The last thing I need is you breaking your neck."

For a brief, wild moment, Cherry thought about falling, accidentally on purpose. She imagined letting go of the railing, allowing herself to drop backward onto the snow, and the frozen ground beneath it. She could twist an ankle, break a leg. Then Cassie would have to put up with her, at least until an ambulance arrived.

She didn't fall. Instead, she stopped filming and put her phone in her pocket, holding still, trying not to shake. At least, not visibly.

"Thirty seconds," said Cassie Griffin. The small dog, the source of the yipping Cherry had heard, had come out of the house to stand at Cassie's knee. It had white fur with reddish spots, pointed ears and big, dark eyes, and it was looking at her, wagging its tail, like it wanted nothing more than to run down the stairs and be petted by this exciting new person. Its appearance served to somewhat diminish Cherry's terror. *At least there'll be a witness if she shoots me*, Cherry thought, a little wildly.

"I'm your niece," she said.

Cassie frowned. She was still holding the gun, but Cherry could feel her scrutiny as she studied Cherry's face.

Cherry tried to stand up straight, core tight, shoulders back. "My name is Cherry Rohrbach. Cherry Grossberg Rohrbach. I'm Zoe's daughter."

Cassie didn't move. She didn't speak. But Cherry saw the information register. The gun barrel wavered the tiniest bit, like her hands had gone briefly slack.

"You're lying." Cassie's voice sounded breathy.

"I'm not."

"You need to go." Cassie's voice was stronger, steadier, only marginally less angry, but Cherry lived in the world of sound. She could hear the difference, as small as it was, and she could see the hungry way the woman was looking at her, like she was trying to commit each of Cherry's features to memory.

"It's true." With one sweaty, shaky hand, Cherry reached into her back pocket, where she'd shoved her phone. "I've got pictures."

Slowly, Cassie lowered the gun to her side, beckoning with her free hand. Cherry's fingers were trembly, and it took her a few tries to open the correct app, but once she had, it didn't take long to find the picture she wanted. It was a shot from the apartment in Bella Vista, at Cherry's fifth birthday party. Zoe had baked a cake, and Cherry had made a construction-paper crown at school, each spike tipped with gold glitter, and they were posing together, smiling in the sun. She realized she probably should have shown Cassie a photograph of a more recent mother-daughter moment, except there weren't a lot where she and Zoe were both in the frame, looking happy.

Cherry handed the phone over. Cassie studied it for a long moment.

"How old are you?" she asked, in a low, gruff voice.

"Eighteen."

"When were you born?"

Weird question, but whatever. Maybe Cassie was into astrology. "May."

"No," Cassie said shortly. "What year?"

"2005," Cherry said, a little impatiently. Did Cassie not know any of this? Was that possible?

It seemed as though it was. Cassie was still staring down at the picture. Eventually, she looked up and went back to scrutinizing Cherry, staring at her eyes, her mouth, her face, possibly comparing what she saw to some checklist in her brain. Cherry found that she was doing the same, looking at her aunt's face, her hands, her posture, checking them for similarities to her mother, to herself.

"Where do you live?" Cassie asked.

"New Jersey," Cherry said, even though she'd been trying to stop thinking of her mother and stepfather's house as home. "With my mom."

"New Jersey," Cassie repeated. Her voice had gotten faint again, and Cherry was getting cold. It was still dark, at almost noon, which was ridiculous, but this weather was like nothing she'd ever felt or even imagined. It was a hopeless kind of cold; a cold without the possibility of warmth; a cold that told you spring was never coming and summer was a lie you'd told yourself.

"Yeah. My mom's remarried. She has two other kids. Noah and Schuyler. My half brothers. Your nephews. I've got pictures, if you want to see them."

"Remarried." Cassie sounded gobsmacked, which was one of Cherry's absolute favorite words. She'd been trying, for years, to put it in a song. "And she lives in New Jersey?"

Cherry wasn't sure why her aunt had seized on that detail as being especially relevant, but she could work with it. "Haddonfield, New Jersey. Right over the Ben Franklin. She's on the PTA."

Cassie made a brief, startled noise—*huh!* Cherry, meanwhile, had started to shiver.

"Can I come in?" she asked. It was rude, but she was past caring. "It's, like, fucking freezing out here."

"Well." Cassie's voice was very dry. "It is Alaska." She fiddled with the gun, holding it loosely by her side, continuing to examine Cherry. After what felt like forever, Cassie turned sideways, and opened the door, waiting as Cherry walked inside.

Cassie
ALASKA, 2024

It can't be, she thought. Except, even while her brain was insisting *no* and *impossible* and *absolutely not,* even as she was thinking that if her sister had had a baby, Cassie would have known that, somehow; that she would have felt it like a faraway volcano's eruption or the after-shocks of a distant earthquake—her eyes were taking in the evidence. The girl had Zoe's nose and chin, the same long neck, and even the same tiny earlobes as her sister. She couldn't see anything of Russell D'Angelo in this stranger's face, but she saw plenty of her sister, and it staggered her. She wasn't surprised that Zoe had had children. That was what normal people did. She was surprised that she was getting to meet one of them, that, after going for so long with no family, this child—this girl who might be Russell's daughter—had shown up at her door.

The girl—*Cherry,* Cassie remembered, and even that was weird—was wandering around her house, picking things up, putting them down. Wesley, the little traitor, was following at her heel, tail and ears erect and quivering. As Cassie watched, the girl stood in the center of the room and stretched her arms out, clearly trying to see if she could touch both sides of the house. It was a near thing.

"How did you find me?" Cassie asked.

The girl puffed out her chest, looking proud. "I used public records."

Cassie frowned.

"And also, someone posted a video of you on Reddit."

Cassie felt herself go cold. "What is Reddit?"

"It's—"

Never mind. "What video?"

"You were singing 'Silent Night' at a supermarket."

Cassie closed her eyes and groaned softly. Her heart was hammering, and her insides felt like they were shaking apart. *Damage control,* she thought. "Which public records did you use to find me?" If she knew that, she'd be able to patch the hole. Stop the leak. Make sure no one else did what this child had done.

Cherry smiled. She seemed so much like Zoe: the way she stood, the tilt of her eyes, the set of her shoulders, and her voice was like Zoe's voice. "How about this? I'll answer two questions if you answer two of mine."

Cassie didn't reply. She sat, motionless, waiting, until Cherry gave a resigned shrug.

"Okay, I knew you were recently in a Safeway in Alaska from the Reddit thing, so I went there and someone who works there told me you buy lots of cleaning supplies."

Cassie heard the low, pained noise coming from her mouth. She made herself be quiet, as Cherry continued. "So I thought you might be a housekeeper, only not in a hotel because they'd buy the stuff. Then I figured that maybe you owned rental properties. It's an easy way to make . . ." She looked up at the ceiling, clicking her tongue against the roof of her mouth. Zoe used to do exactly the same thing when she was trying to remember something. "Like, passive income. I went to city hall and this nice lady helped me do a search." She smiled unexpectedly. "And here I am!"

Cassie was trying to breathe through the pain and the shock, even though she felt stabbed. Gutted. By the fact that she'd been found, by the revelation that this young woman existed. She'd missed so much. "Who knows I'm here? Did you tell anyone else?"

"What, like reporters?" The girl shook her head. "No, I haven't told anyone. And that video I saw of you, like, disappeared after an hour. That was what made me sure it was you. You've got someone doing cleanup, right?"

"Not very well, evidently," Cassie muttered. There were things she wanted to know—about her sister, about her parents, about the world she'd left behind. But she wasn't sure where to start, or how to ask. More crucially, Cassie wasn't sure what she deserved to know, or how much the things she might learn would hurt her. She imagined unwrapping an elaborately packaged gift, tugging at silk ribbons until their bows gave way, working her fingers underneath clear tape, unfolding pretty, patterned paper, only to find something bloody and decaying inside.

"You know, you're still a big deal," the young woman with Zoe's voice said into the silence. "There's this Netflix show that's using your music."

Cassie sliced her hand through the air and shook her head. She didn't want to hear about the band or the music. She didn't know what she wanted to hear about. She wanted the girl to leave. She wanted her never to have come. She wanted to go back in time and never have gone to the grocery store that night. Never have opened her stupid mouth. Never have sung.

Wesley had settled on his belly on the floor, between the two women. Cassie watched his ears swiveling, first toward Cherry, then toward her.

"Your . . . your father," she began.

"He's dead," Cherry said. "You know that, though. You were there, right?"

Cassie closed her eyes and didn't answer. She didn't know what to think. Was Russell really this child's father? The timing suggested it was possible, and Cassie's brain did not know what to do with the information. It just kept spinning, uselessly, stuck on the silliest details, like *Haddonfield* and *PTA* and what kind of a name was Cherry, and her body was in full-on fight-or-flight mode. Her knees were shaking and her heart was thudding and she could taste old pennies in her mouth. She tried to make herself breathe, make herself think. If some part of Russell had survived, had lived on, in this girl—that was good news, wasn't it? Or did it just bring all the awfulness back?

"My turn now," said the girl. She took a step toward Cassie, her face intent. "What happened?"

This time, Wesley did not just swivel his ears. He turned his entire body toward Cassie, sitting up with his eyes bright and focused, like he, too, had been waiting for someone to ask the question, and for Cassie to answer.

Cassie licked her lips. "What happened with what?" she asked, praying for a reprieve.

"What happened to the Griffin Sisters?" Cherry asked. "What happened with my father? What happened at the end? That's what I want to know. That's why I'm here." She paused and seemed to consider. "Well, it's one of the reasons. My mother won't tell me anything. I want to know what happened with my father. How he died. And how you ended up"—Cherry made an abrupt, derisive gesture, with her lips pursed—"here."

"I like it here." *How he died*. The words were tolling in her mind, like a huge bell that would ring forever.

Cherry rolled her eyes. "Your house looks like a prison cell. And it's fucking freezing out there, and it's dark all the time."

"I don't mind the dark." Cassie squared her shoulders, still trying to project calm. "And when the ice caps melt, and the world starts burning, I'm going to be fine."

Cherry's voice was low, sweet, and tuneful as she sang. "And if California slides into the ocean / Like the mystics and statistics say it will / I predict this motel will be standing until I pay my bill."

Warren Zevon, Cassie thought, but did not say. At least this child knew her rock history. That was encouraging.

Cherry gave her what was probably meant to be a beguiling smile. "I'm family," she said. "And I deserve to know."

Cassie considered. Was this true? Did this girl, with her ratty bleached hair, and the tattoo of a treble clef on the inside of her right wrist, have an actual claim on the truth? *She's going to hate me when she hears it*, Cassie realized, and maybe that was fair. Maybe hatred was what she deserved. Maybe this girl had been sent to her so that Cassie would be forced to confess, so she'd have no choice but to tell the whole story and to see the living, breathing consequences of her actions, the end result of the damage she'd done.

"Sit," Cassie said, pointing at the treehouse's single folding metal chair. Cherry sat, looking at Cassie, face calm, palms open and resting on her knees. Cassie closed her eyes, allowing herself a single beat of silence. Then she began.

Cassie
ON THE ROAD, 2003

The video for "The Gift" debuted on MTV on the Fourth of July weekend in 2003, and immediately went into heavy rotation. Within six weeks, the Griffin Sisters had a number one single, one of the songs of the summer, along with Beyoncé's "Crazy in Love," Matchbox Twenty's "Unwell," and Chingy's "Right Thurr." You couldn't spend an hour in your car without hearing the song on the local Top 40 station. Janice and Sam said they'd heard it, on one of their trips to the Jersey Shore. Even Aunt Bess said she'd seen the video on TV.

Two weeks after the video dropped, the album they'd decided to call *Night Ride* came out. Jerry sent the band to open for Thünderstrüt and Toxic Honey, a pair of hair bands whose popularity had peaked in the mid-1990s. At the first few shows, all the Griffin Sisters had gotten were the indifference and the occasional boos that opening acts typically received, but eventually, Cassie began to hear people in the audience singing along, not just to "The Gift," but to every song they played. As their album continued to climb the charts, the balance started shifting, until the crowds were stomping and screaming for encores from the Griffin Sisters, and booing when they left the stage, walking past the assembled members of both bands, all of whom (except for Toxic Honey's female lead singer) were shirtless, in leather pants and matching glares.

After six weeks, Jerry summoned the Griffin Sisters back to New York again and told them that they'd been replaced. "As an opening act," he added, when Zoe opened her mouth to protest. "We'll find someone else to fill that slot. You guys are ready to headline."

Cassie waited for one of her bandmates to tell Jerry that he was delusional. They'd barely been a band for nine months. Prior to their most recent stint as openers, they had only played a dozen or so real shows, gigs that hadn't been organized by radio stations and attended by people who'd been given free tickets. One video, two singles, and a total of thirteen songs did not translate to headlining a tour. But Zoe was staring at Jerry, rapt and breathless, and Russell was looking at Zoe fondly, and Tommy was glaring at Russell, who didn't seem to notice, and Cam was bouncing on the balls of his feet, drumming his fingertips on his thighs, like he couldn't wait to run out of Jerry's office, probably to tell Wendy, his girlfriend, the good news.

So Cassie had to be the one. "We aren't ready," she said.

Jerry looked at her, his small hands clasped, head tilted, his expression almost bemused. "You will be."

There was work to be done. Cassie imagined that, before it started, she and her sister would go back to Philadelphia. Janice said she'd get their bedroom ready, that she'd missed them, that she'd make Cassie her favorite meat loaf and mashed potatoes and Zoe her favorite pancakes and scrapple and take them to Chickie's & Pete's for crab fries and Dalessandro's for cheesesteaks. In the end, the girls only got to spend a weekend at home. The label had rented them apartments in New Jersey, just over the river, an easy drive from the soundstages and recording studios. Cassie and Russell worked with the new musicians the label had brought on board: a quartet of backup singers—two men and two women, soprano and alto, tenor and bass—and another guitar player, a man in his mid-forties who also played the accordion, the Dobro, and the mandolin.

To Cassie's horror, the label had also hired three backup dancers and a choreographer. Cassie prepared herself to tell the woman that under no circumstances would she dance, that she didn't even like standing onstage, that she'd prefer to be seated at her piano at all times, but Lara, who had a mane of dark-blond hair, a constant smile, and the peppy, upbeat, endlessly encouraging attitude of a new mom who was either naturally energetic or highly medicated, never even asked. Zoe was the one who worked with the dancers, spending hours with them at the Broadway Dance Center, shimmying her shoulders and shaking her hips in sequined flapper-style dresses or black patent-leather boots and a red miniskirt.

The show was becoming a spectacle, with costumes and sets; not a concert but a circus-slash–fashion show, with songs thrown in. Cassie hated it. But Russell told her it would be fine. "It's a necessary evil, I guess you could say," he wrote in an AIM message, after she'd told him how she felt. "It's what anyone who pays thirty-five bucks for a concert ticket expects these days."

Cassie told him that none of the singers she'd loved had needed dancers or choreography to make an impact. Their music did that. Joni Mitchell had not worn patent-leather minidresses; Joan Armatrading did not make her entrance on a zip line, a move Zoe was learning, for the part of the concert where they'd perform scenes from the video, and Zoe would come flying onto a set built to re-create the rec room. "I don't like it," Cassie wrote to Russell. "It feels silly and distracting." Also, there probably wasn't a zip line strong enough to hold her. But Cassie was not about to say that.

"Believe me," Russell wrote. "Once you start singing, no one will be distracted. Think of this as a garnish. The parsley on top of your mashed potatoes. It's nice, and people expect it, but it's not what they're there for. You are."

Cassie treasured those words. She'd bought her own laptop, a chunky, hefty Dell, one of the few purchases she'd made for herself with her share of the band money. She'd printed out every message Russell sent her. She kept them in a folder in her tote bag, where she'd once kept her sheet music, and read them when Zoe and Russell were together at night, and she was alone.

The tour began in October, in the Midwest. "Plenty of Cassie's people there!" Jerry had said cheerfully. Cassie had wondered what that meant: Weird people? Fat people? Unfashionable people who'd never had friends? Russell set her straight. "The album's selling well there. I mean, it's selling great everywhere, but especially there."

"Why?" she wrote.

"Who knows?" he wrote back.

And so they piled into three busses: the band, the backup singers, the dancers, the managers, and a security guard, a soft-spoken wall of a man named Richard. Their first show was in Gary. Cassie's goal had been to just get through it, like a tightrope walker who'd be fine as long as she kept herself from looking down. "It'll be okay," Russell told her backstage. "It's just like any other show. Just a few more people."

Just a few more people, Cassie told herself . . . but halfway through their first song, she could hear the audience members singing along, could feel their adoration, a wave of warmth rolling over her, and she stopped being afraid. Their second and third were in Indianapolis. On the morning of their first day off, Zoe had gotten up early to meet Lara and the backup dancers in the hotel gym. Cassie had slept until nine thirty. She'd just gotten out of the shower when she heard the ping of her inbox, signaling a message's arrival. Her heart beat faster as she hurried to her laptop to read it. *U busy?* Russell had written.

No, she typed back. *Never too busy for you*, she thought.

Be right over, Russell replied.

Cassie scrambled into her clothes and spent the next five minutes frantically brushing her teeth, combing her hair, and wishing, desperately, to have been magically transformed into someone who could look good in tight jeans and crop tops, like the ones Zoe wore. The previous week, Zoe and Russell had gotten their picture in *People* magazine, in the "Star Tracks" section, full of candid photos of famous people. They'd been shot on a sidewalk in New York City, right before the tour had started, hands clasped, walking side by side. Russell was looking at Zoe, mouth open, free hand lifted, clearly saying something. Zoe had been looking straight ahead, channeling a supermodel's hauteur. Her hair gleamed in the sunshine; her eyes were bright. *The Griffin Sisters guitar player Russell D'Angelo and singer Zoe Griffin take a stroll in the Big Apple*, the caption read. Cassie was pretty sure that the picture had been staged—that someone from the record company had tipped off the photographer, or maybe someone at CJ's office had even sent the picture in themselves. The week before, there had been a similar shot of Russell and Zoe in *Us Weekly*, and the week before that *In Touch* had been speculating about the hot band's power couple potentially being on the rocks, illustrated with a shot of Zoe having drinks with "a mystery man." Cassie, of course, had instantly identified the mystery man as CJ. Still, she'd been hopeful right up until she asked her sister if everything was okay. Zoe had been smiling as she said, "We're fine. Those breakup stories are just all feeding the machine."

It gave Cassie a miserable, untethered feeling, the same one she got whenever she saw Zoe and Russell holding hands, or kissing, or Russell resting his hand on the small of Zoe's back. She wanted him to want her. She wanted his gaze, his smiles, his attention. And she had no idea whether Russell knew how she felt, and no idea how to tell him or, even, what good it would do.

When he knocked, Cassie smoothed her hair one final time. She looked in the mirror, looked away, and hurried to the door.

"Hey." Russell was wearing a white tee shirt and dark jeans and his battered, unlaced black Chucks. He carried his guitar case in one hand. "I thought we could work on the new song." He looked past her, into the room. "Zoe around?"

Cassie shook her head. "Zoe went to the gym." She and her sister were still sharing a hotel room, which Cassie suspected was a money-saving measure on the label's part. She'd thought about asking for a room of her own, but the truth was that, most nights, Zoe was with Russell, giving Cassie her own room by default.

She opened the door wide, stepping back as he walked in, hurrying to turn on more lights and open the curtains, praying that there wasn't anything embarrassing lying around. Cassie was usually tidy about her belongings. She would prop her suitcase on the stand by the end of her bed, remove only what she needed, hang her pantsuits in the closet, leave everything else neatly packed. Zoe, meanwhile, would dump her entire suitcase out on her bed every second or third day, sorting the dirty laundry from the clean, shaking her head at the state of her out-fits. Her dresses would be left to dot the floor like wilted blossoms; her hand-washed bras and panties would be hung to dry over the shower curtain bar. She'd set her box of tampons on the toilet, cover every inch of the bathroom counter with cosmetics, and strew the room with half-empty cans of diet soda, which would leave sticky rings on the dresser or the desk.

This day, thank God, had not been a dump day. Cassie quickly gathered up the two half-empty cans of Diet Coke, a copy of *The Rules*, which Zoe had purchased at a Waldenbooks in Waukesha and which Cassie had been reading, in the vain hope that she would learn something, some way of attracting Russell's romantic attention. Unfortunately, the book seemed to have been written for women like Zoe: women who already had guys who wanted to date them. Some of the suggestions made it sound like attracting a man meant extinguishing your personality. ("Don't tell sarcastic jokes. Don't be a loud, knee-slapping, hysterically funny girl . . . be quiet and mysterious, act ladylike, cross your legs and smile. Don't talk so much.") Cassie thought that at least she had the quiet part down. Ladylike, she suspected, was beyond her. And her legs were too big to cross.

Other Rules sounded dumb ("make exercise exciting by playing music while you do sit-ups." *As if,* thought Cassie).

And some of the Rules made no sense for their current circumstance. "Don't see him more than once or twice a week" didn't work when you were basically working and living together, spending almost all of your waking hours in one another's company. Cassie was busy, except she was busy doing the same thing Russell was busy with . . . and she knew she'd never be able to lie or pretend with him.

Russell observed her tidying with an amused half smile. Cassie could feel his attention, like something warm and comforting draped over her shoulders.

"Okay!" Cassie said, a little breathlessly. She was always a little breathless when Russell was this close. "Should I go get my keyboard, or . . ." The portable keyboard was still locked in the belly of the tour bus. Some nights, Cassie took it to the room with her. She'd pull her headphones over her ears and play while Zoe slept. She'd have to wait until her sister fell asleep before she started, though. Zoe claimed that the clatter of Cassie's fingers on the keys was enough to keep her awake.

"Nah," said Russell. "I think we're good with just my guitar. I wanted to work on the bridge a little bit."

Cassie nodded. God, she loved listening to him talk. The broadness of his vowels, the crisp taps of his *t*s. The whispering sound when he said her name. That, most of all.

Russell opened his guitar case. Cassie opened her notebook. Half of its pages were already filled with lyrics (plus a single heart she'd drawn, with their initials, together, inside it, and then quickly scribbled over).

He held out his hand, smiling. Cassie handed him the notebook, feeling even more breathless as he flipped through the pages.

"You wrote all that."

It wasn't a question. Still, Cassie nodded.

"Are all of those lyrics?"

"Mostly." Lyrics, and things more like diary entries. Letters to him that she'd never send. *Dear Russell, I know you're with Zoe, but she will never love you like I do.*

Cassie felt her face getting hot as she imagined Russell reading those words. As she licked her lips, trying to think of what to say, he stared at her intently. Heatedly? Was this what romance novels called a heated look? Was it how, for example, he looked at her sister? Cassie wasn't sure.

"God," he said, very softly. "You're incredible. Do you have any idea how talented you are?"

Cassie felt her insides light up, like they'd been brushed in sunshine, painted with gold. She clasped her hands in her lap, looking down, painfully aware of her physical self, her body and its myriad imperfections. Her hair was too thin, her eyes too small and squinty, and her mouth always fell into a frown if she wasn't paying attention.

I have nice feet, she told herself. It was true. Her feet were small, compared to the rest of her, compact and graceful, the toes descending in length from big toe to pinkie toe, like the pipes of a pan flute. They were the same feet Zoe had.

She looked at Russell, remembering how he'd circled her ankle with his fingers, that one afternoon in Wisconsin. His fingers had been warm, but she'd felt like they were burning, like they'd left a mark, a Russell-specific scar, with the shape of his hands and his fingerprints.

Cassie swallowed hard. Russell was still staring at her, with a gaze that might have been heated and might just have been normal eye contact, with her notebook in his hands. He might as well have been holding her heart.

She wanted to stop time and ask him a million questions: What did the house he'd grown up in look like? What color were the walls of his bedroom? What was the name of his elementary school, and who'd been his first best friend? What was his favorite restaurant and his favorite thing to eat? She already knew his favorite musicians, his favorite songs; how he loved Journey and Rush and the Beastie Boys, Liz Phair and Veruca Salt and Bikini Kill and Hole. She'd eavesdropped on him explaining to Zoe that *Live Through This* was a perfect album and that "Miss World" was a perfect song. Cassie could picture her sister, nodding along, her face very serious, even though Cassie knew that her sister preferred Jessica Simpson to Courtney Love and had probably never heard the album Russell loved the best.

She wanted him to tell her his whole life's story. She wanted to make a pillow fort with a bedsheet roof and hide him in there. She wanted to make herself tiny, tuck herself into his pocket, stay with him forever.

"Do you want to get started?" she made herself ask. Her voice was lower than normal, husky.

Russell's own voice was calm as usual. "Sure."

Cassie made herself stop looking at his fingers, or the flex of his shoulders as he pulled the strap of his guitar over his head (the authors of *The Rules* had very strong opinions about how a woman should never, ever stare at a man). Instead, she looked down at the notebook, remembering what she'd written.

Once, she'd read an article that analyzed Broadway musicals. In every musical, the article had said, there is always the "I Want" song, usually, if not always, the very first song the audience hears, where the protagonist sings about his or her animating quest, the reason for the story, the journey, the adventure (and, hence, the show). She'd thought about the prologue from "Into the Woods," how Cinderella wanted to go to the ball, and Jack's mother wished for money, and the baker and his wife wished for a child. *More than life . . . more than riches . . . more than anything . . .*

Cassie had had that song in her head when she'd written her own "I Want" song. The prologue and, also, "Somewhere That's Green," from *Little Shop of Horrors*, where Audrey, the shopgirl, sings about the safe, peaceful, happy life that she will never have. "A matchbox of our own / A fence of real chain link / A grill out on the patio / Disposal in the sink . . ."

She'd let all those lyrics simmer, and then she thought about her own "I Want." Which was Russell. She'd never tell another soul—she'd certainly never tell him—but there it was, as ineluctable a fact as her hazel eyes or her right-handedness or her talent. He was her love, her inspiration. He was her muse, as much as she was his. And a few days after he'd touched her ankle in the car, with Zoe sleeping in the bed beside her, she'd pulled out her notebook and written words to the melody that had established itself in her head.

> Her world is made of dark and water
> Deeper than the eye can see
> Full fathom five, and now they've brought her
> Where she was never meant to be
>
> She couldn't see the traps they'd set
> She mourns the vanished world below
> She cries at night but no one listens
> They tap the glass and start the show

But now he's swimming in her waters
In the dark, her shape obscured
His hands know how to speak her language
All she needs is just one word

Cassie sang with her eyes closed, and wondered if he knew she'd written it about him, and for him. All her songs were now. The room was so quiet, and her voice sounded too loud. She felt completely naked, utterly exposed, because Russell had to know that she was singing about herself. And him. Him too; her savior.

"It's about a whale," she said, her voice abrupt and too loud. Russell blinked, then looked at her, his expression open and curious as Cassie kept babbling. "I saw one once. My parents took us to Florida. We did Disney World, Universal Studios, and SeaWorld. They had whales that did a show. They jumped through hoops, and did tricks. The trainers gave them fish, and everyone clapped, but I just felt sorry for them. They'd been bred in captivity, and spent their whole lives in tanks. They'd never gotten to swim in the ocean. And all these people, you know, looking at them, through the glass." She paused to breathe. Russell was still looking at her. Had she ever told him that boys used to call her a whale? "Free Willy," they'd yell when they saw her coming. Once, one of the boys, braver than the others, had thrown a stick at her. "Harpoon it!" he'd been hollering. The stick had scratched her face, and her mother had come to the nurse's office. Normally, Janice was sympathetic, or, at least, she tried to be, but that day she'd been angry. "Do you think I've got time for this?" she'd asked, walking, stiff-legged, to her car. "Can't you try a little harder to get along?"

Russell was still staring at her. For a moment, she imagined telling him. Cards on the table, beans spilled all over the ground. *I love you. I know you don't love me and that's okay, you don't have to do anything about it, but I had to tell you. I need you to know.*

He would be kind about it, she thought. His voice would be gentle, and he'd look into her eyes and say something like, *Hey, I'm sorry if I gave you the wrong idea. I think you're incredibly talented, but I don't feel that way about you.* Russell was a nice guy, good-natured and well-mannered, goofy and sweet. He would let her down gently. She knew that it would still break her and leave her gutted, and so, so ashamed.

Cassie licked her lips. "Have—have you ever been to SeaWorld?" she asked.

Russell shook his head and nodded at the notebook. "When did you write this?"

Cassie shrugged. "Last week sometime? I think?"

He smiled at her wryly, shaking his head again. "Amazing."

Russell thinks I am amazing, Cassie told herself, trying to put herself back in the present. Fifth grade was a long time ago. *I made it out, and I'm okay now. Some people like me.*

And some people think you're a joke, a voice that sounded like that long-ago classmate said.

Cassie forced herself to ignore it, to return her attention to Russell and the song.

"We built ourselves a castle," she sang. "But the walls have fallen down."

"I have an idea." Russell came to stand beside her. He pointed at the page. "Right here. *Castle* and *ruins.* It should rhyme, right?"

"I know." Cassie shook her head. "I couldn't find a rhyme." She pressed her lips together. "And do we need to say it's a sandcastle, or is that implied?"

"Implied," Russell said. "Let's brainstorm. What rhymes with *castle? Hassle?*"

"*Facile,*" said Cassie.

"Huh?"

"*Facile,*" she said. "It means, like, easy, I think. Or fluent. Like, someone is facile in French."

"Huh." Russell, she'd noticed, had lots of different *huhs.* He could use it as a question, an affirmation, or a noise of pleasure when he'd learned something new. This was his teasing *huh.* His I'm-impressed-with-you *huh.* She liked it. She liked all of them.

"But probably we shouldn't use it in a song. If no one knows what it means."

"There's always *asshole*." Russell raised his eyebrows. "Do we dare?" He strummed a chord and sang, "I built you a castle / but the tide's come in / and it turns out you're an asshole . . ."

"And have always been." Cassie finished the verse, noticing he'd changed the *we* to *I*. I built you a castle. Her heart was doing a swoopy, almost painful thing in her chest, something that felt like bubbles inside of her. She opened her mouth and found that she was giggling. She delighted when Russell started laughing right along with her.

"And you have bad skin," he sang.

"With a double chin," Cassie sang, and then cringed, hoping Russell wasn't noticing her double chin. But Russell was still laughing, bent over his guitar with his shoulders shaking.

"No, no, wait. I've got it, I've got it," he said. He began the chorus again.

> I built you a castle
> But it's made of sand
> Still, I thought that it would last, oh,
> When you held my hand.

He strummed the final chord again. "What do you think?"

His face was so open, so vulnerable, so full of what looked like kindness and affection, that Cassie had to turn away. It was too much. It would break her. Her poor heart would explode. "Play it again," she said. He started to play, and Cassie sang.

> I built you a castle
> That was oh so grand
> But the tide's come in at last, oh
> To wash away the sand.

"Something like that?" she said. "Or should it be something about how the castle's not real? Like, it's only in my . . ." *Shit*, she thought. Shit, shit, shit. "Only in the person's head?" she said hastily. "Or, the whale's head, actually. Because it's about a whale. But do whales build castles? Does any of this make sense?"

"You're fine," Russell said. If had heard what she'd said, if he'd caught the meaning, his face didn't let on. His expression was open and relaxed, not guarded, or, worse, pitying, as if he was getting ready to tell her that he liked her, just not that way. "Maybe it's . . ."

He played the bridge again, changing the second chord, taking it from major to minor and back again, instead of just the major progression Cassie had written.

"Oh," she said, nodding, hearing the rightness of it, the undeniable click of pieces locking into place.

She picked up her notebook and pen and started to write; the song spilled out of her, like that simple key change had opened a locked chest. *Love was what she wanted / a prize she had to win / when his hands find her in the darkness / then she feels the world begin.*

He started to play the bridge she'd rewritten, and they sang together, his voice low and warm, her voice higher, sweeter, twining around his, and then soaring. Together, they made something beautiful: something as shimmering and fragile as a soap bubble, as lovely as a peach-and-golden sunset on the last days of summer.

Russell looked at her. Cassie froze. She could not move, could not breathe. She could only watch as he reached out and cupped her elbow.

"Hey," he said, like he was gentling a horse, trying to keep it from running away. As if Cassie would ever run from him. As if she could. "Hey."

"Hey," she said back, her voice so soft, cracking a little.

Russell took one step toward her. Then another. Her eyes were on his face, his eyes, and she could not have looked away. Not for all the money in the world. Not for all the songs that had ever been written. Not for anything.

They turned their heads at the same instant, at the sound of the door's lock clicking, then the door opening. Zoe was smiling as she sauntered inside.

"Hello there, party people!" Her eyes moved from Russell to Cassie, then back again. Cassie thought she saw, in that tiny span of time, Zoe consider the possibility that something was happening, something she needed to worry about, then immediately reject it. If Russell had done anything to indicate guilt, if he'd lurched backward or looked away or stuffed his hands in his pockets or blushed, there might have been a problem. But Russell stood where he was. His expression did not change. He gave no sign that he was doing anything besides visiting a colleague's hotel room to discuss a business matter. Which, Cassie supposed, was true.

Zoe's smile widened as she crossed the room to take Russell's hand. She was wearing exercise gear, bicycle shorts and a cropped tee shirt. Cassie could see her flat belly, the tanned, lean legs that she'd have no trouble crossing. "You still want to go to brunch?"

He smiled at her. "Absolutely. I'm starving." His voice was casual. "Cassie, want to come with us?"

She shook her head and stood, unmoving, as Zoe went into the shower and Russell went back to his room. For hours, she could still feel Russell's presence, could feel the room ringing with his voice, could still see how he'd looked when he'd touched her.

Zoe
PHILADELPHIA, 2024

I didn't mean for it to happen," Zoe told her great-aunt. She sounded wretched. But nowhere near as wretched as she felt.

"So let me make sure I understand," said Bess, who, clearly, had no intention of making this easy. Zoe was going to have to say it all out loud, going over every shameful act, every deceitful choice. Every lie she'd told, every agonizing memory, every time she'd had a chance to do the right thing and had done the wrong thing instead.

She started at what she thought was the beginning—when the label called them back to New York City, to fill a last-minute vacancy on *Saturday Night Live*.

Jerry had made the call himself. It had been December of 2003, almost a year after the first time she and Cassie had sung together onstage. The Battle of the Bands felt like a lifetime ago, like they'd become completely different people than they'd been in Philadelphia.

They'd been in Washington—Zoe remembered the Washington Monument, rising, ivory white and undeniably phallic, thrusting into the sky, but if it wasn't for that, they could have been anywhere. After all the time they'd spent on the road, everything looked pretty much the same: highways and hotel rooms, the backstages of concert halls, the inside of the tour bus. There was a world outside the bus's windows—sometimes deserts, sometimes mountains; sometimes snowy, sometimes sere, or gray and rainy, or lush and green—but, mostly, that world blurred past while they slept or played cards or leafed through magazines.

After all those shows, the band was tight—so connected that they barely had to look at one another when they played. Tommy would click his drumsticks together, counting off the beats, and Cam's bass would come in, dark and sticky, and then Russell and Cassie would start to play, his guitar layered over her keys. Zoe's arm would lift, her tambourine flashing, and she and Cassie would lean precisely the right distance toward their microphones and start to sing. There were no missed steps or wrong notes; no forgotten lyrics or fumbled key changes. They were young and (mostly) gorgeous, and the *Saturday Night Live* invitation was nothing less than their due.

Jerry had arranged a packed schedule: three days to rehearse and shoot *Saturday Night Live*, then *Total Request Live* on Monday afternoon, where they'd debut their new single, which they'd play again on the *Today* show on Tuesday morning. In between, Zoe and Russell would tape an interview with Howard Stern. They'd asked Cassie, but Cassie had refused.

"Do you remember what he did to Carnie Wilson?" she'd demanded, when Zoe had started begging. Zoe, along with the entire Western world, had, in fact, heard that interview, and what Howard Stern had said, and done, to Carnie Wilson. She knew about the scale Howard's people had hidden underneath the welcome mat, and how Howard had shared the number with both the listening and viewing audience, and had then grilled Carnie's boyfriend. "How can you possibly be attracted to her?" he'd demanded. "Are you gay? Is this a beard situation? Are you just into her for her money?" Zoe understood why Cassie was afraid.

The label had put them up in a hotel on Central Park South, nicer than the places they normally stayed at, and she and Cassie had been upgraded to a two-bedroom, two-bathroom suite. There was a spacious living room, the drapes and carpets and furniture all in shades of blue and silver, full of flowers that the label had sent over, and several bottles of champagne from *Saturday Night Live*. Zoe's clothes, delivered by the label's stylist, were already hanging in the closet. All those years later, she could recall each outfit: the minidress made of golden paillettes with a pair of high gold heels that she would wear when they sang their first song, "The Gift," and a floor-length slip dress made of bottle-green silk that made her feel like a forest nymph for the second song, "Last Night in Fishtown." The third look was a crop top of dark wine-colored velvet, paired with boot-cut flared jeans so tight she had to lie on a bed and suck in her stomach to get them on, and high-heeled leather boots. She would wear the jeans and velvet top when they shot the promotional photos of the band, the ones they'd use in the televised spots, and then the same pants and boots with a white, puff-sleeved top and a cropped blazer for *TRL*.

Poor Cassie had gotten just one outfit for everything: another boxy, shoulder-padded pantsuit with different tops to wear underneath. That one had been navy blue, with silk lapels, a daring departure from the usual black. "Do you want me to say something?" Zoe had asked, walking back and forth across the dove-gray carpet to break in her new gold shoes.

Her sister had just shrugged. "Rosie O'Donnell wears suits like these." Cassie was never what you'd call talkative, but as the band had gotten more successful, she'd gotten even quieter. In the past weeks, her silence had, Zoe thought, a different quality: less watchful and curious, more sullen and morose. Zoe didn't know what Cassie had to be sad about. At every show they played, more and more girls and young women would push their way to the front of the crowds or wait backstage. Plain girls, plump girls, girls with glasses, girls with braces, girls with limp, greasy hair or wild, frizzy curls. Girls no guy would look at twice; girls who'd been lonely all their lives. Those girls would be out by the dozen. They'd cry when they saw Cassie, or they'd try to touch her—her sleeve, her hair, her shoulder—like she was some holy thing. Like she could heal them. Zoe herself would have relished that attention, but this emerging fan club only seemed to make Cassie uncomfortable; sadder, instead of happier.

Zoe told herself not to worry. That, for once, Cassie could be Cassie's problem, not hers. New York City sparkled in December. Skaters in Rockefeller Center went gliding along underneath the giant Christmas tree, the carved lions outside the New York Public Library wore red-ribboned wreaths around their necks, and all the store windows were crammed with gorgeous displays of the most covetable clothes, or toys, or shoes, or handbags. As a Jewish girl, Zoe felt conflicted about enjoying the decorations, but there was no denying the beauty of the season, or how everyone seemed especially cheerful.

On Friday afternoon, the band went to the *SNL* studios to rehearse. The host that week was an actress named Kimmy Brandt. Zoe and Russell were doing a skit, where they pretended to be patrons at a diner where everyone was in a musical and sang instead of talking. The producers had wanted Cassie to participate, but Cassie had turned them down with a simple "No thank you." Zoe supposed she admired her sister's convictions, her boundaries. Personally, she'd decided that there was nothing she wouldn't do, no opportunity to be onstage or on-screen she wouldn't welcome. Maybe some producer or agent would see her and be blown away by her acting, impressed enough to cast her in a film. Maybe she and Kimmy would become best friends. Stranger things had happened.

After the skit, they ran through the songs: first, "The Gift." On a song like that, a thumping breakup anthem, Zoe was fine. She knew that what her voice lacked in nuance and tunefulness, she could make up for in volume and intensity, and that people would be more interested in looking at her than hearing her. But the second song, "Last Night in Fishtown," was a ballad. There was no shout-singing, no thundering guitar licks or buzzing bass line to hide behind. No way to fake it. It was a quiet, introspective kind of song. Cassie sang the lead, with Zoe joining in on the chorus. That was how they'd done it at the rehearsal, a few hours before the real show. But on Saturday night, with the television cameras wheeling around them to catch every note, every expression on their faces, Cassie had nodded at Zoe after the first chorus, and Zoe had taken the second verse, all by herself. She'd never been in better voice, had never come closer to sounding like she belonged on the same stage as her sister.

"Last night in Fishtown / It all rotted from the head down / And it's too dark down here to find our way again . . ."

Cassie joined her for only the final notes, which hung, for a moment, in an unbroken silence. It felt perfect; like the sky had opened up and rained down glitter; like she was glowing, shining, forever marked by this moment. She could picture the studio audience, just past the footlights, gazing at them raptly. She could feel Tommy's attention, the space between her shoulders burning with the intensity of his stare. Best of all, Russell had been looking at her too. Not at Cassie. At her. He'd given Zoe a flash of a smile, a quick thumbs-up . . . and then the applause had started, a thundering wave of it, and it had gone on and on, as Zoe stood there, holding her microphone, smiling shyly, looking down at the fringed Oriental rug that covered the stage, at the Christmas lights that hung behind them, wanting to inscribe all of the details in her mind so she would remember every bit of it, forever.

She'd been with Russell for six months by then, and if someone had asked her to describe the relationship, and she'd answered honestly, she would have said, "Challenging." She and Russell had great chemistry. When they slept together—provided he was not distracted and hadn't been drinking—the sex was great. Or, at least good. Most of the time. Bed was where they connected the best, a place where they didn't have to make conversation, or music, where they both wanted the same thing and could just be bodies, coming together in the dark.

But for the rest of the time, the out-of-bed time, things were harder. Russell wasn't that much older than Zoe, but his experiences were different. All his life, he'd immersed himself in music in a way that she had not. Zoe's focus on the female pop stars of the 1990s and early aughts had been deep but narrow, informed by MTV. Russell was a reader, a serious student of music. And he seemed to know everything about every kind of music there was. Name a record, and he'd heard it. Name a genre, and he could tell you about its best practitioners; name an artist, and he could rattle off a list of that person's albums and songs. Jazz, blues, classical, musicals, even Gregorian chants. Russell knew them all—knew their history, and how they connected and influenced one another. Zoe couldn't talk to him about any of that. Cassie could . . . and so Russell spent more time talking to Cassie than he did to Zoe. Which was fine, Zoe told herself. As long as he came back to her, as long as she was the one holding his hand, sharing his bed, what did it matter who he sat with on the bus? Why should it bother her that he sometimes seemed to be looking for excuses to get away from her? Sometimes she'd sit with him while he talked about Philip Glass and Laurie Anderson with Cassie, who knew who both of those people were, and had listened to their music, but, usually, she'd get bored and wander back to her seat on the bus or her hotel room. Or she'd flirt with Tommy, if she thought that Russell needed a reminder of how desirable she was. "I've got the worst pain, right here," she'd tell Tommy, indicating her shoulder. "Rub my back?" Tommy would rub her back for hours, if Zoe would allow it. He'd probably have learned to braid her hair, if she'd asked. Tommy would happily accompany her to the mall, when Russell and Cam found a nearby park to play basketball during the handful of hours they were free. Tommy was cute, and sweet, and he never made her feel stupid about the things she didn't know. It was relaxing, even restorative, Zoe thought, to spend time with someone who adored her unconditionally, a guy she wasn't constantly trying to win.

Tommy, of course, wanted to be more than friends. And Zoe wasn't completely uninterested. Nor was she uninterested in Anson Kendall, the actor she'd met at the party the label had held when their video debuted, who'd talked to her for twenty minutes by the bar, and had smiled when he'd asked for her number. And there'd been the man in their hotel gym in Topeka who'd handed Zoe his water bottle when she'd gotten off the treadmill, red-faced and panting, whose gaze had been frankly appreciative as he'd asked if she had plans for the night. And the cute guy who'd waited for her, in the rain, after their show in Kansas City, with a bouquet of roses and a handwritten note that said she was the most beautiful woman in the world. Zoe had left that note out on the desk in her hotel room that night, hoping that Russell would see it . . . but, if he had, he'd never said anything.

Zoe tried to tell herself that what she felt for Russell was true love; love that wasn't tainted with fear or insecurity; love that had nothing to do with her place in the band. But sometimes, she'd wake up in the middle of the night. In the darkness, she could force herself to think the truth, to be honest, even if it was only with herself. She liked Russell. He was cute, and kind, and talented. But Zoe knew she was hanging on to him as hard as she could for reasons that had nothing to do with his attributes—his sweet smile, his gentle hands—and everything to do with her own failings. As long as Russell loved her, her place in the Griffin Sisters was secure. And if Russell was done with her, the label would be, too. The Griffin Sisters would become the Griffin Sister, or even just Cassie Griffin. And so she hung on hard, even though she wasn't sure she wanted to. Even though she wasn't convinced that there wasn't a better guy out there for her, somewhere in the world. Even though she felt—or imagined that she could feel—Russell trying to pull away from her. Even though she knew, when she was honest enough to admit it, that she felt drawn to other men.

But that night, in New York, everything between them—everything in the world—had been perfect.

The first after-party began right after the show ended, at a restaurant inside Saks Fifth Avenue. Walking through the store's front doors, past the displays of perfumes and purses on her way to the elevators, still in her green silk wood-nymph dress, with her heels click-clacking on the marble floors, Zoe felt like the heroine of the children's book about the girl and her brother who'd snuck into a museum in New York City after hours. Russell's hand was warm in hers, and she'd passed so quickly from the car into the building that she didn't have time to feel the cold.

They stepped into the elevators, and out again, into a restaurant packed with people—performers and writers and their partners; friends and relatives; random celebrities: a movie star here, a rapper there. There'd been an open bar, waiters passing appetizers—tiny crab cakes and mushroom tartlets on phyllo dough; skewers of chicken with spicy peanut sauce. Zoe hadn't eaten dinner, but she was too excited to have more than a few oysters and a glass of champagne before they'd all piled into a taxi and gone on to the dive bar hosting the next party.

That bar, Zoe remembered, had been down a half flight of steps. It had a low tin ceiling, a pair of vintage pinball machines in the corner, and a spiral staircase in the center that rose up to a restaurant on the ground level. It had been loud, and hot, and there had been trays of sliders on the bar, along with more champagne, and tequila shots. Zoe remembered the burn of the alcohol, the sting of the salt, the sour bite of the lime. One of the *SNL* writers, a freckled, redheaded guy named Kevin Teagarden, had backed Zoe into a corner and yelled his life story in her ear, until Russell had rescued her, swooping out of nowhere with his sweet smile, saying, "Can I have my girlfriend back?" At five in the morning, a few of them had ended up at a Midtown diner, gobbling greasy bacon-egg-and-cheese sandwiches washed down with hot coffee, trying to stave off their hangovers. The entire band was there, except for Cassie, who'd gone back to the hotel after half an hour at the first party. Zoe had felt sorry for her sister . . . but only for a minute.

There had been parties to attend, champagne to drink, and then Russell to slow-dance with, barefoot, in front of his hotel room window as the sun came up and washed them in a gentle, rosy light.

"I love you," Zoe had said, as Russell eased the straps of her dress down, first baring her right shoulder, then her left. Had he said it back? Or had his mouth been busy elsewhere? That morning, their lovemaking wasn't as urgent or hurried. Instead, everything was slow, honeyed, the both of them wrapped in a tingly champagne glow. When Russell was moving inside of her, Zoe had cupped his cheeks with her hands, gazing into his eyes, thinking, *I will never be happier than I am right now.*

She'd slept, and then opened her eyes to find Russell looking at her, tracing the line of her forehead and cheek with one fingertip. "You are so beautiful," he whispered. Zoe had closed her eyes again as he'd spooned her, pressing open-mouthed kisses to her neck and cheeks.

This is good, Zoe told herself. *This is everything I've ever wanted.*

They had showered and gotten dressed in the clothes that had appeared, like magic, on the racks in their rooms. Zoe slipped into a pale-pink velour Juicy Couture tracksuit and a brand-new pair of UGG boots, and Russell wore an Ed Hardy hoodie that he'd rolled his eyes at but had worn at Zoe's urging. They'd gone out together, into the bright, brisk morning, to buy coffee and bagels, and eat them on a bench in the park. They'd rambled through the city, holding hands, looking into the windows of the shops on Fifth Avenue. Russell had waited patiently when Zoe insisted on going to Bergdorf Goodman and to Saks; had pretended to have an opinion on the perfumes she'd sampled and the dresses she tried on; had smiled indulgently when Zoe paid six thousand dollars for an Hermès handbag, and complained that she'd had to add her name to a waiting list for the Birkin bag she coveted. "Don't they know who you are?" Russell had teased.

That night, the label had treated the band to a feast at Nobu. Zoe hadn't eaten much sushi back in Philadelphia, but by then it had become her favorite thing. She could feel other diners' eyes on her, and she swung her hips as the hostess led them through the dining room, where gorgeous platters of sashimi and hand rolls were set out on the long, lacquered table, the slivers of fish glowing orange and ivory, like jewels on beds of rice. The wasabi made her whole face tingle, the bits of salmon and fatty tuna melted on her tongue, and the lychee martinis Jerry ordered were icy cold and went down as soda. Jerry and Helen and CJ had kept the cocktails coming, calling for toast after toast. "To a fabulous performance on *Saturday Night Live*!" "To a huge world tour!" "To your number one song!" "To your number one album! May it be the first of many more!" They'd been in a private part of the restaurant, not exactly a room, more of a large nook, with beaded curtains keeping them mostly out of sight, but Zoe could feel the other diners looking at them, could sense their attention and excitement when they'd realized that they were in the presence of a bunch of capital-*S* Someones.

Midway through the meal, a young woman had approached them. She'd been carrying a notebook, and her hands and voice had both been shaking when she'd said, "You're my favorite band." Zoe hadn't even minded much that the girl had asked for Cassie's autograph first.

"This is perfect," Zoe had whispered to Russell. And then she'd said, "Take me dancing."

There'd been a car at their disposal for the night. Zoe and Russell, Cam and Wendy, CJ and Tommy, and two girls Tommy had met at one of the afterparties had piled into the SUV. They'd gone to Tao, tumbling out of the car in a tipsy, laughing pack, following the security guard past a phalanx of photographers hanging out by the entrance, who knew who they were, and knew their names. "Zoe! This way!" "Zoe! Over here! Zoe and Russell! Give us a kiss!"

Inside there were disco balls glittering from the high, high ceilings. Paper lanterns cast a dim, reddish glow over the dancers; the brick walls were decorated with paintings of dark-eyed geishas. The music was so loud you could feel it in your fillings, and you'd see your skin ripple if you stood close enough to the speakers. Zoe swore she spotted Paris Hilton in the VIP section, wearing a white satin minidress and pink platform shoes, holding court on a couch behind velvet ropes.

The lights and the music bathed her, held her wrapped in their enchantment. Zoe felt like she could dance all night, between the noise and the glow, the thrill of other famous people nearby, and the three bumps of cocaine she'd done in the bathroom. She'd sniffed, wiped her streaming eyes, touched up her lipstick, and smiled at the famous, beautiful goddess she saw reflected in the mirror.

Russell had been waiting outside of the ladies' room. He'd settled his hands on the tanned curve of her waist, bared by her crop top, and she'd leaned into him, her skin suddenly hypersensitive to the textures of his jeans, his shirt, his skin. "I love you!" she'd hollered in his ear.

"What?"

"I love you!" she'd said, yelling even louder.

"What?"

Instead of repeating it, Zoe had closed her eyes, raised her arms over her head, and let the music take her.

They stayed out until almost five in the morning, and she'd barely gotten into bed before it was time to get out. The makeup artist had frowned at the circles under her eyes before pouring Zoe a huge glass of water and waiting until she'd swallowed every drop. "Lucky you're young. You can get away with this," she'd said, in a heavily accented voice, before taking Zoe's chin in her hand and examining Zoe's face in the cool wintry light that came through the window. "Don't take it for granted. It won't last forever." Once Zoe had been made up, her face painted and her hair curled into loose waves, she'd gone downstairs, hearing whispers as she walked through the lobby and into the waiting SUV, where she'd tried to ignore her pounding head, her sweaty temples, and how any sudden movement made her feel like she was going to hurl.

In the MTV studios, she sat, legs crossed in dark-rinse jeans, in an armchair, with Times Square behind her and an audience of two hundred people, mostly teenage girls, in front of her. Through the floor-to-ceiling windows, Zoe could see what looked like a thousand more fans thronging the sidewalk, bundled up in scarves and mittens and winter coats, carrying posters with the band's name, with pictures of Russell and Zoe and Cassie. Carson Daly lobbed softball questions at them, and the fans asked them things like who were their influences and what was their favorite song to perform.

"You two seem very happy," Carson said, nodding at Zoe and Russell. Carson was handsome, but his features were almost too regular, his hair stiff with spray. Russell was better-looking, she decided, and squeezed his fingers.

"Oh, yes," she said. "Very, very happy."

"Any new developments?" Carson asked, his smile turning slightly sharklike. "Any news you'd care to share?"

For a terrifying moment, Zoe felt her mind go blank. What news? What developments?

Russell was the one who answered, smiling gently as he shook his head. "We're very happy," he said, which seemed to satisfy both Carson and the fans. She felt her sister stiffen in the director's chair beside her, and thought, *Poor Cassie.* Cassie could handle the singing just fine, but she was obviously desperately uncomfortable being this close to fans, without the boundaries of a stage or the benefit of darkness. Cassie was wearing a suit identical to the one she'd worn on *Saturday Night Live,* only with a blue shirt underneath instead of a black one. Zoe could see how the arms of her chair were digging into her body, how her hands gripped the seat's armrests.

Poor Cassie, Zoe thought again, and leaned her head on Russell's shoulder.

There'd been a commercial break, when they'd gone to set up for their performance, and that was when Zoe felt that sense of slippage again, that feeling that she was losing her place in the world, hanging on to an unraveling thread. "How about we let Cassie sing 'Fishtown' by herself?" Russell had asked in the huddle.

For a moment, the words hadn't registered, and, when they did, Zoe felt like he'd stabbed her. She'd looked at Cam and Tommy to intervene . . . but Tommy had been eye-fucking some young woman— employee or intern or audience member, Zoe wasn't sure—and Cam had been doing some complicated yoga pose, and Cassie had been as mute and expressionless as ever as she'd nodded, then plodded to take her seat behind the piano.

And then she'd sung brilliantly, as beautifully as Zoe had ever heard her sister sound. Zoe knew she'd been good, when she'd taken the part on Saturday night, but there was the difference between being good and being excellent; between a decently made pancake and an unforgettable seven-course brunch. Cassie had performed with her eyes closed, as usual, with her face mostly expressionless, but she'd infused the song with such feeling, such sorrow and pain, such a heart-rending ache, that even Zoe, who'd heard every word a hundred times, at rehearsals and sound checks and all the takes they'd done recording the album, found herself close to tears. By the time Cassie sang the final words—*your taillights kiss the dark; a long goodbye*—and let the last notes fade, at least a third of the girls in the audience were in tears, and Russell was looking at her sister like Cassie had invented music—like she'd made the world and had started it spinning. Zoe felt like a grape on a greased plate, after someone had tilted the plate sideways, and she was helpless to keep herself from falling.

That night, instead of coming to the suite she was sharing with her sister, Russell invited Cassie to his room. "We've got to finish this song," he told Zoe.

"Sure," she said, her voice and face expressionless. He nodded, and then he and Cassie were gone, and Zoe was alone. She stared at herself in the mirror, trying to be dispassionate, to see herself the way the world did. A few days ago, when they'd arrived in New York, Jerry had called her into his office, all by herself. He'd eyed her up and down, then slid his hand around her waist. His fingers were small, but they hurt when he pinched the flesh at her sides. "Let's keep an eye on this," he'd said. He hadn't said more than that, but Zoe wasn't stupid, and she'd heard the rest: *Stay thin. Stay pretty. That's what you're there for, and you can be replaced.*

For a long time, Zoe had looked at herself in the mirror, as the minutes went by and the skies went dark and Russell stayed away. There, by herself, she'd come up with a plan.

When the alarm clock went off at four in the morning on Tuesday, Zoe had groaned theatrically, dragging herself into the shower. By the time she emerged, wrapped in a hotel bathrobe, the hair-and-makeup team was setting up. Cassie was already parked in a chair, draped in a cape, with a hairstylist eyeing her head, sighing over the task that awaited. Zoe felt that sense of splitting again, her body moving through its day, her spirit hovering to watch from a distance. She put on her jeans and boots and cropped wine-colored velvet top. At six A.M., an SUV collected them and took them to the studio. A stage had been set up in the middle of Rockefeller Center, with space heaters in each of the corners, so that Tommy's and Russell's and Cam's and Cassie's fingers wouldn't be too chilled to play their instruments. A crowd was already gathering as the sun came up, girls and their mothers bundled into wool coats and down puffers, holding signs that said "I ❤ The Griffin Sisters" and "I Luv U Russell" and "I'm Your Flavor," with an illustration of an ice-cream cone beside it.

The five of them sat in the greenroom, smiling and waving at the camera at the producers' direction. "Coming up, just moments from now, we've got the Griffin Sisters, playing their brand-new single . . . only on the *Today* show!" The show's makeup artists touched them up, brushing powder onto Zoe's face, patting a sponge on Russell's forehead. At precisely 7:18, they'd trooped out onto the stage, to the screams and cheers of the audience. At 7:21, Katie Couric, bundled into an overcoat, with leather gloves and a knitted hat, introduced them, and they'd played "When You're Here." Zoe had watched the camera, on its dolly, swooping around her sister, close enough to catch every change in Cassie's expression, every note she played, while Zoe stood, shivering and ignored, feeling the wintry air against her bare skin, barely bothering to open her mouth for her "ooohs" and "aaahs" or shake her tambourine.

When the song was over, and the crowd had stopped clapping, Katie invited the band to sit in director's chairs that production assistants had swiftly lined up at the front of the stage. Zoe heard the familiar words and phrases blur in the air around them: *Congratulations* and *world tour* and *number-one single.* Then Katie Couric turned to her.

"And Zoe Griffin! A number one album, a brand-new single, and a world tour with your sister and your boyfriend! You must be on top of the world!"

Zoe licked her teeth to make sure they'd be gleaming when she smiled. *Here we go,* she thought, as she reached for Russell's hand. "I'm so happy, Katie. I feel like the luckiest girl in the world. For everything you said, and something else too."

"Oh?" Katie asked her, with a conspiratorial grin. Her eyes sparkled. She leaned in close. "Anything you'd like to share?"

"Yes," said Zoe. "Russell and I are getting married!"

The rest of the show passed in a haze of congratulations, joyous screams from the crowd (whether a few of them were pained, Zoe couldn't tell), questions about when the wedding would be. "I'll keep an eye out for my invitation!" Al Roker had said, chuckling. Russell had smiled and nodded, nodded and smiled, gripping her hand tightly enough to hurt. Zoe counted herself lucky that he hadn't immediately pulled back and said, *What are you talking about?* or told her—or Katie Couric—*No, we're not!*

Back in the greenroom, saying goodbye, finding her coat and her bag, Zoe couldn't bring herself to look at Russell, although she did see the shock on her sister's face and the furious look on Tommy's. The band was silent as they piled into the SUV—first Cassie, then Cam, then Tommy. Before she could climb aboard, Russell took her hand. His voice was low and steady as he said, "We're going to walk."

Zoe let him take her hand and lead her toward Central Park. It was funny, she thought—onstage, with her tambourine, she was famous, easily recognizable as prey worth stalking . . . but now, in a black puffer coat, with the hood pulled up and Russell, in a baseball cap, beside her, she was completely anonymous.

The gray clouds seemed to press down on them; the sky threatened snow. Zoe pulled her coat around her more tightly as Russell led them along the sidewalk. He kept a brisk pace, barely looking at her as they joined the throng of pedestrians—moms pushing strollers, attendants pushing wheelchairs, walkers and joggers and happier-looking couples walking arm in arm. Finally, he found a bench and sat, pulling Zoe down beside him. Zoe crossed and recrossed her legs. Russell folded his hands in his lap.

"What the fuck, Zoe," he said, his voice tight. "Why would you—how could you—"

"Because I love you," she said.

Russell turned to face her. There was still *Today* show powder on his cheeks and *Today* show gel in his eyebrows. Underneath them, his eyes were wild.

"Tell me the truth," he said to her. "Is this really what you want?"

Zoe swallowed hard. She'd been so certain, last night in the hotel room, when she'd finally come up with a plan that would assure her spot in the band forever. She really liked Russell. She did. She was happy with him. But now she felt herself gripped with terror. Marriage . . . she was twenty-one! A baby! No one she knew her age was married, except for Julia Darnell, back in high school, and that was only because she'd gotten pregnant senior year.

Zoe made herself stop thinking about poor Julia, who'd brought her newborn daughter with her to graduation, and who was, her friend Sammi had told her, currently getting a divorce. (Sammi had been delighted to renew their acquaintance, once she'd heard the Griffin Sisters' first single on the radio, and had even apologized for kicking Zoe out of Girl Power!, back in the day.) She put out of her mind the man in the hotel gym and the man who'd waited with roses in the rain, the up-and-coming young male movie stars and comedians. She took all her doubts about whether Russell wanted her and whether she wanted him and put them in a box. She pictured a wedding on the beach; bare feet and red lipstick, a simple satin slip dress, like the one Carolyn Bessette had worn to marry John F. Kennedy Junior. Her arms and shoulders lightly tanned, a crown of flowers in her hair. She saw herself, walking on the sand, down an aisle made of seashells and votive candles, as A-list movie stars and pop stars looked on. Her spot in the pop-culture firmament and her role in the band would both be assured; cemented into place with the bonds of holy matrimony. The label couldn't kick her out if she was married to Russell. And no one would ever know that she'd been the one to pursue him, that she'd gotten him drunk that first night and half forced her way into his bed. No one would know that she felt, sometimes, like she was holding on to him the way a mountain climber clings to a rock face, desperate and terrified of falling.

She turned to him, feeling the coldness of the bench and the sidewalk seeping up into her skin. She took his hand. "This feels right," she said, through cold-chilled lips. "Doesn't it feel right to you?" Without waiting for him to answer, she continued, "And it's not like we can, you know. Put the toothpaste back in the tube."

"You could say you were kidding," Russell muttered, but he didn't sound hopeful.

"This will be a good thing! You'll see," she said. "We'll get tons of free publicity, right before the world tour. It'll be the wedding of the year!"

"That's the wedding. What about after? When we're married?" He turned to look at her, full in the face. "We haven't known each other that long—"

"It's been a year," Zoe interrupted. "Almost."

"We've only been together a few months," Russell said, speaking precisely.

"But we're a good fit," she said, before he could. "Aren't we?"

She watched his chest rise and fall, saw his breath emerge whitely in the December air. It was still morning, even though Zoe felt like she'd been awake for a week. For a year. She wondered what he was thinking, if he was trying to figure out how to walk back her announcement, which had probably made its way around the world by now. She could guess what Jerry would tell him: the damage that un-announcing an engagement would cause, how it would set them back, harm everything they'd been working toward. Un-announcing an engagement would set them back, while a wedding would slingshot them forward. She wondered if he could guess what she was thinking, which was that it didn't have to be forever. Nobody's marriage had to be forever. She could say the words, make the vows, and then, in a year or two, or five, or ten, after she'd made herself indispensable and no one could imagine the Griffin Sisters without her, she could change her mind.

Russell's shoulders were hunched, his face tense and shuttered. She thought back to the picture she'd seen, of a long-ago Russell, with his bulky, shapeless body and his curtain of dyed black bangs. Part of him still had to feel incredibly lucky that she wanted him, Zoe suspected. And so she pulled off her hat, and shook out her hair, and smiled at him, touching his arm. "I'm happy with you," she said, and licked her lips, watching his gaze follow the motion of her tongue. "We're good together, right?"

He nodded like he'd been hypnotized. Which, maybe, he had been. Zoe felt a little bit like she'd been hypnotized too. A number one album. A sold-out tour. Riches past imagining; fame beyond anything she'd ever dreamed about. If she could manage to lock it in. If she could convince him to go along with this.

"So?" she asked, eyebrows raised, her heart in her throat and her pulse hammering wildly.

"Okay," he said, in a voice that was almost inaudible. "Okay," he repeated, and took her hand.

In the kitchen, in South Philadelphia, Zoe watched her great-aunt get to her feet. She felt the same way she'd felt on that park bench on that cold December day, like her life was hanging in the balance, like she was waiting for a judge to deliver a verdict, and it would not be a good one.

Bess made her way back to the stove. She collected the kettle, and then carried it to the sink to refill it.

"You remember the wedding, right?" Zoe asked.

"Of course I do." Bess's face gave nothing away. "I was there. You were a beautiful bride."

Zoe shook her head. Had Russell developed feelings for her sister before the wedding, or after? She'd never asked, but, if she had to guess, she would have said before. By the time they were standing on the beach, promising to love and cherish one another, forsaking all others until death did them part, she thought that Russell had already given his heart away. All of the events that would lead to his death had been set in motion. The final verse had already been written. The end had already begun.

Cassie

ALASKA, 2024

Okay," Cherry said. Wesley was sitting at the girl's feet, resting his head against her leg, looking up at her adoringly when she petted him and beseechingly when she stopped. "So, you and Russell were into each other, and then you went to New York for *SNL*, and he and my mom got engaged."

Cassie nodded. She wanted to tell Cherry more; something like, *You say it like it's nothing, like it's ancient history, like it's something you read in a book. It hurt me to breathe,* she wanted to say. *It hurt me to be alive.*

"So what did you do?" Cherry asked. Her voice was hoarse, and there was something in her expression that Cassie recognized—that raw yearning for connection. For love.

"What do you mean?"

"I mean, did you say anything to Russell? Or my mom? Did you tell Russell that you had feelings for him? Did you ask him not to marry someone else?"

You say that, Cassie thought, *like it's possible. Like I would have been able to come up with those words and put them together and say them out loud.* "I didn't know what I wanted," she said slowly. "And, even if I had known, I wouldn't have known how to ask for it. Or make it happen." She wanted to explain, to tell Cherry that she was a tool, built for only one purpose. She could sing, could write songs and perform them. Asking her to do anything else, like actively participate in her own love life, or have difficult conversations with family members or bandmates, was like asking a spoon to take someone's temperature, or thinking a hammer could iron your dress. Cassie Grossberg-turned-Griffin wasn't built to do those things. And the person she'd once depended upon, the one person who'd helped her through the hostile, puzzling world, had become her adversary. Her romantic rival. Somehow, that was a thing that was true.

"What did I do?" Cassie said, repeating Cherry's question. "I congratulated them." She hadn't thought of it in so long, but now all the details of that terrible night came flooding back, overwhelming her.

After the whirlwind of December and the New Year, they'd been given a few days off. Zoe had gone to the Bahamas, with Russell and some of her girlfriends. Cassie had seen pictures of him with her sister, on the beach: Zoe, perfect in her black bikini; Russell's chest glistening from the water, dark hair clinging to his calves.

Tommy had gone to Australia. Cam and Wendy had gone to Jackson Hole. Cassie had gone home, back to the rowhouse where her parents still lived, to the bedroom she and Zoe had once shared. And then, five days into the New Year, Russell had left the resort and flown to Philadelphia, to her, so that they could work on a song.

She remembered how stupidly hopeful she'd been, how she'd told herself a fairy tale, one in which he'd arrive and say he and Zoe weren't really getting married after all. In her fantasy, Russell would walk through the door, windblown and dashing in his navy-blue coat, and say, *I want to be with you.* And then he'd reach for her, and Cassie would let him, and, somehow, magically, she would know what to say and what to do.

But when he'd gotten to their house, with his face tanned from the tropical sunshine, wheeling a suitcase behind him, he'd been quiet, his lips pressed together tightly. Cassie had greeted him, like always. He'd opened his guitar case, like usual. Except Cassie could already tell that this wasn't an ordinary day.

Russell could never hold still when they were writing. He'd sit down, then get up to pace for a bit, then sit down somewhere else. His knee would bounce, or he'd drum his fingers on some surface, like the song was moving inside of him. He'd always been that way, restless, antsy, but that afternoon, in her parents' living room, he'd seemed almost tormented, as if staying in one place would have hurt him. Cassie wasn't good about noticing other people's feelings, but even she had picked up on that. Finally, she had made herself ask him, "Is everything okay?"

He'd stopped pacing. He'd put his hands against his scalp and given his hair a tug that looked painful. And then, low-voiced, his face stormy, he'd said, "The wedding's going to be in May."

Cassie felt her insides crumple, her heartbeat judder to a stop. "Oh," she said, very softly. "Oh." And maybe she was imagining it, maybe she was lying to herself, but she didn't think he looked happy.

"Jerry has the whole thing set up. We're going to do it in Miami. On the beach. *People*'s going to do a big story, and *Access Hollywood* and *Entertainment Tonight* both want to cover it, and there's a hotel out there that's going to host the whole reception. Food and flowers and everything." He gave a rueful smile. "As long as their name's in the pictures."

"Oh," Cassie said again. She thought what he was describing sounded like an advertisement, a promotional stunt, and not two people in love pledging their lives to each other. She made herself step back from him and made herself smile. In her head, she heard herself say *Congratulations* and *I hope you'll be happy*. All of the correct, expected words and phrases—the things Zoe would have told her to say. But she couldn't make herself do it, couldn't force her lips to form the right shapes, couldn't get her lungs to gather enough breath. Russell rubbed at his eyes. "It'll be good for the band," he finally said. "That's what Jerry says. The timing . . . the timing's good. Lots of publicity."

"Yes," she said, a little faintly. "That's . . . yes. Good."

"And that was it?" Cherry was looking at her skeptically. Wesley, Cassie saw, was looking at her too. His head was tilted, and his eyes looked disappointed, like he'd expected better from her. Which was crazy, Cassie told herself. Her dog was not judging her, no matter how it looked. "You didn't fight for him? You didn't tell him how you felt?"

Cassie thought about trying to explain herself. How she'd never been in love, had never even liked a guy before Russell, how, not only was she a virgin, she'd never been kissed. How she was a spoon, and a spoon could not take someone's temperature, how she was a hammer, and a hammer could not say *I'm in love with you*, and *Don't marry Zoe, marry me*.

"I couldn't," Cassie said, acknowledging her failure, her own responsibility in everything that came after.

"So what did you say?"

"I said, 'We should work on the song.' And we did. And, after that, I tried not to feel anything for him anymore."

Cherry snorted, sounding bitter as she asked, "How'd that work out?"

Without looking at the girl, Cassie said, "About as well as you'd think."

Zoe

ON THE ROAD, 2004

If *Saturday Night Live* had been the pinnacle, the peak, the absolute high point of Zoe Grossberg/Griffin's life, the days that followed her announcement were among the lowest.

On Tuesday afternoon, Jerry had summoned her and Russell to his office. "My lovebirds!" he'd said, clapping his tiny hands together, his boyish face wreathed in a smile of absolute delight. "You're brilliant! It's wonderful! Let me see the ring!"

"There isn't a ring yet," Zoe said as Russell stood beside her, in stony silence.

A frown flickered across Jerry's face. Zoe wondered if he'd guessed at what had happened, if he had any idea that this marriage was a trap she'd sprung.

"Not to worry," he said, as his frown disappeared. "I know a guy. You just leave everything to me." Over the next few weeks, the wedding had come together, everything snapping into place with the kind of speed and ease that was only possible, Zoe suspected, when both the bride and the groom were famous. Event planners and hotels, caterers and florists, jewelers and designers, hair and makeup artists, and resorts were all eager to offer their locations and services and wares for free, as long as they were included in the photographs or mentioned in the copy. The date was set for the end of May, during a weeklong break from the tour.

The next afternoon, a jeweler came to their room with a briefcase full of gems. Zoe picked out her diamond, a three-carat stone that glistened with a pure blue light. She had it set in rose gold, and picked out a matching wedding band, plus one for Russell. Three weeks later, the tour resumed in Phoenix. That was when the trouble began.

On their first night back, they'd been in Zoe and Cassie's dressing room for their usual preshow meeting, just the five of them: Zoe and Cassie, Russell, Cam, and Tommy.

Russell clapped his hands. "Okay, let's huddle up."

They stood in a tight circle. This was their tradition: before every show they'd gather with their arms around one another's shoulders, and one band member would speak. Cam would usually bust out something Christian—"Lord, use your voices and our instruments to uplift Your glory." Tommy would stick to the basics: "Stay safe out there." Zoe, the most digressive, would begin with, "I love you guys," proceed to wishes for safety and excellence, and conclude with personal wishes for each of the band members ("Cam, I hope your solo is magic, and Tommy, may your snares sound as crisp as the first bite of a fresh apple on the first day of fall."). Cassie would murmur the same thing each time, "Let's break all the legs." Russell would say, "Teach us to care and not to care. Teach us to sit still." Zoe thought it was from a psalm, but it turned out it was from a T. S. Eliot poem. Cassie, who read poetry, had recognized it. Zoe, who read magazines, had not.

That night, instead of ending with "sit still," Russell ended with, "I think Cassie should sing 'Last Night in Fishtown' by herself again."

"Word," said Tommy, giving Zoe an unpleasant look.

"Fine," said Cam with a shrug.

And so Cassie sang it by herself that night, and again the next night. In Tucson, Zoe came to the stage for the preshow run-through, where she stared at the setup for a long time. She told herself she was being paranoid, that her microphone stand was where it had always been and had not been moved the tiniest increment away from the crowd. But two nights later, in Scottsdale, Zoe didn't go to the hotel with the rest of the band. She went to the arena to watch the load-in. She was there, in the wings, as the roadies carefully unloaded Cassie's grand piano—the one that traveled with them now, in its own U-Haul—and positioned it at the center of the stage. She saw them huddle for a discussion, then move to the microphone stands. The ones for the four backup singers stood, all in a row, to the right of Tommy's drum kit. Zoe's microphone was usually in front of them, and it was, that night . . . only not so far in front as it had been the night before. She didn't have a measuring tape, so she couldn't be sure, except she was sure. In her bones, in her heart, she knew. Cassie's piano had been moved closer to the crowd. Her microphone was farther away.

In the next city—Denver—she'd made CJ come to the arena with her. "Are you seeing this?" she asked. CJ had gotten a squirrelly look, his eyes drifting away from hers as he'd tugged at the hem of the day's Hawaiian shirt. "I think it's just got to do with the camera angles," he said. "Nothing to worry about!" Except after he'd mentioned cameras, Zoe started watching the monitors and noticing how they rarely seemed to be showing her face. She'd look up and see Cam or Tommy. Or, more and more frequently, Cassie. She hardly ever saw herself.

"Don't worry," CJ told her again. He'd been patting her shoulder, his round face earnest, his voice sincere. "You're doing fine. You're do-ing your best, and everyone knows it." Left unsaid was, *Your best isn't as good as everyone else's*. But it was true, and becoming more apparent with every show. The other four members of the band were accom-plished musicians. Tommy and Cassie were both prodigies. And what was Zoe, compared to that? A pretty girl with a tambourine, and a ridiculously large diamond on her finger.

The tour rolled along through the Southwest. Each venue was dif-ferent and all of them were fundamentally the same. The same green-rooms with beat-up furniture and unframed mirrors hanging on the backs of doors. The same photographs of the same big-name artists—always the Beatles, always the Rolling Stones—in cheap plastic frames. The same mazes of cinderblock hallways leading backstage, sometimes with taped arrows on the floor to direct them; the same smells of beer and sweat, overlaid with hairspray and perfume, that had sunk into the walls. The same burly roadies, yelling at each other about monitors and spike tape, dead cases and dB limits. The same marks to hit, the same dance steps to remember, the same set lists and songs to sing.

And the bad news kept coming. Backstage in Pittsburgh, after the venue manager droned through his talking points—the emergency exits; the evacuation plan; the list of friends, reporters, and assorted hangers-on who'd been granted backstage passes—Zoe noticed a new face.

"Zoe, this is Abby Ryan. She's a vocal coach," CJ said. "We've asked her to spend the next few weeks working with you."

"Just with me?" Zoe's voice was sharp.

"She's here for anyone who needs her," CJ said, hands spread in a gesture of conciliation. Zoe bared her teeth and hoped he took it as a smile.

The Internet had still been in its infancy back then. Zoe knew bet-ter than to go looking for reviews, but sometimes it felt like some mi-nor demon took possession of her body. She'd be in the shower, or in the gym, on the StairMaster, or lying next to Russell, her mind on the next show or wedding. Then she'd blink and she'd be at the hotel-room desk in front of her laptop, typing her name into Yahoo or AOL or Ask Jeeves, knowing that what she'd find would be bad; unable to stop herself from looking.

She makes Linda McCartney sound like Whitney Houston, one chatroom commenter had said. The poster had taken the trouble of isolating her vocal track, and Zoe heard her voice, high and thin, nasal and off-key, when she hit play.

"Ten Worst Zoe Griffin Performances," a blog post she'd seen had been headlined . . . and, *Am I crazy? Is anyone else hearing how awful she is?*

How'd she even end up in a band? someone would ask, in the comments beneath a review of the show, one of many where Cassie got glowing notices, the critics emptying their thesauruses to find new words to describe how great she was, and Zoe was barely mentioned at all. *Um, hello? Nepotism,* someone else would respond, and Zoe would sit there, cotton-mouthed and furious, thinking, *If it wasn't for me, none of you would have ever heard Cassie!* Sometimes, there'd be a picture of her, and, instead of words underneath it, there'd just be punctuation marks used to make primitive laughing-crying faces that preceded the invention of emojis. Those, somehow, were worst of all.

The last thing she wanted to do was remind Russell of how little she was contributing, how her place in the band was essentially unearned. But sometimes she couldn't help herself from asking for a little reassurance. *You're being paranoid,* he'd say, a little impatiently, and Zoe would agree, would apologize, even though she could see evidence to the contrary was all around her. When she and her sister walked into a room to meet reporters, she wasn't the one people wanted to hear from. When that reporter from *Rolling Stone* had come backstage in Richmond to interview them, he'd directed almost all of his questions at Cassie and Russell. "Tell me how you guys wrote 'Flavor of the Week'?" he'd asked, and then he'd bent over his skinny rectangular notebook, pen flying. "Cassie gets the credit for that one," Russell said, and Cassie, laughing—laughing!—had shaken her head, saying, "Oh, no, Russell's just being modest. That was all him." Cassie's face had been flushed, her expression animated, hands moving as she spoke, and she'd been standing up straight, not hunched over and hiding. *Has she lost weight?* Zoe wondered. But, no. Cassie had not gotten any smaller. It was, in fact, the opposite. Her sister had stopped trying to make herself small, was no longer trying to hide. Cassie's arms were spread, her legs were planted firmly, and she was talking about major fifths and relative minors, about Bach's French Suites, and why they'd decided to add an oboe to "Flavor of the Week."

"You studied classical piano, correct?" the reporter asked, looking impressed, and Cassie nodded and started talking about the Curtis Institute and all of her professors there, taking the time to spell each one of their names. Zoe felt fury building inside of her, and it only got worse when the photographer arrived. The woman had her assistant set up a ladder onstage, and she'd perched on top, taking test shots with her Polaroid camera, directing Cassie and Russell to the center of the shot, telling Zoe to stand in the back row with Cam. "Nice . . . nice . . . lovely," she'd said, clicking away. Zoe had wanted to hit someone or throw something. *Do you think anyone wants to look at her?* she'd wanted to shout. Instead, she just did what it felt like she'd been doing for her entire tenure in the band. She smiled, and held her tambourine, and looked pretty.

She'd needed her fiancé. She'd needed someone to lean on, someone to love her, to tell her that she was desirable, beautiful, worthy, and that she belonged. Except Russell was pulling away. "Hey, let's get some sleep," he'd said, when she'd turned toward him in bed that night, arms out, needing comfort after the scene with the reporter. In Pittsburgh, he told her he had a cold and that they shouldn't sit together on the bus, in case he was contagious (but, she noticed, he had no compunctions about sitting with Cassie, for hours, to talk about whatever they were writing). In the Marriott in Columbus, Ohio, he said he had a migraine, and in the Hyatt in Cleveland, when Zoe had refused to take no for an answer and had pulled off her pajamas and climbed on top of him, he'd tried to keep her hands from wandering below his waist and had finally told her that he didn't feel up to sex, that he'd had too much to drink.

"Did I do something wrong?" Zoe finally asked, climbing off of him and out of the bed. She was wearing her panties and a lace-trimmed camisole, and Russell had pulled his boxer-briefs back on (a good thing too, Zoe thought—in her opinion, there wasn't anything as insulting as a flaccid penis).

"Of course not," Russell had said. He stood up and took her hands, rubbing his thumb over her engagement ring. For one brief, terrible moment, Zoe wondered if he was going to tell her that the engagement was a mistake and end things for good. Zoe had hurried to the bathroom, taking an extra-long time to floss her teeth, waiting until there was a good chance Russell would be sleeping before she slunk back to bed. She lay awake for most of the night, trying not to think about how the whole world believed they were a couple, passionately in love. They thought Russell wrote his songs for her, that he couldn't keep his hands off her, when the reality was, he wrote his songs with Cassie—maybe not for Cassie, but *with* Cassie, and definitely not with, or for, Zoe. Zoe was the one he kissed, and touched, and put himself inside of . . . but she knew that Cassie mattered to him more.

In Philadelphia, in her great-aunt's kitchen, Zoe made herself tell the rest. "I was lonely," she told Bess. "And angry. I should have talked to Russell and told him how I was feeling." Then she shook her head. "I should have just broken up with him. Or quit the band. That would have been the smartest thing to do." She could remember every detail of those terrible weeks and months. How she'd gotten quieter and angrier as the tour continued, as the fans and the journalists clamored for Cassie, as Zoe got pushed farther and farther to the margins, farther and farther toward the wings.

Aunt Bess looked at her, unblinking. Aunt Bess was Team Cassie for life, Zoe thought wearily. She didn't want to finish the story, but she knew she had to keep going. She'd come this far. Time to get all the poison out.

"I thought about trying to make Russell jealous. Flirting with other guys." She smiled thinly. "Having the security guards pick out cute ones so they'd be waiting for me backstage. But that wasn't what I did."

Bess waited.

"I found someone else." Zoe's eyes were still closed as she spoke a name she hadn't let herself say, or think, in years. "Tommy."

Tommy, the band's drummer, her sister's former Curtis classmate, had always had a crush on her. The worse things had gotten with the band, the more flattering Zoe had found his attention. It soothed the sting of the cruel comments, and the vocal coach's presence, and Russell's indifference, and the way her microphone kept inching backward. Maybe the fans weren't calling her name; maybe the big screens were showing her sister, but Zoe knew that at least one pair of eyes would always be looking at her. "Can I get that for you?" Tommy would ask, reaching for her tambourine as they came offstage, placing it carefully in its cinched velvet sack. He dubbed himself the Guardian of the Velvet Bag. "Milady," he'd say, waving his arm with an elaborate flourish, urging Zoe to walk ahead of him as they boarded the bus on their way to the shows, taking her hand to help her off when they arrived at their destination. "Come sit with me," he'd urge her, every time they boarded the bus. Sometimes she would. She'd hold his hand as they walked from the bus to the hotel, swinging their arms up and down jokingly. On the bus, she'd pretend to fall asleep with her cheek against his shoulder, willing Russell to turn around and look. Russell hardly ever did. Zoe kept trying, sitting with Tommy, touching his arm or his face, asking him flattering questions, gazing at him while he spoke.

And, eventually, Zoe realized that she wasn't just flirting to be strategic or manipulative and that Tommy was not just a means to an end. Zoe found that she actually liked him. He was cute, with his sharp haircut and the little rock-star swagger he'd acquired in their months on the road. *Maybe I'm marrying the wrong guy,* she found herself thinking, one night in May, as they drove through the darkness somewhere in South Carolina, with Tommy sitting beside her and Russell sitting up front, next to her sister. But by then it was too late.

Russell D'Angelo and Zoe Griffin got married in Miami, as planned, on a beach at sunset, in front of three hundred people, maybe forty of whom they actually knew. The rest of the guests were other famous people: musicians, actors, reality TV stars, celebrities represented by the same agents or publicists or working with the same corporations, who could benefit from the exposure. It was all transactional. At least Zoe looked just like she'd imagined, barefoot, in a bias-cut slip-style gown of ivory silk with spaghetti straps, with her hair in loose waves, topped by a crown of pale pink roses.

Cassie wore a long-sleeved navy-blue gown that fell to her shins with a matching bolero jacket with rhinestone details, an outfit so hideously nondescript that it zoomed past mother-of-the-bride-wear and settled comfortably into a niche for grandmother of the bride.

The morning of the wedding, in the bridal suite, as Janice fussed with Zoe's veil, and Sammi Johnson, who'd flown in the night before, drank champagne and giggled, and Bess sat silently in the corner, Cassie had said, "I'm happy for you," in a muted voice.

"Thank you," Zoe said graciously. Maybe Cassie would have said more, but the wedding planner, with her earpiece and her clipboard, was knocking on the door, saying, "It's time." Sam walked Zoe down the aisle, and Cassie held her bouquet, and Janice cried—in bewilderment, Zoe suspected, as much as joy. Less than a year and a half ago, Zoe had been an indifferent student at the Community College of Philadelphia. Now she was famous, and there were movie stars and musicians standing on the sand, craning their necks for a glimpse of her, counting themselves lucky to be in attendance. Best of all, her sister, the one destined for fame and glory, had been relegated to a secondary role. *For once,* Zoe thought meanly, *Cassie is my backup singer.*

At the reception, in a candlelit ballroom, Zoe and Russell entered through an archway of roses. Russell sang "God Only Knows" to her, and they slow-danced to "Never My Love." Cam and CJ both gave speeches, as did Sammi Johnson, Zoe's friend from home and former bandmate. Zoe hadn't even asked Cassie if she wanted to speak, knowing that her sister wouldn't. Nor did she ask Cassie if she wanted to sing. The last thing Zoe wanted was to be upstaged on her own wedding night.

Zoe and Russell fed each other bites of lobster and filet mignon in red wine reduction, tiny mushroom tartlets, and lemon wedding cake with raspberry fondant, and they danced, first in the ballroom, then, later, on the sand, as a DJ played club music. They went to bed at four in the morning, too footsore and exhausted to make love. That happened the next morning. For the first time in a long while, Russell was an enthusiastic participant, reaching for Zoe, first in bed, then in the oversized shower. They flew to Tahiti on a borrowed private jet that Jerry had procured and spent three nights in a cabin that stood on stilts above the turquoise-blue sea. They swam, and made love, and feasted on dorado and squid and oysters pulled right out of the water and, at night, the sound of the waves lulled them to sleep. Zoe barely minded when, on the second day, Russell spent three hours on the phone with her sister, working through the pre-chorus of the song they were hoping to debut soon.

"I love you," Zoe said to Russell, as the plane touched down in St. Louis, where the rest of the band was waiting.

Her husband had smiled and touched her cheek. His face was tanned, and his eyes looked especially clear. "You're my girl," he told her, and cupped her cheek in his hand. "Ready to go back to the salt mines?"

Zoe smiled and nodded. Later, she would think that it was the last time she'd been happy with Russell, when they were still inside the airplane, on the runway, in that placeless, liminal nowhere, where she was no longer a bride, but not yet a wife, or a musician on a world tour.

Zoe had thought that being married would change things. But other than officially sharing a hotel room with Russell instead of her sister, not much was different. Russell continued to spend more time with Cassie than with her. On the bus, he and Cassie would sit together, humming phrases of music or listening to a song on Russell's portable CD player, or with their heads bent over one of Cassie's notebooks. During the shows, they would sing together, with Cassie at her keyboard and Russell standing center stage. Cassie would have her eyes closed, and Russell would have his eyes on her. Zoe would be watching the monitors, watching her husband being awed by someone who was not her.

It hurt. So did the nights where Russell said he was too tired to have sex with her . . . or when he'd be asleep, or pretending to be asleep, by the time she finished taking off her makeup, before she could even get into bed. When he did stay awake long enough to attend to his conjugal duties, the lovemaking felt perfunctory, like no matter what she did, or how beautiful she looked, she only ever had half of his attention.

And Tommy, when he wasn't indulging the female groupies clamoring for his attention, was always there, watching her, loving her, hoping for his chance.

Tommy kissed her for the first time after the show in Arlington, Virginia, as they stood in the wings between their second and third encores. He'd drawn Zoe into a dark corner, between a curtain and a stack of amps, and, while the crowd clapped and stomped and chanted the band's name, he'd wrapped his arms around her, pulling her close, kissing her cheek, then the corner of her mouth, and then, very gently, her lips. "I've been wanting to do that forever," he whispered.

Zoe remembered how her skin prickled with heat. She felt flushed, weak-kneed, aroused in a way she hadn't been in weeks by his desire. *All I want is to be wanted*, she'd think on the tour bus, as she stared at the back of her husband's head bent close to her sister's.

"We kissed for the first time in Virginia, and we slept together ten days after that, in Tampa," Zoe told her aunt. She remembered Tampa specifically—how the humid Florida air threatened to make her straightened hair go frizzy, and left the hotel carpet feeling slightly spongy under her feet. She remembered getting back to their room at two in the morning—two A.M. was an early quitting time, in those upside-down days, where, sometimes, they'd party after the shows, then climb onto the bus at dawn and sleep all day. That night, they'd all gone right back to the hotel. Russell had been brushing his teeth in the bathroom when Zoe came and wrapped her arms around his waist.

"C'mon, Zoe. I'm exhausted," he'd said.

"So you're not up to performing your marital obligations?" she'd asked, hoping that humor might build a temporary bridge over the space between them. Their eyes had met in the mirror, and Russell's face had looked tired, and sad. He'd climbed into bed without glancing back.

Zoe had taken off her makeup and gotten into her nightgown. She'd laid herself down beside him, then, almost immediately, she'd gotten up again, knowing she'd never be able to sleep. She'd gone outside to stand on the balcony instead, and looking to her right, she'd seen Tommy, standing on his. He was shirtless, with drawstring cotton pajama bottoms hanging low on his hip bones.

"Hey," he'd said, lifting one hand in an ironic salute.

"Hey."

"Can't sleep?"

Zoe had shaken her head.

"You should come over." The offer hung in the humid night sky.

"I should go to sleep."

"I'll rub your back," Tommy had offered.

I've got a husband for that, Zoe had thought. Except she didn't. Her husband was in bed, snoring softly, his head full of dreams and music and, possibly, her sister. He didn't see her. But Tommy looked at her like she was the only thing he could see, like she was bigger than the sky and brighter than the moon.

Zoe had barely felt herself deciding. One minute she had been out on the balcony, and the next she'd been moving silently through the hotel room, her bare feet silent on the spongy carpet, then slipping out the door and into the room next door, where Tommy had been waiting for her.

The lovemaking had been exactly what she'd craved. Tommy had spent what felt like hours just touching her—her hair, her eyebrows, the insides of her elbows. He'd planted a line of slow kisses along her collarbones, then turned her over and traced the bumps of her verte-brae with the tip of his tongue. He'd run his fingertips up and down her thighs, long, slow teasing strokes from her knees to her belly, first gen-tle, then more insistent, coaxing her legs open, waiting patiently, until her hips started to rise and fall, until she was pushing herself at him with her mind blissfully empty—no words, no thoughts, just desire.

Tommy cherished her. Tommy adored her. Tommy seethed with jealousy every time Russell touched her, every time he saw a picture of Zoe and Russell together, every time the photographers called for a shot of the two of them. "Hey, Zoe! Russell! This way," they'd say, or "Give him a kiss!"

And so he wooed her, leaving her little gifts, sending flowers to her dressing room, tucking love notes into her pockets. In Hartford, Rus-sell had gone off with Cassie, and Zoe had barely waited for the door to shut before she'd gone to Tommy's room. He'd filled the tub for her, scooping her into his arms, settling her into the warm water, scented with bath salts. She'd closed her eyes, and he'd washed her hair.

In Boston, she'd found a heart-shaped gold locket in her dressing room, with the words *Be Mine* and Tommy's initials engraved on the back. In New York, during a four-day stand at Madison Square Gar-den, he said, "I want to be with you forever."

Tommy's declaration had thrilled her and terrified her, filling her with dread and delight and confusion. What was she supposed to do? Dump Russell and be with Tommy? Leave the band, go back home, start another life? Find the thing that she was really good at, which wasn't music, and would probably not end up with her being famous and rich and adored?

"I was trying to come up with a plan," she said to Bess. "Trying to find a way out, I guess. Tommy wanted me to end things with Russell." She gave a humorless laugh. "Even though it felt like Russell had al-ready pretty much ended things with me, we were still a couple, as far as the public was concerned. Tommy hated that. He kept pushing me to tell Russell what was going on. But I was worried it would . . ." She gestured vaguely.

"That it would break up the band?" Bess asked.

Zoe started to nod. Then she shook her head. "No," she said. "Honestly? I wasn't even thinking about the band. I was thinking about myself. How I'd get blamed for the breakup, even though Russell was the one who wanted out. I was thinking about that, and I was thinking about Cassie winning. If I let Russell go, if I went off with Tommy, it would mean that Cassie had won. And I couldn't stand that."

Bess looked at her steadily.

Zoe touched her hair, then clasped her hands on her lap. She'd been wondering whether Bess would get there by herself—if she'd ask, or make Zoe say it. "And I got pregnant."

"Oh." Her great-aunt's voice was soft and uninflected. Her expression wasn't angry. Nor was it particularly surprised. Zoe looked down. "The night that Russell died, I was going to tell him that I was with Tommy. I thought he was probably getting ready to dump me, and I figured, if I ended things first, at least I'd have my pride. Only then . . ."

She shut her mouth and closed her eyes, shuddering all over, remembering.

Cassie
ON THE ROAD, 2004

They'd been in Austin, Texas. She'd been sleeping, she remembered. She'd been sleeping as much as she could, since Zoe and Russell's wedding. It made things easier. When she was asleep, she didn't have to think about Russell, putting a ring on her sister's finger, kissing Zoe, singing to her in a ballroom full of candlelight and flowers. During shows, when she sang, she could imagine that there was nothing but that moment, where she and Russell were together. She could lie and tell herself that he was with her, and not with Zoe. And when she slept, she didn't have to think about anything at all.

And so, she spent as much of her time as possible in bed. Which was where she'd been at midnight, when she woke up to the sound of someone knocking.

Cassie got to her feet, swung the door open, and stared at Russell, who never just showed up; who always messaged first. It was one of the dozens of tiny ways that he accommodated her weirdness, one of the things he did to make the world easier for her.

"What is it?" Cassie asked. "Is something wrong?"

But Russell didn't look upset. He was beaming and his cheeks were flushed, hair disarranged. He reached for her hands. "Did anyone from the label call you?"

"What?" Cassie's brain felt thick and sluggish, like a bowl of cooling oatmeal.

"It went gold. The album went gold!"

"Oh," Cassie said. That was all she said before Russell grabbed her by the shoulders and whirled her into her room, dancing her past the bed, toward the window, then back toward the door again. He was laughing, and Cassie found that she was laughing too, laughing and whooping and feeling his hands against her.

Finally, Russell flung himself onto her bed, on his back, and Cassie flopped down beside him (but gently, so the bed wouldn't shake too hard and the bed frame wouldn't groan). She wondered if he'd told Zoe already, if the two of them had screamed with delight and gone bouncing around the room. She decided that she didn't want to know.

"Can you believe it?" Russell asked.

"No," she told him. Which was the truth. The album's release, the singles that had hit the charts, the band's entire existence—all of it felt like a dream to her, as improbable and unlikely as winning the lottery, or putting a tooth underneath your pillow and finding a million dollars there when you woke up.

"We could go platinum. We could win a Grammy," Russell said, sounding dreamy.

"Do you think so?"

"We've at least got a shot. Of course the album's been selling like crazy, but sometimes that kind of success can work against you," Russell was explaining. "They want to give prizes to something obscure, not something popular."

"Why?"

"To show how smart they are."

What would a normal girl say? What would she ask, what would she do? *Think*, Cassie told herself, and rolled onto her side, to find Russell looking at her. He was wearing a dark tee shirt and loose gray sweatpants. His feet were bare. "We're smart," she said. *You're smart,* she thought.

"Indeed we are," Russell agreed. "And even if we end up getting nominated, God knows they don't always get it right."

"What do you mean?"

Russell grinned at her and assumed his radio-announcer voice, one he'd probably honed after all those weeks listening to actual radio announcers. "The year was 1990, and the National Academy of Recording Arts and Sciences gave its award for Best New Artist to none other than Milli Vanilli."

Cassie grimaced. "Oh no."

"You don't remember?"

She found that she was smiling as she shook her head. "I would've been eight years old. I wasn't really paying attention yet."

"Ah, right. Of course. I forget you're such a baby." Cassie was pleased, even though she knew that thinking of her as a baby wasn't the same as calling her baby. But babies were small, and sweet, and cute. People loved babies.

Russell was still talking. "The real tragedy is that they beat the Indigo Girls. And I know it's extremely uncool to like the Indigo Girls, but they're the real deal."

"What happens if we win?"

He shrugged. "More fans. More attention. More money. More touring. More—just. Well. More."

"More," she repeated.

He must have heard something in her voice, or seen something on her face, because his own voice was gentle when he said, "Hey." He reached out. Cassie thought he was going to touch her face, and maybe that had been his intention, but he pulled his hand back and patted her shoulder. "What's wrong?"

She shrugged. "I don't know. Maybe I'm . . ." *Normal,* she told herself. *Sound normal.* "Homesick?"

She cringed as soon as she'd said it, but Russell just nodded. "Do you miss Curtis? Playing classical music?"

She shook her head no before she'd had a chance to think it over.

"Are you liking any of this at all?" His voice was as gentle as his hand had been, and he was close enough for her to get a hit of his scent, hotel soap and warm male skin. "I know being onstage isn't your favorite thing."

"I don't mind." Her voice was too loud; she'd spoken too abruptly. "I—I'm getting used to it. I guess."

"People love you."

She shook her head. "No, they don't. Not me. They love the songs, maybe. Or, you know. The band."

"No," Russell said. His voice was steady. "It's you. You're what makes us special. They love *you.*"

They love you was not *I love you.* Still, Cassie felt pleasure, warm and sweet, blooming inside of her, at the same instant a question occurred. Where was Zoe? Had he left her behind, asleep in their bed? Had he wanted to give Cassie the news first? Or did Zoe know already?

At the thought of her sister, Cassie closed her eyes, thinking that she could feel her heart aching. She'd always thought heartache was just another made-up thing that songwriters put in their songs, but, lying next to Russell, still tingling from his touch, she could feel an actual physical throbbing in her chest. She wanted to wrap her arms around him and hold him close and tell him how much she loved him; how much she understood him, how she'd be so much better for him than Zoe.

But she couldn't. Of course she couldn't.

She opened her eyes and found that Russell was still looking at her. For a long moment, she looked back, holding his gaze, unblinking, barely breathing.

He took her hand and got to his feet, pulling her upright.

"Come here," he said. He held his arms open, and she stepped close, leaning into him. Russell wrapped his arms around her, drawing her against his chest. His scent was all around her, and when she turned her head to press her cheek against his chest, she could feel his warmth, and hear his heart, beating in her ear.

It felt like a long time that they stood and swayed together, holding on like the other person was a raft in a storm-tossed sea. More clichés that also felt true.

When Russell moved one of his hands up her back, to gently cradle the base of her skull, she thought she would die of pleasure, that her body, unable to contain this amount of bliss, would simply explode. Being this close to him, feeling him, hearing him—it was almost too much. If she looked at Russell—if she remembered that Russell was looking at her—she would die.

"Hey," he whispered. They were so close that Cassie could feel the push of his breath on her lips as he shaped the words. She made herself open her eyes. Russell caressed her cheek with his thumb, then cupped her face in his hands. "Cassie," he whispered, and bent his head, gently brushing his lips against hers.

At first, Cassie stood motionless, frozen with disbelief, then shame. She'd never been kissed. She didn't know what to do with her hands or her lips or her tongue. But Russell was careful with her, his mouth gentle, respectful, like this, too, was a dance, only now he was showing her the steps. He brushed his lips against hers, lightly, and she pressed back, shivering as she felt his tongue touch the seam of her lips, and it was like some undiscovered part of her brain took over, and, just like that, her body knew what to do. She let her hands reach out, touching the soft skin of his neck, feeling along the broadness of his shoulders, the length of his back.

Russell kept one hand at the base of her neck, rubbing gently, the other around her shoulders, keeping her close. When he deepened the kiss, it felt like Cassie's entire body had been poured into just her lips and her tongue, like every nerve ending she had was there. When he slid his hand down her back, then reached under her sweatshirt, gliding his palm against her bare skin, she gasped.

"Okay?" Russell whispered.

She wanted to tell him yes. To close her eyes, press herself against him, let whatever had started to happen keep happening. Her body, mute and sullen for all her life, was suddenly speaking up, fiercely and urgently, telling her that it knew what to do.

Instead of listening, Cassie pulled back. "You're married." *To my sister* was left unsaid.

Russell kept his hand on her back, rubbing gentle circles. She felt him struggling in the brief silence, until he said, his voice low and angry, "It isn't real."

She looked at him, certain that she'd heard wrong or, somehow, misunderstood. "What do you mean?" She'd been there, at the wedding— had held the satin-wrapped stems of her sister's bouquet, had stood, stoic, under the branches that were not exactly a chuppah but, Zoe had explained to her mother and her grandmother and her great-aunt Bess, not exactly *not* a chuppah either. "And we'll raise the kids Jewish. Isn't that what matters?" she'd asked, when they'd made mention of the absence of a rabbi and the carefully nondenominational ceremony, which did not include the traditional seven blessings and ended with the groom stomping on a glass only because Zoe had decided it was "fun." Cassie had heard Zoe and Russell say their vows, had watched him put a ring on her sister's finger, and it had felt like she'd swallowed broken glass. Cassie could feel Great-Aunt Bess looking at her sharply, her eyes narrowed behind her bifocals as her gaze moved from Russell to Zoe to Cassie, then back again. Cassie had left the party as soon as she could to escape that scrutiny.

Russell took a step away from her (*No, no,* Cassie's newly awake and vocal body cried, *come back, come back!*). He yanked at his hair again. He said, his words clipped and precise, "When Zoe told Katie Couric we were engaged? We hadn't even discussed getting married. Not once. I had no idea she was going to do that."

Cassie stared at him. Of all the things Russell could have told her, this was the very last one she'd expected.

"And then—well, there wasn't any way that toothpaste was going back in the tube. Jerry was thrilled about all the publicity. And if we'd had to make an announcement to say it wasn't happening . . ."

"You would have looked like a jerk," Cassie said. She found that there was a part of her that could admire her sister's manipulations; a part that could marvel at how expertly Zoe had trapped him.

"And so." Russell squared his shoulders, a lone football player facing an onrushing horde of defenders. "I went along with it. What choice did I have?"

No choice, Cassie thought, feeling the words setting her blood alight. He didn't have a choice. Zoe had made him do it, against his will. Of course the marriage didn't feel real to him. In a rusty, croaking voice, she asked, "Do you love her?"

Russell pressed his hands against his eyes and muttered something Cassie couldn't hear. She waited, until he dropped his hands and sighed. "I'm an idiot," he said.

"No, you're not," Cassie said, her voice surprisingly steady. "But I need to know. Do you love her?"

Russell reached for her hand. Cassie let him take it, but when he tried to pull her closer, she resisted, settling her weight in her heels, so that he wouldn't be able to move her, until she had her answer. *She'll never love you like I do*, she wanted to tell him . . . but she made herself wait.

Russell gathered up both of her hands, squeezed them, and brought them to his heart. His eyes were very dark, and his voice was low and rough. "I don't love Zoe," he said. And then he bent his lips close to her ear, as Cassie thought, *Oh, please, oh, please, oh, please oh please oh please.*

And Russell whispered, "Not like I love you."

It was too much. Too much for her poor heart. Cassie looked up at him, certain that all of her fear and yearning were right there on her face, completely obvious, unmissable and unmistakable. "Even though I'm not pretty?"

Russell cupped her head again, touching his lips to her temple, and said, "You are. To me."

Inevitable, she thought, when they were in bed, and she was underneath him, her hands on his shoulders, her legs wrapped around him. *This was inevitable.* It was as if they were two stones that had been rolling toward each other since the world was made, working their way slowly around the earth's diameter until they met. It could not have happened any other way.

It took approximately sixty seconds from the time they'd stopped having sex for the guilt to swoop down and leave Cassie feeling sick with shame. She and Russell were lying on their sides, facing each other. His hand was on her shoulder, his fingertips touching her hair, and she didn't want to ask, didn't want to say her sister's name in the dark room, which conferred the same kind of invisibility that the stage lights did. She wanted to stay in the safe dark forever. But she made herself ask. "Tell me how it happened. You and Zoe," she said. "Tell me what happens now."

Russell made a humming noise, and Cassie could feel his hesitation. His voice was gruff, and he sounded ashamed as he said, "At first, she kind of . . . threw herself at me." Hastily, he added, "And I wasn't complaining. Zoe's a great girl. A lot of guys would be lucky to have someone like her interested in them." He turned onto his back, rolling his head from side to side on the pillow. "It was never going to be anything serious. Only then the tabloids started covering us, and Zoe clearly wanted to be with me." He snorted. "That sounds a little vain, doesn't it?"

"Zoe had her reasons." Cassie's voice was cool. She sounded detached, and unbothered, even though that wasn't how she felt. "I know the band was her idea, but—" She closed her eyes, like a true believer getting ready to blaspheme in a church. "She's not very good, is she?"

"No," Russell said. "She's not."

"And so, the marriage?" She wanted to ask about his plans; if he was going to stay with Zoe forever, or if he'd thought about an end point. She wanted to know if there was a world where she and Russell could be together.

"It's real for now," Russell said. He sounded glum. "I don't think she loves me. Not really. I think she loves the attention. And . . ." Russell exhaled noisily, then said, "I don't love her."

Cassie's heart felt like a kicked, starving dog that had smelled food, and heard someone calling to it kindly. She felt hope flaring inside of her, sharp-edged and bright.

"We haven't slept together in weeks," Russell said. "Not since the honeymoon, really." Cassie wondered what *really* meant, what ground it covered, what behaviors it might encompass. She decided that she'd been brave enough for one day, and didn't ask.

"Are you going to stay together?" she asked instead. "Is there a plan?"

The pause felt like it lasted a lifetime. "When the tour's over," he finally said. "If the band takes some time off. I think there's a way we can . . ." He sent his hands into the air, side by side, pressed against each other, then veering apart. "The issue is finding a way to do it where Zoe doesn't get blamed. Where the band doesn't suffer."

Cassie nodded eagerly. Zoe not getting blamed, the band not suffering, that all made sense. And now she understood how this had happened, how neatly Russell had been trapped. It seemed horribly unfair, ridiculously cruel. But Cassie knew she had limits. There were lines she wouldn't be able to cross without hating herself. "Russell . . ." She squeezed her hands into fists and made herself say it. "We can't do this again if you're still with her."

Her heart was beating very hard as Russell nodded, then reached up to grasp a lock of her hair. Her stupid hair that never looked right, that always frizzed or tangled, no matter what the stylists did to it. Russell touched it like it was beautiful. Like it was rare and lovely and precious. He stroked her cheek, ran the ball of his thumb lightly over her lips, until Cassie felt her eyes flutter shut. "All I want," said Russell D'Angelo, "is you."

"We didn't mean for it to keep happening," Cassie said, in her little treehouse, as Cherry leaned forward, listening carefully, and Wesley sat at her side. "And then, when we couldn't stop, when we couldn't keep away from each other, Russell wanted to tell people. He thought he could talk to Zoe, and make her understand, and then they would figure out a way to end things so it didn't look like either of them was at fault. And then we would give it some time, and after a while, we could be together."

"Did you believe him?" Cherry asked.

Cassie sighed. "I wanted to believe him." She did not add, *And I was very young.* "We talked about how to handle it. We tried to come up with a plan and, when we couldn't do that, we tried to stay away from each other. Which didn't really work." She swallowed hard and wiped her eyes. "We made each other happy."

"For ten minutes?" Cherry asked.

"For three weeks." Cassie let herself remember that handful of precious days they'd had, that brief, glorious interval when Cassie had loved someone and been loved in return. She and Russell truly had tried to be careful, but as the days went by, they got a little less attentive. Once, right before a show, Russell pulled Cassie into his dressing room, kicked the door shut, and kissed her until Cassie felt like she was swooning. Backstage, a few minutes later, Zoe had given Cassie her regular preperformance pep talk, telling her that she was talented, that she deserved to be there, that everything would be fine. For the first time, Cassie did not feel grateful or relieved. She'd been impatient for Zoe to stop talking. She'd felt guilty, and terrified that Zoe would be able to smell Russell on her, somehow, or that she'd look at Cassie and know.

They'd had close calls. In Toledo, Russell had gone onstage with the tiniest bit of Cassie's lipstick on his cheek. Cassie had been dismayed when she'd noticed, but part of her had been proud, that she'd claimed him, somehow, and had marked him as her own.

Then, on their way to Cleveland, they'd been on the tour bus late at night, bodies turned toward each other, talking quietly, their faces moving closer and closer together, until their hands were touching and they were close enough to kiss, when Cassie had heard Zoe's voice, and pushed Russell away from her, hard.

"Oh, hey, you two," Zoe said, her voice light, her expression untroubled. But Cassie knew her sister well enough to see how her eyes had narrowed, so briefly that it would have been easy for someone else to miss. Cassie saw, and was pleased. *That's right*, she imagined saying. *He's mine.* Except, Cassie thought, with a spasm of anger, her sister probably wouldn't believe it, wouldn't believe that Russell could want her, could choose her over Zoe. Not unless Zoe saw them in bed together, naked. In the ensuing years and months, she'd have time to wonder: Had she wanted it to happen? Had she wanted to obviate the possibility of the conversation, to do an end run around Zoe's skepticism, her inevitable disbelief? *You and Russell? Oh, Cass. Whatever you think is happening, it isn't real.* Cassie could picture the precise look her sister would get, the cloying sympathy on Zoe's pretty face. *Did Russell say something to you? Is he teasing you? Don't worry*, she would say. *I'll talk to him. I'll get him to stop.*

Boys had done things like that before. Boys had played cruel tricks. Laughed at her. Back in sixth grade, in February, Matthew Munson had left a Valentine in her desk—on a dare, it turned out. In eighth grade, a boy had walked up to her in the cafeteria at lunchtime, asking, with a perfectly serious look on his face, if she'd go to homecoming with him. By then Cassie knew not to trust any kindness extended to her by the opposite sex. She'd built armor up, constructing an internal world, a secret realm for just herself, the piano, and the songs that could explain how people were. And her sister. She'd let Zoe in. And then she'd let Russell in too.

She knew Russell loved her, that what they had was real. She knew, too, that Zoe would never believe her. Not unless she had evidence to the contrary. Maybe a part of Cassie resented Zoe for her beauty, and envied Zoe for her ease in the world, for always knowing what to say. Maybe that part of Cassie hated herself, too, for needing Zoe to help her navigate regular human contact.

Maybe that part—that small, hateful part—had caused what had happened to happen.

Three weeks after Cassie and Russell had first kissed, they'd had a rare night off in Detroit. The band had gone out to dinner, at an old-fashioned steakhouse downtown. The restaurant was below street level, with a speakeasy atmosphere: red velvet swags, dark leather banquettes, wood-paneled walls, and an old-fashioned phone booth tucked into the corner. At that point, every meal was a celebration, every day brought some bit of good news: another week with the number one album, a third single entering the Hot 100, ticket sales so strong they'd crashed the Telecharge network. There was always wine at those dinners, always cocktails beforehand, usually a bottle of champagne that someone would send over or the restaurant would give them for free. Fans would stare, or stop by their table, asking for autographs, or pictures snapped with hastily purchased disposable cameras, and if she'd had a glass or two of wine, instead of cringing, or hiding in the bathroom, Cassie would pull her shoulders back and smile.

That night, when dinner was over, Zoe announced that she was meeting a friend, a former high-school classmate attending the University of Michigan, who'd driven in from Ann Arbor to see the show. Cassie and Russell had gone back to the hotel, to Cassie's room, where they'd planned to enjoy the luxury of uninterrupted time together.

They'd had no idea that when CJ had handed out the hotel-room keys after dinner, he'd accidentally given Zoe a key to Cassie's room instead of her own. Or that Abby, the vocal coach, who'd tagged along for the night, had started feeling sick on their way to meet Zoe's friend. They didn't know that Abby and Zoe had turned around and come back without even reaching their destination. They'd had no idea, until they were in bed together, both naked, with Russell on top of her, and Cassie heard the click of the lock, the sound of her sister's indrawn breath.

Cassie had pushed Russell off of her, sending him scrambling for his pants. She made herself sit up, but, beyond that, she couldn't think of what to do or what to say. Part of her was terrified, and part of her was glad, relieved that this confrontation had finally come, that she and Russell wouldn't have to hide any longer. And how much would it matter? Russell had told her that he and Zoe weren't really together, and Cassie had believed him. Maybe Zoe would be relieved that she'd be able to stop pretending. Maybe she'd even be happy for her sister.

"Russell." Zoe's voice was cold, her face pale and still.

Russell turned his head to look at Zoe. He'd worked his jeans up over his hips, but his chest was still bare. Zoe had pointed toward the hallway.

"Outside," Zoe had said to him. Russell picked his shoes and shirt up off the floor and followed her out the door, without so much as a look back. Cassie had never seen him again.

Zoe

ON THE ROAD, 2004

All these years later, and Zoe could still recall, perfectly, how it had felt to find her husband and her sister, in bed, naked, together: how her head had felt like it was full of thunder, a great, crashing emptiness between her temples and behind her eyes. How everything seemed to be moving very slowly, as she stood there, frozen and shaking with rage and shock.

Russell had flung himself out of bed, grabbing for his pants (no flopping, flaccid penis in sight, Zoe noted coldly). Cassie had just lain there, looking across the room at Zoe, her cheeks pink, pale moon face perfectly calm. *I stole your man just like I stole your dream, and what are you going to do about it?* Zoe saw her life crashing down: being forced out of the band, her reputation shredded, because, of course, no one would ever believe that Russell had wanted her sister. They'd think that she'd been the one who'd cheated, that she'd broken his heart. They would blame her. It was the end of everything. And, with that vision, everything Zoe had meant to say, all of her plans to tell the truth, disappeared, obliterated by that eruption of rage.

"Outside," she'd hissed at Russell, and turned on her heel, hair flying as she went out into the hallway. He came after her, bare-chested in his jeans, his shirt and shoes in his hand and his head hanging down, pulling a key card out of his back pocket, letting her into their room. The bed was neatly made. A bouquet stood on the dresser, a profusion of flowers, roses and lilies in cream and gold, filling the room with its heavy, heady scent. There was champagne in an ice bucket. Zoe pictured herself lifting the bottle and swinging it at him, imagined the sound it would make when it hit Russell's head.

She turned toward him, breathless and shivering with shock. She felt very far away from herself, like she was watching this scene unfold across a distance of many miles and many years—herself, in her high ponytail and her going-out clothes: high-heeled black boots, glossy patent-leather leggings, and a long-sleeved halter top made of silver lamé knotted underneath her breasts. Before she could say a word, Russell started to talk.

"Zoe," he began. "I'm sorry this happened. I shouldn't have done it this way. I should have told you . . ." He paused to drag his hands through his hair. Zoe knew how that hair felt, sleek and soft against her fingers, except for the bristly bits at the nape of his neck, and she knew she would never touch it again. The thought kindled rage like a wall of fire.

Zoe kept her voice soft, kept her body still. "Explain it to me," she said.

He shrugged, giving her a sad smile. "I don't understand it either, to tell you the truth. But Cassie and I . . ." He was still smiling, but less sadly. His face looked almost dreamy, which enraged her even more.

"I'm pregnant," she said, without preamble. That slapped the dreamy look off his face. His mouth fell open. She saw his Adam's apple jerk as he swallowed.

"What?" he asked.

"Pregnant," Zoe pronounced, loudly and slowly, and watched the news land. Russell's eyes got wide. He put one hand, fingers splayed, on the room's wallpapered wall, like he'd fall down without its support.

He asked if it was true. She told him that it was. He asked how long she'd known. Just a few days, she'd told him. "I was waiting for the right time to tell you," she'd said . . . and then she'd told him how it was going to be. "I'm having this baby, so don't even ask. I'm keeping it. And if you think that you're going to be with my sister, while I have our baby all by myself, you've got another think coming."

She remembered that he'd pulled on his tee shirt and stood, slump-shouldered and silent and utterly defeated, as Zoe berated him, as she called him a liar and a cheater and informed him that he had broken her heart—that he'd been her first love, that he'd destroyed her. And the band. And that he was going to pay.

"It was true," Zoe told her aunt. "What I told him. Everybody would have blamed me. They'd never have believed that he'd picked Cassie instead of me."

Bess was looking at her steadily. "Why? Because of how Cassie looked?"

Zoe nodded. "They would have treated me like I was a joke." She was remembering the coverage of Britney and Justin's breakup, the tabloid covers with headlines like "Did She Betray Him?" and "The War Is On." She recalled, too, the televised interview Britney had done with some middle-aged journalist. "You did something that caused him so much pain. So much suffering," the woman had said, leaning toward Britney, all hairspray and earnestness and fake solicitude. Zoe recalled, too, how angry people had been when Jessica Simpson had shown up onstage, a few pounds heavier than she'd been in her *Dukes of Hazzard* days, how they'd acted betrayed, injured, as if she'd thrown a grenade into the crowd instead of just choosing the wrong pair of pants. People back then—and, probably, people right now—thought that they owned their female stars, that their fandom gave them a say in what they wore, how they looked, who they loved. When the stars failed to follow the script, people felt perfectly entitled to make their displeasure known. Jessica Simpson was supposed to stay thin and hot and Britney was supposed to stay virginal and faithful and sweet, and Zoe was meant to stay married, even if some of the band's fans, the fat girls, the mousy girls, the girls with glasses or braces, the weird, lonely girls wouldn't be amused or horrified if they learned that Russell was with Cassie. They'd be delighted. Thrilled. They would think that, if someone like Russell loved Cassie, maybe there was hope that someone could love them too.

"So what did you want?" Bess asked.

Zoe bowed her head. She realized that she'd been foolish to expect sympathy. It wasn't like she deserved any, and she certainly wouldn't get it from Bess, who'd loved her sister, and who probably blamed Zoe for driving her away. "Did you want to be with Russell?"

"Did I want to be married to a man who was in love with someone else? Did I want to have a baby with a husband who would spend the rest of our lives making cow eyes at my sister every Thanksgiving?" Zoe smiled thinly and shook her head. "I wanted to hurt him. To make him suffer the way I was suffering."

"Did he know about Tommy?"

Zoe shook her head again. "I don't think it ever occurred to Russell to think that I was cheating. He was probably feeling so guilty about what he was doing that he wasn't paying any attention to what I was doing."

Bess sipped her tea, waiting. Zoe remembered how she'd been terrified when she'd realized that her period had failed to arrive, how she'd rubbed herself raw with toilet paper every time she peed, praying to see blood. She'd sent Abby to buy a test, after swearing her to secrecy, and when the test had confirmed what she'd already known, she'd buried her face in a stack of pillows and howled in anguish, her whole body shuddering in primal, animalistic fear. At that moment, the pregnancy had been an obstacle, a problem. As soon as she'd seen Russell and Cassie, it had transformed into a weapon: a sword she could wield against her faithless, two-timing, heartbreaking asshole of a husband and then use on her sister. In Zoe's mind, in that moment, everything she'd said to Russell had become true. He was the love of her life. He had betrayed her, broken his vows, broken her heart. And it was not just a pregnancy anymore, but a baby. His baby.

In their hotel room, Russell had half collapsed against the wall, pressing his hands to his eyes. His face was anguished. Zoe had relished his misery, like an exotically spiced dish she'd sampled and found delicious. She wanted to gobble it down, to stuff herself full.

"I'm keeping it," she'd said, her voice mean and gloating. As soon as she'd said the words, the part of her that had spoken and the part that was floating somewhere near the ceiling, watching, came together long enough to realize that this was insane. She was twenty-two years old, with no desire to be a mother. She was too young, and too busy being a rock star, albeit a mostly extraneous one, and pregnancy fit that dream about as well as a pair of her stilettos and a thong would have fit the eighty-year-old tortoise she'd once seen on a class field trip at the Camden aquarium. She had gotten her happy ending: a life, and a man, that a million girls would have killed to have as their own. There was no room in her life for a baby. Only now . . .

"Picture a little love nest," she sang, her voice high and mocking and, for once, sounding just as good as her sister's. "Down where the roses cling." She didn't continue, but she was sure that Russell, who knew every song ever written, could hear the rest of the verse: *Picture the same sweet love nest /And think what a year can bring.*

Even when she was threatening him, taunting him, telling him the way it was going to be, there was a part of her watching, shocked and grieving, aching from the betrayal. That part knew the truth. She didn't want to have a baby. A baby was not going to bring Russell back, or keep them together. At least, not forever. Maybe he'd end things with Cassie, maybe he'd come back to Zoe. But, eventually, she'd be left with a child she didn't want, and a man who, she knew, didn't really want her. Not to mention a band that had no place for her. It was more than she could stand.

But Zoe hadn't let herself dwell on any of that. "I'm going to keep it," she'd said. "And you're going to stay with me."

Russell had managed a single, short nod. Zoe lifted her chin, stood up straight, and, with as much dignity as she could muster, walked out of the room.

She'd gone to the lobby, where she'd half fallen into an armchair and pulled off her boots. She sat, in her leather and her silver lamé, and waited for someone to find her—maybe Russell, to beg forgiveness; maybe Cassie, to apologize.

No one came. Zoe sat alone, in the lobby, all night long, unwilling to go back to the room where she'd fought with Russell, determined that he should come to her. To comfort herself, she thought back to one of her fondest memories. The band had been in LA, driving to the airport, at the end of their radio-station tour. No gold record; no record at all, just their first single. Zoe hadn't been sleeping well, after too many hours of snuggling up to Russell in the vans, or trying to spoon him in bed, only for him to push her away, telling her that he was tired, that he had heartburn or a scratchy throat, that they both needed their sleep. She'd been grouchy, PMS-y, feeling bloated, and the first twinges of a headache, when the DJ said, "And now, a brand-new single from a brand-new band. This is the Griffin Sisters." Zoe had screamed so loud she was surprised the car's windows hadn't shattered, and Cam and Russell were whooping right along with her. "Turn it up, turn it up!" Cam was chanting. They'd rolled down the windows, and all of them, her sister included, had stuck their heads out into the highway traffic, screaming, "THAT'S OUR SONG!" while the label rep had veered into the slow lane, yelling at them to be careful, because Jerry would never forgive him if one of them got decapitated, but also laughing at the same time, as delighted for them as they were delighted for themselves. Zoe thought about that day, and about the wedding, dancing with Russell, the taste of champagne on her lips, the guests' attention, the photographers' cameras; seeing her own beauty reflected back at her in their gaze, and in her husband's eyes. They'd been happy. Hadn't they?

All night long, Zoe sat in the lobby and waited for Russell to come, to apologize, to tell her that he'd come to his senses, that . . . what? That it had been an accident? That he'd tripped, and fallen into her sister? That Cassie had seduced him? That seemed impossible. How could Russell want to sleep with Cassie when he had her, Zoe? How could any man? It would be like a diner in a restaurant sending a perfectly cooked steak back to the kitchen and requesting roadkill instead. Zoe knew how her sister looked without shapewear and clothes. Cassie was flabby; she was squishy; her belly sagged and her breasts drooped; and even if a guy didn't let himself see her body, he wouldn't be able to keep from feeling it. Had Russell wanted to touch her? Or had he, somehow, been attracted to Cassie's personality, to her talent, so much so that it had canceled out her sister's looks?

It didn't make sense. It barely seemed real. Except Zoe had seen them together, in bed. Russell had not seemed repulsed. And Cassie, for all her fat, hadn't seemed hideous. Her hair had been tangled, her face had been flushed, and she'd been smiling, her hands gripping Russell's shoulders, as he'd . . .

Zoe swallowed hard. As he'd looked at her adoringly; with a tenderness she'd never seen on his face when they'd been together. She'd had plenty of sex with Russell, and it had been exciting, and thrilling, sometimes with a fine edge of danger, but it had almost never been tender. Russell seemed to have been saving that side of himself for Cassie.

In the hotel's empty lobby, Zoe sat, legs crossed, one foot flicking up and down, and waited, hot-eyed and sleepless, as the night dragged on. Later, she would wonder if she'd heard the sound of the car that had killed him. Had she noticed the screech of the tires, the thudding of flesh against metal? Had she raised her head at the wail of the sirens, as the cop cars had gone racing by? She didn't remember hearing, or seeing, or sensing anything unusual, lost, as she was, in her own pain.

At six o'clock in the morning, finally, someone had come. Zoe stood up, grimacing at the prickles in her feet, but it was just a yawning guy in khakis and a clip-on tie, looking more asleep than awake as he set urns of coffee and hot water up on a table by the front desk. A half hour later, she saw CJ. She'd called his name, but he'd hurried past her without a glance, running through the lobby and through the hotel's sliding doors. Zoe had stood, staring after him. Part of her wanted to follow, and part of her was already dreading what she'd see past the hotel doors.

So she'd waited. Eventually, CJ had come back, flanked by a pair of police officers. Then, finally, he'd seen her.

"Zoe," he said. "Oh God." His round face was ashen. His cheeks glinted with stubble, and his Hawaiian shirt was on inside out. "Oh Jesus. What a shitshow. What a mess."

"What are you talking about?" Was CJ crying? He was. Tears were rolling down his cheeks, and for a moment, Zoe thought that he'd found out about Russell and Cassie. "What's going on? What happened?"

"There's been an accident." He reached out and took her hands in his. "It's Russell," he said. "Russell's dead."

She stared into his eyes. "No," she said. "No."

"The police called me." CJ ducked his head and said, as if he were reading from cue cards, "He was hit by a car. It's him, Zoe. They found his driver's license. He had his wallet in his pocket."

All of Zoe's fury was gone. Her brain was a blackboard against which someone had hurled a bucket of soapy water. It was wiped clean, completely empty, absolutely blank. "No," she said again. This wasn't real. It couldn't be. None of this was real—not Russell sleeping with Cassie; certainly not Russell dying. It was all some horrible dream, and she'd wake up, any minute now.

Only CJ was still gripping her hands, and she could smell his sour breath and could see the creases the pillow had left on his cheek. "I'm so sorry, Zoe. I am so sorry."

Zoe's knees had wobbled. She'd staggered back, collapsing into one of the lobby's armchairs. CJ stood next to her, shaking his head, muttering to himself. "Gotta tell the promoters . . . gotta call the venue . . . gotta let Jerry know what happened." Zoe was too afraid to interrupt and ask for details. Had Russell gone out into the night, believing that Zoe was going to have a baby and force him to stay with her? Had he been preoccupied, distracted enough to wander into a car's path? Or—she cringed, moaning at the thought—had he done it on purpose? Had he been so full of despair that he'd seen no way out except death?

I should be crying, she thought. *My husband is gone.* But there were no tears, just that faraway feeling, like she was a spectator in a theater, watching her own life unfold.

She realized that CJ was talking to her. "I'm so sorry, Zoe. I hate to have to even ask, but—maybe you can tell your sister?"

Zoe nodded without thinking. *Take care of your sister*, she heard her mother saying in her head. That had always been her job. Giving Cassie this terrible news would be just one more version of her eternal assignment.

It had been, again, like watching a movie. There were her feet, carrying her to the hotel's front desk. There was her voice, asking for a key. There was her hand, with its long, red-lacquered nails, beringed fingers, and braceleted wrists, inserting the key card into its slot and opening the door to the room she'd been meant to share with Russell. She'd planned on going to the bathroom, to wash her face, and try to collect herself a little before going to her sister, but as soon as she walked into the room, she saw the piece of paper on the desk. Hotel stationery, folded in half. Zoe picked it up, unfolded it, and saw Russell's handwriting. *I'm sorry*, read the first line. The *sorry* was wavery and splotched, as if it had been blurred by a drop of water, or a tear. And then, six words. *I never should have touched you.*

Zoe stared dully at the paper. The message was for her. She was the "you." She knew it, in her bones, in her heart. But, without a name, how could she be sure? How could anyone?

Her leggings had no pockets, so she tucked the scrap of paper into her bra and walked down the hall, to Cassie's room. When she knocked, the door opened so quickly that Zoe wondered if Cassie had spent the night on her feet, standing in the vestibule, waiting for Russell to come back. Cassie wore pajama bottoms and a man's white undershirt. Zoe was certain it was one of Russell's. She wondered if it still carried the scent of his skin.

"There's been an accident," she said.

Cassie rubbed her eyes and tucked her hair behind her ears. "What? What accident? What happened?"

"Russell was hit by a car. He's dead."

Instead of looking stunned or hurt, Cassie just looked irritated. Her brow furrowed, her lips pursed. "I know you're mad, Zoe. But why would you say something like that?"

"It's true. There are cops in the lobby. Go ask them, if you don't believe me."

Cassie gave Zoe a long, unfriendly look, before turning around to grab a sweatshirt and her shoes. Zoe waited as Cassie walked off down the hall. She sat on the bed, waiting, and a few minutes later, Cassie came back, her face slack and blank and shocked.

"It can't be true," she said, more to herself than to Zoe. "This can't have happened. He can't be gone." She squeezed her eyes shut, clenched her hands into fists. "No," she was saying, under her breath. "No, no, no, no, no."

Zoe pulled Russell's note out of her bra and held it out, waiting, until Cassie looked.

"What's that?" Cassie asked dully.

"He left a note," Zoe said, holding it out for her sister.

Cassie took it, unfolded the little piece of paper. Zoe watched her face as she read, and there, finally, was what Zoe had wanted to see: shock and sorrow; shame and guilt.

Her sister turned away and started crying. Zoe, who still hadn't cried, got up from the bed and stalked across the room, bringing her face close to Cassie's. "This is your fault."

"No," Cassie whispered.

"Yes," Zoe said. "He felt terrible for cheating."

"He said . . ." Cassie's voice was tiny. "He said you were the one who wanted to get married. He said it was all your idea. That he didn't want to. That it wasn't real."

"Yeah, well, men lie, don't they? They lie when they want things. But Russell loved me. Whatever he told you, whatever he said, he was my husband. My husband. He loved me." Cassie flinched, turning away. Zoe grabbed her sister's chin and held it hard, forcing Cassie to look at her, to listen. "If he hadn't felt so guilty about what he'd done, he wouldn't have drunk half a bottle of whiskey and gone running out into the dark."

"No," Cassie repeated, almost moaning the word.

"Yes," Zoe said again, gripping her sister's face, digging in with her nails, hissing the words. "This happened because of you." *Not true*, she thought, as she kept talking. "You might as well have put a gun to his head."

Cassie shook her head some more, and finally managed to pull herself away from Zoe. "No," she began whispering. "No, no, no." She walked to the window, rocking back and forth, arms wrapped around her shoulders, keening.

In her great-aunt's kitchen, Zoe bowed her head.

"So Russell left you a note," Aunt Bess said. Her voice was emotionless, and soft, in a way that let Zoe know precisely how disappointed she was. "He left you a note, and you gave it to Cassie, and you made her think it was her fault."

Zoe nodded miserably. She squeezed her eyes shut, resting her face on her fisted hands, rocking a little in her seat and crying, great, wrenching sobs that racked her frame and made it hard to breathe. All the tears that hadn't been there the morning she'd gotten the news.

She wept, and wiped at her dripping face, and remembered something that had happened when she'd been a girl, some trick she and her friends had played on Cassie, some lie they'd told her, something mean they'd done. She couldn't recall the specifics of her transgression, but she could remember how furious her aunt had been, along with every word of what Bess had said back then: when you hurt someone's feelings, it's the same as if you broke their leg. *It's even worse, because it takes longer to heal. Sometimes, it never does.*

"I'm sorry," she said, in a gasping, choked voice, when she could manage to speak again. "I'm so sorry. I know how much I hurt her."

"Do you?" Aunt Bess said, in a cool tone that said, more than words ever could, *I doubt it.* Zoe found herself devastated all over again, disgusted with herself, positive there was no way forward. This was why she'd only looked ahead for so long, only forward, never back. This was why she'd refused to let herself think about what had happened—no, not what had happened. What she'd done. Who she'd hurt. Because there were some breaches you couldn't repair, some harms you couldn't undo, some transgressions so terrible that forgiveness was impossible, and all you could do was try to live with what you'd done, and what kind of person it made you. *I'm not a good person,* Zoe thought. But she didn't say it, knowing it would sound self-pitying, self-involved, like she was the victim, the one who'd suffered. Her, and not Cassie.

"What can I do?" she said instead. Which, she realized, was the wrong question. *Can I fix this?* she should have asked. *Can this be fixed? Ever?*

She raised her head, looking for advice, or sympathy, or absolution. Aunt Bess stared back at her and didn't say a word.

"I never thought," Zoe began, and then stopped, resting her elbow on the table and her forehead on one fisted hand. *I never thought he'd cheat on me. I never thought he'd die. I never thought Cassie would leave. I never thought that anything could hurt so much, for so long.*

She closed her eyes and just repeated, "I never thought." Because there was nothing else left to say.

Part Six

US WEEKLY "STAR TRACKS"

August 23, 2004

Rock-and-roll royalty and Hollywood stars turned out in force on a rainy morning in Boston for the funeral of guitar player Russell D'Angelo of the Griffin Sisters, who died from injuries he sustained after being struck by a car on August 19 in Detroit. D'Angelo's grieving bandmates, including his wife, Zoe Griffin, who he married in May, attended the funeral mass at St. Christopher's. "He was the love of my life," Zoe Griffin said.

Relic Records president Jerry Nance remembered meeting D'Angelo in 1997, when Relic signed D'Angelo's first band, Sky King. "In my forty years in the business, he was one of the most talented people I've ever encountered, and one of the kindest. He had so much more he could have accomplished—so many more songs to write," Nance said. "It's a tragedy that we've lost him."

Others who came to see D'Angelo laid to rest included musicians Lenny Kravitz, Nancy Wilson of Heart, Melissa Etheridge, and Sheryl Crow and actresses Drew Barrymore and Demi Moore. A notable no-show was Cassie Griffin, the band's lead singer. When asked about Cassie Griffin's absence, Griffin Sisters manager CJ Carver declined to comment.

Cherry
ALASKA, 2024

So wait." Cherry stared at her aunt, blinking. "Hold up. Russell D'Angelo was sleeping with both of you?"

"Not at the same time. He slept with your mother first. Then me." Cassie was standing in the corner of the single room that comprised the kitchen. Wesley was curled up on his dog bed in the corner. Cherry was sitting at Cassie's table, on her single folding chair, still bundled in her inadequate winter coat. Her bleached hair stood in a spiky halo around her head.

"And my mom walked in on you with him, and that was the night he died?"

Another nod. Cassie cleared her throat, and asked, "Does your mother talk about it at all?"

Cherry snorted. "I only found out my mother had been in a band because I saw the CD in a used bookstore. She didn't talk about the band, or Russell, and she never talked about you." Cherry reached down to pat Wesley's head. "Not any of it. Not ever. All she wanted was to be a fancy lady in the suburbs. With a husband and an SUV and a goldendoodle."

Wesley picked up his head. His ears swiveled toward Cherry, as if he knew his species had been invoked. Cassie gave a half smile. "There are worse things than New Jersey and designer dogs."

"Do you hate her?" Cherry asked.

"I—do I hate her?" Cassie paused, then shook her head. "We hurt each other," she said. "But I don't hate anyone anymore."

"Hmm," said Cherry. An unpleasant warmth was building in her chest, and she could feel her breath coming faster. It was strange. She'd come here to find Cassie Griffin, the musician she respected more than any other artist in the world. Cassie, the brilliant pianist; Cassie, with her once-in-a-lifetime voice. She'd spent so much time thinking about Cassie from the Griffin Sisters, and no time at all thinking about Cassie from the Grossberg family. Cassie, who could have been her aunt, if she hadn't run away. That Cassie could have stood up for Cherry, when Cherry fought with her mother. That Cassie could have been her partner in crime, and in music making. That Cassie could have been her friend.

Focus, Cherry told herself. She could be angry and disappointed later. Right now she had to think about the show. She remembered the notebook she'd peeked at when Cassie had been in the bathroom: all those repetitions of *I'm sorry*, suggesting that maybe her aunt did hate someone, and maybe that someone was herself. Guilt, Cherry had thought. She could work with guilt.

"Look," she said. "I get that what happened was, you know. Tragic. But you got some great songs out of it."

Cass looked horrified. "Russell died. I hurt my—your mother. And you didn't have a father at all."

"Or an aunt," Cherry couldn't keep herself from saying.

Cassie blinked, looking startled. Then she nodded. "Or an aunt. No song is worth that."

Cherry shrugged. "Which would you have picked—Stevie Nicks and Lindsey Buckingham staying together, or the world getting *Rumours?* Adele staying with . . ." Cherry groped for the name of the guy who'd broken Adele's heart, then gave up. If she'd ever known his name, she'd forgotten it. *Lost to the mists of time,* as Jordan liked to say. "One person's broken heart doesn't compare to writing a song for the ages."

"It was more than just broken hearts." Cassie's voice was low. "Someone *died.*" She crossed the room and perched on the edge of her bed looking down at the floor, then up at Cherry. "Who is Adele?"

"Who is . . ." Cherry gawped for a moment, then shook her head. Time for a change of topics. But before she could figure out how to turn the conversation around, Cassie said, "What are you doing here, really?"

Cherry was startled, but quickly smoothed her face into a semblance of calm. "Can't a girl be curious about her family?"

Cassie didn't answer. She crossed her arms over her chest. Cherry realized she'd never get a better opening. Speaking rapidly, like if she got her request out fast enough Cassie wouldn't be able to refuse her, Cherry gave her aunt the condensed version of her life's history. She told Cassie that she'd always wanted to be a musician, and that her mother wouldn't let her, had opposed her at every turn. She described her audition for *The Next Stage,* and how she'd made it to the finals, and the mentor they'd assigned her, and how she'd wanted to find her own. Before she could finish, Cassie was shaking her head.

"No."

Cherry pretended she hadn't heard. "So if you help me, that would be, you know . . ." She groped for a phrase she'd heard on the news a lot in the summer of 2020. "Reparative justice."

Cassie's expression was somewhere between chagrined and amused. "Reparative justice," she repeated. Cherry leaned forward.

"Maybe it sounds crazy, but it isn't. My mom's the way she is because of what happened. That hurt me. If things had gone differently—"

Cassie rolled her eyes. Cherry pressed on.

"If things had gone differently, she would have wanted me to be a musician. She would have helped me. Maybe we'd be touring together right now. Me and my mom. And like you said, I never got to meet my father." She bit her lip, arranging her features into a mournful expression. "And you weren't there to stick up for me." She swallowed hard, realizing that she was no longer faking sorrow. Thinking about how Cassie could have been there for her actually did hurt.

"I'm sorry about that," Cassie said steadily. "But no."

Cherry forged ahead, thinking about the notebooks, weighing risk and potential reward. "Why are you so sad?" she asked. "What are you sorry for?"

Cassie looked startled. "What? I'm not—"

"What are you doing here?" Cherry interrupted. "For real. Why did you run away? How come nobody knows where you are? Why aren't you singing?"

"Weren't you listening? It's my fault Russell died!" Cassie said, her voice loud.

"Did you pour a bottle of whiskey down his throat and push him in front of a car?" Cherry asked.

Cassie shook her head. "You don't understand."

"No, I do. I get it. He was cheating on Zoe, she flipped out, and he got drunk and ended up . . ." Cherry saw how Cassie was glaring at her and decided not to finish the sentence. "But you didn't make that happen."

"He left a note." Cassie's voice was flat. "He said it was a mistake. He said he never should have touched me."

"Yikes," Cherry said, before she could stop herself. That certainly explained why Cassie would feel guilty, but it still didn't *make* her guilty. Unless . . .

Cherry leaned forward again, elbows on her knees. "Do you think he killed himself?"

Cassie looked anguished. "I don't know. I don't know whether it was an accident or if he meant for it to happen, but, either way, it wouldn't have happened if we hadn't been together."

"Or maybe," said Cherry, "it wouldn't have happened if he hadn't been with my mom. Maybe that was his big mistake. Maybe she was the one he never should have touched." Cherry leaned back, pleased with her argument. "You can't blame yourself—"

"Yes," Cassie said, her voice heavy. "I can." Her shoulders lifted as she inhaled, then let out the breath in a long sigh. "You should go. And you should let—" She stumbled, very slightly, before saying, "—your mom know where you are. I'm sure she's worried about you."

"My mother," Cherry said, speaking each word precisely, "does not give a single tiny shit about where I am or what I'm doing. She doesn't care."

"That's not true." Cassie shook her head. "She isn't like that. She cares."

"You haven't seen her in twenty years! You have no idea what she's like!" Cherry shook her head angrily. "I don't fit in the picture of her perfect little blended family. She's probably thrilled that I'm gone." If guilt didn't work, Cherry thought, maybe pity would. Maybe she could make Cassie feel sorry for her, and then Cassie would agree to help. "She didn't want me taking guitar lessons. Didn't want me joining a band. She doesn't even know I auditioned for *The Next Stage*." She checked to make sure Cassie was still listening. "I hated school, and I didn't want to go to college. I only wanted to make music. And Zoe wouldn't let me."

Cassie hadn't spoken. But she was still listening. Cherry could tell.

"I won't go home," Cherry said. "No matter what happens, with . . ." She made a gesture encompassing herself and her aunt and the possibility of mentorship and *The Next Stage*.

"New Jersey was that bad?"

"You really seem hung up on the New Jersey of it all," Cherry observed. "And it wasn't just New Jersey. Or my mom, even. I have a stepbrother." She didn't have to fake the shudder that ran through her at the memory of Bix's wet eyes and red lips. "He's a creep."

Cassie's forehead furrowed. "Does Zoe know he's a creep?"

"She ought to know. I've told her. Over and over and over."

"And she didn't do anything about it?"

Cherry shrugged. "He's sneaky. He doesn't really do anything you can nail him for. He just gets in my personal space, and he stares at me. All the time. It's intensely creepy."

Cassie was frowning. "That sounds unpleasant."

"Unpleasant," Cherry repeated, and rolled her eyes.

"But still. If I picked up the phone and called your mother, right this minute, what would she say?"

"You mean, once she finished being shocked that she was hearing from you, after all these years?"

"She'd say," Cassie continued doggedly, "that you should come home. Am I right?"

"Yeah, but it isn't her choice," said Cherry. "I'm legally an adult. She's not the boss of me." She struck a pose, hand over her chest, face tilted toward the heavens. "Music is my mistress. I must follow her where she leads."

"Are you sure this is what you want?" Cassie asked. "I don't know what it's like, trying to be a musician, these days. But for me—for your mother—for your—for Russell . . ." She shook her head. Raised her hands and let them fall. "It ruined our lives."

"You made great music," Cherry said.

"We hurt people."

"You hurt one person," Cherry said.

"Russell died. And your mother got hurt too."

"Okay, two people," Cherry allowed.

Cassie raised her eyebrows and gestured wordlessly, first at Cherry, then at herself.

"Fine," said Cherry. "Four people. That's still not exactly a trail of devastation. And Russell dying was an accident, anyhow." She had no idea whether this was true or not, even after reading everything she could find. Opinion on the Internet was divided as to whether Russell had been suicidal or just drunk and careless, and nothing she'd read had mentioned even the possibility that he and Cassie had been together . . . although there were certainly people who shipped the two of them. They'd post videos of the band singing "The Gift" or "Stay the Night," or the cover of "Silver Springs" they'd done at an early show, and talk about the way Russell's eyes stayed locked on Cassie's face, not on Zoe's, and how Cassie's body leaned toward Russell's, even though she never looked at him.

"And even if I wanted to perform with you—which I don't," Cassie said, "I haven't played, or sung, in years." Cassie stood up. Three steps brought her to the door. She set her hand on the knob. "You should go."

Cherry knew she looked petulant, but didn't even try to arrange her face in a more pleasant expression. "I came all this way to find you."

"I didn't ask to be found."

"And I didn't ask to have no extended family, but here we are," Cherry shot back. Oops. She hadn't meant to say that. Cassie stared at her for what felt like forever.

"Sorry," she finally said.

In that moment, Cherry felt an opportunity, and knew she'd be stupid not to seize it. "So how about this," she said. "You play, like, one song with me, in public, somewhere around here. Just once. If it's a total disaster, I'll get on a plane and go home. Well, not home. Back to Los Angeles. I'll tell the judges that I couldn't get you to mentor me, and someone else will win the competition." She rolled her eyes at the ceiling. "And then I'll just go back to posting my stuff on TikTok and SoundCloud."

"I don't know what those are," Cassie said, mostly to herself.

Cherry ignored her. "And I won't have any family. My father's dead. Zoe doesn't want anything to do with me. I'll be all alone in the world." She'd meant for it to sound melodramatic, but as she heard the words, she found that she was feeling them too. All alone in the world. A motherless child. More or less.

Cassie met Cherry's eyes before she looked down at the floor. "You don't understand. I can't."

"Can't what?"

"Can't sing in front of people."

"Have you tried?"

"You don't understand," Cassie repeated.

"So explain it to me!"

Cassie shook her head again, her face resolute. And Cherry was out of strategies, out of arguments. She felt jet-lagged, suddenly, tired and sad. *A motherless child.* When Cassie said, "You should go," again, Cherry nodded and zipped up her coat. She walked out the door, back into that cruel cold. She was halfway down the stairs, her car keys in her hand, when she turned around. "I'm coming back tomorrow."

Cassie's voice was muffled but still audible through the door. "I won't be here," she said.

Cherry decided to pretend she hadn't heard. She didn't believe it, anyhow. Her aunt did not impress her as a woman with a packed social calendar. And where would she even go, in this ridiculously cold, stupidly dark world? Cherry kept walking, boots crunching through the snow as she trudged back to her car. Her plan was to go back to the hotel, regroup, come up with a new plan, except the last thing she'd said to Cassie seemed to have gotten stuck in her head, like a sesame seed between her back teeth. *I won't have any family. I'll be all alone in the world.*

She'd told her aunt that the band's implosion hadn't caused that much pain. She'd never thought to add herself to the list of people the Griffin Sisters had destroyed, but maybe she'd been wrong. Maybe she, too, was a victim of three young people and their bad choices. Maybe her life, too, had been affected, her dreams derailed before she'd gotten them underway. Maybe she'd been cursed, the way Cassie seemed to feel she'd been cursed. But, Cherry decided, she wasn't giving up. Curses could be lifted. And, if Cassie had been one of the people who'd hurt her, that made her aunt responsible for undoing what she'd done.

Zoe

For the first days and weeks after Russell's death, Zoe had been too numb with disbelief, and then too full of anger and sorrow, to do more than keep herself upright and breathing. She didn't sleep, didn't eat, barely spoke. She let other people make decisions, letting herself be just a body to be moved and directed, as the world went on around her.

The rest of the tour had been canceled, of course. The label had made an announcement; refunds had been issued. Russell's funeral had been arranged, in Massachusetts. Zoe had attended—or, really, Zoe had permitted herself to be moved by people who were capable of action, from the hotel in Detroit to the airport to a hotel in Boston and, finally, on a gray Thursday morning, to a church in Medford, Massachusetts, where Russell had grown up.

Cassie wasn't there. Zoe hadn't seen Cassie since that morning in Detroit. She supposed that her sister had gone home, to Philadelphia, and their parents, but no one had said anything about where Cassie was, and Zoe hadn't asked.

There were clothes waiting in the hotel room in Boston: a black satin dress, a hat with a black lace veil. Black shoes with a modest heel and sheer black hose. Zoe stood in the shower with the lights out, her forehead resting on the marble wall, letting the water beat down, feeling nothing. There was something awful waiting for her, on the other side of the numbness. There were wild animals, huge and heavy-hooved, sharp-toothed, waiting to run her down, to trample her, until she was just a bunch of bloodied rags on the ground. Cassie had once talked about a crowd that way when they'd been backstage, listening to the restless murmurings of three thousand people on the other side of the curtains. "It sounds like a monster, doesn't it?" Cassie had asked, and gestured toward the crowd. "Like something that wants to eat us up."

Zoe remembered shaking her head, then, when she'd realized Cassie was serious, taking her hands and reassuring Cassie that there was no monster, that they'd both be fine. Now she thought that her sister had been right. That night, the name of the monster had been Fame. This night, it was a different monster, one named Grief. Grief waited on the other side of the wall, pacing and panting, waiting to swarm her, to stomp her, to break her bones and tear her to pieces with its sharp-edged hooves. The wall Zoe had built would not hold forever. Eventually, the monster would break through and be upon her . . . but in that moment, in the water, Zoe was still numb, and still safe.

In her Boston hotel room, she wrapped herself in a towel and went to the bed, where she lay on her back, open-eyed and sleepless. Around midnight, she heard knocking, and Tommy calling her name. She ignored him. She stared at the ceiling, hands laced over her belly, and thought, *I want to die.* Except death would have required action, movement, a series of choices: Knife or gun? Pills or falling? Zoe couldn't act, couldn't move, couldn't think. Her brain was circling in an endless loop of grief and guilt, each lap digging the ruts deeper, chanting, *this is all my fault.*

In the morning, she got up, feeling her stomach lurching, as it had, every morning, for the past week. She hurried to the bathroom and crouched in front of the toilet, the tiles cold against her knees, vomiting up stringy bile until it felt like she was turning herself inside out. She brushed her teeth, pulled on the clothes they'd sent, and waited to be collected and moved to the next place.

CJ knocked on her door, and brought her down to the lobby, then out to the limousine. He helped her into the back seat, where she sat, motionless and mute as a doll, between Cam and Tommy, ignoring Tommy's kicked-puppy look, declining Cam's offer of a pill from the little bottle in his pocket. A fusillade of camera flashes greeted them as they pulled up to the church. As soon as the car's door was open, Zoe could hear the paps shouting her name. "Zoe! Zoe, over here! Zoe, this way, please! Zoe, who told you Russell was dead? How did it feel when you found out?"

How did it feel, Zoe repeated to herself. She was shivering, her shoulders shaking involuntary. "Don't listen to them," Tommy had muttered. "Fucking animals." Zoe had barely spoken to Tommy since the night Russell died. She knew Tommy was, still, so angry. He'd begged and cajoled and all but ordered her to tell Russell that it was over, that they were together, that she loved him, not Russell, but she hadn't. And now, as far as the media and the photographers and the whole wide world knew, Zoe had been Russell's one true love, and he hers, right up until the moment the car sent him flying and the impact of his body against the pavement snapped his spine. To the world, Zoe was now the grieving widow. Tommy was just the band's drummer, her sister's former classmate, nothing to Zoe at all.

At the last minute, Tommy had pulled off his black leather jacket and draped it over her shoulders. CJ extended his hand to help her out of the car, then handed her a bouquet of roses to lay on Russell's coffin, and he and Cam and Tommy formed a kind of scrum around Zoe as she made her way up the church's stone steps. The leather was stiff and heavy, and Zoe could feel sweat trickling down the small of her back, the insides of her thighs, as she kept her head up, eyes forward. One of the photographers had snapped what would become the iconic image that appeared on the covers of *People* and *Us* and inside the *New York Times*: Zoe, framed by the men, with the black lace veil covering her eyes and the black leather jacket hanging from her narrow shoulders. Zoe with her head bent and her arms full of roses and her wedding band hanging loosely on her left ring finger. She'd looked fragile and lovely and devastated, a broken flower in a rainstorm. A victim of a tragedy, and not its perpetrator. *Good*, she'd thought, when she'd seen the picture. *I can work with this.*

Tommy had found her, in her hotel room, after the funeral, which Zoe had endured, sitting motionless, with her father on her left side and her mom on her right, patting her back. "God, what a mess,"

Tommy had said, raking his fingers through his hair. "But, Zoe . . . it's okay now." He'd knelt down before her and taken her hand. "We can be together."

In that instant, Zoe was given a gift: a flash of perfect clarity. She saw all the possibilities in front of her, as clearly as if someone had handed her a road map, and, with that vision, she understood a number of things. The first was that a young woman whose bandmate-husband had died and who went on to date someone else in the band was a far less compelling figure than a grieving young widow who stayed single, or who had her dead beloved's baby on her own. The fans would not want her to move on. They'd hate her for desecrating Russell's memory. They would see Zoe's decision to love again as a betrayal, especially if it was with Tommy. And Tommy might have been twenty-three in calendar years but was closer to thirteen in terms of actual maturity. He was sweet, not too smart, talented, but not a person with whom she wanted to have a baby and build a life, even if he claimed to love her. Even if she was absolutely certain that the baby was his, instead of just ninety percent sure. Even if she could trust him when he told her that he loved her.

Zoe couldn't be with Tommy. Not if she ever hoped to keep the public's attention and maintain her reputation—her *brand*, as CJ and Jerry called it, an odious word, but a useful one. And as for a baby . . .

She pictured the spread in *People* magazine, a gauzy, soft-focus shot of her cradling her little bundle of joy. Maybe the magazine would pose them in a field of wildflowers, or under a magnolia tree, the baby pink and tiny, Zoe draped in something flowy and forgiving. She imagined how she'd tell the reporter how overjoyed she was, that there was still this piece of Russell for her to love.

And then she imagined more reporters, less-friendly questions. *Who's with the baby while you're on tour?* Nobody ever seemed to ask new fathers that one, but new mothers got it all the time. They had to account for themselves, for their choices, and woe betide them if they didn't have a good answer, even though no answer could make everyone happy. She knew that the world, and the fans, would treat her kindly as a grieving widow. They'd be even more generous with their sympathies if she was both a grieving widow and a single mother. But Zoe knew that sympathy would lessen, if not vanish outright, for a single mother who'd gone back on the road to perform, who'd left her baby with a grandmother or, worse, paid help. Even bringing the baby with her would be wrong, because babies needed routines and schedules. They were not meant to be carted around the country like luggage while their mothers worked nights. Men were supposed to be providers and breadwinners. Mothers were supposed to be mothers. Mothers were supposed to stay home. Maybe that would be different, someday, but it would take women braver than Zoe to be at the vanguard of that change.

When Tommy reached up to touch her cheek, Zoe leaned back, turning her face away. "I'm sorry," she'd said, her voice cracking. "I can't. I'm sorry."

"What do you mean, you can't?" Tommy asked, looking bewildered. "Can't what?"

"I can't be with you."

He'd looked at her, lips trembling. "What do you mean?"

Zoe didn't answer.

"Where will you go? What will you do?"

Zoe had made up her mind, right on the spot, coming up with an answer to the first question, if not the second. "I'm going home."

Tommy kept talking, but Zoe didn't listen, and, finally, he'd left. She'd watched the hotel door swing closed, and then she watched her body moving, her hands gathering her clothing from the closet, unzipping her suitcase, putting the clothes inside; her feet, walking along another hotel hall. She'd found CJ in his room, and she told him what she'd decided.

CJ hadn't seemed especially upset when she'd given him the news . . . or, at least, not more upset than he'd been since Russell's death and Cassie's disappearance. Cassie and Russell were the important ones, and with one of them dead and the other missing, there would be—could be—no more Griffin Sisters. Tommy and Cam could join another band. There'd be other girls, coming down the pike, girls for David to discover and Jerry to sign and CJ to manage and all of them to profit from. Another bunch of innocents, lining up at the mouth of the cave, eager to offer themselves to the dragon, or the troll beneath the bridge. She, Zoe Griffin, now Grossberg again, was done.

She let her parents bring her back to Philadelphia. The house hadn't changed. The narrow staircase was still lined with school pictures: twelve years of Zoe smiling brightly and Cassie looking like she wished she could disappear. It had been less than two years since she'd left, but it felt like an entire lifetime had elapsed between David Katz coming to the house over Christmas break and Zoe returning with a suitcase in her hand and a baby in her belly.

Her father had given her a single, hard hug. "Love you, kiddo," he'd said, and then he'd gone off to work. Janice followed her upstairs, never meeting Zoe's gaze, behaving like her older daughter was a ghost who'd vanish if Janice looked at her directly, or for too long. "Is—is Cassie coming?" her mother had finally asked. Zoe, who'd been considering asking her mom the same thing, had shrugged, and Janice must have seen something in her daughter's face that forestalled additional questions.

Zoe had wandered through the house. Nothing had changed, but everything was different. All the furniture—the off-white love seat, her dad's ancient recliner, the coffee table with a chip at its corner, where the wood veneer had peeled away—seemed to have shrunk, like it had been reduced by some small but meaningful percentage. When their first big check from the label had arrived, Zoe and Cassie, giddy at the prospect of what seemed like a fairy-tale sum of money, had agreed to send their parents a portion of it. Zoe guessed that Sam and Janice had put the money in their savings account instead of spending it on lavish vacations or home improvements. Maybe they'd wisely figured that the band's success would not last, that the money the girls had sent them would be all the money they'd get.

Zoe felt her sister's absence in the empty bed in the bedroom, the empty seat at the kitchen table, the empty space at the piano's bench where Cassie should have been. She felt it, most of all, in the quiet. She'd gotten so used to the house being full of music, the sound of Cassie practicing, for four or five or six hours a day, difficult, dense pieces without any fun, hummable bits. She never thought she'd miss it, only without her sister, the silence seemed as loud as an explosion. She'd braced herself for questions from her parents—*Where is your sister? What happened, exactly? Are you okay?* So far, though, they'd barely spoken to her, and they'd looked at her like she'd become someone else. A stranger. Zoe supposed that, in a way, that was exactly what had happened. She'd had her picture in magazines; she'd been on TV. She'd become, at once, larger than life, and smaller; thinner, flatter, less real.

Zoe took to her bed. She barely spoke to her parents and, when her friends called, she wouldn't pick up her cell phone or come downstairs to talk on the landline. She slept eighteen hours a day, and when she wasn't sleeping, she was listening to music, lying in bed with headphones on and her eyes closed. She played her sister's CDs, stared at her sister's empty bed, and let the songs pile up, like snowflakes, until they formed a cool drift in her brain. It wouldn't fill her empty places—not for long—but Zoe listened, and listening kept her from thinking. When she did think, the guilt and the shame of what she'd done, of what she'd caused to happen, clung to her like a second skin, oily and gritty, heavy and invisible, impossible to shed. The mirror showed her the same pretty face, but Zoe knew the truth of it . . . that, inside, she was as ugly as anyone could be.

Finally, one morning in October, she knew she couldn't delay the inevitable any longer.

In the bathroom, she'd shucked off the pajama pants and sweatshirt she'd been wearing for days, and took a shower, washing her greasy hair, carefully combing out the tangles. She applied moisturizer and put on her makeup. Back in her bedroom, she found jeans and skirts and sweaters in a dresser drawer, but nothing fit. She had to go into Cassie's drawers for leggings and a loose button-down plaid shirt.

When she came downstairs, barefoot, her mother's eyes widened. "Zoe," Janice said, "are you . . ."

Zoe followed her mother's gaze down to where the swell of her belly pushed at the shirt. "Oh," she said. In all the weeks she'd been in bed, she'd forgotten about the pregnancy. Or, not forgotten, exactly, but she'd managed not to think of it. To put it on hold. When she'd come home she'd planned on ending it, on arranging and getting an abortion at some point. From the look on her mother's face, Zoe suspected that "some point" had come and gone.

"Zoe," Janice had whispered, wide-eyed, one hand splayed against her chest.

Zoe realized she'd need to be careful. She said the words in her head, testing them out, tasting them, before she spoke them out loud, in her mother's kitchen.

"I don't want anyone to know."

Janice gawped at her, mouth hanging open, giving Zoe a view of the fillings in her mother's back teeth. "So you want to, what? Keep it a secret?" Janice shook her head. "It won't work. People will know. Your doctor . . . everyone in the doctor's office . . . everyone in the hospital . . ."

"They won't tell," Zoe said, with a confidence she did not feel. "It's, like, an ethical thing. Medical ethics. They're not supposed to talk about private health . . . stuff." Even as she spoke, she was thinking. The paparazzi and the gossip blogs knew to watch hospitals in Beverly Hills and New York City when they were expecting famous people to give birth, but Philadelphia was a blessedly celebrity-free city, a place where the romantic lives of the local newscasters and meteorologists were as avidly chronicled as the lives of movie stars were in New York and LA . . . and no one knew she was here. Of course, that didn't mean some unscrupulous roommate or nurse or orderly or janitor wouldn't recognize her and tip off the press. But there was a way to limit the number of people who'd know about the blessed event.

"A home birth," Zoe announced. "I'll have a home birth."

The baby came on a cold spring morning, which felt fitting, some-how: like an echo of when she and Cassie had been discovered. This time, instead of a record-label executive rushing to their house, ea-ger to see something amazing, it was the midwife, a taciturn woman named Kayla who'd brought babies in the hundreds into the world and who knew not to hurry. Kayla was perfect. She wore teddy-bear-printed scrubs, only listened to sports radio, and had never heard of the Griffin Sisters. Unlike David Katz, Kayla did not lavish her with praise, saying only, "big push," or "rest now," or, very occasionally, "good work." The only music was Zoe's moans, getting hoarser as the night went on. "I can't," she said, after some endless-seeming span of time. "I can't do it. I can't anymore."

"You can," Kayla said, rubbing her back. "And you don't have much of a choice right now." Zoe had closed her eyes, had pushed with all her might, making a noise that felt like it would tear her in half. The baby had slid out, into Kayla's waiting hands.

"A girl," Kayla announced. She clamped and cut the cord, bathed the baby in the basin of warm water Janice had prepared, swaddled the tiny body in a soft blanket, and handed the bundle to Zoe, who lay on her bed, sweaty and limp and bleeding.

"What are we calling her?" Janice asked.

"You pick." Zoe felt bereft. Bereft and empty, and confused, too, because who was she missing? Russell? Tommy? Her sister? The band? The person she'd been, who still believed in happily ever after?

"What do you think about Cheryl?" Janice said, a little hesitantly. Cheryl had been Janice's aunt, one of Bess's sisters. She'd died years before.

"Nobody names babies Cheryl anymore," Zoe said.

"How about Cherry?"

Zoe's eyes were sliding shut. She waved one hand. "Fine," she said, and closed her eyes, pretending that she couldn't hear the baby crying, crying, crying. Once they'd cleaned her up, the baby was beautiful, pink and small and sweet. How could Zoe, as bad as she was, with all the ugliness she contained, have made something so lovely? And how could Zoe, as broken as she was, be a mother, and not infect this child with her darkness and her selfishness?

It all felt impossible. As impossible as the fact that Russell D'Angelo was gone, forever. That she'd never hear his voice again.

In the months since his death, she'd had plenty of time to think, and what she'd eventually realized was that she'd been wrong about fame. Fame wasn't a monster. It was more like an animal. A horse. A wild horse could hurt you if you weren't careful. But horses could be tamed. They could be broken. You could train them to the saddle and the bridle, and they'd take you where you wanted to go.

That had been her mistake. She'd let the horse ride her. She'd been stupid and incautious, trusting and blind. But now she knew better. She'd be careful this time. She'd make sure that she was the one holding the reins.

Zoe stayed with her parents as long as she could, as the baby got bigger, right up to the moment she'd sensed her mother's patience fraying, and she could feel an ultimatum hanging in the air—*Zoe, you're a mother now. You can't stay here forever.* She thought about trying to explain her fears—that she was bad, that she was broken, that she was the last person who'd be able to raise a whole and happy daughter. Except that would have involved telling Sam and Janice what had happened with Russell, how he'd died, and why Cassie had gone running, and Zoe knew she could never tell anyone that story. Not ever.

She made an appointment at a new hair salon to get her ends trimmed and her highlights refreshed. At home, she unzipped the makeup bag that had come home with her and applied cosmetics carefully, wiping her face clean, starting over when she made mistakes, when the eyeliner looked crooked or she'd put on too much blush. With the help of some shapewear and an underwire bra, she'd wriggled into a leather miniskirt and a white silk blouse. Pregnancy had left her feet half a size larger than they'd been, and her shoes pinched viciously. She told herself to just keep walking, and did her best to ignore the pain.

She'd taken a train to New York City, then walked toward Relic's offices, trying to mimic her old swagger, feeling her hips swing and her hair bouncing on her back. She could feel men's eyes following her as she went. Maybe they'd recognized her, or maybe they just thought she was pretty. When they looked at her, they couldn't see her tragic backstory. No dead husband, no runaway sister, no unwanted baby at home; no big dream that had come true and then come crashing down to crush her. Just a pretty young woman on a soft spring day, with the wind in her hair and her whole life ahead of her, walking like her feet did not hurt her.

At the label, the receptionist's eyes got wide, and her mouth fell open a little when Zoe presented herself. At least, thought Zoe, someone remembered who she was. "Is Jerry available?" Zoe asked sweetly.

"Do you have an appointment?" the receptionist replied.

Zoe hadn't imagined she would need one, but she was careful not to let her surprise register on her face. Instead, she'd smiled.

"Tell him Zoe Griffin is here, please. And that I'm ready to make music again."

Cherry

ALASKA, 2024

Okay," said Cassie. "So, they're called boygenius, but they're actually girls?"

"Correct." Cherry had shown up at Cassie's treehouse that morning, her third in Alaska, with a bag full of pastries from Two Sisters, a bakery in Homer that she'd spotted the night before. She'd shown up at five minutes after nine, and already there'd been a line out the door. Cherry had waited, and had eventually been able to fill a bag with iced cinnamon buns, maple butter cookies, savory Danishes filled with butternut squash and goat cheese, and BLTs on fresh-baked rolls. It had all cost more than sixty dollars. On her way to Cassie's treehouse, Cherry told herself it was an investment, a necessary outlay of funds that would yield dividends in the future. When she knocked, her aunt had ignored her, but Cherry had been ready for that. She'd torn a piece of bacon from one of the sandwiches and bent down, holding it to the bottom of the door so Wesley would be able to smell it. She heard him whining, then the sound of his nails, scrabbling at the door, followed by Cassie's displeased mutter. "Wesley! Cut it out!"

Luckily, Wesley, who Cherry had started to think of as an ally, hadn't stopped, and eventually Cassie had been forced to yield. When the door had finally opened, revealing her aunt, in all of her scowling, plaid-shirted glory, Cherry was waiting, a box of pastry in one hand, a cappuccino in the other, a smile on her face. "I come in peace," she'd said.

"That's a lie," Cassie had grumbled . . . but she'd opened the door wider and hadn't stopped Cherry from coming inside.

"I brought breakfast." Cassie was still frowning, but Cherry saw that there was a second folding chair set up near the metal-legged table. She looked around the kitchen, which didn't take long—there was a single cupboard, a toaster oven, and a single-burner hot plate. She gathered plates (there seemed to be only two in the entire house) and set out the treats, letting Cassie have first dibs after she and her aunt both reached for the same pastry, a savory goat-cheese-filled croissant.

Cassie took a bite. She cleared her throat. "I'm glad I got to meet you. But I'm not going to perform with you."

"Oh, no worries, no worries," Cherry said. "I'm in Alaska for another few days, so I figured we could just hang out. Get to know each other." She had picked up her phone. "I also need to shoot some footage of you turning me down."

Cassie looked worried, and perplexed, and a little bemused. "You need video of me telling you no?"

"Yeah. If I decide to keep trying, the producers will probably splice it into the video package."

"I don't want to be on camera," Cassie said, her voice curt. "I don't want people knowing I'm here." She pressed her lips together, rolling them in, then out. "And 'if' you keep trying? Are you—you're not sure?"

Cherry shrugged. She kept her face placid as, with the sound of a mousetrap snapping, she thought, *Gotcha!* Ignoring Cassie's question, she said, "I won't show you on camera. No one will know where you are, I promise. Look, I'll put my phone in selfie mode, so people will hear both of us, but they'll just see me." Before Cassie could object, Cherry did as she'd promised, propping the phone up on a mug she'd fetched from the cupboard and starting to record. "Hey there, everyone in TV land. This is Cherry Rohrbach, and I've traveled a long way to find a singer who has chosen to remain anonymous, and who has declined to work with me." She looked at Cassie, who'd fled the three steps required to get to the other end of the house. "Hey, Anonymous Singer, are you interested in coming to Los Angeles and being my mentor?" *Say no*, she mouthed, leaning away from the camera.

"No," Cassie said. Her voice was almost inaudible from her spot in the farthest corner of the room.

Cherry popped back on-screen. "There you have it," she said, and ended the recording. She nodded at her aunt. "Thanks."

Cassie came back to the table. She didn't sit. "When do you go back?"

"My ticket's in three days."

Cassie frowned. "Don't you want to get back sooner, so you can work with April?" Cherry had told her aunt the name of the mentor she'd been assigned. Cassie—big surprise—had never heard of her.

Cherry waved her hand, feigning nonchalance. "Like I said, I'm not sure I'm going to do the show after all."

Cassie looked just as surprised as Cherry hoped she would. "I thought this was your dream."

"Well, even being on one of those shows doesn't mean you get to be a working musician. Or that anyone's going to pay for your music. It's just exposure. I guess I've been thinking, you know, what's the point?" Those were all of Zoe's lines, practically verbatim—*shows won't get you anywhere. Why even try?*

Cassie, she noted with satisfaction, looked bewildered and guilty. She'd probably expected Cherry to renew her assault, to beg and to threaten. She hadn't expected this meek acquiescence, or for Cherry to quietly accept defeat. But Cherry had realized that pleading and guilt-tripping hadn't worked. She'd decided that maybe this would. "I thought about it last night," Cherry continued, "and if you don't want to perform—"

"I can't," Cassie interrupted. "It's not that I don't want to; it's that I can't."

Cherry flipped her hand. "Can't. Won't. Whichever. It's fine. And it's none of my business. I don't have any right to force you to do something that makes you uncomfortable." She smiled a gentle, benevolent smile, and hoped it looked sincere. "I don't have a lot of family, you know. That's why I thought I could just hang out with you a little, before I have to go."

At the words *hang out*, she saw, or thought she saw, Cassie's back stiffen, her posture become defensive. Quickly, Cherry reached for her phone. "Want to hear some of my music?" she asked. Cassie shrugged, then nodded.

"Do you have Bluetooth speakers?" Of course Cassie did not, and so Cherry had played her music on her phone, scrolling through her SoundCloud and starting from the first song she'd recorded to the most recent. The sound was shitty, her voice, coming through the phone's speaker, was thin and tinny and small, but Cassie had either been genuinely impressed or she'd been polite enough to fake it for the duration of three of Cherry's original songs.

"Hey, so listen," Cherry said, moving on to the next step of the plan. "I know we're never going to perform together, but, before I go, do you think . . ." She kept her expression soft, her body still and voice gentle, as she asked, "Would you sing a song with me? Just, here, with no one listening?" She gestured toward the tiny treehouse, and Wesley, whose ears swiveled. She sent up a fast, silent prayer to the gods of music and held her breath as Cassie's shoulders hunched forward, her lips pressed into a straight line. Cherry hurried to keep talking.

"It would mean a lot to me. It would be fun. It would be something I could take with me when I go."

And, for a wonder, Cassie wasn't immediately saying *No* or *I can't* or *You should go.* Cassie, instead, seemed to be actually thinking about it.

"One song," she finally said.

Cherry felt like there were fireworks going off in her chest. She wanted to jump in the air, cheering, but she kept her face calm and her voice steady. "Oh, that's awesome! Wait here!" She hurried out the door and raced down the stairs, out into the brief span of daylight, car keys in hand. Her guitar was in the trunk, along with a cheap keyboard that she'd borrowed from a friend of a friend of her new buddy Aline, the clerk at the Land's End Resort, who'd been willing to help her. The plastic keyboard had sixty-four keys, instead of eighty-eight keys, and there was Magic Marker and what looked like glitter decorating some of its upper octave, but it had the benefit of being available, nearby, and free.

Cherry trotted back up the stairs, carrying both instruments. "I brought this, just in case you want to play," she said, showing her aunt what she'd gotten. "Where can I plug it in?"

Cassie, she saw, was staring at the keyboard, gaping at it like . . .

well. Cherry knew that *like she'd seen a ghost* was a cliché, but it was accurate. Her aunt's face had gone pale, and her eyes looked enormous as she pointed.

"Where did you get that?"

"I borrowed it," Cherry said. "Why?"

Cassie seemed to collect herself. She shook her head. "I had one just like that. When I was—" She stopped, then started again. "A long, long time ago."

Cherry filed that away for future consideration. She opened her guitar case. Her mind was whirling, racing through the Griffin Sisters catalogue—or would that be too much, too soon? Should she start with something else?

She tuned her guitar and tried to look calm, running through possibilities: Show tunes? The Great American Songbook? A song about family, something in a minor key, with lyrics about wanting something or missing someone? Or would that be too on the nose? She should have had something ready, she realized, but she hadn't wanted to jinx anything, or get too far ahead of herself. Cherry cast her mind back, remembering that there were twenty years of songs her aunt wouldn't have heard.

"Do you know 'Sunny Came Home'?" she asked.

Cassie nodded. Cherry started to play, and started to sing: "Sunny came home to her favorite room / Sunny sat down in the kitchen . . ."

She'd thought that Cassie would start to sing with her, but, instead, her aunt started playing the keyboard, finding the key immediately, weaving the notes through Cherry's voice and her guitar.

Cherry sang the first verse and chorus by herself, then nodded at her aunt. Cassie's eyes were closed, her voice almost inaudible at first, getting louder, steadier, as she sang, "'It's time for a few small repairs,' she said . . ."

Cherry could hardly breathe. It felt like she'd been trying to start a fire and had finally managed to get the tiniest flicker of a flame going, and if she wasn't super careful the spark would go out. She made herself keep singing, trying not to stare at Cassie, thinking that maybe, if she worked very hard for the rest of her life, she'd be able to sound half as good. Cherry knew that she could sing. Certainly people had told her so—music teachers and bandmates, friends and social media fans. But there was singing, and there was this: the thing Cassie could do. Those things were related. Cousins, maybe. But to be able to open your mouth and produce a sound with so many dimensions and shades, with such richness; to possess a voice that could reach inside of you and pull out memories, a voice that could thrill you or soothe you or make you ache—what would it be like? And what, Cherry found herself thinking, would it have been like for her mother to grow up with Cassie as competition? To know that you had a book of matches, and your sister had a flamethrower?

It ruined our lives, Cassie had said. *We hurt people.* Cherry had spent the night thinking about the story she'd heard, what she knew, or thought she knew, dismantling the picture she'd constructed with the scraps of information she'd gleaned from her mother and the Internet, adding what Cassie had told her, trying to fit it all together. Cassie loved Russell, but he'd married Zoe. Why? And Cassie was convinced that she'd taken away the one thing Zoe had wanted, that she'd killed Russell, that she'd deprived Zoe of a husband and, now, Cherry of a father. Was that true?

For the first time in a long time, Cherry wanted to call her mother. To get her on the phone and ask her questions; to tell her what she'd learned in Alaska and hear what she had to say.

Meanwhile, here was Cassie, in the cold and the dark, alone with a dog in a house barely the size of a handicapped bathroom stall, and just about as comfortable.

You could have saved me, Cherry thought. *You could have helped me.* But in a day's time, those ideas had lost their teeth. Now what she saw was a victim. A princess who'd shut herself in a tower. Cherry wanted to rescue her aunt. To bring her back to the comforts of family and home. To have her not be lonely. To have her sing again.

Wesley was staring up at her, his expression rapt and solemn. Cassie was staring at her feet.

"So you can sing," Cherry said.

Cassie shifted her weight. "Yes. Here. With you. But in front of people . . ." She shook her head, and appeared to be thinking. "You know, if you don't have to be in LA for another few days . . . if you didn't change your ticket yet. I mean, you don't have to . . ."

Cherry felt her heartbeat quicken. Wesley's ears swiveled toward his mistress. "One of the cabins hasn't been rented for this week," Cassie said. "You could move out of the hotel and stay. For a few days. If you want."

Again, Cherry felt that percolating sensation, like she'd swallowed a Roman candle and it was fizzing inside of her, that feeling of wanting to jump and cheer and celebrate. "That would be very nice," she said demurely.

"Come on," Cassie muttered. "I'll show you."

"And we can sing some more!"

Cassie just grunted. Which wasn't a *yes*, Cherry thought, but it wasn't a *no* either. *Baby steps*, she thought. She put her guitar down and followed her aunt out into the dark.

Zoe
PHILADELPHIA, 2024

On the elevator ride up to Jordan's office, Zoe touched the piece of paper in her pocket, checking for the tenth time in as many minutes to make sure she hadn't lost it. It turned out that Bess not only had Cassie's phone number; she also had an address. Zoe had stared down at the words and numbers Bess had written, then up at her aunt. "Alaska?" she'd asked.

Bess gave her a cool look. "She told me she wanted to be as far away as she could."

"Oh," said Zoe. Then, "When? When did she tell you this?"

"The day Russell died." Bess looked at her steadily. "She said she was going away, so she wouldn't hurt anyone else."

Zoe felt her knees going watery. She leaned against the counter and made herself nod, accepting responsibility; aching with how badly she'd screwed up. *It wasn't her fault*, she thought. *I should have told her it wasn't her fault*. During the drive to Center City, the walk from the parking garage to Jordan's building, and the elevator ride, Zoe tried to organize her thoughts, to figure out the best way to make her case to a man who made cases for a living, but the memories she thought she'd banished had started to come back and she couldn't stop remembering how it had been, after Russell had died, and Cherry had come.

At first, Jerry had welcomed her return. "It's been a minute since people heard from you," he'd said. "But they'll remember. It's not too late. Not yet." He'd made it clear that they'd need to move quickly, and he'd paired her with half a dozen likely songwriters, men and women, young and old. Cam and Tommy were long gone. Cam had married Wendy, and they'd moved to Los Angeles, where she worked for Nickelodeon and he played in studio sessions, and Tommy had returned to his classical-music roots, and the Midwest, joining the Cleveland Orchestra.

Jerry, as promised, had worked fast, and had built a band around her. A year after Cherry's birth, Zoe was back on the road again, with a band called Night Becomes Her and a single called "Twenty Questions," on which no fewer than four songwriters were credited. The song had been launched with great fanfare and had been greeted with ringing silence. The album that had followed earned a handful of lukewarm reviews. A few radio stations played the song, probably out of residual affection for the Griffin Sisters—or, more likely, memories of how well their music had sold. But the single hadn't charted, and the album hadn't even cracked the top 100.

By then, streaming platforms were emerging, and CD sales were starting to drop. Instead of paying fifteen dollars for an album's worth of music, kids were downloading songs at ninety-nine cents apiece, or they were pirating copies and paying nothing at all.

Looking back, years later, Zoe could see that her comeback was doomed before it had even begun. She was attempting it at what was a low moment in the history of pop music, even for artists far more talented and established than she'd been. Jerry and CJ both reassured her, promising that her pathetic album sales and poorly attended live shows were not due to lack of talent or hard work, but just bad timing. Zoe wanted, badly, to believe them when they told her that anyone would have struggled, even though she knew that her sister would have done just fine, if Cassie had been the one with a new band. Even if there wasn't a single radio station left, even if record stores had closed and album sales had cratered, even in a crowded marketplace with a new crop of debut artists every week, Cassie still would have found listeners and made a living. Cassie was special. Zoe was not.

Night Becomes Her had lasted less than a year. Jerry's next idea was to launch Zoe as a solo act—probably, Zoe thought, with a cynicism that was becoming more habitual, because it was cheaper than hiring another band. More songwriters were dispatched to the rowhouse in Fishtown, to sit where Russell D'Angelo had once sat and try to coax a song into existence. Except nineteen-year-old Zoe had been delighted at the prospect of fame, hardworking and eager and full of ideas, even if they weren't especially useful ones. Twenty-three-year-old Zoe, who'd lost a husband and had a baby, was a lot less delighted, and significantly less eager, and had no ideas at all. "Maybe it's a song about loss," she said, to the young woman songwriter with long, brown hair. "A song about a woman who loses her love," she said, to the middle-aged guy with tired gray eyes. "A song about loneliness. About being alone. About thinking you're always going to be alone." Loss and loneliness were the only things on her mind. "It's okay," she'd end up telling them all, thinking that the best thing she could do would be to get out of their way. "You write it. I'll sing it."

It took over a year for her to scrape together enough music for an album. Zoe was pretty sure that most of what the songwriters had given her were songs that had been cut from someone else's album, or demos that had never been released. She couldn't bring herself to protest. With no ideas of her own, no ability to write, she had to be grateful for what she got, even if it felt like crumbs from a rich man's table.

The label sent her to a recording studio in New Jersey, where she spent ten days in a soundproofed cubicle two stories underground, hoping she was imagining the bored look on the engineer's face on the other side of the glass window, and that the backup singers were not rolling their eyes at her ineptitude.

"There's a photographer in the Village," Jerry told her, once the sound engineer signed off on the album, saying, "I think that's as good as we can get. He just shot his first feature for *Vogue*." Zoe had expected the label to make arrangements with a stylist, to schedule her hair and makeup and come up with a concept for the cover, the way they had for the Griffin Sisters and Night Becomes Her, but when she'd arrived at the guy's studio—a fourth-floor walkup in a building with a steep, narrow staircase covered in thin gray carpeting and white-painted brick walls—she hadn't found the expected racks of clothing or boxes of shoes. No makeup artist, no hairstylist, no assistant either . . . and, when she knocked on the door, no one had answered.

She checked the new BlackBerry she'd purchased, making sure she had the time and the address right. When she knocked again, and there was still no answer, she pushed the door open. A man, about her age, in a loose-fitting crewneck sweatshirt and dark-blue sweatpants, was standing in the corner of a high-ceilinged room with his back toward the door and a cordless phone tucked under his chin. Light fought its way in through a grimy skylight and through south-facing windows, illuminating the dust on the hardwood floors. Zoe saw a white paper backdrop on a roller, collapsible reflectors and diffusers stacked untidily in the corner, lights on wheels, a stepstool, and a ladder.

"Yeah . . . the Griffin Sister," the guy was saying into the phone. "Sister, singular." He paused, listening, then said, "No, no. The other one." His laughter had a nasty edge.

"Hello?" she all but shouted. The guy turned and eyed her up and down, not even trying to pretend he wasn't. Zoe pushed her hand at him, waiting until he shook it.

"I'm Zoe Griffin."

"Yeah. You are. Brian Halvorsen." He had a long, narrow face, with shaggy brows, a beaky nose, and pockmarked cheeks. His dark hair was thinning on top. His arms and legs were spindly; his belly pushed at his sweatshirt's hem. Zoe tried to give him the same treatment he'd given her, moving her gaze up and down the length of his body. She found that she couldn't. It felt too invasive, too weird.

He clapped his hands together, the sound as loud as a shotgun in the mostly empty space. "Okay, what are we doing?"

"Um. An album cover?"

He laughed like she'd told a joke. "Yes, but what, exactly?"

No one had spoken to Zoe about the concept for the cover, or given her—or, it seemed, Brian, the photographer—any direction. Which told her exactly how much of a priority she was to the label these days. "A portrait," she said, after thinking it over. "Black and white. Chest up. Three-quarter profile." There. That sounded like something. She could picture it too: her expression, thoughtful and sober, her eyes clear. Maybe with her hair blowing over her shoulders. She looked around hopefully for a fan.

"Okay, then." Brian was loading his camera. He jerked his chin toward the backdrop. Zoe walked over, wondering if she had time to primp. She'd worn a loose-fitting black sweater with a cream-colored silk camisole underneath, boot-cut jeans, low-heeled black boots. Nothing fancy. Nothing sexy. But that was fine. She was going for more of a singer-songwriter vibe these days. No more prancing party princess; no more miniskirted, bare-midriffed dancer. Her belly, once as golden-brown and flat as the desert, had stretch marks and a little bit of pooch below her navel.

"All set?" Brian asked, without looking at her.

Fuck it, she thought, and walked onto the roll of white paper, standing, facing him with her hands in her pockets. Brian hit a switch.

Zoe found herself blinking in the sudden glare of a brilliant white light.

"Chin up." Zoe could hear his voice, but couldn't see him. She blinked, feeling mole-like, hoping her eyes weren't watering. Over the click-click-click of the camera, his voice sounded bored. "Lean forward a little. Weight on your back foot. Hips toward me." Zoe felt herself start sweating at her hairline, above her upper lip. After a few minutes, Brian walked toward her, the camera still at his eye. Without a word, he reached out and pushed her sweater off her shoulder. Zoe looked at his hand on her skin. *Don't touch me*, she wanted to say. But she didn't say a word.

"Okay to try some with the sweater off?"

Zoe's fingers felt like frozen sticks as she worked the buttons and tossed the sweater into a corner.

"There you go," he said, still click-click-clicking away. He dragged a white plastic stepstool over, unfolded it, and climbed on top of it, shooting down. "Very nice."

"Did you get what you need?" Zoe asked, when the camera stopped.

Brian climbed back down and circled around her, holding his camera, then stopped, shaking his head. "Can you take your shirt off for me?"

Zoe stared at him.

"I'm not going to show anything," he said. "Just the tops of your shoulders." His voice wasn't even cajoling, just flat and matter-of-fact.

Zoe told herself not to make trouble. She knew she was running out of chances, and if this album didn't work, there would not be another attempt to give her a career. Zoe wasn't ashamed of her body—at least, she knew she wasn't supposed to be—and she wasn't shy. She'd gotten changed in a hundred dressing rooms, with people all around her. She was a professional, Zoe told herself, and pulled off her camisole.

Brian reached toward her. With two thick fingers he pinched her bra strap, then slid it off her shoulder. First the left strap, then the right. Click-click-click, went the camera, before Brian stopped and looked at her again.

"Let's lose the bra."

Zoe blinked. "What?"

"Take it off." He'd turned away, was walking back toward a folding table, where there were two other cameras set out, along with boxes of film. Zoe stared after him. She felt like her spirit was hovering, somewhere in the air above her, staring down at this unhappy scene.

"No," she finally said. Her voice was so faint she could hardly hear it. She cleared her throat. Tried again. "No."

Brian had his back to her as he fiddled with his camera. "If the straps show up in the pictures, I'll have to retouch them. And you're on a pretty tight budget." He finally turned around to face her. "You're not a prude, are you? Nah," he said, answering his own question. "You're a rock-and-roll girl, right?" He flipped a switch, the sounds of drum machines rattling and vocals glitching as the lyrics of Nine Inch Nails "Starfuckers, Inc." filled the room.

Zoe looked at him, at herself. *It doesn't matter*, she thought. *Nothing matters. And this will be over soon.* She unhooked her bra, tossing it on top of her discarded sweater. She crossed her hands over her breasts, trying not to shiver, turning her face, lifting her chin.

Click . . . click . . . click, went the camera. Brian was sweating now— she could see widening circles of wetness underneath his armpits, could smell it too, the ripe odor of unclean male body, as he circled her, coming closer with each pass. "Relax," he whispered in her ear. The music had changed. Zoe heard a discordant shriek of guitars, the ominous thud of a bass line, and recognized Marilyn Manson's "The Dope Show." *Cops and queers . . . to swim, you have to swallow . . .*

Zoe felt his hands on her shoulders, then sliding down to grip her upper arms. He was leaning toward her, close enough that she could see a fleck of dried egg on his chin. He pushed her arms down, rolling her shoulders back, leaving her breasts exposed. "Come on," he whispered. "Who are you saving it for? You want people to buy what you're selling, right?"

Buy what I'm selling, Zoe thought numbly. Which, clearly, was not her music. Had Jerry called this guy beforehand, given him a heads-up?

Don't spend too much time on this. Don't make a big deal. She's nothing special. Girls like her are a dime a dozen.

"Come on," he said again, and reached out to cup a goose-pimpled breast. When Zoe flinched, he pinched her nipple, hard enough to hurt. He rolled it between his fingers, left, then right. "Let's give the people what they want."

In her mind, Zoe pushed him away. In her mind, she said *Stop* and *No*; said *What are you doing*, and *I'm going to tell Jerry.* She saw herself, bending, scooping up her abandoned clothes, running out of the studio, letting the door slam behind her.

In real life, she let him move her, let him touch her, let him pose her, like a doll.

"Hot," he said. "Sexy." He had her straddle a chair, still topless, hair tossed over one shoulder. "Like this," he said, climbing behind her, pressing into her, his fingers all over her skin and his breath hot and damp in her ear. She told herself that it didn't matter, that it was just her body, that this was her last chance.

Later, at home, in the shower, trying to scrub away the feeling of his hands on her body, trying to get his stench out of her nose, Zoe would think, *Why didn't I stop him?* But the answer was obvious. She still wanted success, fame, fortune. If she didn't have the talent she needed to acquire those things, she'd use what she could. If that meant trading her body for a good album cover, she'd do it. Her body wasn't her, she told herself, as the hot water turned her skin pink, then red.

When the photographs arrived, Zoe went to New York to see them. The shots were black and white, bare neck and shoulders. Her hair looked limp and her eyes looked sad. "Nice," Jerry said. "Very nice."

They sent her on a three-week tour, in support of the album that Zoe had called *One Time*, which was the name of the first single, a song she hadn't written. Three weeks, seventeen shows, in bars in big cities and clubs or halls in smaller ones. Vienna, Virginia, and Frederick, Maryland, instead of Washington, DC; Princeton, New Jersey, smallish towns in Maine and Connecticut. None of the larger venues in Philadelphia had been interested. Instead, Zoe had been booked at the Scottish Rite Auditorium in Collingswood, one night after a Led Zeppelin tribute band called Get the Led Out.

To save money, she was driving herself to her gigs in her mother's ten-year-old Toyota, staying in Hampton Inns instead of fancier places. She'd finally learned to play the guitar, after six months of intensive study with an eighteen-year-old teacher moonlighting from the School of Rock. She'd done her best . . . but the album, like the one before it, had flopped. She'd spent a year after its release flogging it, playing at any bar or club that would have her. That was when she'd met Jordan, at a bar in West Philadelphia, at one of the last shows she'd played.

"Sorry we don't really have a greenroom," the bar's owner had said, ushering Zoe to a cramped back office, indicating, with a sweep of his hand, a desk with an elderly desktop computer, a cardboard box filled with foam beer cozies, and a rolling chair with a torn fabric seat. A tiny adjoining bathroom breathed an odor of industrial cleanser and sewage.

"It's fine," Zoe said.

"Just let me know if you need anything." He had the grace to look apologetic as he said, "I can comp your dinner if you want anything, but drinks are full price."

"It's fine," Zoe said again, and tried not to think about the bottles of top-shelf liquor, plus garnishes and mixers, and the platters of fancy cheese and fruit and charcuterie that would be waiting backstage for the Griffin Sisters during their tour, or the designers who'd send her dozens of free outfits, dresses and blouses and shoes, right off the runway, with the hope that she would deign to wear one of their pieces. It had felt endless—a cornucopia of riches that would pour out until the world ended.

There were only a dozen people at the bar. Zoe had noticed Jordan right away. He was in his mid-thirties, nursing a glass of whiskey, dressed in a dark-blue shirt and a loosened tie, with his suit jacket hung neatly over the back of his chair. Zoe was used to men looking at her—used to being appreciated—but Jordan was not just looking; he was listening too.

"Hey, make sure you do some Griffin Sisters stuff," the manager had told her, right before she'd gone on. That was what her audiences, such as they were, wanted from her. It was all they wanted, really. Sometimes, just to be perverse, Zoe would only play new stuff, the songs she'd written for Night Becomes Her, or covers of old songs that she liked. Mostly, though, she did as she was told, knowing that if she refused, word would make its way back to CJ. Then she'd get a lecture. *Zoe, if you want to make this work, you've got to give the people what they want.* CJ would say those words, and she'd feel the photographer's hands on her shoulders again. It wouldn't be worth it.

Normally, Zoe sounded okay to her own ears . . . but that night, with the stranger's flattering attention, the rapt way he listened, the way he looked at her, barely blinking, like he didn't want to miss even a second of the show, Zoe sang better than she had in a long time. She ran through her usual set, which included some covers, some of her original stuff, and enough Griffin Sisters songs to keep the crowds, and the club owners, happy. There was muted applause when she finished up with "Last Night in Fishtown," except for the man in the suit, who had clapped and clapped, with his eyes on Zoe's face.

The bartender caught her eye and nodded at the manager, who, Zoe saw, was tapping his wrist where a watch would be. Zoe pretended not to see him. "This is a new song," she said, and sang, for the first time, the song she'd been working on for almost a year, staying up late at night while Cherry slept in Cassie's old bed beside her. It was the only song she'd written completely on her own. Writing it had been the hardest thing she'd ever done, every word and note wrestled into being, like she'd clawed them out of the rock face with her bare hands. The process had left her jealous of her sister all over again.

I want a love like a death row pardon
A back-bent smile, a pretty little weed
Growing wild in a witch's dark garden
Behind wire walls that don't care if you bleed

She hadn't been surprised when the handsome man had clapped enthusiastically, getting off his chair and onto his feet, eventually shaming the other patrons into joining his ovation. He'd looked at her the way people used to look at her sister. The thought filled her with shame and remorse again, like she was a glass and there was a bottomless pitcher somewhere that could just keep pouring it into her, topping her off, making sure that the story of how she'd betrayed her sister and killed Russell D'Angelo was the first thing she thought of every morning and the last thing she thought of every night.

But she was still pretty . . . and she wasn't surprised when she'd been walking to her car and the guy from the show had called out to her and jogged to catch up.

"Hey," he said, slightly breathless, smiling a boyish smile. "Hi. I just wanted to tell you that you were incredible."

"Thank you. That's nice of you to say."

"I . . ." He swallowed. Zoe felt herself tensing. She wondered if he'd say he was a Griffin Sisters superfan, if he had questions about Russell, about Cassie. But he surprised her. "I feel so lucky I was here tonight."

"You don't come here often?" Zoe thought she'd judged her tone perfectly—light, but not flirty. Interested, but not desperate.

He shook his head. "It's the first time I've been out in . . . God. Over a year." He swallowed. "My wife's been sick."

Wife, thought Zoe. Well. Of course there was a wife. Of course some other, wiser woman had married this handsome, attentive, kind-eyed man. "Oh, I'm sorry," she said. "I hope she's better?" She heard her voice getting higher, tilting the last statement into a question, even as she looked at the guy more closely, and saw his pallor, the circles under his eyes.

"No. Not better. She's dead," he said. "She died . . ." He tilted his head briefly at the sky. "Six months ago," he said. "My God. Sometimes it feels like it just happened yesterday," he said, mostly to himself.

"Oh," Zoe said. "I'm sorry." Up close, she could see that the guy was no older than forty, probably closer to thirty-five. His wife must have been a young woman too.

"Yeah," the guy said. "It's—it's been hard. I haven't been sleeping. And I knew if I went home tonight, I'd just lie awake, staring at the ceiling, and so . . ." He gestured back in the direction of the bar. "I was walking around, and I just wandered in, randomly. And there you were!" His face lit up. "I've never heard of you, or the band you were in. Which I apologize for."

Zoe felt herself smile. Once, that admission would have hurt her. Now it made her glad.

"I think you're amazing," said the guy. Zoe could feel her smile soften, as she thought, *Oh, honey. You should have heard my sister.*

"I'd love to buy you a drink. Or dinner," he said.

Zoe hadn't kissed a man since Tommy. Hadn't touched one since her last fight with Russell. Hadn't been touched by one since Brian the photographer, and hadn't wanted to be touched since then. Between her grief, and the pregnancy, and the exhaustion of new motherhood, she hadn't felt even a flicker of desire. Now she looked at this man and wondered how it would feel if he put his hands on her hips. She wondered how he'd smell, up close; how he'd kiss her. "I'd like that," she said, and gave him her number.

The elevator doors to Jordan's office slid open. Zoe walked down the short length of a hallway, opened the heavy paneled wooden doors, and announced herself at the front desk. "You can take a seat," the receptionist said, indicating the comfortable armchairs that stood on fringed wool carpets. Colorful modern art hung on the gleaming dark wood of the walls; fresh flowers wafted their fragrance from the receptionist's desk; and magazines—*Fortune, Real Simple, Bon Appétit, The Atlantic*—were neatly fanned out on the coffee table. The atmosphere was hushed, reverential, like something holy was going on beyond the doors the receptionist was guarding. *The First Church of the Almighty Dollar*, Zoe thought, and smirked.

In less than a minute, Jordan emerged. He'd removed his suit jacket. His sleeves were rolled up and his tie was loosened, and he looked so handsome, so dear to her, that Zoe felt her eyes burning, the back of her throat prickling.

"Zoe? What's wrong? Did you hear from Cherry?"

She shook her head. "I need to talk to you."

Jordan nodded. Murmuring something to the receptionist, he led Zoe past her, through a doorway, down a hall, and into his office, which had a floor-to-ceiling window that looked east, toward the Delaware River. He moved a stack of files from the chair across from his desk to the floor, then took a seat behind his desk and gestured toward the now-vacant chair. Zoe stayed on her feet. She wondered how she looked to him, if he guessed that there was trouble, if he had any idea at all what it was.

"What's been going on with Cherry and Bix?" she asked.

Jordan stared at her. Zoe tried again.

"Do you know what Bix has been doing to Cherry?"

Jordan's expression was baffled. Zoe didn't think he was faking . . . but would she know for sure if he was?

"Did Cherry say something happened?" he asked. Jordan's desk was a slab of lacquered wood, an unbroken stretch of glossy black, without a single latch or handle or ornament. His hands rested on it, palms tipped open toward her. "Did she accuse him of something?"

Instead of answering, Zoe swiped her phone to life, opened the file she'd prepared, and slid the phone across the black hole of the desk, watching as Jordan scrolled through the pictures she'd found on Bix's phone.

"How did you get these?" he asked, when he'd reached the last one.

Zoe's hands clenched. "That's your first question? Not 'Why is my son taking creepy pictures of my stepdaughter?' It's 'How did you get these?'"

Jordan just looked at her, his expression calm, his voice patient. "Zoe—"

"For God's sake," Zoe said, "does it matter? Can we focus on the pictures? They're gross, they're weird, it's a violation . . ."

A little stiffly, Jordan said, "Looking at his phone without his permission is a betrayal of his trust."

Zoe felt breathless with fury. "Jordan, he took pictures of Cherry in the bathroom. Pictures while she was sleeping. And you think *he's* the victim?"

Jordan pressed his fingers to the bridge of his nose, massaging the red dents his glasses had left there, a gesture she'd seen him make a thousand times. "I don't know what to tell you," he said. His voice was thin, frustrated. Zoe could see the tight line of his lips, and how angry he was in his helplessness. "What do you want me to do? Kick him out? Tell him he can never come home again?"

"Yes. That's what I want. I'm not comfortable—"

She knew what Jordan was going to say before he said it. She'd heard it so many times. "Zoe. He's my son."

That was usually where the conversation ended, because what reply could she possibly make? What could she say? Except, this time, there was something. "Yes. He's your son. And she's my daughter. And she's gone now. And it's your son's fault."

Jordan pressed his lips together. "Well," he said. "That's convenient."

"Which means what?"

"That if it's his fault," said Jordan, "it's not your fault. And I think at least some of her leaving has to do with you refusing to listen to what Cherry was telling you, about what she wanted to do with her life."

Zoe recoiled. "Well, that's very convenient for you," she said, when she could speak. "Because if it's my fault, it's not his."

They'd gone round and round, neither one yielding. Jordan admitted that the pictures were problematic, but refused to concede that Bix had anything to do with Cherry running away. Zoe said that she was happy to own her part of the mess, but she couldn't countenance Bix's continued presence in their home. Jordan, who hardly ever got angry, had yelled at her. Zoe, who hardly ever got emotional, had cried. She'd wept, and she'd pleaded, but she hadn't relented. Hadn't said, *Okay, we'll do it your way*, or agreed that Bix could come home if Jordan promised to watch him more carefully and insist on more therapy and never leave him alone with Cherry. *He can't stay with us ever again*, Zoe said. *If he's there, I'll leave.* She made herself look at the wall, and the framed diplomas that hung there, instead of her husband's hurt expression. "I'll take the boys with me. And you'll never see Cherry again."

She saw bafflement on Jordan's face, followed by anger. "I'll fight you if you do that." His voice was cool, detached, almost thoughtful. "I wouldn't just let you walk away with my children."

Zoe didn't reply. Jordan had adopted Cherry after they'd gotten married. And he loved her. Cherry was as much his daughter as the boys were his sons. But Cherry was an adult now. If Zoe told her daughter what she'd done, told her that Jordan knew about Bix's actions, would she still want to see him? Or would she cut him out of her life, wall herself off from him, the way she'd closed herself off from Zoe?

"You can fight me," she told her husband. "But I have to keep Cherry safe. I'm her mother. That is my job." Even as she spoke, Zoe wondered if this newfound strength would last, if she'd be able to make good on her promise. Maybe she'd end up alone again, broke and single again, only this time with three kids instead of one. Maybe the shame of a divorce, the pitiable and impecunious life of a single mother, was what she deserved for what she'd done.

"Look," Jordan finally said. "Zoe, if it happened—if Bix was watching Cherry, or taking pictures—"

"He was," she interrupted. "There's no 'if,' Jordan. It happened."

"At least he didn't touch her. It could have been worse, right?"

"If it hurt my daughter, that's bad enough." Jordan looked up at her unhappily. Helplessly. But he wasn't helpless, was he? He could do the right thing and live with the consequences. Or he could lose her. When Cherry was little, when Zoe had been so broken, the prospect of walking away from a marriage would have undone her, left her paralyzed with terror. But now she was older, and stronger, and the world hadn't broken her yet.

"I think I know where Cherry is. I'm going to find her," Zoe said. "And when I come home, if Bix isn't gone, then we'll leave. Me, and Cherry, and the boys."

Jordan had his lawyer look on. His *Let's not be hasty* look. His *I'm sure there are options* and *Let's talk it through* look. It was a conciliatory look, but Zoe could also see mulishness behind it: a man prepared to dig in for a long siege.

"I'm not kidding," she said. "This has gone on for too long, and I ignored it. I looked the other way; I stuck my head in the sand. Because I love you." *And because it served my purpose to ignore my daughter*, she thought. The churn of guilt that lived just under her breastbone tried to swell, to rise up and choke her back into silence, but Zoe wouldn't let it. "And because I'd been hurt—that way—I couldn't stand to think about it happening to Cherry."

She'd never told Jordan about the photographer, had only talked in a vague, nonspecific way about the industry and the harm it did to young women. When the #MeToo movement had gotten under-way, and it seemed like every day brought new revelations about some prominent man's wrongdoings, Jordan had asked if anything like that had ever happened to her, and Zoe had given him a humorless laugh and said, "Where do you want me to start?" He'd looked surprised, then saddened.

"That bad?" he'd said, putting his arms around her shoulders, pull-ing her close.

Zoe picked her words out carefully. "We didn't have a way to talk about it then. It was a different time."

He'd drawn her against him, kissed her cheeks. "My poor darling," he'd said. She could see him getting ready to ask for details. *Do you want to talk about it?* he'd ask. Zoe didn't. So she'd said, "It was a long time ago." She'd never offered more information, and Jordan hadn't pressed.

"Zoe—"

She looked across the office, considering her husband, who seemed, in that moment, like a handsome stranger, a man she'd never kissed, never slept beside, a man she didn't know.

"You're a good father," Zoe said. "I know you love your son. But I can't let him keep hurting my daughter." She walked to the door. Her knees weren't trembling; her voice wasn't wobbling; her gaze was steady and her palms were dry. "I'm leaving now."

Jordan got to his feet. "Where are you—"

"I'm going to bring Cherry home, and, Jordan, believe me when I tell you that I mean what I say. Either he's gone, or we will be."

Zoe knew she'd never come up with a better exit line. And so she'd gone, leaving Jordan behind his desk, looking bewildered, praying that she'd done the right thing. She'd go home, book a flight, go find her sister and give Cassie the apology she'd owed her for decades, and hope that Cassie could lead her to Cherry. *Let me be forgiven*, she thought, as the elevator descended. *Let this all not be too late.*

Cherry
ALASKA, 2024

I can't do this."

Cass and Cherry were in downtown Homer, at a table in the corner of Alice's Champagne Palace, a dimly lit bar that had a stage up front. It was five o'clock, two hours before Tuesday's open mic night began, and the fourth day of what Cherry thought of as her Alaska residency. Three days previously, she'd packed up her things and moved from the hotel to Cass's vacant cabin, and had spent all day, every day, with her aunt. In the morning, she helped Cassie with the cleaning. The rest of the time, they'd been making music together.

On the first day, they'd started with covers: "(You Make Me Feel

Like) A Natural Woman" and "Piece of My Heart" and even an acoustic, lo-fi version of "No Scrubs," which Cassie somehow turned into a soul-wrenching lament. In the restaurant, Cherry patted her aunt's shoulder. She tapped out the drumline on the table, and sang the way Cassie had sung: "Hangin' out the passenger's side of his best friend's ride . . ."

At their table, at the sound of Cherry's voice, Cassie groaned quietly. Cherry squeezed her aunt's arm, encased in a black hooded sweatshirt.

"You're going to be fine."

"I'm going to be sick," Cassie replied . . . but at least she hadn't bolted. At least she was still here.

On the second day, after a lunch of ramen noodles cooked in low-sodium chicken broth and green apples that were almost painfully tart (Cherry had started to notice that her aunt's food tasted like either punishment or nothing at all), Cherry had tentatively suggested trying one of the Griffin Sisters songs. "Night Ride" or "Flavor of the Week." Immediately, Cassie had shaken her head.

"Why not?" Cherry had asked.

Cassie hadn't answered for a long time. "I wrote those songs with Russell," she'd finally said.

"You miss him," said Cherry.

Cassie shoved her hands in her pockets and didn't respond. Cherry hadn't pushed . . . but, the next morning, she'd strummed the opening chords of "Take You Down," and Cassie hadn't told her to stop.

Baby steps, Cherry thought again, and started to sing. "I feel your eyes move over me, / Like car wash brushes slap and scrub / And when it's through, I'll be made new / I say it hurts, you say it's love."

Cassie wasn't singing, or playing her keyboard. But she hadn't left the room. "Does it make you think about him?" Cherry asked.

Cassie's lips moved briefly upward, a flicker of amusement too small to be a smile. "I wrote it with him, not about him," she said. "Russell wasn't like that. He would never . . ." Her voice had caught. "He never hurt me."

Cherry wondered if her aunt ever thought about how her life could have been if Russell hadn't died. Would he have left Zoe? Would he and Cassie have gotten married, had a family? Would they have made music together for the next twenty years? Of course, in that version, Cherry herself either wouldn't have existed or would have been raised by a single and undoubtedly bitter mom, who might never have met Jordan. But at least her father would have still been alive. And Cassie would not have run away.

"Did you ever think about marrying Russell?"

"He was married," Cassie replied, her voice low.

"Yeah, but . . ."

"We never talked about the specifics," Cassie said. "We talked about being together, someday. But not marriage."

"Did you want kids?"

Cassie made a scoffing sound and gestured at herself. "Do you think I would have been a good mother?"

Cherry honestly wasn't sure. "I don't know. Did you want to be a mom?" As soon as she'd asked, she realized that maybe she should have phrased it differently; asking Cassie, *Do you want to be a mom?* Her aunt was in her early forties, which wasn't too late, Cherry thought, and there were many ways for women to become mothers. But Cassie was shaking her head.

"I didn't want children."

"You're an art monster," said Cherry.

Cassie's head went back. Her eyes narrowed. Before she could get too insulted, Cherry said, "I just mean, you're a woman who cares more about creativity and art than domestic stuff. It's a good thing!"

"Is it?" Cassie looked unconvinced.

"I'm one, too," Cherry said. "No kids for me." Zoe had heard Cherry giving this speech, and would say things like *You can't be sure*, and *Just give it time*, but Cherry was sure. And she thought she saw a glimmer of understanding in her aunt's expression, and that Cassie's feelings didn't seem hurt. She looked almost amused as she repeated the words "art monster" under her breath.

Cherry picked up her guitar and started singing "Take You Down" again. On the second repetition of the chorus, she held her breath, not even daring to look, as she heard—very faintly—Cassie singing with her. "Take you down the broken staircase / Take you down to water's end / where we're drowning while we're breathing / where we fall as we ascend."

"I love that song," Cherry said, when it was over.

Cassie's face had taken on a musing look. "We wrote it on the tour bus, from Buffalo to New York City. The leaves were changing."

"That sounds nice," Cherry ventured.

"It was a long time ago." Cassie hadn't talked much the rest of the afternoon, and Cherry hadn't even tried another Griffin Sisters song. "Sleep well," she'd told her aunt, after a dinner of black bean burgers and baked sweet potatoes, served without butter or salt. Cassie had smiled weakly: the look, Cherry thought, of a woman resigning herself to a sleepless night, where she'd lie awake, gnawed by nerves and by memories.

The next morning was Tuesday. Cherry had offered to do all the cleaning, but Cassie had refused. She was always quiet, but that morning, she'd said almost nothing, sweeping and scrubbing with her forehead furrowed, her lips pressed together, and Wesley shooting worried looks at her face. They'd had bread and soup for lunch, and Cherry had gone back to her treehouse to shower and dress. She hadn't missed the way Cassie's hands had trembled as she'd set her keys in the car's center console, or the way Cassie sat, rocking a little, hands curled into fists, fingernails digging into her palms, when they'd gotten to the bar and grill.

In the restaurant, a harried-looking waitress, in a black tee shirt and black jeans, with an apron tied around her waist and brassy red-blond hair piled on her head, swung by to refill their water glasses. "You guys want to do a sound check before it gets busy?" she asked. Cherry had brought her guitar, and one of the bands that was signed up to perform had a keyboard that Cassie could play. She started to nod, then looked at Cassie, who shook her head.

"We're fine," Cherry said.

The waitress looked dubious, but didn't argue.

There were two other bands set to perform—locals, the manager had told her. Amateurs. Cherry figured that people whose full-time jobs involved leading tourists on hikes or through glacial lagoons on pack rafts couldn't be much competition—that this could be the lowest of low-pressure situations, the easiest of easy ways back in. She'd begged and pleaded and threatened until, finally, Cass had agreed to try. "You'll see," her aunt had said darkly. Cherry hadn't wanted to ask exactly what Cassie thought she would see. "It'll be fine," Cherry had said instead.

In her borrowed treehouse, decidedly more comfortable than the one Cassie herself occupied, Cherry had bleached her hair for the occasion, and used extra-strength hairspray to freeze it into spikes. She wore high-waisted jeans, a black bodysuit, and a loose flannel shirt. Cassie wore black jeans, a black hoodie over her flannel and her thermal, and a look of abject misery. Cherry pulled out her phone. She filmed the stage and the bar, panned back over the crowd of about twenty, and pointed the camera at her aunt, who immediately yanked her hood up over her head, covering her hair, hiding most of her face.

"I can't do this," Cassie repeated.

"Sure you can!" Cherry said. Her voice was too loud, and it sounded too insistently upbeat. She leaned closer to her aunt and lowered her voice. "You're going to be fine."

Cass just shook her head.

"You've done this before," Cherry reminded her. Cass muttered something, so quietly that Cherry couldn't hear. All she caught was the word *sister*. It took a minute for her mind to fill in the blanks: *not without my sister.*

Oh.

Cherry cast her mind back, over every Griffin Sisters performance she'd ever seen or heard: the single video, for "The Gift"; the bootlegged concerts on YouTube; the television appearances she'd found online. Cassie had been on a hundred stages; she'd sung for audiences of thousands. Millions of people had seen her, if you factored in the band's TV appearances. But, as far as Cherry could recall, Cassie had never sung in public without Zoe. Not even going all the way back to that legendary Battle of the Bands in Philadelphia. She'd always sung with her sister at her side.

Cherry realized that this could be a problem. "You're going to be fine," she told her aunt, with as much conviction as she could muster.

Cassie shook her head. "I don't want—" she began. Then she stopped, shook her head again, and started over. "I can't have people looking at me. I don't want them looking, and I don't want them knowing where I am. I just want . . ." Her voice trailed off, and she turned toward the door again, with such a look of longing that Cherry was left breathless. Was it just that Cassie had stage fright, or suffered from anxiety? Was there some other explanation for the way she was?

Cherry thought back to Jordan, talking about one of Noah's friends, who'd been diagnosed with autism spectrum disorder. "When your mom and I were his age, kids like him were just called weirdos," he'd said. Before Cherry could start telling him all the ways that was wrong, and all the neurodivergent people she knew, he'd said, "Thank God we've made progress. It's a good thing, that they're getting help and support now. That the world's more understanding about differences like that." Cherry, who'd been ready for a fight, had been forced to back down. She'd barely noticed her mother, looking stricken. Now, she wondered if Zoe had been remembering something specific; if she'd been thinking about her sister, and whether the world had misunderstood Cassie. Or, Cherry thought, maybe her mom had felt guilty because she'd been the one who hadn't understood.

"What can I do?" she asked her aunt. "How can I help you?"

Cassie said, "You can't. I can't do this. I'm sorry, but I can't. I want to go home." She said it again—"I want to go home"—but she made no move to leave. It was almost like she couldn't get out of her chair, like fear and bad memories had left her paralyzed.

What happened to Cassie out there? Cherry wondered . . . and then, for the first time in a long time, Cherry found herself thinking about her mother, without any of the anger and resentment that had accrued over the last months and years. Both sisters had been damaged, Cherry realized. Cassie lived in exile, in this cold, dark, lonely place where she never sang at all, and Zoe had stopped making music, had retreated completely into the life of a wife and a mother. Maybe Zoe needed Cassie, to write the songs, the same way it seemed like Cassie needed Zoe to get on a stage.

Maybe they really couldn't do it without each other.

The manager came back to their table. "Ten minutes," she said. "Just giving you a heads-up."

She hurried off. Cassie shook her head. "I think I'm going to be sick," she said faintly.

Fuck.

Cherry could see her dream coming apart. She'd go back to LA, alone and empty-handed. She'd be eliminated from the competition, right back where she'd started. This would be the end. She could feel a spike of adrenaline in her blood; her body revolting at that idea, and then she was up and moving, kneeling down in front of her aunt and taking her hands.

She put her hands on Cassie's knees and looked into Cassie's face, as she sent a quick prayer to the gods of rock and roll, wherever they were, whoever they might be (she imagined Janis Joplin and Jimi Hendrix, together in heaven, dressed in leather and sequins, smiling benevolently down).

"Listen to me," she said. "You have so much talent. You can do this. You are going to be fine, and I will be there with you."

Cassie stared down at her. From the look on her face, it was like she'd never seen Cherry before. Her voice was hoarse as she asked, "What did you say?"

For one brief, frantic instant, Cherry couldn't remember. Then the words came back. "You have so much talent? I will be there with you?"

Cassie's eyes were locked on hers, and she looked frightened but, also, Cherry thought—or hoped—determined. Cherry felt a fragile breath of relief. For a second or two, she thought, *I can make this work.* Then Cassie pressed her hand to her mouth, stood up, fast. Cherry heard her retching as she went racing toward the door.

Fifteen minutes later, Cherry glumly loaded her guitar in the trunk of Cassie's car. They drove back without speaking. Cherry's thoughts were coming fast and furious. *This is a disaster,* followed by *There is no way she'll agree to come to Los Angeles with me.* And then, hard on the heels of that thought: *God, but she's so good.* Except if the prospect of singing in front of a few dozen friendly locals made her aunt physically ill, how would performing in front of cameras and a televised audience affect her?

Cherry sat in the passenger's seat as the car sped through the dark, and, slowly, a new plan came together. If it was true that Cassie had never sung onstage without her sister, if she found it physically impossible to do so, it meant, Cherry realized, that she'd need to engineer a bigger reunion. She'd have to do the thing she'd long dreaded—the thing she'd hoped, desperately, to avoid. She'd have to call her mom.

"Hey," she said, as Cassie turned onto the dirt road that led to the treehouses. Cassie had left the lights on in her house, so that Wesley wouldn't be alone in the dark, and the windows glowed like squares of gold, making the house look like a tiny ship afloat on a great, dark sea. "Is there any chance . . ."

"Any chance of what?" asked Cassie. Her voice was wary.

"I'd like it if you came to LA with me. Not to sing," Cherry said hastily, before Cassie could object. "Just to be there. If I decide to go through with it. All the other contestants will have family there, or boyfriends or girlfriends." She made her voice small and mournful. "I won't have anyone."

"You could ask your mom." Cassie's voice was expressionless.

"Could," said Cherry. "Won't." *Can,* she thought. *Will.* Cassie was not going to like it, but that couldn't be helped. When you had a voice like Cassie's, a gift like Cassie's, you couldn't just stay holed up in Alaska and not let anyone hear you. It was like spurning your destiny, turning your back on the gifts God had given you—maybe, even, on God Himself. And Cassie was so lonely. Cherry couldn't allow it. She had to help her aunt. She had to give the world the gift of Cassie's voice. She had to balance the scales, fix what was broken. And if it ended up helping her music career, was that the worst thing?

Cherry decided that it was not.

Zoe

PHILADELPHIA, 2008

By the time she'd met Jordan, that night at the bar in West Philadelphia, Zoe had spent almost four years trying to make it, first with a band, then as a solo artist. Then two things had happened, to hasten the end of her second attempt at stardom.

The first was that Jordan had called her, even before she'd gotten home, asking to see her again. The second was that she'd opened the door to the Fishtown rowhouse to find her mother, wild-eyed and terrified-looking, standing just inside the door with Cherry in her arms, as if she'd been standing there, waiting, for hours.

"You have to go," Janice said, pushing Cherry toward Zoe. Janice's lips were white around the edges, and her expression was frightened and unhappy. Cherry, for her part, looked delighted at being up so late.

"Hi, Momma!" she said, waving.

"What?" Zoe asked her mother. "Go where? What happened?"

What happened, it turned out, was that, just before bedtime, Cherry had toddled over to Cassie's piano, hoisted herself up onto the bench, pushed back the wooden lid, put her pudgy toddler fingers on the untouched keys, and started playing "Für Elise." Neither Janice nor Zoe had any idea where she'd even heard the song. Nor did it matter.

"I can't go through it again," Janice whispered.

Zoe did not need to inquire what *it* was. She knew what Janice meant: that she could not live with another musical prodigy, and the sorrow that talent brought with it, the barbwire string tethered to the gaudy balloon.

"You need to find your own place," Janice said. "It's time." In the kitchen's lights, her mother looked haggard, and haunted, and old. She looked as if she'd seen a ghost . . . which, Zoe supposed, she had.

Zoe had taken stock of her options. And her savings. As a kid, she'd figured that anyone who was part of a band that was on MTV and had a number one album would be rich, and it was true that a single hit album and half a tour had left Zoe with a decent hunk of cash, even after she and Cassie had gifted their parents a generous sum. When the record had been selling, Zoe had gotten royalties—her portion, plus Russell's. But Zoe hadn't denied herself much during the Griffin Sisters' heyday, which meant that instead of stocks and bonds, she had shoes and bags; instead of investments and property, she had jewelry and designer dresses—the accoutrements of another life—things that had started losing value the second she'd bought them and wouldn't do her any good in Philadelphia. By the time Janice told her it was time to go, she had a tidy nest egg, but no idea of how she'd earn any more.

She could have gone back to school and studied teaching, or nursing, but she'd never been a very good student or had an appetite for bodies and their frailties. She could have found a job in fashion, maybe reconnecting with one of the stylists who'd dressed her for photo shoots or the band's one video . . . except that would have meant a reckoning with her former life, acknowledging who she'd once been, and how far she had fallen. She wasn't ready for that.

What she wanted, Zoe decided that night, was security. A big house, in a town with good schools for her daughter. Money in the bank; enough so that she'd never have to worry. What she had was her face. Her body. Her good-enough voice. A little money, still. The remnants of her fame.

Zoe did the math, balancing what she had to offer versus what she wanted, factoring in how many years she'd be likely to look this good, and how many men might be willing to take on a woman with a child. The next morning, she returned Jordan's call and told him she was free that Friday night.

He'd been thrilled. "Where do you want to go?" he'd asked. "I'll take you anywhere."

"Just dinner is fine," she'd said, laughing. And, at first, it had been lovely. After years of bashing herself into the brick wall of not-quite-good-enough and a husband who—she could admit it now—had never wanted to marry her; after all of that, she'd met a man who looked at her like she was a goddess, some celestial creature who'd stepped down from the heavens and deigned to let him into her bed.

Jordan was thirty-seven, with a law degree from Penn. He was older than Zoe and much more educated, but her former fame, the cachet that it gave her, seemed to make up for her working-class background and her lack of a college degree . . . although, Zoe wondered if her beauty alone wouldn't have been enough for Jordan to overlook all the ways she was not his equal. She knew what their life would be: A house in the suburbs. Good schools. Vacations. More children, because she knew he wanted them, and Zoe decided that she was fine with that.

Jordan proposed after a year. Six months after that, they were married, with just twenty-five guests; an intimate ceremony in one of the city's small, historic gardens, underneath blooming magnolia trees. Then she and Cherry moved across the river, to Haddonfield, where Zoe slipped into her new identity as if it were a dress that had been sewn to her measurements.

She could have been happy, living in that four-bedroom house, driving her Range Rover, spending summers at the shore, skiing out West each December and spring breaks in the Caribbean sun. She could have been content, if it hadn't been for Bix . . . and for Cherry. Because Cherry, it seemed, had inherited both Cassie's outsized talent and Zoe's single-minded intensity. And Cherry, like her mother, wanted to be a star.

In third grade, Cherry had used her stepdad's laptop to go online and find out about auditions for the new Mickey Mouse Club. Cherry hadn't seen the shudder that racked Zoe's body at those words when she held up the page she'd printed so her mother could see it. "There's an open casting call at the Cherry Hill Mall. I just need a ride!"

Zoe told her no. Cherry's face, normally cheerful, had gotten thunderous. "Why not?"

Zoe stuck with the most expedient answer. "Because you're not moving to California."

She had hoped that would be the end of it. It was not. Cherry had wanted dance lessons, which she and Jordan had been happy to pay for, and guitar and voice lessons, which Zoe felt a little less thrilled about, but had agreed to, nevertheless. When Cherry and her friends had formed a band, in sixth grade, Zoe assumed it would last a week or two. She'd had a cold feeling in the pit of her belly, a coppery taste in her mouth, when Cherry had told her they were entering a talent show, but what could she do?

When Cherry had wanted to go to a performing-arts summer camp, Jordan had been all for it. Zoe had been the one to say that she thought a regular kind of camp, with archery and swimming lessons, would be a better experience. When Cherry had asked to enroll in a performing-arts high school, Jordan had said, "If this is what she wants, we should encourage her." Zoe had, again, argued that being well-rounded would set Cherry up better for a successful adulthood. She'd given her husband David Epstein's book that argued against early specialization, telling him, sweetly, that she wished her own parents had let her try more things before settling on music, and, again, Jordan had agreed.

But Cherry kept pushing, and the fights got worse. When she was fourteen, there'd been a big blowup over whether she could miss a family trip to Disney World to stay home and play a gig with the School of Rock house band. Zoe and Jordan had finally agreed to let her stay with a friend for the weekend of the show, then fly out to meet them . . . except Cherry had missed her flight. "Accidentally," Cherry told them, but Zoe suspected that it hadn't been an accident at all. "And I can stay with Andi for the rest of the week. Her parents say it's fine."

By fifteen, Cherry was spending more of her weekends out of the house than in it; staying with friends, or, Zoe suspected, her boyfriends; lying about where she was going and what she was doing. Zoe started to notice money missing from her wallet, blank checks disappearing from her checkbook, charges she hadn't made appearing on her credit card statements. Cherry chopped off her beautiful, long light-brown hair and used Clorox to bleach the fuzz that remained a shocking white. She wore black eyeliner, black lace bodysuits with ripped jeans, or petticoats layered on top of them and stack-heeled black Doc Marten boots underneath them. The first time Zoe found a vape pen in Cherry's pocket, and condoms in her dresser drawer, there'd been a fight. By the fifth or sixth time, Zoe just sighed, replacing the offending items, telling herself that Cherry could be doing worse things than vaping, and that the condoms, at least, meant she was being careful.

Bix, too, was a challenge . . . but by the time he was fourteen, and Zoe's boys were toddlers, he'd been enrolled in (or, in Zoe's mind, banished to) boarding school. He came home on vacations, and for a few weeks each summer, when he wasn't in camp. Despite her best efforts, Zoe never warmed to her stepson. But neither Bix nor Cherry was her primary concern. By then Zoe was busy with what she sometimes, guiltily, thought of as her real family.

Zoe doted on her boys. She watched in dismay, then resignation, as Cherry's grades and her behavior got worse. It was clear Cherry was barely attending high school, and not paying attention when she was there . . . and she and Zoe were fighting whenever Cherry was home. It made everyone in the house tense. Schuyler would go to his room when his sister walked in the door. Noah would cry as soon as the shouting began, and Jordan, Zoe suspected, would come home late even when it wasn't strictly necessary, to avoid the misery that Cherry's presence guaranteed. When she found out Cherry had left, Zoe had been worried. And, shamefully, she'd felt a not-inconsiderable amount of relief.

You're a terrible mother, the Cassie who lived in her head whispered. *You're as bad a mother as you were a musician.* Zoe would not disagree. She'd never wanted Cherry. She would have abandoned her completely, would have left her with Janice to raise, if Janice had allowed it. And, as the weeks had gone on, and Cherry stayed missing, Zoe realized that she had no idea how to fix what had gone wrong between them, when—if—she saw her daughter again.

Back at home, after giving Jordan her ultimatum, Zoe sat at her desk in her beautiful kitchen. She looked at the marble countertops, the flowers, the rugs, and the glossy floors, and wondered how long it would be hers. Then she opened her laptop and began looking for flights. When her phone rang with an unknown number, she'd ignored it. But when it had rung again, she'd sighed, picked up the phone, and said, "Hello?"

And had almost fallen down on the kitchen floor when a voice she hadn't heard in weeks said, "Hi, Mom!"

Cassie

LOS ANGELES, 2024

Cassie sat in the dressing room backstage, hearing voices, the tumult of a live show getting ready to begin, thinking that everything felt different; but, also, everything felt exactly the same. The fashions had changed, and, obviously, everyone had iPhones now, but the feeling before a performance, the crackling energy, the smells of hairspray and anxiety, the sounds of high heels clicking and headsets squawking and the ambient hum of the audience, not too far away—all of that was the same. Except, this time, she had nothing to worry about. This time, Cassie wasn't the one performing.

A PA knocked at the door and stuck her head inside, calling, "Twenty minutes to places."

"Thank you," said Cherry. The dressing room was tiny, with barely room for a full-length mirror and a vanity with a narrow counter running its length. There was just one chair. Cassie was sitting in it, and Cherry, who'd said she was too nervous to sit, stood behind her, practically trembling with anticipation. The hair and makeup people had sprayed Cherry's two inches of bleached hair into spikes. They'd put circles of kohl around her eyes, and slicked her lips with pink gloss. She wore black leather leggings (vegan leather, she'd taken pains to explain), a loose black lace top with billowing sleeves, and studded platform-soled black boots. Cassie thought Cherry looked like a punk Peter Pan, androgynous and adorably fierce, like a kitten that would swipe at you with its tiny claws before it curled up in your lap.

Cherry stopped bouncing and swung one hip up to perch on the countertop, next to the litter of makeup and tissues. Cassie could hear her niece breathing—in for a four-count, hold it, a slow, eight-count exhalation. With Cherry occupied, Cassie forced herself to look at her own face in the mirror. She, too, had been made camera-ready. The hair and makeup people had tried their hardest, but her face was still soft and round, skin pale, and her body . . . well. At least they'd mostly managed to disguise her, in a flowing caftan made of vivid pink silk. She wore leggings underneath it, in a complimentary shade of pink, and gold beaded slippers. Her hair had been augmented with extensions, piled on top of her head in an updo, with curls falling down to frame (read: disguise) her face.

"All this trouble, for a five-second reaction shot?" she'd asked. The makeup artist just smiled. "We want everyone to look their best," he'd replied.

The Next Stage had been airing for six weeks. There'd been four shows devoted to auditions held in each of the four cities the producers had visited, and two weeks about the winnowing that had taken place in Los Angeles, and the mentor assignments. Tonight, the first six finalists would be performing with their mentors. Cassie knew that Cherry, who'd agreed to work with April, was going to sing "Alone," by Heart, with April, and "When You're Here," a Griffin Sisters song, which she'd do alone.

Cassie knew that Cherry was still hoping that she would change her mind, that she'd agree to sing, no matter how many times Cassie had told her that it wouldn't be happening. Just being here was almost more than she could handle. Getting on the plane had been hard, even with Cherry beside her, and Wesley, in his traveling crate, at her feet. She'd felt, or imagined she could feel, people's eyes on her. She told herself that what she felt was just the judgmental scrutiny every fat lady got for the crime of existing in public or daring to board an airplane—hostile stares, people hoping that you wouldn't end up sitting next to them and not even trying to hide it. She kept her head down until she was buckled into her seat, praying that no one had recognized her and that the inspection wouldn't morph into recognition. *Oh my God, aren't you . . . ?*

More than once, Cassie asked herself why she was doing this. Why she was bothering. Why she was leaving the nest she'd built, why she was venturing back out into a world that had done nothing but hurt her. The answer was rarely a few feet from her side . . . or, for a few hours on the flight, it was sleeping, with its head on her shoulder and its mouth open, snoring softly, eyes moving underneath her lavender-colored eyelids as she dreamed.

She'd told her niece the truth. She'd never wanted children. Maybe because she'd been, more or less, a child herself when she'd fallen in love with Russell. She'd never imagined them having a family, never pictured herself as a mom. Or as an aunt, once she'd run away and knew she would never see her sister again. But then there was Cherry— funny, prickly, talented Cherry, with her sweet voice and her spiky hair. Cherry, who'd pulled her back into the world, even though she hadn't wanted to rejoin it.

The world still hurt. Cassie had always hated being looked at, feeling like, in any room she entered, she never knew what to say or how to stand or where to put her hands, and that feeling had not subsided at all since that terrible morning in Michigan.

But Cherry needed her. And Cassie liked Cherry, who was all hustle and drive, all platform-soled Doc Martens and ambition. It was possible that Cassie even loved her a little bit . . . and she wanted to keep her safe, safer than she'd been, when she'd been young and trying to make it. And so she'd boarded the plane, and, when they'd landed at LAX, she'd followed her niece through the airport, keeping a sweaty grip on Wesley's carrying case. Cherry moved briskly, cutting through the crowds, leading her outside, across six lanes of traffic, onto an island, where they waited for a car to come and get them.

The Griffin Sisters had played only a few shows in Los Angeles, back in the day, but Cassie could still remember the look and the feel of the city, the vertiginous roads that wound up the mountains and down through the canyons and left her carsick with their twists and tight turns; the endless concrete strip malls, the monochrome landscape of beige and off-white buildings and black roads; the flat, glaring light. When their Uber driver had taken them past the Hollywood Bowl, she'd had to clench her hands together tightly and close her eyes, praying that she wouldn't throw up, or pass out, that coming hadn't been a mistake. *I'll sit in the audience*, she'd told Cherry. *And you can't say who I am. Just that I'm a friend.* Even that, Cassie knew, was risky . . . but, as much as she feared being recognized, even more she hated the idea of Cherry being up there, onstage, without anyone to support her. She could be there for her niece, wishing her well, cheering her on.

At dress rehearsal the previous afternoon, Cassie had watched as the producers had walked Cherry through the beats of the show—the emcee's introduction, the camera operator who would follow her from backstage as she took her place. They'd edited the songs down to ninety-second versions, and there'd be a drummer, a bass player, a keyboard player, and, for the second song, a cello and a violin. Cameras up front; cameras overhead and in the wings; cameras there, in the audience, to catch Cassie's reaction to Cherry's performance. *It's been twenty years*, Cassie told herself, when the panic of being in public, on camera, threatened to overwhelm her. *No one will be looking for me. No one even remembers me, and I don't look the same.* She'd cram herself into the aisle seat they'd designated for her use, and she'd try to make herself as small as possible to keep her body from overspilling the armrests, and she'd do what she'd come to do. She would support Cherry, and cheer her on, and then she'd go back home, to be an art monster. Or a former art monster, a retired art monster who ran rental cottages and lived alone, but who talked to her niece from time to time.

In the dressing room, Cherry fiddled with her phone, then propped it against a makeup kit. It was filming, but Cassie didn't think much of that. Cherry had been filming everything, including her plane trip from Alaska to LA, her purchase of a Frappuccino that morning, and Wesley's encounter with a purse dog on the sidewalk the previous afternoon. Cherry's fingers looked a little shaky, and Cassie heard her swallow hard as she got to her feet.

"Hey. So. You know how you told me that you've never been on-stage singing without my mom?" Cherry asked, in a tone that was trying for casual and not quite getting there.

Cassie nodded.

"Well," said Cherry. "What if . . ." She cleared her throat. "What if I could make that happen?" she asked. "What if we could all sing together? The three of us?"

"What?"

Cassie's pulse quickened as someone knocked at the dressing room door. "Come in!" Cherry called . . . and Cassie felt her heart stop. Because this time, it wasn't a PA or a makeup artist. It was not Braden or Tori or one of the other contestants, stopping by to tell Cherry to break a leg.

It was her sister.

Zoe looked the same. Older, but still pretty, maybe even more beautiful than she'd been. She wore a navy-blue silk top, cropped, sharply creased black trousers, and high-heeled shoes. A camera guy and someone holding a boom mic stood behind her, the better to catch every sound, every expression, every instant of the reunion.

Cherry had moved to stand at her aunt's side. She shot Cassie a look that was both anxious and proud, as if this reunion was a wonderful bit of magic she'd engineered, a gift she'd set in Cassie's lap. Cassie sat, frozen, watching one of Zoe's hands drift up, slowly, to cover her mouth, red-painted nails splayed over red-lipsticked lips.

"Cassie," Zoe whispered. "Oh God. Cassie."

Cassie wasn't in a dressing room in Los Angeles any longer. Instead, she was back in the hotel lobby, in Detroit, where three police officers and CJ were standing in a huddle, and one of the cops' radios was squawking, and people were clustered in front of the hotel's windows, staring out at the scene, and CJ's face was tinted red, then blue, then red again, washed by the ambulance's strobing lights. *I'm sorry*, CJ was saying. *Cassie, I am so sorry.*

"So listen!" Cherry was saying brightly, for the benefit of the cameras. "Mom—Cassie—I know this is a big surprise for both of you, but I'm hoping—and I know I'm not the only one—that you guys would be willing to sing with me." When neither sister spoke, Cherry touched the spikes of her hair, then fidgeted with the microphone pack wrapped around her waist. "I hope you'll do it." She pressed her lips together, shot the camera operator an apologetic glance, then said, lowering her voice, "Because I kind of told the producers that you would. And they're really, really excited for that to happen."

At that, Zoe and Cassie both turned to stare at Cherry.

Zoe spoke first. "Wait," she said, lifting one hand to her temple. "Cherry. You told me Cassie knew about this! You said—you told me—"

Cassie decided that whatever Cherry had told her sister did not matter. She couldn't be here. She got to her feet and pushed past Zoe and the camera guy and the guy holding the boom mic, blundering through the door, down the hall, her feet, in their stupid twinkly gold shoes, going faster and faster, speeding her toward an exit, daylight and fresh air and escape. She would get Wesley and she would go home, where no one knew who she was and no one wanted anything from her. Where she could hide in her treehouse, hide in her parka, hide in the dark.

"Cassie!"

At the sound of her sister's voice, Cassie quickened her pace. Of course Zoe was coming after her. Of course Zoe wouldn't leave her alone. Zoe probably wanted to review Cassie's cruelties and transgressions; she'd want to pick through all the trouble Cassie had caused and demand recompense.

"Cassie, wait!"

Cassie pushed past a wardrobe assistant wheeling a rack of clothes, half running as she dodged rolling lights and moving bodies, until she finally spotted an exit sign. She opened the door it marked, feeling the daytime heat blast her, pulling in a breath of desert air, trying to orient herself and figure out where the street was. And then Zoe was there. Zoe had her hand on Cassie's shoulder, Zoe was saying, "Cassie, wait, please. Don't run away. I need to talk to you."

Cassie stopped. Mostly because she knew she couldn't outrun her sister. Without turning, without looking, she asked, "What?"

Zoe touched Cassie's shoulder again. "Can we go somewhere? Please? Can we sit down and talk?"

Helplessly, Cassie turned back toward the soundstage. A small part of her wondered what Cherry was doing; how Cherry was trying to explain this turn of events to the producers. Cherry was supposed to be onstage soon, maybe even now.

Part of her wanted to run. But another part wanted to hear what Zoe had to say . . . and to stay with Cherry. To be there for her niece, the way she'd planned.

When Zoe asked again, Cassie managed a jerky nod. She let her sister lead her toward the parking lot, where Zoe unlocked a car and got behind the wheel, waiting until Cassie opened the passenger's door and climbed in beside her. Cassie didn't ask where they were going, just snuck glances as Zoe drove, trying to superimpose her sister's current, adult face over the face of the younger woman Zoe had been when she'd last seen her. Zoe's hair was shorter—shoulder-length and straight, where, before, it had fallen to the small of her back in waves— and her posture was stiffer, controlled and contained. Once, Zoe had twirled and danced across the stage, arms loose, eyes closed, heedless and free, exuberantly taking up room and making it everyone else's job to get out of her way. Cassie could not imagine this woman, in her sharply creased trouser pants and her high heels, dancing at all. And it was her fault. All her fault. Cassie had stolen her husband; she'd taken Zoe's dream away; she'd turned her sister into this stiffened, diminished version of herself. Married to a lawyer. Estranged from her daughter. A PTA mom.

I need to tell her I'm sorry, Cassie thought. *I need to say that to her face.*

Zoe consulted a map on her phone's screen and drove them up into the hills, to a park that wound along a hillside, with benches, and green grass, and weeping willows giving shade, their fronds rustling in the hot wind.

Cassie unbuckled her seat belt. She followed Zoe out of the car, to a bench, set a little way off from a path. When Zoe sat down, she sat, too, taking in the scene. The park was full of people walking their dogs or hiking or working out with their trainers. Cassie wondered how she looked to her sister—if she seemed older, if she looked changed.

"Where to begin," Zoe said, almost to herself.

Cassie decided that she should be the one to start. "I'm sorry," she said.

Zoe had been on the verge of saying something. She closed her mouth and turned toward Cassie, looking startled. "You're sorry? For what?"

For sleeping with your husband, Cassie thought, but could not make herself say. Instead, haltingly, she tried to tell Zoe why she'd done what she'd done. "Russell told me . . . when we were together . . . he said it wasn't real. That you were the one who'd wanted to get married. That you'd said you were engaged on TV." Cassie swallowed hard, a little astonished that she'd managed to get the words out.

Zoe pressed her lips together, then nodded. "Yes," she said. "That is true."

"Did you love him?" Cassie asked.

"I wanted him," said Zoe. She had stopped looking at Cassie and, instead, was staring straight ahead, like a prisoner who'd refused the blindfold and was waiting for the firing squad to start shooting. "I felt like I didn't matter very much. Like I wasn't essential to the band.

I knew I wasn't as good as the rest of you. And I thought, if Russell wanted me, if we were together, that would be . . . something to hold on to, I guess. Or a reason for the band to hold on to me." Her shoulders slumped. "I wanted to be a star. I wanted all of it, so badly, and then, to get it, and to find out that I wasn't good enough . . ." Her voice trailed off. She licked her lips. "So I went after Russell. But he told you the truth. He never wanted me. Not really. He certainly never wanted to get married. He was willing to go along with it, because it helped the band's image, you know? It was free press, and Jerry, and CJ, and everyone else, they were all for it." She stopped talking, then turned to Cassie. "But you were the one he loved."

Cassie could barely swallow around the lump in her throat. "So it wasn't real?"

Zoe shook her head. "No." She clasped her hands together in her lap. "And I wasn't even being faithful."

"What?" Cassie asked. Then, "Who?"

"Tommy," Zoe said.

Cassie blinked. For a moment, *Tommy* meant nothing. "Tommy Kelleher? Tommy the drummer? Tommy from Curtis?"

"Tommy from Curtis," Zoe confirmed.

"You were with Tommy?" Cassie's voice was a squeak.

"More than I was with Russell, by the end," Zoe admitted. "And there's something else I need to tell you."

Cassie's skin was prickling, and the muscles in her legs and her back were tensed, like her body had decided before her mind could that she did not want to hear whatever it was Zoe had to say.

Zoe looked down. She pinched the crease of her pants. "You remember the note. The note Russell left."

Cassie made a noise. The noise meant, *Yes, of course I remember the note, I remember as if I had it tattooed on my heart.* Her voice was leaden, uninflected, as she recited the words. "'I'm sorry. I never should have touched you.'"

"That's the one," Zoe said, wincing. "But the thing is . . . that note? I don't think it was meant for you."

Cassie's heart stopped. Her entire body went still, like a watch someone had smashed with a hammer. A great roaring sound filled her ears. When she opened her mouth, what emerged was not quite a word, more like a sound: *Wha?* If Russell hadn't written the note for her, had it been for Zoe? Was her sister the one he should never have touched, the one he couldn't be with?

Cassie groaned out loud and buried her face in her hands, feeling the false eyelashes, the airbrushed foundation, all of that strangeness covering her skin.

"You know he loved lyrics you could read a few different ways," Zoe said wryly.

Cassie shook her head. She felt the oddest mixture of fury and relief. As angry as she was at Zoe, for letting her believe, all this time, that she'd been the one at fault, she also felt relief, like something tied tight inside of her had loosened, like some knot had been unpicked.

"It wasn't your fault," Zoe said. "If anyone was to blame, it's me."

Cassie's body, her entire world, might have stopped, but the world around her rushed on. A car pulled into the parking lot, cruised slowly past the occupied spots, then backed up toward the entry, where it idled, waiting for someone to leave and make room. The wind stirred up an eddy of dust. Two hikers, sleekly clad in technical fabric leggings and tops, greeted each other, then started walking, side by side. A bird trilled its song from a tree.

"There's more," Zoe said.

Cassie shook her head. There couldn't be more. She couldn't survive more.

"The night Russell died," Zoe said. "After I walked in on you two, I told him I was pregnant, and that it was his. But I wasn't sure if that was true. I'm still not."

It took Cassie a minute to put the words together, to fit what Zoe had just told her into her own memories of the night. When it finally made sense, when she came back to herself and could hear again over the roaring in her ears, Zoe was still talking.

"He was ashamed, and I was angry, and I just kept going at him, and going at him . . ." Zoe shook her head. "I told him that we'd have to stay together, and that he couldn't be with you." She sounded so normal, Cassie thought. So calm and controlled. She could have been talking about her flight to Los Angeles, or what she'd had for breakfast, and not the end of Russell's life. "And I think—I think that's why it happened. Why he got drunk, and went out in the dark." Staring straight ahead at nothing, Zoe said, "I think he decided that he'd rather be dead than have to spend the rest of his life with me."

She sat back against the bench, looking smaller, and older, and drained. Like all of the rock-star glamour had faded and all her well-heeled housewife elegance had disappeared. The disguises were off, and she was just a regular middle-aged woman, not famous, not special, not immune to heartache, or to time.

"I should have told you the truth a long, long time ago. And I'm sorry." Zoe paused for a breath. "And if you can't forgive me—if you never want to see me again, if you want to go back to Alaska and never speak to me again—I will understand."

Cassie didn't answer.

"But if you want to come home—if you want to make music again, or not make music again, or if you want to go back to the Curtis Institute, pick up where you left off, if that's even possible, whatever—anything. If you want to see Mom and Dad, and Bess, and get to know Cherry, and meet my husband, and my sons . . ." Zoe's throat bobbed. She was still looking straight ahead. Not at Cassie. "If you want anything, any part of me, or my family, I would love that. Because I've missed you. So much."

For a long moment, Cassie didn't speak. She barely breathed. Zoe had lied to Russell, about the baby. She'd lied to Cassie, about the note. Cassie had spent *twenty years* atoning for a sin she believed was hers alone, only that wasn't true. Part of the blame had been Zoe's. Part of it had been Zoe's fault, all along.

"Cassie?" Zoe's voice was tiny. "I know you're angry. And you should be. But I have missed you. So much. I feel like I lost a part of myself when you went away. And I want it back. I want you to come back." Cassie didn't move. *You lost a part of yourself,* she thought. *I lost all of you. All of Russell. I lost everything.*

"Can you forgive me?" Zoe was asking.

Cassie sat, not moving. Not speaking.

"I don't know," she finally said. And then, before Zoe could tell her anything else, or ask her anything more, she got to her feet and walked away.

Part Seven

Letter to Cassie Griffin, care of Relic Records

September 14, 2005

Dear Cassie Griffin,

I don't know if you will ever see this letter—probably you won't!—but I had to write it anyhow.

My name is Amy O'Brien. I am fifteen, and I look like you. I have been over-weight/obese/fluffy/chunky/fat for my whole life, and I have spent my whole life trying to change the way I look. My pediatrician put me on my first diet when I was eight years old. My mom took me to Weight Watchers when I was eleven. I've done low-carb diets and low-fat diets and pineapple and cabbage soup di-ets, and nothing ever worked (at least not for long).

I never saw anyone who looked like me on a stage or on TV (unless it was a Jenny Craig commercial or *The Biggest Loser*). I will never forget the night in 2003 when I was babysitting and I was so excited to see you on *Saturday Night Live*, because I already loved your songs, and I felt like the lyrics were speaking to me, or could be about someone like me. I know that sounds confusing but that is how I felt.

You looked like me and you were on that stage, on TV, and you weren't there as a "before" on a weight-loss show or commercial. You weren't a problem to solve or something that had to change. You were the star. You were singing, and you sounded so beautiful, and you looked so fierce and so powerful, like you knew that was where you belonged. I never forgot it.

You made me feel like I could be someone, and do something big with my life, even if I never lost weight. You made me think about all the time and energy I was spending on diets, and counting calories and tracking my fat grams, and measuring my portions, and whether I couldn't spend that time doing some-thing I love as much as you must love music (I don't know what that thing is yet—I'm not as good at anything as you are at singing or playing the piano!—but I am trying to find it).

You changed my life, and I wanted to say "thank you." And I hope someday you'll make another album, and I'll get to see you singing again.

Sincerely,
Amy O'Brien
Lenox, MA

Cherry

Cherry had, of course, been cut from the competition, fifteen minutes after her mother and her aunt disappeared. She'd more or less promised the producers that she'd be able to get Cassie and Zoe for the show, and when it turned out that both of them had vanished, they'd replaced her with one of the alternates. *I knew this could happen*, Cherry told herself, as she sat in her dressing room, auntless, motherless, waiting for the bad news to be confirmed. A stone-faced PA had marched her to Sebastian's office backstage. Sebastian was waiting for her, his expression cold, eyebrows lifted.

"Well?"

Cherry told Sebastian what had happened. Sebastian's face was impassive as he listened.

"The Griffin Sisters were always kind of a package deal," he'd finally said.

Cherry nodded. "I could sing with someone else. Tomorrow. Maybe, if April isn't busy . . ."

"Oh, no. You're done," Sebastian said, almost indifferently. He'd turned back to Cherry with an indulgent smile that put his veneered teeth on display. "But I'll tell you what. If you can manage to get the Griffin Sisters back together, we'll come and film the concert. Anytime, anywhere in the world." He'd patted Cherry on the shoulder, a benediction and a dismissal. "I'll give you my assistant's contact information."

The PAs ignored her as she left Sebastian's office, turning their faces away like she had the plague and it was catching. Cherry couldn't blame them. Sending April, her assigned mentor, away, asking her mom to fly out, then springing her mother on Cassie was the definition of a high-risk/high-reward situation. She'd hoped for the best—a joyous reunion, tears and hugs and kisses, after which Cassie and her mother would go onstage with her. Cherry would come clean about her lineage, thrilling the audience in the process. *The Griffin Sisters, reunited at last, after all those years!* The judges would be delighted, and then Cassie would take her place at the keyboard and Cherry would pick up her guitar and her mom would be there, for moral support and possibly backup harmonies, and they would sing, and it would be everything.

Cherry had stayed through the show's taping. She'd sat backstage, away from the cameras, and watched on a monitor as the other contestants performed, hearing the judges' critiques, observing her former competitors come offstage, some of them elated, some of them looking shell-shocked or terrified. *That could have been me,* she thought, as the girl they'd tapped to replace her sang "And I Am Telling You I'm Not Going," from *Dreamgirls,* and wasn't half as good as Cherry knew she could have been.

When it was over, Cherry went back to her dressing room, to comb the gel out of her hair and put her street clothes back on. Eventually, a knock came, and Cherry opened the door to admit her shamefaced mother. Zoe's carefully applied makeup was mostly gone. Her highheeled shoes were dusty, and she looked like she'd been crying.

"What happened?" asked Cherry, as Zoe stepped inside and closed the door behind her. "Where's Cassie?" Her mom just shook her head.

"I owe you an apology," she said, in a muted voice Cherry had never heard.

Yes, Cherry thought. *Yes, you do.* She stood up, put her hands on her hips, narrowed her eyes, and waited. But when Zoe began, she didn't say a word about scaring Cassie away, or ruining Cherry's performance, or getting her disqualified from *The Next Stage.* She smoothed her hair, hands twitching anxiously, and said, "When you told me Bix was bothering you, I should have listened."

Cherry blinked. Of all the things her mother could have said, of all the conversations she'd imagined they'd be having, that one hadn't made the list. But if that was where Zoe wanted to start, she could work with it.

"So why didn't you listen?" she asked.

Zoe looked down at her feet. In that moment, with her shoulders hunched, shaking her head, she looked so much like Cassie that Cherry found herself a little breathless. She'd never seen much of a resemblance before, but in that moment it was unmissable. "I guess because it was easier not to. Easier to tell myself that Bix was just annoying." She looked at Cherry, glancingly, then looked away. "Easier for me. Not for you." She hung her head. "It was my job to take care of you. And I didn't."

Cherry felt staggered. She felt like she'd gotten herself geared up to punch her fist through a board, and had ended up shoving her knuckles into a pile of marshmallow fluff; something that offered no resistance and didn't feel the way she'd imaged. It should have been a relief, but instead, she felt unsettled, off-balance. Wrong-footed.

"I was a terrible mother," Zoe said. "But I'm going to do better. I promise."

Just words, Cherry thought, not wanting to hope. *Of course she can say the right things, it doesn't mean that anything will change.* She'd barely finished thinking it when Zoe said, "I told Jordan that Bix can't live at home. I don't want him around you, or the boys," she said, then looked anxiously at Cherry. "You don't think he—bothered—them too, do you?"

"No." Cherry was disgusted to find that her voice had gone a little wavery. "I think I was the only one who got that honor." She blinked hard, then wiped at her eyes, hoping her mother didn't notice. "What did Jordan have to say?"

"He isn't happy." Zoe sniffled a little. "He loves Bix. And he feels guilty, still, that Bix lost his mother. He thinks that whatever Bix has done is because he's troubled. Not bad."

"What do you think?" Cherry asked.

"I'm not interested in the why of it." Zoe's voice was a little steadier. "All I know is that he doesn't get to hurt you anymore."

Cherry couldn't bring herself to look at her mother. "You did your best," she said, her voice sounding thick, her tongue feeling heavy. "You couldn't have known all of it. He was sneaky. And he never touched me. And I just stopped talking about it, after a while."

"Because I wasn't listening!" Zoe raised her fisted hand to her forehead and struck herself, once, then again. Cherry grabbed her hand.

"Hey," she said. "Don't. It's okay."

"It isn't," said Zoe, with her voice like a sob. "It is not."

"Okay," Cherry said. "But maybe it will be. You know. At some point."

Her mom made a noise, half sob, half laugh. Cherry decided she could be magnanimous.

"I know that it must have been hard for you. With the band breaking up. With my father dying."

Zoe sniffled. She wiped at her eyes. "Ah. Well, that's another thing."

"What?"

"I'm not actually entirely sure who your father was."

Again, Cherry felt that sense of dislocation, of expecting one thing and getting something completely different. "What?" she asked. Then, like a baby owl, "Who? If it wasn't Russell, then who?"

"Maybe Tommy. Tommy Kelleher. The band's drummer."

Cherry still felt staggered. Russell, maybe, wasn't her father? Her father was, maybe, still alive? She struggled to picture Tommy Kelleher and could come up with only the vaguest memory of a generic dark-haired man behind a drum kit. "Does he know?"

Zoe shook her head.

Before Cherry could ask more questions, starting with why Zoe had lied to her, her mother said, "One more thing."

Cherry waited, breathless, wondering what revelation could possibly be next.

Zoe pushed her hair behind her ears. She stood up straight and looked her daughter in the eye. "If music is what you wanted, I should have let you pursue it. I'm sorry."

"It's fine," Cherry said, a little faintly.

"I got hurt. A man—hurt me." Zoe's throat jerked. "I can tell you about it, sometime . . . Anyhow, the thing is, I wasn't as careful as I should have been. I was ambitious, and I let that . . ." She shook her head. "It made me stupid. I made bad choices. I got hurt, and I didn't want that for you. But if music is your dream, Cherry, you should go chase it." She let her hands fall, palms out, at her sides. "I won't stand in your way ever again."

"What happened?" Cherry asked. Part of her didn't want to hear any more. But she needed to know. Maybe knowing would help her understand.

Zoe shook her head again. She sounded anguished as she said, "It was a long time ago. There was a photographer . . ." Her voice trailed off as one of her hands wandered—unconsciously, Cherry was sure—to rub at her cheek. "It doesn't matter. Just—well. If you made it all the way to Alaska and nothing bad happened, I guess you can take care of yourself."

"I can," Cherry said, speaking half to herself. "I always could." She looked at her mother. "And whatever happened to you, it wasn't your fault."

She wanted to grab her mother's shoulders and shake them; wanted to tell Zoe what she was sure her mother would have said if Cherry had been the one who'd gotten hurt. "He was the one who did something wrong. Not you."

"I know. You're right. You are." Zoe didn't sound entirely convinced. Cherry wondered if her mother believed what she was saying. Zoe was still looking at the ground when she said, "I wasn't much of a mom to you."

Cherry stared at her curiously. She remembered the years in the apartment in Bella Vista, the time before Jordan. Her mom had been tired, short-tempered and prickly, and Cherry could remember nights and weekends spent with her grandparents and Aunt Bess and random babysitters, seemingly anyone Zoe could find to care for her. She remembered sitting at the window, watching her mom heading down the sidewalk, toward her car, carrying her guitar case, walking away. She'd had a cropped leather jacket, and her hair had been loose, and Cherry remembered feeling a little sad, but also proud. Other kids had parents who were doctors and lawyers and nurses, parents who worked in offices and in restaurants and yoga studios. Their parents were regular-looking people with normal kinds of jobs. But her mother was beautiful, and she did something amazing. Her mom made music. Even after Zoe had married Jordan, even after they'd moved, even after the guitar disappeared and Cherry never heard her mom singing in the shower or humming an insurance-company jingle, Cherry never forgot how her mom had looked, and how it had made her feel.

"I wanted to be just like you when I grew up," she said.

Zoe laughed, and wiped her eyes. "Maybe not just like me," she said. "Maybe better."

Cherry's boots clomped on the floor as she crossed it, and gave her mom a hug. She felt Zoe stiffen, then relax. She could smell perfume and expensive hair products, and could hear her mother sniffling against her shoulder . . . but, when they separated, Zoe's eyes were dry.

Cherry wondered whether asking about Cassie would be a mistake, in the moment. She decided to risk it.

"Do you know where . . ." *Your sister?* she wondered. *My aunt?* ". . . where Cassie went? Did she go back to Alaska?"

Zoe's shoulders lifted in a brief shrug.

"Is she coming back?" Cherry asked.

Zoe shrugged again. In a muted voice, she said, "I did things that hurt her. Things she hadn't known about. I told her everything, and she . . ." Zoe gestured in a way that indicated disappearance.

Cherry ground her teeth together, and her voice was brittle. "Whatever you had to say to her . . . did it occur to you to maybe not say it until after my performance?"

"Oh, she wouldn't have gone onstage with you." Zoe's voice was almost absent. "She only sings with me."

"You're wrong. She did sing with me," Cherry said, not hiding the fact that she was, suddenly, furious. All the anger that had dissipated after her mother's confessions had come roaring back. "She's changed. People do that when you don't see them for twenty years. But I knew she wanted to sing with you. That's why I asked you to come."

Her mother looked at her. Cherry couldn't read the expression, could only identify parts of it—sorrow and regret. Maybe a bit of amusement. Maybe, even, a touch of pride.

"These shows don't guarantee anything," said Zoe.

"No," Cherry said. "I get that. You've told me a hundred times. But you know what? Making it this far tells me I've got talent. That I'm actually good. And if I'd won the competition, at least it would have given me a shot." She inhaled, remembering what she'd said to Sebastian, the first time he'd interrogated her onstage. When he'd asked her if she wanted to be rich and famous, and she'd told him that singing was her way of communicating, her way of telling the world her story.

"You are," Zoe said. "You are good. You've always been good. You . . ." She paused, inhaling deeply. "Whatever Cassie has, you inherited it."

For all the good it's done me, Cherry thought, feeling frustrated and furious, and—still—sorry for her mother, to whom bad things had happened. She touched Sebastian's card, tucked in her pocket. "Do you think she'd ever sing with me?"

Zoe shrugged.

"Will you talk to her?" Cherry asked. Her voice was getting louder, sharper. "Can you try to convince her? It would . . ." *Make a difference. Help me. Get me on TV. Launch my career.* "It would change my life. And hers, too, I think. I think she's pretty lonely." Huge understatement, Cherry realized, but, in the moment, it was the best she could do. Cassie might have been an art monster, a woman who lived for music, and music alone. But monsters got lonely, too.

Her mother looked at her. "Let's go home," she said. "And when we're back, I promise, I will help you as much as I can."

"What about Cassie?"

Zoe's expression became complicated again. "What happens next is her choice. We just have to wait and see."

This was not what Cherry wanted to hear. "So what happens now?" she demanded.

Zoe sighed, and nodded toward the door. "Now, we go home."

Cassie

Can you forgive me? her sister had asked.

I don't know, Cassie had answered.

After Zoe's revelations, all Cassie wanted was to run away and hide: under a bed, inside a closet, someplace dark where no one would find her and tell her anything else that would erase any more of her certainties and upend her world.

She'd started walking: out of the park, through a residential neighborhood, up one hill, down another. And, as she walked, she started thinking.

What if it's true?

What if I was the one he loved? What if it wasn't my fault that he died?

It was too much for her to consider, too big a revision to hold in her head. And so she'd walked and kept going, barely noticing where she was, moving herself through the city until her feet hurt too badly for her to go on.

She found herself sitting in a bus shelter, with no idea of where she was or how far she'd come. Instead of the Los Angeles landscape—six lanes of street, a stucco mini-mall with a vape shop, a doughnut shop, a karate studio, a used-car lot—she was seeing Russell, as he'd been, soft cheeks, pale skin, dark hair. The way he'd gesture, talking with his hands when he got excited. The way he looked onstage, with his guitar. It felt, in a way, like losing him all over again, only it felt even more cruel—to know, for sure, that he'd loved her, and not Zoe! To know that they could have had a life together! They could have written more songs together; they could have played shows all over the world. Only what did it matter? Knowing did not change anything. Russell was still dead. It felt like more than she could bear, more than she'd ever be able to endure.

Cassie dug for her phone, and tried to remember what Cherry had shown her about the ride-sharing apps. Eventually, she'd managed to summon a car and get a ride back to her hotel. Wesley was waiting in the room, whining unhappily, even though Cassie knew he'd been walked around lunchtime (Cherry had shown her an app for hiring dog-walkers, the same way there was one for summoning cars—how the world had changed, while she was hiding away!).

When she unlocked the door, Wesley had been sleeping on the hotel-room bed, and he was delighted to see her, prancing around her legs, licking her face when she bent down to leash him. Was he comforting her? Did he have any idea that her life had just been blown apart, that every certainty had been pulled out from under her? She'd taken Wesley for a walk, noticing, with faint amusement, the way he seemed to lift his paws extra-high, looking especially jaunty as he strutted down the sidewalks, turning his head from side to side, possibly hoping to spot someone famous, or, maybe, be discovered, like Lana Turner at the soda fountain. "Trust me," she told him. "You don't want to be famous. I know it looks like fun, but it's not." Back in the room, she'd showered away as much of the day as she could, and lay on the bed and closed her eyes, as Wesley curled up beside her. *Who am I now? Where do I go? What do I do?*

She thought about the treehouses, and the life she'd made in Alaska. A small, quiet life, where she didn't hurt anyone, and no one hurt her. She had Wesley, and her work. Her routines. She had enough money, and the pleasure of offering a useful service: a comfortable bed, a cozy room, a place to stay the night. A life with no surprises.

It's not enough, a voice in her head said. Was that Bess's voice? Her mother's? Was it Jerry's voice, or CJ's? Was it Zoe, or Cherry? Was it Russell?

It's not enough. You have more to give.

Cassie pressed her fisted hands to her eyes, groaning. She didn't want to give more. She didn't want to have to be in the world at all. She didn't want to risk being stared at, or laughed at, being despised.

Or is it, asked this cool, new voice, *that you don't want to risk being loved?*

"Please," Cassie heard herself saying, before she realized she was going to say anything. "Please stop. Please just don't." Her throat was tight; her voice sounded hoarse. She'd probably spoken more in the days since Cherry's arrival than she had in the twenty previous years combined. She'd built herself a life without voices, a life without people. She'd needed the silence and the distance to keep herself safe.

And now look.

Wesley stood, stretched, turned himself in three circles, and settled his snout against her leg with a tired sigh. Cassie stroked his ears. Everything felt impossible. Every choice seemed wrong. Stay? Go? Sell the treehouses, come back to Philadelphia? Or New York? Make music again? Or find some third option, go somewhere else, and hope that this time, no one would find her?

You shouldn't be hiding. The voice was growing stronger, more certain, even though Cassie still didn't know whose it was. *You have a gift.*

"Fuck my gift," Cassie said hoarsely, loudly enough for Wesley to lift his snout and give her a concerned look.

"Sorry," she muttered. And thought, *What good is a gift, if all it does is hurt me?*

She groaned . . . and then found herself remembering a time that she'd been happy. Singing, and happy. It hadn't been in her house, singing with her niece, even though Cassie could admit that she'd liked it. It was something else she'd done, almost against her will, and found herself enjoying.

There's your answer, said the voice. *Go to the joy. Find the thing that makes you happy. Try it again.*

I don't want to, Cassie thought. *What if I just get hurt?*

The voice—she wanted to believe that it was Russell's, or at least partly Russell's—was kind. *Just try.*

Cassie used another one of the apps her niece showed her to order Thai food for dinner, then went online and bought a plane ticket. The next morning, she and Wesley flew from LAX to Seattle. By that after-noon, she'd landed in Anchorage and retrieved her car from long-term parking. By eight o'clock, they were pulling down her driveway, with Wesley giving happy little whimpers. She let him run outside, sniffing at the snow, lifting his leg at every tree trunk. She fed him, checked the treehouses, built a fire in her woodstove, so that she wouldn't leave Wesley in the cold, and climbed back into her car.

At eleven o'clock, she was back at the Safeway, walking slowly up and down the aisles, until, in the baked goods section, she found who she was looking for.

"Hi, Carl," she said.

He'd been mopping the floor. When Cassie said his name, he'd put the mop carefully into the bucket, then looked at her. For a moment, she was sure he didn't recognize her; that he didn't remember. Then his face broke into a broad smile.

"You sang that song!"

"That's right," she said.

"I remember," Carl said. His chest puffed up. "It was my birthday, and you sang 'Silent Night.'"

Cassie cleared her throat. "Yes," she said. "I wondered . . . you like to sing, right?"

Carl nodded. "Singing is my favorite thing. My favorite and my best thing."

Before Cassie could ask anything else, a woman with a meringue-like scoop of white hair came bustling down the aisle. "Carl, who are you . . ." She paused, eyes widening when she saw Cassie. "Oh my goodness. Oh, it's you!"

Cassie nodded. "I came to ask Carl if he wanted to sing with me again." She wasn't sure, but she thought the look on Marcia's face was approving.

"Well. Well, that's very kind of you."

"Singing is my favorite and my best thing," Carl said again.

"And you're very modest about it," Marcia said with a smile.

"I thought—I don't know, if there's a place where we could sing,"

Cassie said. "Carl, and other people, if they wanted. A school, or a classroom, or . . ."

Marcia nodded. "Carl's in a day program. I bet they'd be very glad to have you," Marcia chattered. "They're desperate for volunteers, you know. They get state funding, and some federal, but they're always scrounging, and I don't think they've had any kind of music program since Carl's been there."

Cassie nodded, and said, "Maybe I can help."

That night, in the Safeway, she sang with Carl. The next day, she drove to a single-story office building, presented herself to a receptionist, and filled out a stack of forms. She gave them her address and her phone number and agreed to a background check. Under *relevant experience*, she wrote, *I am a former classical piano student. I used to be in a band.* Under *time available*, she wrote, *I have a very flexible schedule.* Under *references*, after a long moment of thought, she put her niece's name.

Are you happy now? she asked the voice that was maybe Russell's voice. No reply came. Cassie supposed the satisfaction she felt, the calm that enfolded her, was the only answer she could expect. It was confirmation that she'd done the right thing, that she was honoring her gift. That she was, just maybe, leaving things a little better than she'd found them for other people who were lonely, who felt like outcasts, or who, maybe, just needed a song.

Would it be enough? she wondered. Now that she'd met Cherry and seen Zoe, and heard about her sister's husband and sons, could she stay here, keeping herself apart from them, for another month, another year, the rest of her life? Or would the voice that was maybe Russell's demand more things from her?

Zoe's transgressions seemed so monstrous that she couldn't see her way over them or around them. She'd spent all those years with the weight of Russell's death hanging on her shoulders, and now that weight was gone . . . but Zoe had let her carry it. And Russell D'Angelo was gone too. Forever and forever, no matter whose fault it was.

They'd both loved him, Cassie thought. And Zoe had burdens of her own. A baby! What would Cassie have done, if she'd known her sister was pregnant? Would she have resented her, for holding on to what was—perhaps—a remaining piece of Russell, for keeping it to herself? Would Cherry have brought them back together? Would Cassie have found a way to forgive Zoe, and let her back into her life?

"I don't know," she said out loud, as she climbed the steps to the treehouse, where the air was warm and faintly wood-scented, and where Wesley was waiting. She sat down on the metal chair, and thought, *I want a couch. It is ridiculous that I don't have a couch.* And then she smiled, because, after the dark, blank expanse of all of the years, she felt like she was coming back to herself. No, she thought. Not coming back. She was moving toward a better version of herself, one who could believe she deserved small comforts, and that she had something to give to the world; that it wasn't too late, and never would be.

Russell, she thought, would have approved.

Zoe
HADDONFIELD, 2024

Zoe hadn't realized how much she'd missed her sister until that afternoon in Los Angeles, when, after almost twenty years had gone by, she'd finally seen Cassie again. She hadn't understood how much it had hurt, how much pain and shame she was carrying, until the moment that Cassie was actually standing in front of her, with her hair done and her face painted and an anguished look in her eyes. Zoe had seen that look and felt lacerated. Flayed. Torn open.

She'd done her best. She'd spent the entire flight to Los Angeles making a plan. She was going to apologize. She was going to try to explain herself, to tell Cassie how it had felt, being pushed out of the band, and tell her why she'd done what she'd done. Not that it justified her actions, but, maybe, she could make Cassie understand it. Had she accomplished any of that? Had she made her sister understand? Or had she only made things worse?

I hurt my sister, Zoe thought. *I hurt my daughter. I'm a terrible mother, and a terrible person.*

Back home, she'd tried texting Cassie, tried calling. She'd sent long, handwritten letters to the PO box that Bess had given her, explaining it all again, saying she was sorry again. She'd gotten no reply.

At least things were better at home. Jordan had been stiff-shouldered and palpably resentful when Zoe brought Cherry home, but Bix's room was empty . . . and, after a day or two of barely speaking to her, Jordan hadn't turned to his side facing away from her the instant he climbed into bed, but had settled on his back, as usual. Her third night back home, Zoe switched off the lights and slipped under the covers. After a minute, Jordan reached for her hand and asked, "Do you want to tell me about it?"

"I think . . ." Zoe's voice caught in her throat. "I don't think you're going to like me very much when you hear the whole story." Her voice was very small. "I don't think you'll be able to love me anymore."

"Oh, Zoe." He'd pulled her close, kissing her forehead, her nose, her lips. "Sweetheart. I could never not love you."

"Just wait," she'd said, sniffling. Even though it was dark, she kept her eyes closed while she told him about Russell, and Cassie, and what had happened at the end. He'd held her hand, and handed her tissues, and, when it was done, he'd pulled her close, settling her against him, so that her head was on his chest.

"I lied," she said. Her voice was flat. "I told Cassie it was her fault that he died, but it wasn't her fault. It was mine."

"Maybe," said Jordan. For a wonder, he didn't sound judgmental or disgusted or angry. He wasn't telling Zoe that she was a monster, or demanding that she leave his bed, his home, his life. He was using his lawyer's voice, cool and analytical. "Or maybe it was Russell's fault. Or the driver's fault. Or the person who sold him the whiskey. Or the person who designed the road. Maybe it was just a tragedy, and it would have happened, no matter what."

Could that be true? Zoe wondered, as Jordan stroked her arm, then her hair. Could she let herself believe that Russell's death had been predestined, somehow, and that she wasn't to blame? Could she let herself be forgiven?

Zoe felt a lightness pouring through her, a sense of happiness, and contentedness, as Jordan held her, letting his body warm her. "It's over now," he told her. "You're safe. You're here."

Zoe nodded, crying with her eyes squeezed shut, knowing she didn't deserve any of it—not safe harbor, not happiness, or forgiveness, not a home with a man who loved her.

"You can't change anything that happened," Jordan said. "All you can control is what you do now. What happens next."

"You're very wise," Zoe said, laughing a little before she started crying again. "When did you get so smart?"

"Born this way," Jordan said modestly, and Zoe laughed. *What happens next?* she thought. Next, she'd help Cherry, as much as she could. Next, she'd reach out to Cassie, and apologize again, and again, for as long as it took. And then she'd do the hardest thing of all. She would wait.

Cherry had called her old bandmates to tell them she'd come home, and by that weekend, she was playing with them again. She returned to posting her music on social media and started sharing clips of her time on *The Next Stage*, once her segments had aired. Zoe promised to send her songs to her contacts at Relic, whenever Cherry was ready. "How do I know when I'm ready?" Cherry had asked, and Zoe hadn't known how to answer. Cassie would have been the best judge, but Cassie wasn't talking to either one of them. Zoe knew that her sister was ignoring Cherry's calls and the texts Cherry sent her: funny memes, pictures from Alaska, mostly of Wesley stretched out in front of the fireplace, or sitting attentively, listening to them sing, followed by emojis—musical notes, treble clef, snowflake, smiley face, heart, heart, heart.

Zoe had bought Cherry the Les Paul guitar she'd been lusting after for years, and attended three of Cherry's band's shows, standing in the back, earplugs in her ears. She'd spent hours after dinner in the basement, listening to Cherry's songs, holding the phone to record her daughter singing; offering all of the encouragement she could, knowing that her praise wasn't what mattered to Cherry, that her judgment was no substitute for her sister's.

Time went by. Spring slipped into a hot, mostly rainless summer, which, eventually, gave way to fall. The days got shorter; Halloween came and went. And then, one night in November, after the boys were asleep, and Cherry and Zoe and Jordan were in the den, watching the British crime drama they'd all become obsessed with, Zoe's phone rang, and the name she'd been waiting to see was flashing on the screen. She stabbed at the buttons and lurched to her feet.

"Hello?"

There was a long pause. "I was wondering," Cassie asked, "if I could come for a visit. If you're going to be around this week." Like she lived around the corner, instead of on the other side of the world, Zoe thought.

"Of course," she said, hearing her voice cracking. "Of course we'll be here."

Cassie bought a ticket for the following week and sent Zoe her flight information. Zoe had offered to pick her sister up at the airport, but Cassie had declined. She'd be renting a car, she said. She'd drive herself. Zoe hadn't wanted to push. She figured the car might have something to do with Cassie needing an escape plan, a way to get herself back home, if she felt like she had to run. And so she waited, until on Wednesday night, at ten o'clock, there was a knock at the door. Zoe opened it, and there was Cassie, with her suitcase handle in one hand and a dog's leash in the other. The leash, she saw, was attached to a smallish terrier-type dog, who was looking up at Zoe with friendly curiosity.

"Hi," said Cassie.

Zoe exhaled, feeling like she'd been holding her breath for days. Possibly weeks.

"Do you want to come in?" she asked.

Cassie nodded. And then Cherry was there, hugging her aunt, scooping the little dog into her arms.

"Cherry, can you give us a minute?" Cassie asked. Cherry gave Cassie another quick hug, then carried the little dog downstairs. Cassie was looking around, at the family photographs on a table in the foyer, the big windows in the living room that offered a view of the yard. Zoe followed her sister's gaze to the photograph of Schuyler and Noah stuck to the refrigerator with a pickle-shaped magnet. The boys were grinning at the camera, holding terrapin turtles. Schuyler was missing one of his front teeth.

"Your nephews," she said. "They're asleep, but you can meet them in the morning."

Cassie made a soft sound, and sat up very straight, her hands folded on the marble counter. "I wish I'd known," she said, her words slow and halting. "About them. About Cherry."

"I didn't know how to reach you."

"I didn't want to be reached," Cassie said. She closed her mouth, pressing her fingers against her lips like she was trying to keep more words from escaping. Zoe felt her skin prickling with heat. *I deserve it,* she thought. *Whatever she wants to say to me, whatever she wants to do, I deserve it.*

"Are you hungry?" Zoe asked, needing something to do, to focus her thoughts on a task.

Cassie shrugged. From the refrigerator, Zoe gathered butter, cheddar cheese, sourdough bread. She found a tomato in a basket on the counter, pulled a cast-iron pan out from a sliding drawer. She put the pan on the stove, turned on the flame, and began buttering slices of bread for grilled-cheese-and-tomato sandwiches. "Remember how Mom used to make these?" Zoe asked.

"Wonder Bread and margarine," Cassie said immediately.

Zoe's bread was sourdough from the Mighty Bread Company. Her tomatoes were heirloom and organic. She told Cassie this, aware that she was babbling, unable, in her nervousness, to stop. Cassie sat at a stool at the breakfast bar, silent, until Zoe paused for a breath.

"I was so jealous of you," Cassie said. "For so long. You had friends, and you knew how to talk to people, and what to wear, and how to be in the world." She licked her lips. "I never wanted to be famous. The only thing I liked about performing was that I could forget that there were people looking at me. I could just be a voice." She looked down at herself, at her body. "I loved that." Cassie licked her lips again. "And I liked being with you. I liked feeling like I mattered to you. Like there was something I could give you, so I could help you the way you'd helped me."

Zoe made a small, mournful noise. She found that she'd clasped her hands together and was pressing them against her chest like she was trying to hold her flayed, torn self together. *Listen*, she told herself. *You have to listen.* She could feel herself trembling, her legs shaking, desperate to run. Downstairs, to her daughter; upstairs, to her husband; anyplace but here. Anyplace where she wouldn't have to hear this list, the careful accounting of what she'd done and what it had cost.

"I felt guilty about being with Russell," Cassie said. "I loved him, and I believed him when he told me you weren't really together. It was what I wanted to be true. And we should have told you. We shouldn't have been sneaking around." Cassie delivered this speech without looking at Zoe, with her eyes straight ahead and her face expressionless. "I've spent twenty years thinking that he died because of me."

Zoe couldn't help another one of those small, pained sounds from escaping her lips. She wondered how she'd be able to live with the guilt of what she'd done, if it would even be possible.

"Did you love him?" Cassie asked softly. "Did you ever love him at all?"

Zoe looked at her sister. She saw how Cassie had changed, how the years had changed her, how her body looked strong and her face looked determined. She made Zoe think of a carved mermaid on the prow of a ship, facing the cold waves, thrashed by storms and salt water, bleached by sunshine. Enduring whatever the world threw at her.

"Did I love him," Zoe said. She tried to think back, to remember the girl she'd been, so full of dreams and envy, so desperate to be seen.

"The night you walked in on us . . ." Cassie leaned on the counter, looking at Zoe. "I told myself you didn't love him, that you didn't care for him at all, but that night, it looked like you did."

Zoe turned off the stove. She slid the sandwiches onto a cutting board, using a knife to slice them diagonally. "I think," she said carefully, "it was the shock of seeing the two of you together." She smiled, a little sadly. "It was a dog-in-the-manger situation. Even if I didn't want him, I didn't want anyone else to have him." She put the sandwiches onto a pair of plates and handed one to her sister. "I'm sorry I couldn't be more generous. I could see how good you two were together. I'm sorry I didn't just let it happen."

"I could have been more generous too," said Cassie. "I knew how much performing meant to you. How much you got from it. I could have spoken up more, when they started . . ." She paused. "You know. Pushing you to the side."

"That was where I belonged," Zoe said. "If it wasn't for you, I wouldn't have been on those stages at all."

"Well," said Cassie. "Same here." She was speaking slowly, like the words were pieces she'd just shaken out of a puzzle box, and she was taking her time fitting them together. "I never knew how much I'd like it until you dragged me onstage that first night."

"At Dobbs," Zoe said, remembering.

"It gave me something," Cassie said. "It was a way to be in public and be hidden at the same time."

"And I'm grateful," said Zoe. "Even if it wasn't perfect. I'm glad that I got the chance." She took her plate and sat at the counter next to her sister. *We were so young*, she was thinking . . . and was startled when Cassie said those exact words out loud.

"We were so young."

Zoe nodded her agreement. "And it was a long time ago."

Cassie bit into her sandwich. She chewed, and swallowed, and turned to Zoe. "Being mad at you won't bring Russell back. Being mad at myself didn't. I think I would like to be done with all of that, and just not be mad at anyone." She took another bite. "I think I'd like to try being happy."

"Oh," said Zoe, in a very small voice.

"I can forgive you," Cassie said. "I guess maybe the question is, can you forgive yourself?"

"Oh," Zoe repeated. Her heart felt light as a bag of feathers, released to float up toward the sky. She hadn't let herself realize how much she'd longed for Cassie's forgiveness until she had it.

Cassie looked down at her plate. Then she looked up, her gaze steady on her sister, the question still hanging, waiting for Zoe's reply.

"Can you? Can you forgive yourself?"

Zoe took a minute to think before finally saying, quietly, "I can try."

The first night, Cassie stayed in a hotel room in Cherry Hill. On the second night, Zoe offered the guest room, but Cassie said she thought that it would be too much, too soon, so Cherry helped Cassie find an Airbnb, a one-bedroom apartment in an old Victorian house a few blocks away. Every morning, Cassie walked Wesley over to Zoe's house, and she'd join Zoe and Cherry in the soundproofed basement, where the Steinway baby grand that Jordan had purchased stood in the corner, behind a pair of new microphones on stands. Cassie would sit in the corner, with Wesley on her lap or by her feet. At first, she just listened, as Cherry played the piano, and Zoe played the guitar and sang with her daughter. Then, after a few days of listening, Cassie stopped them in the middle of a song. "Try it like this," she said, and went to the piano to play a line of the melody from "A Long December," before she started to sing. Her voice, as always, was a shimmering miracle. Zoe met her daughter's eyes and stepped back, holding her breath, not wanting to disrupt the magic.

By the next afternoon, Zoe was the one in the corner, with the dog on her lap, listening quietly as Cassie played the piano and Cherry played the guitar, better than Zoe ever could, even after all her lessons and hours of practice. She would have been happy to stay there all day, witnessing this beauty—her daughter and her sister, making music, together. But after an hour, Cherry said, "Mom, why don't you sing with us on the chorus?" Zoe looked at her sister, who nodded, beckoning her toward the piano. At first softly, then more confidently, Zoe joined her voice with theirs, thinking about how lucky she'd been, to sing with her sister; how lucky she was now, to be able to do it again.

For days, then weeks, they sang together, taking breaks to make meals or snacks or taking Wesley for walks. In the afternoon, they'd climb upstairs to make dinner. The boys would set the table, Cassie and Zoe would do the cooking, and, when Jordan arrived, they'd sit down together and tell stories about their days. They were some of the most pleasant, most peaceful nights Zoe could remember. When the dishes were done and the leftovers put away, they'd watch movies or TV, the boys petting Wesley, Cassie sitting on the couch with Cherry next to her, on her phone, on social media, posting outtakes from the day's performance that didn't feature Cassie's face. *Big things happening*, Cherry would write. *Watch this space!*

Cassie still insisted that she wasn't interested in playing in public, that she wasn't ready. But, eventually, Zoe decided to make a very low-stakes request.

"The PTA winter fundraiser?" Cassie looked skeptical, but she was smiling a little, and her voice sounded amused. "Not *The Next Stage?* Or the Vegas residency? Or that Broadway thing?"

"I thought we'd start small," said Zoe. "I know how it'll go. I'm on the planning committee."

"Impressive," Cassie said, deadpan.

"The kids sing some nondenominational winter songs. Then there's a silent auction, and some kind of entertainment. Last year it was one of the kids' dads who does magic tricks." Zoe paused, then said, "I think we'd be at least as good as he was."

Cassie smiled a little. "And it's in the school auditorium?"

Zoe nodded. "There's maybe a hundred people. It'll be over by nine o'clock, because it's always on a school night."

Cassie didn't say yes immediately. It took the better part of a week, before Cassie told Zoe, "I'll try."

It was Cherry's idea to let Sebastian at *The Next Stage* know about the concert. Zoe saw the way her sister's spine had stiffened, and the frightened look on her face when Cherry raised the possibility. "It would help me," Cherry said. "So much."

Just leave her alone, Zoe wanted to say. It's too much, too soon . . . but, before she could step in to defuse the bomb, Cassie had said, "Okay."

"Really?" Zoe asked.

Cassie shrugged. "Your daughter says that talent is a gift, and that gifts are meant to be shared, not hoarded. I like singing." She closed her mouth, seeming to consider the words, then said them again. "I like singing. And I think I can handle a show in a school gym."

If they tape it, Zoe thought, then the whole world will be watching. But Cassie knew that. And if she wasn't objecting, Zoe wasn't going to provoke her refusal.

The *Next Stage* people, unsurprisingly, had been over the moon. *Anything you want,* they'd said. *Anything you need, just let us know.* They'd offered to pay the sisters, but, when Cherry conveyed the offer, Cassie asked the show to make a donation, to some music program she was starting back in Alaska, for disabled kids and adults. Zoe, who was pretty sure the producers would have sent millions of dollars in unmarked bills to anyplace her sister cared to name, had told Cassie she was confident they'd agree.

"I'm so glad you're doing this," Zoe told her sister, later that night. "Cherry's thrilled too. And maybe it's a way to honor Russell's memory."

Russell's name seemed to hang in the air. For a moment, Zoe imagined she could see him, as he'd been the day they'd met: curly brown hair brushing his collar, cheeks red from the cold. She could hear how happy he'd sounded, how eager to begin when he'd said, *Let's write a song!* Was Cassie remembering that too?

"We can try," said her sister. She nodded, like she'd answered her own question, and repeated the words: "We can try."

Cherry

HADDONFIELD, 2024

Ladies and gentlemen! Here in Haddonfield, New Jersey, for one night only . . ."

"You can do this," Zoe whispered, and squeezed Cassie's hand. Cherry took Cassie's other hand and said, "I believe in you."

"I believe in you too," Cassie said, to both of them, which made Cherry snort and Zoe smile. Then the three of them walked onstage together, as Principal Deakins, the emcee for the night, said, "Put your hands together, and let's give a great big Haddonfield Elementary PTA welcome to the Griffin Sisters!"

For a moment, there was silence. Cherry heard a few whispers— *Griffin Sisters?* and *Is this a joke?* Then the lights came up, and Cassie walked toward her piano. After a moment of shocked, awed silence and more whispers—*Is that really them? Is that really her?*—the applause began. It went on and on, growing louder and louder as people finally understood that this was happening, that this was real. Cherry couldn't see past the spotlights' glare but imagined hands creeping into pockets and reaching into purses, phones coming out to record this unprecedented, unbeliev- able, once-in-a-lifetime event, along with the cameras that *The Next Stage* producers were using for their own recording. Then Cherry heard her bandmates, recruited for the night, begin to play: the snap of the snare drum, the murmur of the bass. For a single terrifying instant, her hands seemed to belong to someone else, but, after a breath, they knew just what to do as they found their way to the strings and the fretboard.

Cherry looked at her aunt. There was color in Cassie's cheeks and her eyes were clear. She looked excited. Happy. Best of all, she looked comfortable—like she was completely at home and exactly where she was meant to be. And then she started singing.

Cassie's voice was, as always, a revelation, strong enough to rattle the floorboards, delicate and restrained as a thread of gold. Rare and precious. A wonder and a miracle. Cherry sang with her, and she'd never sounded better, with her mother harmonizing with her, their voices braided with Cassie's. Somewhere in the crowd were Bess and Janice and Sam, cheering for them. Jordan was there, and Schuyler and Noah, and David and Tori, her friends from *The Next Stage*, who'd flown in special for the show.

"No one ever saw me / And I was so alone," Cassie sang. Cherry could hear that famous ache in her voice, but she could hear happiness too. "But you were right there with me / And your heart was my home."

And then the guitar and bass were roaring, and Cassie was looking at Zoe, singing right to her.

And I know
Even so
If you come back, I won't say no . . .

Cherry wondered what would happen next. Maybe there'd even be an entire, official reunion tour. Cherry could hope. She could dream. It would be everything Cherry had ever wanted, and, maybe, more than anyone deserved.

Cassie sang, and Zoe harmonized with her, and, as Cherry played, she realized that, as many times as she'd listened to the song, she'd heard it wrong. Or, at least, she'd missed something. She'd never realized that it could be about a lover who'd broken your heart, but also about a sister, or anyone you'd loved who had cared for you, then hurt you; a person you loved in spite of yourself, because you couldn't do anything else.

One by one, the instruments went silent. Cherry and Zoe's voices fading away, until it was just Cassie, holding the final notes, all sorrow mixed with longing, regret leavened by hope.

Take me in, take me back, take me home.

There was a brief, ringing silence when the song ended before the audience exploded. The applause was loud enough to shake the walls of the auditorium. The people in the auditorium looked astonished and stunned, as if they'd been woken up from a dream. They clapped and whistled and whooped and hollered and shouted and called for more. It went on and on and on. Cassie and Zoe looked at each other. *Thank you*, Cassie mouthed. Zoe blew her sister a kiss. Cherry's heart ached fiercely, so full of pride, and regret at the years the two of them had wasted, and excitement for everything to come. And gratitude. That too. For her mother and her aunt, who had found their way back to each other. For the boy, or the girl, who was out there somewhere, waiting to meet that special person, or to find out who to be. For all the songs that she would write. For the talent she'd inherited. For the mother who loved her, imperfectly, as best she could.

For these gifts and more, make me grateful, Cherry thought. And then, along with her mother and her aunt, Cherry kissed her fingertips, and raised them to the sky.

Acknowledgments

Every book goes into the world with its author's name on the cover . . .
but every book (like every song, or album, or concert) is a collective
effort, the work of many hands. I was very lucky to be uplifted by so
many smart, talented women.

I am grateful to my editor, Liz Stein, who steered the ship with
compassion, understanding, enthusiasm, and a great deal of care. Here's
to many more stories together!

Thanks to HarperCollins CEO Brian Murray and Morrow Group
president and publisher Liate Stehlik.

At William Morrow, I'm grateful to deputy publisher Jennifer Hart,
president of sales Ed Spade, vice president of marketing and publicity
Kelly Rudolph, senior publicity director Danielle Bartlett, marketing
director Kelsey Manning, senior publishing director Kaitlin Harri,
senior publicity manager Julie Paulauski, senior marketing manager
Rachel Berquist, rights director Carolyn Bodkin, senior production
editor Stephanie Vallejo, and copy editor extraordinaire Stephanie
Evans, who kept my timeline straight and made sure I didn't use the
word *thwart* in three consecutive paragraphs.

Thanks to my agent, Celeste Fine, to John Maas, who offers such
insightful, thoughtful comments on draft after draft after draft, to
Andrea Mai, Emily Sweet, Abigail Koons, and Yelena Gitlin Nesbit,
who are so smart and savvy about the publishing industry, and who
work so hard to get my stories out into the world. Thanks also to
Charlotte Sunderland, Haley Garrison, and Ben Kaslow-Zieve.

And of course I have the very best readers in the world. I was delighted to get to hang out with so many of them in person on Cape Cod in the spring of 2023, and I'm grateful to every single woman or man who's read my blog, followed me on social media, watched my videos on Instagram, signed up for my newsletter, or subscribed to my Substack, or who's picked up one of my books. Special shout-out to all the readers who helped me come up with names for the hair bands the Griffin Sisters toured with. Thünderstrüt came courtesy of Jill Grunenwald, and Tabitha Landry gave me—and now you!— Toxic Honey.

Thank you to Kate Seng and Chloe Seng, for their support of the arts, and Settlement Music School here in Philadelphia, where I take piano lessons (and if you're ever in Milton, Georgia, go check out Kate's bookstore, Poe and Company!). I am grateful to Chloe for her generous donation to Settlement School (and for lending her name to a character!).

In writing about the early aughts, and how it was for women in the public eye during that specific era, when diet culture was ascendant and tabloids were at the peak of their power, I'm grateful to every woman musician who told her own story.

My reading list included Britney Spears's *The Woman in Me*; Jessica Simpson's *Open Book*; Carnie Wilson's *Gut Feelings* and *I'm Still Hungry*; Rosanne Cash's *Composed*; *Shine Bright: A Very Personal History of Black Women in Pop* by Danyel Smith; Carrie Brownstein's *Hunger Makes Me a Modern Girl*; Beth Ditto's *Coal to Diamonds*; *Hooked: How Crafting Saved My Life* by Sutton Foster; Sheila Weller's *Girls Like Us*; Carole King's *A Natural Woman*; *Respect: The Life of Aretha Franklin* by David Ritz; and Liz Phair's *Horror Stories*.

Diana Degarmo of *American Idol* fame gave me invaluable information about auditioning for a reality TV show. Lucy Kaplansky walked me through the beats of writing a song. And Dixie Tipton told me all about the music industry and taking a new act out on the road.

On the home front, Meghan Burnett makes my writing life possible, and is the most thoughtful, cheerful person in the world. None of this would happen without her good nature and hard work.

I am grateful to my husband, Bill, the quiet unsung hero of our family. Our dog, Levon, is a first-rate bedfellow and muse.

And my biggest thanks of all goes to my daughters, Lucy and Phoebe, who have somehow grown up into adult-sized human beings. They make me laugh, they teach me things, and they expose me to new ideas, concepts, and social media platforms, and help me see the world differently. I am grateful for their willingness to share me with imaginary worlds and characters, and endlessly impressed by their courage and good humor. They give me hope for the future.

About the Author

JENNIFER WEINER is the #1 *New York Times* bestselling author of twenty-two books, including the novels *Good in Bed*, *In Her Shoes*, *Mrs. Everything*, and *The Breakaway*. She has appeared on many national television programs, including the *Today* show and *Good Morning America*, and her work is frequently published by the *New York Times*. Jennifer lives with her family in Philadelphia. Visit her online at JenniferWeiner.com.